LATINOS IN LOTUSLAND

Bilingual Press/Editorial Bilingüe

Publisher
Gary D. Keller

Executive Editor
Karen S. Van Hooft

Associate Editors
Adriana M. Brady
Brian Ellis Cassity
Amy K. Phillips
Linda K. St. George

Address:
Bilingual Press
Hispanic Research Center
Arizona State University
PO Box 875303
Tempe, Arizona 85287-5303
(480) 965-3867

LATINOS IN LOTUSLAND

An Anthology of Contemporary Southern California Literature

Edited by
Daniel A. Olivas

Bilingual Press/Editorial Bilingüe
Tempe, Arizona

Library of Congress Cataloging-in-Publication Data

Latinos in lotusland : an anthology of contemporary southern California literature / edited by Daniel A. Olivas.
    p. cm.
  ISBN-13: 978-1-931010-46-7 (cloth : alk. paper)
  ISBN-10: 1-931010-46-3 (cloth : alk. paper)
  ISBN-13: 978-1-931010-47-4 (pbk. : alk. paper)
  ISBN-10: 1-931010-47-1 (pbk. : alk. paper)
 1. Hispanic Americans—Literary collections. 2. American literature—Hispanic American authors. 3. American literature—California, Southern. 4. American literature—20th century. I. Olivas, Daniel A.
  PS508.H57L43 2007
  810.8′086807949—dc22

                                  2007036821

PRINTED IN THE UNITED STATES OF AMERICA

Front cover art: Heart Like a Boat *(2002) by Maya González*

Cover and interior design by Bill Greaves

Permissions and source acknowledgments appear at the end of this volume.

For Sue and Benjamin

Contents

Acknowledgments

Mil gracias to the wonderful *gente* at Bilingual Press who, once again, have shown a commitment to produce important works of literature. In particular I am grateful to Gary Keller, Karen Van Hooft, and Adriana Brady for all of the time and energy put into this anthology.

A special thanks to my editor, Linda St. George, who continues to pour heart and soul into the manuscripts that pile up on her desk. And thank you for very patiently answering my many e-mails and phone calls . . . I know I can be a pain.

I thank all of the authors as well as their representatives and publishers for making this project possible. This was no easy undertaking and your cooperation stoked my enthusiasm throughout the process. I am honored to have my name associated with the powerful and beautiful works that fill this anthology.

I want to thank the artist, Maya González, whose painting *Heart Like a Boat* graces the cover of *Latinos in Lotusland*. Even though you live a few hundred miles north of Southern California, the piece perfectly captures the spirit of this anthology. I hereby make you an honorary citizen of Lotusland!

I thank my parents for their unconditional support of my writing and for introducing their children to the magic of books and storytelling.

Many hugs and kisses to my wife, Sue Formaker, who continues to offer moral and emotional support for my writing and editing. And of course thanks to our wonderful son, Benjamin, who fills our life with joy and excitement.

Preface

In spring of 2005, after receiving a "green light" from Bilingual Press, I set upon the waters of the Internet the following call for submissions:

> I am editing an anthology of short fiction by Latinos/as in which the City of Los Angeles plays an integral role. I am interested in provocative stories on virtually any subject by both established and new writers. Stories may range from social realism to *cuentos de fantasma* and anything in between. Los Angeles may be a major "character" or merely lurking in the background. I'd like to see characters who represent diverse backgrounds in terms of ethnicity, profession, age, sexual orientation, etc.

What happened next both surprised and delighted me. My call for submissions quickly spread like a happy virus through the Web, showing up on numerous literary sites, personal blogs, and even on the home page of the Department of Urban Planning at the UCLA School of Public Affairs. With the exception of several pieces I solicited from authors I knew, submissions started pouring in over my virtual transom from writers who found my call on the Web or learned of it through an e-mail from a friend, agent, or writing instructor. It was almost overwhelming. After making some tough decisions, I chose the pieces that make up this volume.

The stories presented here span sixty years, with the earliest being "Kid Zopilote" by the late Mario Suárez, which first appeared the *Arizona Quarterly* in 1947. I begin the anthology with this piece not only because of its literary merit and historical importance, but because it sets the stage for the stories and novel excerpts that follow. In Suárez's story, the teenage Pepe García ventures out of his seemingly boring Tucson barrio to experience the more exciting life in Los Angeles. His friends and family are shocked when he returns a full-fledged *pachuco*, decked out in a zoot suit and smoking marijuana. He eventually slides into selling dope and pimping and eventually winds up in jail after the police round up (and harass) other Chicanos who have donned the *pachuco* style. On one level, it's a cautionary tale of what big city life can do to young people. But on another level, Suárez explores the economic struggles of barrio life in postwar Tucson as well as law enforcement's endemic bigotry and abuses of power with respect to young Chicanos.

Latinos in Lotusland concludes with a chapter from the 1970 novel *Chicano* by the late Richard Vásquez that was first published by Doubleday. In 2005, Rayo, the successful Latino imprint of HarperCollins, reissued this landmark novel in honor of its thirty-fifth anniversary. As Rubén Martínez notes in his introduction to the reissue, *Chicano* had long been out of print despite its importance within the relatively young canon of Mexican American literature. Martínez tells us that prior to *Chicano*, the only other Mexican American novel was José Antonio Villarreal's *Pocho*, which Doubleday also published—in 1959. The selection from *Chicano* brings us to postwar Los Angeles and the construction of the now-ubiquitous freeways; by joining unions and taking advantage of the city's need for skilled laborers, we see Mexican Americans working toward the dream of economic stability and upward mobility. It also stands in stark contrast to the vision offered by the first story of this anthology: where Suárez paints Los Angeles as a dangerously intoxicating and ultimately successful corrupter of Chicano youth, Vásquez envisions the city as a land of opportunity for those who wish to learn new trades and comply with the requirements of union bosses.

The stories and novel excerpts sandwiched in between "Kid Zopilote" and the excerpt from *Chicano* bring us to modern-day Latino denizens of Los Angeles and the city's surrounding communities. And what a complex and diverse group of people we observe: young and old, gay and straight, rich and poor, the newly arrived and the well established. There's a Cuban American screenwriter trying to pitch the "real" story behind the Bay of Pigs fiasco. We see a Mexican woman struggling with barrio life who believes she's seen a miracle. There are youths trying to avoid gang life and others embracing it. And we're introduced to aggressive journalists, cement pourers, disaffected lovers, drunken folklórico dancers, successful curanderos, teenage slackers, aging artists, wrestling saints, aimless druggies, people made of paper, college students, and even a private detective hot on the heels of a presumed-dead gonzo writer. These actors perform on a stage set with palm trees, freeways, mountains, and sand in communities from East L.A. to Malibu, Hollywood to the San Fernando Valley, Venice Beach to El Sereno. The storytelling comes in all packages: social realism, lyrical fantasy, tough-talking noir.

No anthology can give a complete picture of its theme because that would require a book of infinite pages. This is particularly true with this volume, which draws its stories from a wildly diverse group of people who can be loosely categorized under the umbrella of "Latinos" and who live in one of the largest metropolitan areas in the world. But if I had one goal in editing this anthology, it was to bring together some of the best contemporary Latino fiction about my home. In doing so, I believed readers would not only be entertained, but also be reminded that no group of people is monolithic and that Los Angeles literature is not limited to stories about scheming movie moguls and dazzling starlets with surgically enhanced figures (though several of this anthology's stories do concern the movie and television industries albeit through a decidedly Latino prism). And notwithstanding the fact that the characters who populate this anthology may have feasted on the City of Angel's lotus flowers, they do not live in blissful oblivion and they certainly have not forgotten who they are.

I once had the opportunity to interview Luis Alberto Urrea (whose work is featured in this anthology) about his magnificent novel *The Hummingbird's Daughter* (Little, Brown), which is based on the miraculous life of Teresita, Urrea's great aunt. One question I asked was why Urrea rendered Teresita's life in novel form rather than biography. He said, "The simplest answer is you can't footnote a dream." I'd like to borrow this sentiment with regard to *Latinos in Lotusland*. While I could have recruited a scholar to write an extensive introduction analyzing the historical and literary significance of the pieces included in this anthology, I did not want to footnote a dream. So, without further ado, we invite you to partake of these stories and novel excerpts and enjoy them for their beauty, power, and eloquence.

KID ZOPILOTE

Mario Suárez

When Pepe García came back from a summer in Los Angeles everybody began to call him Kid Zopilote. He did not know why he did not like the sound of it, but in trying to keep others from calling him that he got into many fights and scrapes. Still everybody he associated with persisted in calling him Kid Zopilote. When he dated a girl with spit curls and dresses so short that they almost bared her garters, everybody more than ever called him Kid Zopilote. It annoyed him very much. But everybody kept saying, "Kid Zopilote. Kid Zopilote." When he reasoned that it was a name given him because he dated this particular girl, he began to go with another one who wore very shiny red slacks and a very high pompadour. But to his dismay he found that he was still Kid Zopilote. All the girls who were seen with him were quickly dubbed Kiddas Zopilotas. This hurt their pride. Soon even the worst girls began to shun poor Kid Zopilote. None of the girls wanted to be seen with him. When he went to the Tira-Chancla Dance Hall very few of the girls consented to dance with him. When they did, it was out of compassion. But when the piece ended the girls never invited Kid Zopilote to the table. They thanked him on the run and began talking to someone else. Anybody else. Somehow all of this made Kid Zopilote very sad. He blamed everything on his cursed nickname. He could dance as well as anybody else and even better. Still he was an outcast. He could not understand what his nickname had to do with his personality. It sounded very ugly.

When he came back from Los Angeles he had been very happy until he went out to see his friends. He had come back with an even greater desire to dance. To him everything was in rhythm. Everywhere he went, even if it was only inside the house, he snapped his fingers and swung his body. His every motion and action was, as they say, in beat. His language had changed quite a bit, too. Every time he left the house he said to his mother, "Ma, I will returniar in a little while." When he returned he said, "Ma, I was watchiando a good movie, that is why I am a little bit late." And Señora García found it very hard to break him of saying things like that. But that was not the half of it. It was his clothes that she found very odd. When he opened a box he brought from Los Angeles and took from it a suit and put it on, Señora García was horrified.

"Why, Pepe, what kind of a suit is that?" asked Señora García.

"Ma, this is the styleacho in Los Angeles, Califo."

"Well, I certainly do not like it Pepe."

"Ah, mama, but I like it. And I will tell you why. When I first got to California I was very lonely. I got a job picking fruit in no time at all and I was making very good money. But I also wanted to have a good time. So— one day I was down there in a place called Olvera Street in Los Angeles and I noticed that many of the boys who were Mexicans like me had suits like this one. They were very happy and very gay. They all had girls. There were many others, but they were not having any fun. They were squares. Well, I tried to talk to them, but it seemed as though they thought they were too good for me. Then I talked to the ones that were wearing drapes and they were more friendly. But even with them I could not go too far in making friends. So I bought this suit. Soon I went down to Olvera Street again and I got invited to parties and everything. I was introduced to many girls."

"But I do not like the suit, Pepe. It does not become you. I know now that you came back from California a cursed pachuco. A no-good zoot suiter. I am very sorry I ever let you go in the first place. I am only thanking Jesus Christ that your father is dead so that he would not see you with the sadness I see you now."

"Well, ma, I will tell you something else right now if that is the way you feel about it. I am not the same as I used to be. I used to think that I would never want to wear a suit like this one. But now I like it. If the squares in Tucson do not wear a suit like this one, is that my fault or is it for me to question? No. And I do not care. But if I like it and want to wear it I will. Leave me alone, ma, and let me wear what I please."

"You will not leave this house with that suit on, Pepe," said his mother, as she stood before the door, obstructing his path. "I will not have the neighbors see you in it."

"The neighbors do not buy my clothes, ma, so if they do not like my taste they can go to hell," said Kid Zopilote, as he gently moved his mother from the door and went out.

After that Señora García said nothing. Whenever Kid Zopilote went about the house with his pleated pants doing the shimmy to the radio, she merely sighed. When he clomped his thick-soled shoes in rhythm, she left the room in complete disappointment. When Kid Zopilote put on his long finger-tip coat, his plumed hat, dangled his knife on a thick watch chain, and went out of the house, Señora García cried.

Every day Kid Zopilote walked past the Chinese stores, the shoeshine parlors, barber shops, bars, and flop houses on Meyer Street. Sometimes he spent the entire day at Kaiser's Shoeshine Parlor. This was where, through time, a few lonely zoot suiters had been attracted by the boogie woogie music of the juke box. All day they put nickel after nickel into it to snap their fingers and sway their bodies with the beat. On other days Kid Zopilote went uptown to the Pastime Penny Arcade. Here again, the zoot suiters came in hour after hour to try their luck with the pinball machines. They walked by the scales a few dozen times a day and instead of stopping to weigh, they took out a very long comb and ran it through their hair to make sure that it met in back of the head in the shape of a duck's tail. Then they went outside to lean on the window. They sat on the sill and conversed until very late at night. Here they followed the every action of the girls that passed. They shouted from one side of the street to the other when they saw a friend or enemy, their only other action being that of bringing up cigarettes to the lips, letting the smoke out through the nose, and spitting on the side-walk through the side of the mouth, leaving big yellow-green splotches on the cement.

One morning Kid Zopilote got up very early and went to visit his uncle who was from Mexico. When he got to the house, Kid Zopilote walked in the front door and found his *tío* was still asleep in street clothes. But it was very important to Kid Zopilote to find out the true implication of his nickname. So he woke his uncle. After the two started a fire, made and ate breakfast, with an inquisitive look on his face Kid Zopilote began, "Tío, you are a relativo of mine because you are a brother of my mother. But I know and you know that my mother does not like for me to visit you because you are a wino. But today I came to ask you something very important."

"What is on your mind?" asked the uncle.

"Well, before I went to Los Angeles everybody I knew used to call me Pepe. But since I came back everybody now calls me Kid Zopilote. Why? What is the true meaning of Kid Zopilote?"

"The zopilote is a bird," said his uncle.

"Sí—?"

"Yes, the zopilote is a bird . . ." said his uncle, repeating himself.

"What more, tío?" asked Kid Zopilote.

"Well—in truth, it is a very funny bird. His appearance is like that of a buzzard. I remember the zopilotes very well. There are many in Mazatlán because the weather there is very hot. The damned zopilotes are as black as midnight. They have big beaks and they also have a lot of feathers on their ugly heads. I used to kill them with rocks. They come down to earth like giant airplanes, feeling out a landing, touching the earth. When they hit the earth they keep sliding forward until their speed is gone. Then they walk like punks walk into a bar. When the damned zopilotes eat, they only eat what has previously been eaten. Sometimes they almost choke and consequently they puke. But always there is another zopilote who comes up from behind and eats the puke of the first. Then they look for a tree. When they ease themselves on the poor tree, the tree dies. After they eat more puke and kill a few more trees, they once again start running into the wind. They get air speed. They become airborne. Then they fly away. "

"So you mean that they call me Kid Zopilote because they think I eat puke?" asked Kid Zopilote as his eyes became narrow with anger. "Tell me, is that why?"

"Not necessarily, Pepe, perhaps there are other reasons," said his uncle.

"The guys can go to hell then. If they can't call me Pepe they do not have to call me anything."

"But I would not worry about it anymore, Pepe. If once they began to call you Kid Zopilote they will never stop. It is said that a zopilote can never be a peacock," said his uncle, "and you probably brought it onto yourself." So Kid Zopilote went away from the house of his uncle very angry.

One night there was a stranger at Kaiser's Shoeshine Parlor. While he was not a zoot suiter he had the appearance of one of those slick felines that can never begin to look like a human being even if he should have on a suit of English tweed and custom-made shirts. He was leaning against the wall, quietly smoking a cigarette, when Kid Zopilote arrived. As usual Kid Zopilote saluted the zoot suiters with their universal greeting, "Esos guys, how goes it?"

"Pos ahí nomás. Oh, just so-so," said another *pachuco*.

"Well, put in a good jitter piece," said Kid Zopilote. Before the pachuco could slip the nickel into the slot, the stranger slipped in a coin and the juke box began to fill Kaiser's with beat.

Kid Zopilote and the other *pachuco* were thankful. After the stranger sized up Kid Zopilote he said, "Have a cigarette, won't you?"

"Thank you," said Kid Zopilote. And from that day Kid Zopilote smoked the man's cigarettes. In time he was being charged extravagant prices for them but Kid Zopilote always managed to get the price. He walked into the Western Cleaning Company and walked out with pressing irons. He went into business establishments and aways came out with something. He stole fixtures off parked automobiles. Anything. Kid Zopilote needed the cigarettes at any price.

One day the man said to him, "You know, Kid, I can no longer sell you cigarettes."

"I always pay you for them," said Kid Zopilote.

"Yes, I know you always pay for them. But from now on you can only have them when you bring your friends here. For every friend you bring me I will give a cigarette. Is that fair?"

"Fair enough," said Kid Zopilote. So in time many young *pachucos* with zoot suits began hanging around Kaiser's. Every day new boys came and asked for the stranger and the Kaiser directed them up a little stairway to the man with free cigarettes. In time he no longer gave them. He sold them. And the guys who bought them were affected in many ways. Talaro Fernández crept on the floor like a dog. Chico Sánchez went up and down Meyer Street challenging everybody.

Gastón Fuentes opened the fly of his pants and wet the sidewalk. Kid Zopilote panted like a dog and then passed out in a little back room at Kaiser's. Even Kid Zopilote was not getting the cigarettes for nothing because in no time at all he brought in all the potential customers. He had to pay for his smokes as did everybody else. In order to get the money he went to work hustling trade for Cetrina, who gave him a small percentage from her every amorous transaction. In the morning when trade was not buzzing Kid Zopilote stayed in her room and listened to dance records. When he tired of that he headed uptown to the Pastime or Kaiser's. Sometimes he walked into Robert's Cafe for a cup of coffee. There, when any of the squares that knew Kid Zopilote from the cradle asked him why he did not go to work, he got mad.

"Me go to work? Are you crazy? I do not want to work. Besides, I have money. I sell kick smokes and I can get you fixed up for five dollars with a vata that is really good looking," he said.

"That is no good. You will get into a lot of trouble eventually," they said to him.

"No, I won't. Anyway, I haven't got a damned education. I haven't got no damned nothing. But I'll make out." Then Kid Zopilote got up and snapped his fingers in beat and swayed his body as he walked out.

One day Kid Zopilote was caught in a riot involving the *pachucos* and the Mexicans from the high school whose dignities were being insulted by the fact that a few illogical people were beginning to see a zoot suit on every Mexican and every Mexican in a zoot suit. It ended up with the police intervening. The Mexicans from the high school were sent home and the pachucos were herded off to jail. The next day they were given free haircuts. Their drapes and pleated pants were cut with scissors. They crept home along alleys, like shorn dogs with their tails between their legs, lest people should see them.

"I am glad it happened to you, Pepe," said Señora García, "I am glad." But Kid Zopilote did not say a word. His head was as shiny as a billiard ball. His zoot suit was no more. All day he stayed at home and played his guitar. It was strange that he should like it so much, but now there was nowhere he could go without people pointing at him should he as much as go past the front door.

"Pepito, " said his mother, "you play so beautifully that it makes me want to cry. You have such a musical touch, Pepe, yet you have never done anything to develop it. But you do play wonderfully, Pepe."

One day as Kid Zopilote strummed his guitar, a boy looked over the fence and said to him, "Tocas bien. You play very well." But Kid Zopilote said nothing. This boy looked like many of the other American boys he knew that never had anything to do with him. "I play too," continued the boy, "so I hope you will not mind if I come into your yard and play with you. I will bring my guitar and perhaps we can play together. I learned from my Mexican friends in Colorado. I am attending school here."

"You can come if you wish," said Kid Zopilote. So the boy did and in time they were good friends.

One night the boy said to Kid Zopilote, "You were not meant to be a damned pachuco."

"Look. I like to play the guitar in your company but I do not want you or anybody else to tell me what I should be and what I should not be," said Kid Zopilote in an angry tone.

"I am sorry. We will just let it go at that," said the boy.

So, while Kid Zopilote's hair did not grow, he spent hour after hour with his friend who was thoroughly overcome with the beauty with which Kid Zopilote executed and with the feeling he gave his music. When Kid Zopilote's hair began to respond to the comb the friend took Kid Zopilote to visit friends. They went from party to party. They played at women's luncheons. They played on radio programs. Both were summoned for any event which demanded music.

"Pepe will be the finest guitar player in the whole Southwest," said Kid Zopilote's friend.

But when Kid Zopilote's hair grew long and met in the back of his head in the shape of a duck's tail, he no longer played the guitar. Anyway, most zopilotes eat puke even when better things are available a little farther away from their beaten runways and dead trees. As Kid Zopilote's uncle had said, "A zopilote can never be a peacock." So it was. Because even if he can, he does not want to.

from the novel

THE MIRACULOUS DAY OF AMALIA GÓMEZ

John Rechy

When Amalia Gómez woke up, a half hour later than on other Saturdays because last night she had had three beers instead of her usual weekend two, she looked out, startled by God knows what, past the screenless iron-barred window of her stucco bungalow unit in one of the many decaying neighborhoods that sprout off the shabbiest part of Hollywood Boulevard; and she saw a large silver cross in the otherwise clear sky.

Amalia closed her eyes. When she opened them again, would there be a dazzling white radiance within which the Blessed Mother would bask?—a holy sign *always* preceded such apparitions. What would *she* do first? Kneel, of course. She might try to get quickly to the heart of the matter—in movies it took at least two more visitations; *she* would ask for a tangible sign on this initial encounter, proof for the inevitable skeptics. She would ask that the sign be . . . a flower, yes, a white rose. Then there would follow a hidden message—messages from Our Lady were always mysterious—and an exhortation that the rose and the message, exactly as given, be taken to a priest, who would—What language would the Virgin Mother speak? "Blessed Mother, please, I *do* speak English—but with an accent, and I speak Spanish much better. So would you kindly—?"

What strange thoughts! Amalia opened her eyes. The cross was gone.

She *had* seen it, knew she had seen it, thought she had. No, Amalia was a logical Mexican American woman in her mid-forties. There had been no real cross. No miraculous sign would appear to a twice-divorced woman with grown, rebellious children and living with a man who wasn't her husband, although God *was* forgiving, wasn't He? The "cross" had been an illusion created by a filmy cloud—or streaks of smoke, perhaps from a skywriting airplane.

Amalia sat up in her bed. The artificial flowers she had located everywhere to camouflage worn second-hand furniture were losing their brightness, looked old and drab. She heard the growl of cars always on the busy streets in this neighborhood that was rapidly becoming a barrio like others she had fled. Looking dreamily toward the window, she sighed.

It was too hot for May! It's usually by late August that heat clenches these bungalows and doesn't let go until rain thrusts it off as steam. Amalia glanced beside her. Raynaldo hadn't come back after last night's quarrel at El Bar & Grill. Other times, he'd stayed away only a few hours after a spat; usually he was proud of the attention she drew, liked to show off his woman.

And Amalia was a good-looking woman, with thick, lustrous, wavy black hair that retained all its vibrant shininess and color. No one could accuse her of being "slender," but for a woman with firm, ample breasts and sensual round hips, her waist was small; any smaller might look ridiculous on a lush woman, she often assured herself. "Lush" was a word she liked. An Anglo man who had wandered into El Bar & Grill once had directed it at her, and that very night Raynaldo had called her "my lush brown-eyed woman, my lush Amalia."

Daily she moistened her thick eyelashes with saliva, to preserve their curl. She disliked downward-slanting eyelashes—but not, as some people of her mother's generation disdained them, because they were supposed to signal a predominance of "Indian blood." Unlike her mother, who repeatedly claimed "some Spanish blood," Amalia did not welcome it when people she did housework for referred to her—carefully—as "Spanish." She was proud to be Mexican American.

She did not like the word "Chicano"—which, in her youth, in El Paso, Texas, had been a term of disapproval among Mexicans; and she did not refer to Los Angeles as "Ellay." "The city of angels!" she had said in awe when she arrived here from Texas with her two children—on an eerie day when Sant' Ana winds blew in from the hot desert and fire blazed along the horizon.

Raynaldo was not her husband, although—of course—she had told her children he was. Gloria was fifteen, and Juan seventeen. They slept in what would have been a small living room, Juan in a roll-out cot, Gloria on the pull-out sofa. When Teresa, Amalia's mother, was alive, she occupied the small other "bedroom," a porch converted by Raynaldo. The last time he was out of jail, Manny, Amalia's oldest son, shared it, sleeping on the floor next to his grandmother's cot. Now the improvised room was vacant, surrendered to two deaths.

On a small table in Amalia's room were a large framed picture of Our Lord and one of his Blessed Mother, next to a small statue of the Virgin of Guadalupe on a bed of plastic flowers. There, too, was a photograph of President John F. Kennedy. When he was murdered in her home state, Amalia and her mother—her father was on a binge and cried belatedly—went to several Masses and wept through the televised funeral, the only time Teresa did not resent "Queen for a Day" being pushed off the black-and-white television.

Amalia made her slow, reverential morning sign of the cross toward the picture of Christ, hands outstretched, his bright red Sacred Heart enclosed in an aura of gold; and she extended her gesture to the Blessed Mother, resplendent in her blue-starred robe. *They* would certainly understand why it was necessary that she tell her children Raynaldo was her husband, to set a moral example, why else?

Almost beefy and with a nest of graying hairs on his chest nearly as thick as on his head, Raynaldo was not the kind of handsome man Amalia preferred, but he was a good man who had a steady job with a freight-loading company, and he helped generously with rent and groceries. He had been faithfully with her for five years, the only one of her men who had never hit her. Once he had paid a *mariachi*—who had wandered into El Bar & Grill from East Los Angeles in his black, silver-lined charro outfit—to sing a sad, romantic favorite of hers, "A punto de llorar"; and he led her in a dance. God would forgive her a small sin, that she pretended he was a handsome groom dancing with her one more time before their grand church wedding.

Amalia pulled her eyes away from the picture of Christ and the Holy Mother because she had located the place on the wall where the plaster had cracked during a recent earthquake. She had felt a sudden trembling in the house and then a violent jolt. As she always did at the prospect of violence, she had crouched in a corner and seen the crack splitting the wall. Now every time the house quivered from an idling truck, she thought of rushing out—although she had heard repeated warnings that that was the worst thing to do. But what if the house was falling on you? She wished the talk of earthquakes would stop, but it seemed to her that constant predictions of a "Big One" were made with increasing delight by television "authorities."

My God! It was eight-thirty and she was still in bed. On weekdays she might already be at one of the pretty houses—and she chose only pretty ones—that she cleaned. She preferred to work at different homes in order to get paid daily, and for variety. Too, the hours provided her more time with her children, although now they were seldom around. She was well liked and got along with the people she worked for, though she felt mostly indifferent toward them. She always dressed her best, always wore shimmery earrings; one woman often greeted her with: "You look like you've come to visit, not work." Amalia was not sure how the remark was intended, but she *did* know the woman was *not* "lush." Lately Amalia had begun to feel some anxiety about her regular workdays because "new illegals"—Guatemalans, Salvadorans, Nicaraguans without papers—were willing to work for hardly anything, and one of her employers had laughingly suggested lowering her wage.

Amalia sat on the edge of her bed. A strap of her thin slip fell off her brown shoulder. Had it really happened, in the restaurant-bar, after Raynaldo left and that young man came over? Amalia pushed away the mortifying memory.

She walked to the window. One side of her bungalow bordered the street. At the window she did not look at the sky.

Daily, the neighborhood decayed. Lawns surrendered to weeds and dirt. Cars were left mounted on bricks. Everywhere were iron bars on windows. Some houses were boarded up. At night, shadows of homeless men and women, carrying rags, moved in and left at dawn. And there was the hated graffiti, no longer even words, just tangled scrawls like curses.

When she had first moved here, the court looked better than now. The three bungalows sharing a wall in common and facing three more units were graying; and in the small patches of "garden" before each, only yellowish grass survived. At the far end of the court, near the garage area taken over by skeletons of cars that no longer ran, there remained an incongruous rosebush that had managed only a few feeble buds this year, without opening. Amalia continued to water it, though, hating to see anything pretty die.

Still, she was glad to live in Hollywood. After all, that *was* impressive, wasn't it? Even the poorest sections retained a flashy prettiness, flowers pasted against cracking walls draped by splashes of bougainvillea. Even weeds had tiny buds. And sometimes, out of the gathering rubble on the streets, there would be the sudden sweetness of flowers.

There were far worse places inhabited by Mexicans and the new aliens— blackened tenements in downtown and central Los Angeles, where families sometimes lived in shifts in one always-dark room, tenements as terrible as the one Amalia had been born in—at times she thought she remembered being born within the stench of garbage. . . . Still other people lived in old cars, on the streets, in the shadows of parks.

As she stood by the window of her stucco bungalow, Amalia did not think of any of that. She was allowing her eyes to slide casually across the street to a vacant lot enclosed by wire—and then her eyes roamed to its far edge, past a row of white oleanders above which rose jacaranda trees with ghostly lavender blossoms. Even more slowly, her eyes glided toward the tall pines bordering the giant Fox Television Studio that extended incongruously from the end of the weedy lot to Sunset Boulevard; and then her gaze floated over the huge HOLLYWOOD sign amid distant hills smeared with flowers, crowned with beautiful homes. Finally, she looked up into the sky.

The cross was not there!

Of course not—and it had never been there. And yet—

Yet the impression of the silver cross she had wakened to had altered the morning. Amalia was startled to realize that for the first time in her recent memory she had not awakened into the limbo of despondence that contained all the worries that cluttered her life, worries that would require a miracle to solve.

Trying not to feel betrayed, she turned away from the sky. She heard the sound of tangling traffic on the nearby Hollywood Freeway, heard the cacophony of radios, stereos, televisions, that rampaged the bungalow court each weekend.

Amalia touched her lips with her tongue. Last night's extra beer had left a bitter taste. No, it was the memory of it, of that man she allowed to sit with her last night at El Bar & Grill. Released with a sigh, that thought broke the lingering spell of the morning's awakening and her worries swarmed her.

Worries about Juan!—handsomer each day and each day more secretive, no longer a happy young man, but a moody one. He'd been looking for work but what kind of job would he keep?—proud as he was. He had made terrible grades that last year of Manny's imprisonment. Was *he* in a gang? She had fled one barrio in East Los Angeles to keep him and Gloria from drugs and killings and the gangs that had claimed her Manny. Now, students carried weapons in school and gangs terrorized whole neighborhoods. Yesterday she thought she had seen bold new graffiti on a wall. The *placa* of a new gang? That is how *cholo* gangs claim their turf. And Juan was coming home later and later—recently with a gash over one eye. He had money. Was he selling *roca*—street crack?

And who wouldn't worry about Gloria? So very pretty, and wearing more and more makeup, using words even men would blush to hear. What had Gloria wanted to tell her the other morning when she hadn't been able to listen because she was on her way to work and came back too late to ask her? Gloria had turned surly toward Raynaldo, who loved her like a father all these years. Did she suspect they weren't really married? . . . Amalia was sure God knew why she had to live with Raynaldo, but she wasn't certain He would extend His compassion, infinite though it was, to a sullen girl. . . . *What had she wanted to tell her that morning?*

Something about her involvement with that Mick?—that strange young man who rode a motorcycle and wore a single earring that glistened against his jet-black long hair? Although he was Mexican American, he had a drawly voice like those Anglos from the San Fernando Valley, and he wore metallic belts and wristbands. *What had Gloria wanted to tell her?*

And Raynaldo! If he didn't come back—but he would—there would be mounting bills again, constant threats to disconnect this and that. There was still the unpaid mortuary bill—Teresa had demanded that there be lots of flowers at her funeral. Amalia could afford this bungalow, small and tired as it was, only because of Raynaldo. Had his jealousy really been aroused last night so quickly because the man staring at her at El Bar & Grill was young and good-looking? Or had he used that as an excuse for anger already there, tension about Gloria's—and, increasingly, Juan's—abrupt resentment of him?

Of course, of *course*, Amalia missed Teresa—who wouldn't miss her own mother?—dead from old age and coughing at night and probably all her meanness, thrusting those cruel judgments at her own daughter. Who would blame her for having slapped her just that once? Certainly

God would have *wanted* her to stop the vile accusations she was making before Gloria and Juan during those black, terrible days after Manny's death. And who could blame her for having waited only until after the funeral to pack away the old woman's foot-tall statue of La Dolorosa, the Mother of Sorrows? . . . Of course, however you referred to her, she was *always* the Virgin Mary, whether you called her Blessed Mother, the immaculate Conception, Our Lady, the Madonna, Mother of God, Holy Mother—or Our Lady of Guadalupe, the name she assumed for her miraculous appearance in Mexico to the peasant Juan Diego, long ago. Still, Teresa's La Dolorosa, draped in black, wrenched in grief, hands clasped in anguish, tiny pieces of glass embedded under agonized eyes to testify to endless tears, had always disturbed Amalia, had seemed to her—God would forgive her this if she was wrong—not exactly the Virgin Mary whom she revered, so beautiful, so pure, so kind in her understanding—and so miraculous!

Yes, and now there wasn't even her trusted friend, Rosario, to turn to for advice, crazy as her talk sometimes was when they both worked in the "sewing sweatshop" in downtown Los Angeles. That tiny, incomprehensible, strong woman was gone, fled—*where*?—had just disappeared among all those rumors that she was in trouble with the hated "migra," the immigration, for helping the illegals who tore her heart.

And Manny—

Manny.

Her beloved firstborn. His angel face haunted her. A year after the blackest day of her life, she still awoke at night into a stark awareness of his absence. Did he hear the guards approaching along the desolate corridor toward his isolated cell? Did he recognize them in the gray darkness as the two he had broken away from earlier, the one he had hit across the face with handcuffs? Did he know immediately what they were going to do to him?

The horror of it all would push into Amalia's mind. She saw the guards tightening the shirt around his neck. Did he cry out to her as he had each time he was arrested? . . . What were his last thoughts?—that he would never see her again, about his love for her, of course. No, she would not even open the letter that had arrived yesterday from the public attorney. She knew what it would say. More investigations! She could not go through any more pain, listen to any more filthy cop lies. Let her son rest!

And then last night—

She cursed the extra beer that allowed last night to happen. She had said yes when the young man offered it to her, but only in defiance—the Blessed Mother would attest to that—because Amalia was a moral woman who had never been unfaithful to any of her husbands, nor to a steady "boyfriend." She spat angrily now. The hot humiliation of last night grasped her—Raynaldo stalking out of the bar, accusing *her* of flirting with that young man, who had kept staring at her. And so—

"Yes, I will have that beer," she had told him. He joined her in the "family" section of the restaurant-bar. He brought his own beer and a fresh one for her. Yes, he was good-looking—why deny what everyone could see? He had dreamy dark eyes, smooth brown skin, and he wore a sacred cross on a tiny golden chain on his chest. He was from Nicaragua, his family displaced; where? . . . Like her he spoke English and lapsed into Spanish. She was sure he thought she was younger than she was. She attracted all types of men, after all, and she was wearing one of her prettiest dresses, watery blue, with ruffles—and her shiniest earrings, with golden fringe.

"Bonita Amalia," he had said.

"How do you know my name?" She was not flirting, just asserting that it was *he* who was interested in her.

"I heard the man you were with." Then he told her his name: "Ángel."

Ángel! Amalia had a weakness for handsome men with holy names. Her first husband's name was Salvador, savior; her second was named Gabriel. She hated it when "Ángel" was mispronounced by Anglos as "Ain-jel." It was "Áhn-hel." . . . The holy cross on his chest, the sadness about his family, his beautiful name, and his eyes—and Raynaldo's unfair accusation—that's what had goaded her.

Amalia drank the extra beer with him, and then—

In her bedroom now, Amalia's eyes drifted toward the window. It would be a beautiful summer-tinged spring day, she told herself. Yet a sadness had swept away the exhilaration of this day's beginning.

She stood up to face the day. She could hear Gloria and Juan talking in their "bedroom." They were so close she sometimes felt left out of their lives. . . . And why shouldn't they sleep in the same room? After all, they *were* brother and sister, weren't they?—and of the same father. Soon one of them would be moving into Teresa's room, where Manny had slept—and they had adored their reckless half brother. They were avoiding moving into that room, Amalia knew, but there was just so long that you could avoid things, and that's what she must tell them.

She dressed quickly. Now she would leave this room with its aroused worries. She would allow no more, none, not about Juan—Hiding what with his new moodiness? Was he using drugs? Who was that Salvadoran boy he had let sleep in the garage; hiding from what? . . . No more worries! Not about Gloria. She had thrown up recently. Was she pregnant by that odd Mick with his colorless eyes and dark, dark eyebrows? *What had she wanted to tell her that morning?*. . . No more worries! Not about Raynaldo, either— What was really bothering him? Would he come back? *No more worries!*

And she was not going to give one more thought to the white cross— no, it had been silver!—that she had seen—thought she had seen this morning . . . although it had been *so* beautiful.

And certainly no more about last night!

Last night—

"Una flor para la bonita Amalia." Ángel had said that last night.

"What?" She had wanted to hear it again.

"A flower for pretty Amalia." He had already called to the girl selling flowers in the bar-restaurant. He placed the bud in her dark hair, as if he had known her for long, from her girlhood, yes, and he had made her feel the way she had wanted to feel as a girl, and that's why she said yes to him when he asked to join her, because—

Because—

Because he had given her a gardenia, the color of the pearl-white wedding dress she had never worn because at fifteen she had already aborted one child by a man who raped her and whom she was forced to marry.

THE WHITE GIRL
Luis Alberto Urrea

2 Short was a tagger from down around 24th St. He hung with the Locos de Veinte set, though he freelanced as much as he banged. His tag was a cloudy blue/silver goth "II-SHT" and it went out on freight trains and trucks all over the fucking place. His tag was, like, sailing through Nebraska or some shit like that. Out there, famous, large.

2 Short lived with his pops in that rundown house on W 20th. That one with the black iron spears for a fence. The old timer feeds shorties sometimes when they don't have anywhere to go—kids like Lil Wino and Jetson. 2 Short's pops is a *veterano*. Been in jail a few times, been on the street, knows what it's like. He'd like 2 Short to stay in school, but hey, what you gonna do? The *vatos* do what they got to do.

2 Short sometimes hangs in the backyard. He's not some nature pussy or nothing, but he likes the yard. Likes the old orange tree. The nopal cactus his pops cuts up and fries with eggs. 2 Short studies shit like birds and butterflies, tries to get their shapes and their colors in his tag book. Hummingbirds.

Out behind their yard is that little scrapyard on 23rd. That one that takes up a block one way and about two blocks the other. Old, too. Cars in there been rusting out since '68. Gutiérrez, the old dude runs the place, he's been scrapping the same hulks forever. Chasing kids out of there with a bb gun. Ping! Right in the ass!

2 Short always had too much imagination. He was scared to death of Gutiérrez's little kingdom behind the fence. All's you could see was the big tractor G used to drag wrecks around. The black oily crane stuck up like the stinger of the monsters in the sci-fi movies on channel 10. *The Black Scorpion* and shit.

The fence was ten feet tall, slats. Had some discolored rubber stuff woven in, like pieces of lawn furniture or something. So 2 Short could only see little bits of the scary wrecks in there if he pressed his eye to the fence and squinted.

One day he just ran into the fence with his bike and one of those rotten old slats fell out and there it was—a passageway into the yard. He looked around, made sure Pops wasn't watching, listened to make sure G wasn't over there, and he slipped through.

Damn. There were wrecked cars piled on top of each other. It was eerie. Crumpled metal. Torn off doors. Busted glass. He could see stars in the windshields where the heads had hit. Oh man—peeps died in here, Homes.

2 Short crept into musty dead cars and twisted the steering wheels.

He came to a crunched '71 Charger. The seats were twisted and the dash was ripped out. Was that blood on the old seat? Oh man. He ran his hand over the faded stain. Blood.

He found her bracelet under the seat. Her wrist must have been slender. It was a little gold chain with a little blue stone heart. He held it in his palm. Chick must have croaked right here.

He stared at the starred windshield. The way it was pushed out around the terrible cracks. Still brown. More blood. And then the hair.

Oh shit—there was hair in strands still stuck to the brown stains and the glass. Long blonde strands of hair. They moved in the breeze. He touched them. He pulled them free. He wrapped them around his finger.

That night, he rubbed the hairs over his lips. He couldn't sleep. He kept thinking of the white girl. She was dead. How was that possible? How could she be dead?

He held the bracelet against his face. He lay with the hair against his cheek.

When he went out to tag two nights later, 2 Short aborted his own name. Die Hard and Arab said, "Yo, what's wrong with you?"

But he only said, "The white girl."

"What white girl? Yo?"

But he stayed silent. He uncapped the blue. He stood in front of the train car. THE WHITE GIRL. He wrote. It went out to New York. He sent it out to Mexico, to Japan on a container ship. THE WHITE GIRL.

He wrote it and wrote it. He sent it out to the world. He prayed with his can. He could not stop.

THE WHITE GIRL.

THE WHITE GIRL.

THE WHITE GIRL.

TEARS ON MY PILLOW
Helena María Viramontes

Mama María learned me about La Llorona. La Llorona is the one who doing all the crying I've been hearing all this time with no one to tell me who it was til Mama María. She told me La Llorona's this mama, see, who killed her kids. Something like that. How does it goes? Something like there's this girl and some soldiers take her husband away and she goes to the jail to look for him, asses why these soldiers took him. And she gots I don't member how many kids all crying cause their daddy's gone, you know. And the soldier being mean and stupid and the devil inside him (but that's okay cause God knows everything says Mama María), he points a gun to her head and says "I gonna kill you." But she looks at him and says "Do me the favor." That's like something Arlene would say, you know. But the girl she don't know when to stop. "You kill everything so go ahead and kill me," she tells the soldier, "but first kill my kids cause I don't want 'em hungry and sick and lone without no *amá* or *apá* or TV." So the devil says "OK," and shoots all the kids, bang, bang, bang. But you know what? He don't kill her. Cold shot, huh? She goes coocoo and escapes from the nuthouse like my grandpa Ham used to do before he got dug in at Evergreen. And to this day, the girl all dressed up in black like Mama María cause she killed her kids and she walks up and down City Terrace with no feet, crying and crying and looking for her kids. For reallies, late in the dark night only.

You could hear her crying, for reals, I swear. When you hear her crying far away that means she's real close so don't go out at night. She's as close as your bed, so don't sleep with your feet to the window cause even she can pull you out. She'll get you, I swear. Ask Mama María. She's too old to lie.

Arlene don't believe me either. Not til she's home on a Friday night with nowhere to go but here. She heared it, too, herself, covered my ears. Ssshhh, my Mama Arlene said. Make it stop, I told her. Make it stop. I wished to God for Gregorio to come home. He's mean and can kick La Llorona's ass to the moon. Arlene took me to her bed, and I pulled up my feet real close to her. She smelled like cigarettes and warm beer and Noxzema cream. Her *chichis* was soft and cool under her slip, where I put my head. Please, mama, make it stop. I asses her to put the TV on real loud, do something, cause La Llorona was crying so crazy, she was breaking windows.

Ssshh, Arlene said, turning off the light, ssshhh.

■

La Llorona only comes at night. When it's day, Veronica will always stay. That's what I say. I don't like Veronica. Not cause her skin was all scaly and yellow and pus-y 'round the elbows and neck and behind her knees. Not even cause she's been hold back a few grades and just gets taller, or the way spit always dried at the corners of her mouth and turned white. I'm ascared of her cause her mama died a few months back, when the hot so hot you could fry your toes on the tar street. And every time I seen her, I remember if it's possible for my mama to die too. And my stomach burns bad to see her, tall and ugly and bad luck stuck to her like dried pus.

I have to sit next to Veronica on account of both our last names begin with G, no relation. She smells like pee and no one talk to her 'cept for Miss Smith, but she don't answer to nobody, not even Miss Smith. Veronica forgets that her name begins with V, puts spit on her eraser to erase the T on paper. Watching her smear the T all greasy black, then seen her scratching, scratching makes me want to tear out to anywheres. But Veronica, she lives close to me too.

Veronica and the brat brothers live 'cross the street from us in City Terrace Flats. Everybody ugly in her family, 'cepting her mama, Lil Mary G. Arlene knew her mama cause they went to Belvedere Jr. High together and hung around at Salas drugstore afterward. Then they got old.

Once when Arlene and me are in the bra section, First Street Store, cuz Arlene needs a new bra cause the thing that makes the straps go up and down broke and so her *chichis* hang down like a cow's she told Pancha, Veronica came up with Lil Mary G. For the first time, I seen Veronica's mama up front. She was short, kinda lumpy in a Arlene sorta way, which even made Veronica look more longer and ropey with knots for hands. Arlene said:

"Hey Lil Mary G! Member when we had to wear these, member?" Meaning Arlene picked up this kinda crippled bra for beginner *chichis* to show her. Lil Mary G. don't look like she even related to Veronica. I'm thinking about how someone so purty could have someone so ugly for a kid. She had glued, black Maybelline falsie lashes, black liner on top and at the bottom of her eyes, raccoon style. And, she gots these gray eyes like rain clouds. Ain't never seen color in eyes like that before. She wore her hair beehive teased, looked bitch'n cause you couldn't even see the bobby pins. But even, I seen the way Veronica looked at me staring at her mama, the way I check her out her skin so tissuey and Veronica gets all proud at her mama.

"Ain't buying this for Veronica," said Lil Mary G, and grabbed Veronica's *chichis* and Veronica gets all bareassed, unknots her hands and flapped Lil Mary G. chichis back, kinda laughing, kinda pushed out of shape. "It's for me," and Arlene and Veronica's mama had a good laugh between the rows of boxes with them bra girls pushing out their starched up tits, thinking they all look Hot. No one 'cepting me don't even pay no attention to the way Veronica always scratching, scratching her arm, behind her legs, or the spit all white on her mouth even in the bra section at the First Street Store.

■

Arlene was in the kitchen. Got her rollers the size of candles all waxed stiff with Deb gel. She looked to be a shadow at the kitchen window, sitting in the dark, and for a snap of a minute, cause maybe I woke up all sleepy-head, I think it's a ghost. Mama? but she don't answer me, just the radio real low, a man singing Arlene's favorite song. You don't member me, but I member you, was not so long ago, you broke my heart in two—I peek over her to see what she's looking at.

"Crying shame" was all I heard, shaking her head like she does when Grandpa escaped and no one ever knowed where he was. The peoples down below all grouping next to Lil Mary G.'s house, the ambulance doors scream open and the bed rolls out like a tongue. I seen a plastic bag and lots of tubes, red period spots on white sheets, the tongue swallowed up by the ambulance mouth. I don't see Veronica nowheres, and I stick my head out to look for her but Arlene grabbed me back in real hard, like she's piss at me for something. "I hope they blow his fucking dick off," she tells no one.

∎

Veronica don't talk to no one, and purty soon no one talk to her. She just wants to be left alone til everybody forgets she's around. I think that's what it is. Then she can disappear like Lil Mary G. without no one paying no attention. You don't need bras or nuthin' when you just air.

But to me, she just gets taller and rashier and her scratching sounds louder, like someone always rubbing sandpaper together. For reals.

Miss Smith yelled to me in a voice coming from a deep cave, "Ofelia, answer my question!" cause she been calling me and who cares, I don't know the answer anyways and I said "I dunno the answer anyways" the bell rings. I ain't allowed to stay after school and play with Willy on account of he bit me like a dog, and Arlene and Tía Olivia had a fight, sos I ain't allowed to go to Tía's house either, and I dunno where my brother Gregorio is sos I guess I just go straight home, put the TV on loud or something.

When the door opens and its Arlene, my stomach burns stop. Her face makeup is all shiny sweat. Last week, me and Arlene and Pancha, who can drive a pickup truck, go to where Arlene works on account of I might get this job there pulling pant pockets inside out and getting money for it. Pancha can't find no parking so it's just me and Arlene that goes into this big room with pipe guts for ceilings and no windows. All these sewing machines buzzing, buzzing, eating up big balls of string about big as my head spinning dizzy and so much dust flying 'round, makes it hard to breathe where Arlene works. Even I sneeze to no God bless yous. Nobody even to look up to say hello, not even Mr. Goldman who's so red he's pink 'n' says I'm too young anyways. Arlene said everyone at the machines ascare to go pee cause when you come back, might some other girl be in your place and no more job for you. Sos she got to hold her piss—'til my pussy 'bout to pop—she said to Pancha at the Kress lunch counter and I heard.

"Turn off the TV," she always says before hello. "Get me some aspirins." And I does both. I know it takes a long time for the buzzing of the machines in your head to stop. I know it after last week. Arlene kicks off her tennies, goes straight for the couch. The gummy black mascara lashes close like Venetian blinds, puts her arm over her forehead, asses me, "Where's Spider?"

"I dunno."

"Was he home?"

"I dunno."

"Did he go to school?"

"I dunno." And in a snap of a minute, she's asleep.

Sos not to wake her, I go to the kitchen, look out the window for Gregorio. I see Veronica across the street, sitting on the porch, licking her lips, and I act like I don't see nuthin'. She act like she don't see nuthin' either.

"What the fuck's wrong?" Arlene yells, running into the bathroom, her hair wrapped in a towel like a vanilla Foster Freeze ice cream. "Well?" She's pissed, unwraps her towel, bows to rewrap it.

"Oh," I says, wiping my nose with the back of my hand, feeling stupid. "It's nuthin', Amá. I just thought you . . ."

"Cheezes, *mija*. Don't do me that again, sabes?"

I dunno what to say. One minute I seen her in the tub, next minute I run into the bathroom and stand there and the tub is empty and I only seen the water circling and circling into the drain and I screamed for I dunno why. Ain't nothing worser could happen than for a mama to die, you know. They ain't supposed to. Not even with such a purty name like Lil Mary G.

Just they never say hello and they never say good-bye. Mama María never said good-bye, she just left and that's that and nobody to tell me why Tío Benny don't live with Tía Olivia any more or when is Gregorio gonna come home or if Arlene is fixed up to go dancing at the Palladium tonight. No one to say nuthin'.

Arlene is getting ready in front of the mirror, pulls the top of her hair up, teases it with a brush, brushes it back, forks it high with her comb. I trip out cause she can do this and blow bubble gum at the same time without missin' a beat. Sprays Aqua Net back and forth, back and forth til her hairdo as shiny and hard as candied apples.

See what I mean? They just never say hello and never say good-bye. They just disappear, leaving you alone all ascared with your burns and La Llorona hungry for you.

PITCH 2506

Jorge Saralegui

He sat in the outer office, examining the credits on the framed movie posters that covered the walls. This was one of the studios that had downsized its water offerings. Instead of the traditional twelve ounces in a cold plastic bottle, Ted's assistant had given him a half-full, room-temperature tumbler. He doubted he'd take more than a sip during the entire pitch. Served like this, the water seemed used.

Ten minutes after the meeting was supposed to start, Ted emerged from his office. It was a Friday: Ted wore jeans, sneakers, and an untucked polo shirt.

"Dude."

"Hey, Ted."

They bumped fists and went inside, closing the door behind them.

Ted told him to sit wherever he wanted. He took the seat opposite the one that was clearly Ted's. In between the shelves lined with movie scripts, there were photos of Ted jumping out of an airplane, and Ted doing a pull-up on the gun barrel of a tank. He was definitely in the right office.

After some small talk about how neither could complain about his circumstances, Ted got down to business. "So. You have a war movie for me. You know . . ." Ted held out his hands. No need to state the obvious.

"That's why I'm here."

"It's not about Iraq, is it? That's been done to death, and it hasn't even been done yet."

Movie projects were like groceries: everything had a shelf life. One day on the shelf too long, or one similar project too many, and the freshest idea suddenly seemed stale. "This hasn't been done yet, either. But no one has this story. Which is amazing, because it's been there for 45 years. And it's got everything. Think Gallipoli. With tanks and jets."

"I'm psyched." Ted leaned forward, giving him his full attention. "My junior's out sick, so it'll just be the two of us."

He crossed his legs. "What do you know about the Bay of Pigs?"

"It's what they called the game between Tampa Bay and Green Bay, back when both of them sucked."

They laughed. Ted was fifteen years younger than him, but he knew his football.

"The Bay of Pigs is Cuba's Gallipoli." That wasn't exactly right. It was the Cuban exiles' Gallipoli. But splitting hairs in a pitch was a bad idea.

"Cool."

"Should I just launch?"

"Go for it."

■

Guatemala is nobody's idea of a good time. Not even the Cubans who come from the country. There is no break from the humidity or the mosquitoes. For those of us from Havana, the absence of women or decent music on the radio has us itching for a fight. Maybe it would be different if we already had the discipline that the army is supposed to bring. A few of the guys served in Batista's army, but most of us just want to kick Fidel's ass out of Cuba.

Our flight arrived two weeks ago. They trucked us from San Jose to the training base. One of the vets told us it used to be a coffee plantation. We joined the original contingent that trained in Florida, and the guys who followed from Alabama and Louisiana. The first thing we asked was why Guatemala instead of Florida. The answer was not Florida, to keep us out of the newspapers. And Guatemala because the CIA thinks it looks just like Cuba, which is scary. The CIA bought our plantation and another base about twenty miles away for the pilots they're training.

There's about 1,500 of us, but our serial numbers start at 2500 to make our force seem bigger. Our first casualty was serial number 2506. He was killed in a training exercise long before we got here. They named our unit in his memory: the 2506 Assault Brigade. Why padding our numbers to 4000 makes a difference when the Communists have 300,000 is something only the CIA spooks can answer, and they don't, mainly because none of them speaks Spanish. What we hear is that we can't lose—the U.S. government won't let us. Kennedy is officially committed to overthrowing Castro. They'll provide the sort of air superiority that GIs had fighting the Nazis. They better. We get $400 a month, more for the guys with families. Nobody's doing this for the money.

Our pilots are going to fly B-26 bombers, which date back to World War II. The explanation is that they match the Cuban air force, so the U.S. can claim that they didn't train anybody, that the planes dropping bombs on Fidel's head are really rebel pilots from his own air force. Although the jungle keeps us from visiting the airmen's base, we hear how their training is going. It seems that the pilots can fly, but the gunners can't shoot. At least not from the air. The B-26s would take off every day from the base's runway and do target practice at some bamboo poles, pine boards, and 55-gallon drums that they set afloat in a small lake. Each plane has six .50-caliber machine guns installed on the nose. When the CIA pilots arrived, the target was still afloat. The CIA pilots destroyed it the first time out. That was embarrassing.

Over on our base, we learn how to use small arms and set off demolitions. At night, we study insurgency techniques. The radio operators may disagree, but this is fun, if we can forget for a moment that the fun is happening in a state of permanent sweat, and that we have bug bites on our bug bites. The guys with the most self-control are trained to operate mortars, bazookas, and 75mm recoilless rifles. There are even five tanks. The jungle around here gets some serious shredding.

After a couple of months, we are ready to fight. And with no word as to when we will, we start bitching. What we're most pissed off about is that the CIA is running this operation. They picked our commander—Pepe San Román—and didn't let the heads of the movement even visit our bases. Supposedly this was to maintain secrecy, but there had already been articles in the papers spelling out exactly where we were and what we were up to. Arguments about pride are hard to resolve. In the end, 200 of our men wind up under arrest and behind wire in the jungle. It's time to go—before we lynch the CIA guys and start fighting with ourselves. The Americans make it official in March, saying that we want to strike before fifty of Fidel's pilots return from Czechoslovakia trained to fly MiG fighters. Right now his air force is about a dozen bombers like ours, four jet trainers, and a bunch of prop odds and ends.

The CIA lays out the invasion plan to Pepe, and he lays it out to us. First our B-26s knock out Castro's planes. Paratroopers then drop in and secure the Santa Clara airfield, which is in the country's center. Together with commandos already in place as well as the anti-Castro underground, they sever communication lines, cutting the island in half. Nino Díaz lands with 168 men in Oriente, creating a diversion. With the army distracted, we land on the southern coast at Trinidad, far from where they're concentrated. The brigade could then move in, protected by American fighter planes. At this point, our government-on-exile would officially ask for help from our American friends. And a naval task force would comply, supplying and reinforcing us.

There it is. Pepe shouts out, "On to victory!" and our kettle blows its lid. We cheer, sing, hug, cry. The Americans are swept up by our emotions, and throw their hats in the air as well.

The next morning we cross the border into Nicaragua, and board the transports assembled in Puerto Cabezas. The Nicaraguan president, Somoza, tells us to bring back some hairs from Fidel's beard. Most of us laugh. We're feeling pretty cocky until we learn that there has been a change in plans. Kennedy is worried that the original plan exposes too much of the American involvement. Instead of landing near Trinidad in the morning, where we can duck into the mountains if we have to, we are going to land at Playa Girón, in the Bay of Pigs. U.S. intelligence reports that, apart from two railroads, it's isolated from the rest of the island by swamps. The only military in the area is a small detachment in the village. Since there's no rapid communications between Girón and Havana, we will land, capture the airfield at Girón, and fly in war supplies before Castro realizes what's happened.

We look at each other. They're changing the plans for a military operation that's been in the works for more than a year. Changing it in four days, and making us land at night on a coral coastline. The specifics of how we're going to do it are sketchy. And then we learn why: the only successful night-time amphibious landing happened in World War II. A guy who grew up near Girón says that if we are forced to retreat to the mountains, we won't be able to. The CIA guys tell us that, thanks to the U.S. air umbrella, there won't be anybody to retreat from. Somebody says that Kennedy just announced that under no conditions will U.S. armed forces intervene in Cuba. We want to know how that affects our air cover. The spooks claim it's a misdirect to lull Castro into a false sense of security. We look at each other again. They wouldn't bother sending us if it weren't true. We wouldn't have a chance.

■

Ted's assistant came in to hand Ted a note. Ted read it and shook his head. The assistant left.

"Is that the end of the first act?"

"Yeah."

"I like it. Kennedy throws them a curve ball, and now they have to rise to the occasion."

"You got it."

"So what was his problem?"

"Politics. He ran on an anti-Communist foreign policy, then had second thoughts when it was time to pull the trigger."

"That dude, man." Ted shook his head. "Hey, didn't Oliver Stone already do this? I'm all for remakes, but I think Warners did that one."

"No, that was about the Cuban Missile Crisis. It happened one year later." A grin. "This is the prequel."

He can see that Ted still doesn't like the connection.

"Who's the hero—the guy the U.S. put in charge? Now he has to prove himself to his men, that sort of thing?"

"Yeah, he proves himself to his men. But it's an ensemble story."

Ted raises an eyebrow. "At a budget that can swing an amphibious landing?"

"*Gallipoli* was an ensemble story with an amphibious landing. *Saving Private Ryan* was an ensemble story with an amphibious landing."

"Come on, man. *Gallipoli* was like a million years ago. *Private Ryan* had Tom Hanks. And it was a Spielberg movie."

He was about to say that just about all war movies were ensemble stories. But it was the studio's money, so Ted made the rules.

"I hear you. There's parts for Andy García, Jimmy Smits, and Ben Bratt."

He hoped that Ted wouldn't focus on the fact that this was an ensemble cast.

"How about George López as the funny one?"

"You mean the one who comes through in the clutch? Absolutely."

"Is there a role for a black guy?"

"Sure. We're talking a representative cross-section."

"Morgan Freeman."

"Morgan Freeman." They laughed and moved on. "Anything else?"

Ted looked at the notes he had been taking on a legal pad. "Yeah. Lose Somoza. With friends like that, who needs enemies?"

■

In the early hours of April 15, we are in the Caribbean, sailing east to Girón. Overhead, our B-26s head for Castro's three airfields. We have little to do but imagine Fidel's surprise at dawn as we bomb, rocket, and machine-gun the two dozen parked planes, and his air force disappears. By the afternoon, we learn what happened. At the last minute, Kennedy decided that a sixteen-bomber raid would create too much exposure. Only six planes took off from Nicaragua—two for each airfield. They reached the rendezvous point where they would be joined by an escort of American fighter jets near Cuba. But the fighters never showed.

The six planes go ahead. Our pilots try to make up for their reduced numbers. Instead of the planned two bombing runs per airfield, some of them make as many as five, flying fifty feet from the ground, making sure the hangars and aircraft are destroyed. Later, U-2 reconnaissance photos show that most of the destroyed planes are decoys. Castro has dispersed his air force. Our pilots are back on the runway, about to fly back and finish the job, when Kennedy calls off the clean-up strikes. The last word from the base is that the American air force general in charge of training says, "There goes the whole fucking war."

A few guys think he's right, and are hoping that Kennedy will call off the invasion. The spooks tell us that none of that matters. There'll be air cover throughout. Castro's air force won't be able to fly against us, and that's the bottom line. We have no choice at this point but to believe them. We are pissed at ourselves for having let the Americans run things, even though we know there'd be no invasion without their money. As the sun starts to set, we grow quiet, wondering what awaits us. We think about those pilots flying to Cuba and suddenly finding out that their escort wasn't there to meet them. We look at the darkening sea, and imagine how empty and alone the sky must have felt right then.

Our seven little transports meet up with the U.S. naval task force the day before we hit the beach. There are seven destroyers and an aircraft carrier. We feel a little more reassured. Around midnight, six of our frogmen approach the beach to mark it for us. Their boat gets stuck fifty yards offshore on a reef the CIA said was just seaweed. A militia jeep surprises them, and one of the spooks opens fire. It doesn't take long for a truck to pull up and 25 militiamen to hop out. It's now or never. The frogmen radio for us to come ashore.

We board our landing craft in the early hours of the 17th, say nothing, and plow toward the shore. The first thing we encounter is the teeth of the coral. Our vessel ruptures and starts to sink. We know the water is shallow, but the darkness says otherwise. Cursing furiously, we gain control of ourselves and wade to shore, firing into the bungalows that line the beach. Bungalows none of us expected. Soon after, another landing craft sinks. That no one drowns is a miracle. That the militiamen retreat despite our confusion is an even bigger one. And before the first rays of light appear, two battalions land at Playa Girón and a third at Playa Larga, twenty miles away. Word reaches us from the fleet that Castro still has aircraft operational, and that air strikes from Nicaragua to knock them out have been nixed. Any further air strikes will have to come from Girón, once we secure the local airfield. We also are told to expect no protection from the navy. That means we probably have until dawn to finish unloading all of our supplies before the ships are hit. At this point, nobody is complaining. There's no time. We secure the beachhead. A local tells us that the bungalows are part of a new tourist colony being built because Fidel likes to fish for trout nearby. As a result, there are now three paved roads cutting through the swamp. So much for our being safe against counterattack.

We have to seize the roads before they are used against us. The sky is already pink as we hear a rumble overhead. It's six C-46 transport planes. Each one carries about thirty of our paratroopers. Their mission is to drop them in position to cut off the invasion site. They probably flew over the aircraft carrier and thought we couldn't lose. A short while later, two of them pass by on their way back from the drop. Castro's B-26s are in pursuit. We never thought of how slow those C-46s are, because it wasn't supposed to be a factor. But it's a factor now that they have no fighter support. One goes down, smoking. The other makes it out to sea, skimming low over the waves.

There is enough light by six for us to count nine of Castro's planes as they go right for our cargo ships, which have yet to unload our supplies. The ships are all but unarmed, their decks laden with fuel and arms. They disable the *Marsopa*, our command ship. The *Río Escondido* goes up in a ball of flame. The *Houston* also sinks. Together, they carried all of the food, water, medical supplies, and fuel we need to survive. They also bore enough weapons for 20,000 additional soldiers. Thinking of what that means for our cause, we barely notice the other landing ships that also go down.

Our CIA guy with the fleet radios us. Washington has instructed them to go to sea and not return until dark. Pepe understands. He only asks that they not desert us. The spook says that they won't.

■

"Ouch." Ted makes a pained face. "That is cold, dude. This is definitely not a Camelot movie."

"No, it's not."

Ted scribbled some notes on his pad. "Don't you worry about trashing our military after 9/11?"

"We're not trashing the military. It killed those guys not to be allowed to help. A lot of them broke down in tears afterward."

"Is that going to be in the movie, too?"

He made a quick decision. "Yeah."

Ted wasn't there yet. "We have to sell this movie in all fifty states, not just California and New York."

"Don't forget Florida. It's full of Cubans. Plus international. On a movie like this, foreign's much bigger than domestic. And the whole world hates us."

Ted didn't find enough comfort in that. "Could we drop them getting fucked over? Government bad guys have been done to death."

"But that's what happened," he said, crossing his legs. "You can't change history."

"Who's talking about changing history? D-Day happened. Vietnam happened. But nobody tried to save Private Ryan. Nobody played

Russian roulette for a living in Saigon. That's what makes it a movie, and not a documentary on the History Channel." Ted paused. "Is there a documentary on this?"

"Yeah, but it's more about Kennedy. Not the guys who put their lives on the line."

"My point exactly. They catered to their audience. We're doing the same thing. This is a war movie. Our audience doesn't want all that geopolitical shit. They want to see guys coming out of a swamp firing automatic weapons." Ted glanced at his notes. "You said there was a swamp there, right?"

"There's a swamp," he replied, then returned to the original point. If he didn't, the politics of the situation implied that he had conceded it. "It's not about being accurate. It changes the whole story. If they hadn't been fucked over, things might have turned out differently."

"Hey, no offense, but how about giving some credit to Castro? Sort of like in a Civil War movie. You don't have to trash the South just because they were fighting for slavery."

He hesitated.

"Dude, I'm just trying to find a way to get this done," Ted said, unconsciously flexing his muscles.

"I hear you," he said. The odds of his setting up this pitch had always been low. He could see the tote board recalculating them right out of the realm of possibility.

Ted glanced at his watch. "So where are we? End of the second act?"

"Just about."

"The low point." Ted said this hopefully.

"Sort of."

∎

From Playa Larga, Oliva orders two B-26s to attack 900 militia racing toward the beach in about 60 vehicles. Our bombers rout the caravan, only to be shot out of the sky by Castro's faster planes. We see the entire invasion taking place in the air above us. A Sea Fury is on the tail of one of our B-26s. The B-26's port engine is already on fire. Behind the Sea Fury appears a navy jet fighter. We cheer. We know what the navy pilot is doing—radioing for permission to blow the Sea Fury out of the sky and save our men. Then the jet backs off, and the Sea Fury closes in for the kill. Again and again, navy pilots zero in on their targets, then pull away. We know what they're hearing: permission denied. If Kennedy were here, we'd rip him limb from limb. As the morning wears on, five more of our planes go down. They're sitting ducks. And by now they know it. Some of us break down as we watch. They came to die for us.

Word arrives that Díaz refused to disembark his 168 men in Oriente when he found out how things were going. We can't blame him. Our brothers in the mountains have been sealed off and radio messages to our infiltration teams and the underground blocked. There'll be no more resupplying, no more air support. We are on our own.

Our only chance is to get out of here and into the mountains. From there we can do to Fidel what he did to Batista. But by midnight, our scouts estimate there's about 20,000 militia in place, corralling us in. Artillery shells rain down on us. The rain never stops. With daylight, tanks move forward. Even those of us who hate mosquitoes are happy to be in a swamp right now. It's not going to be easy for them to break through. The launching pad of our offensive turns out to be a great place to defend. The swamps provide some cover against shrapnel, so if an artillery round doesn't land on our heads, we're usually OK. And as long as we have ammo, those militiamen are going to get stung by a lot worse than mosquitoes. Who wants to walk into a jungle that's shooting at you? It goes against a person's common sense, and Cubans have nothing if not common sense.

Not that we showed much, trusting another country to do the right thing for ours. But even that doesn't matter any more. All we need is to know that the guys next to our unit, and the guys down in Playa Larga, will hang in there as long as we will. What we're hanging on for is another question, and we're not wasting any time wondering about that. Not out loud, anyway.

It's funny how little you need to know to do a good job, when you don't have any choice. Everything gets easy then. We can't look up without seeing artillery shells buzzing toward us. Castro's militia keeps coming at us in waves. And we keep stopping them. Somebody says we're like the 300 Spartans holding off the Persian army at Thermopylae. Except we're not defending the gates of Greece, but the fucking ocean. The ones who get the reference laugh. The ones who don't tell him to quit talking shit.

Oliva's men join us the next morning. In between explosions, they tell us about their night in Playa Larga. After about 2,000 shells dropped on them in about four hours, Castro sent in his Stalin tanks. One of our tanks knocked out a Stalin with its last shell, then rammed another Stalin until its gun barrel split. Then there was some crazy little guy who kept running around a tank firing a recoilless rifle at it until the tank surrendered. The Stalins pulled back around midnight. Of the 370 men in Oliva's battalion, twenty had been killed and another fifty wounded. Knowing they'd be attacked at dawn, they made their way over to Girón.

Our reinforcements put their experience to good use on our second day. Castro again throws his tanks at us, and is beaten back with the three tanks and seven bazookas that Oliva still has left. Our mortars fire so many times that the tubes start to melt. We look at each other. It is amazing, like something out of a World War II movie. Except we are running out of mortars. Castro's tanks pull back, leaving behind three hulks.

If only the artillery barrage would stop, this would be the time for a cigarette. We watch a T-33—a trainer, but a jet trainer—strafe whoever it can find on the beach. Another navy jet closes on it. We watch with frustration as it does what they all do—pull away. If we had one goddamn jet, somebody says, we could have pulled this off. A shell lands nearby and the ifs fade away.

The militia keeps pushing, and by our third morning here, we are twenty feet from the water. We are almost out of ammunition. There is no more food or water. Nobody has slept in over 48 hours, and some of us are delirious. Castro's planes have nothing left to do but drop every last bit of ordnance on us. There is a very short conversation about surrendering as the 2506 Brigade. We decide that we cannot do it. Pepe radios the offshore fleet and says we are destroying our communications equipment and slipping off into the marshes in little groups. We have nothing left to fight with, he explains in a voice cracking with anger and apology. "How can you people do this to us, our people, our country? Over and out."

We head into the swamp.

■

"That's it?"

"That's the end of the movie. Sooner or later, the ones who survived were all captured. They were in prison for about two years, until Kennedy traded Castro $50 million in food and medicine for them. But you don't want to end the movie on any of that."

"No shit. How many of them died?"

"114."

Ted did some quick math. "That's like ten percent. Not too bad. I mean, it's not exactly Custer's last stand."

"I guess not."

"What are you going to call it—*Bay of Pigs*? You can't sell that title."

He took a sip of water. "I didn't say it was the title. And not that it matters, but 'pigs' is 'cochinos' in Spanish. But 'cochinos' is also the name of a fish found in that bay. So the Bay of Pigs is really the bay of a fish called cochinos."

"It could be a fish called Wanda. How is an audience going to relate to the story of a group named after the inflated serial number of a guy who died in a training accident? I mean, doesn't that tell you everything?"

It was time to lean forward. "Ted, they were guys like you and me. Half of them from Havana. Half of them were married. Most of them had no previous military training. And yet they pulled off a nighttime amphibious landing. Air operations. They held off a vastly superior force until they ran out of fucking bullets. If they had some air support, they might have pulled it off." He realized that in making excuses for the Brigade, he was making excuses for the pitch. So he shut up and finished his water.

Ted liked him. "Look. I know you well enough to know that you wouldn't pitch me something just because you're Cuban. When I think of you, I think event movie. Tell me why you're so hot on this one. Because dude, I don't get it."

An image of himself in knee pants at the airport in Havana flashed through his mind. "It has those moments that choke me up. Like *Gallipoli. The Charge of the Light Brigade*. Those moments are all you need."

Ted lowered his head, and came up taking the deep breath he needed to deliver his judgment. "We've known each other for a long time, so let's not play the usual game. I'm going on vacation next week and I want to get this off my desk." Ted held the legal pad out. "Look at my notes."

Scrawled across the top was "Pitch 2506." "That's not what I'm calling the pitch. That's how many pitches I've heard in my career, know what I mean? I have to ask myself—what's memorable about this one? I feel for those guys, dude, and I respect the hell out of your passion, but there's no hook. No hero. No title. No one-sheet. Bottom line, they're a bunch of guys nobody ever heard of who got their butts kicked. Next, right?"

He had been in the business long enough to know a lost cause. "I don't agree, but I know what you mean."

Ted gladly settled for that. Then his assistant entered to say that the head of production wanted him to come down. As they walked down the corridor together, Ted mentioned that he and some buddies were planning a trip to Cuba over Thanksgiving. "Cigars and mojitos 24-7. Peterson goes every year. He says the chicks are really cool, and everything's dirt cheap. But hey, I don't have to tell you that." Ted whacked him on the arm. "You should join us, dude. You speak Spanish, right? It'll be awesome."

Ted entered his boss's office, and he left the building. There were other studios, he thought, although Ted had definitely been his best bet. Rolling with the punches was part of his job description, and he would pitch it again. It just wouldn't be anytime soon.

He had wanted to say a lot more. That the name of the brigade was pronounced "Twenty-five zero six." That people relate to those who have fought and failed. It had been true for him since he was a child, watching war movies where someone took it for the squad or the squadron. He wasn't sure why that sort of death affected him so deeply. He had traced the feeling back to when he was seven, and left Cuba.

Everything about that day—from driving to the airport in tears, to the militiaman who made it clear he knew his family wasn't coming back, to landing in Montreal and feeling the cold on his bare legs—was more likely to be a story his mother had told him than something he remembered. He was happy to have grown up in the United States, but he had lost something back there, and the men of the brigade had tried to get it back for him. That was what he would have told Ted, had he been showing rather than selling. He wanted to let them know that they hadn't been forgotten, even if what they had fought for had been. To give them a Hollywood ending.

The hammering from inside a stage made it hard for him to sustain his thoughts. Ted's mind had long since shifted to whatever his boss had called him about. Some grips carried a shell-pocked wall past him, and he wondered for which war it would be used. He entered the visitors' parking lot and unlocked his car with the remote. Be it on Malibu or Playa Girón, he thought, we are sand; history washes over us.

DO YOU KNOW THE WAY TO THE MONKEY HOUSE?

Kathleen Alcalá

One night after work, Serena met Bullitt at Lucky John's for pizza.

"What do you want to do? A movie?"

"I don't know," she said. Since her trip to Tijuana with Julio-call-me-Mike, she had been subdued. It didn't matter, she kept telling herself. She had known she would lose him as soon as he moved to the East Coast.

"Still brooding about Julio?" asked Bullitt.

"I guess so," she said. She had told him the rudiments of the adventure. "I'm not sure why I'm still upset."

"Probably because you didn't have a say in the matter," said Bullitt. "It's always more pleasant to be the dumper than the dumpee."

"Yeah," said Serena. "Thanks. That makes me feel *much* better."

"I know something that will cheer you up."

"An execution?" asked Serena. "Baby torture?"

"Better than that. I want to take you to a place you haven't been before."

"Hmmm," said Serena, toying with her chocolate milkshake. "Does this involve fútbol?"

"No, not that I know of," said Bullitt. "Although my father asks about you all the time. He was quite smitten by you."

"Oh, well that's nice. At least someone is."

"Serena," said Bullitt, taking her hands in his and trying to look into her downcast eyes. "You know how I feel."

"I do?" she asked, looking up.

"Come on," said Bullitt, standing up. "Let's check this place out."

They got in the car and drove north up to Laurel Canyon. Two miles into the hills, they were surrounded by trees and shrubbery.

"It's like a little jungle up here," said Serena. "One minute you're in the city, the next you're far away."

Bullitt slowed the car at a side street. "I think it's up here," he said, turning.

The street narrowed and they passed a No Outlet sign. Beyond that, the road turned to dirt. The houses here were invisible behind barriers of trees and oleander run wild.

"Are you sure this is the way?" asked Serena. "Where are we going, anyway?"

"Trust me," said Bullitt. "I got careful directions from a friend."

Bullitt had not consulted notes or a map the entire time. Serena had noticed before that Bullitt could remember a lot of things that she could not.

They came to a neon yellow plastic ribbon that marked a dirt track.

"This is it," he said, and pulled the car into a gap in the weeds. A home-made Private Property, No Trespassing sign leaned dangerously over an embankment above them. Serena squirmed nervously in her seat. Some of these places had armed private guards, she had heard. Reasons to keep people out. Celebrities. Drugs. The vices that, even in L.A., needed to be kept secret.

The track leveled out, and Serena thought she could glimpse some walls or buildings ahead.

Although it was nearly dark, Bullitt kept the headlights off. As they rounded a bend, Serena could hear odd, high-pitched sounds.

"What is this?" she asked.

"You'll see."

They pulled into an open area from which they could see a pink hacienda-style mansion with a red tile roof. Bullitt turned off the engine, and Serena leaned forward, straining to see more detail. A light was on inside, and she could make out a moving figure now and then.

"Is this a party?" she asked, placing her hand on the door.

"Wait," said Bullitt, putting his hand on her arm without looking away from the house. "Don't get out just yet."

One of the figures came closer, and as her eyes began to adjust to the darkness, Serena could see that it was some kind of animal. It sat up, regarding them.

"Why, it's a monkey!" she said, delighted.

The monkey opened its mouth and let out a shrill scream, and what seemed like hundreds of monkeys came toward them out of the bushes, the building, and the surrounding trees.

"Lock the doors," said Bullitt.

The car was swarmed by screeching monkeys that tried to open the doors, fingering the antennas and wipers, clambering on the hood and roof of the car, and baring their teeth in the windshield. When it was clear that Bullitt and Serena were not coming out, a few began to lose interest, then more and more dropped off and sauntered back to the main building.

"Wow," said Serena, stunned. She could now see the dilapidated condition of the building, the hanging, shredded screens, the broken windows. Still, there was a light on inside.

"Does someone live here?" she asked.

She and Bullitt had been gripping each other's arms all this time. Now he relaxed.

"I don't know," he said. "Someone at work told me about it. People come up here and feed them."

"We don't have any food."

"I know. I forgot."

Serena could see that it had once been a beautiful place with a courtyard off to the right flanked by shaggy palm trees. Now this, too, was overrun with monkeys, all the same kind, scratching, eating, screaming in each other's faces.

"I can't believe no one takes care of them," she said. "Even if they didn't, the city or the county couldn't just leave them here."

"Maybe they'll take over the city," said Bullitt.

"Maybe they already have."

Bullitt laughed. "That would explain a lot."

As night fell, it became more and more difficult to see. Once in a while, one of the monkeys came back to the car as though checking to see if they had changed their minds about getting out or distributing some food.

"I can't believe all this," said Serena. "I wonder if this used to belong to some famous actress. It looks abandoned, but then there's that light."

"Maybe monkeys like light, too."

"Then someone's paying the electric bill for them. I'm going to check it out." She started to open her door.

"I don't think that's a good idea," said Bullitt. "They look like they could be dangerous."

"I just want to go close enough to look in the window, see where the light is coming from. Maybe there's someone in there."

"Then I'll go with you," said Bullitt, without much conviction.

"Why? We'll just make more noise."

Serena cracked her car door. None of the monkeys seemed to notice. She carefully climbed out, then crouched down, her fingertips touching the earth. Slowly, she made her way closer to the window, where she could now see the remnants of jagged bamboo blinds hanging in one corner, the light from inside coming through them.

A low, crumbling wall separated the driveway from the courtyard. Rather than trying to open the rusted gate, Serena leaned out over the wall, trying to see into the window beyond the blinds.

Just then, a sentinel's shriek pierced the air as a monkey that had been strolling the veranda spotted her. Serena raced for the car as the monkey hordes descended. She slammed the door, leaving a few ends of her hair outside that were promptly snatched out by the enraged monkeys.

"Ow! Ow! Ow!" she said, pulling her hair away from them.

The monkeys pressed their faces to the glass, demonlike now in the dark, howling their fury at the two of them. Their tiny hands were like dark starfish on the windshield, constantly moving as the monkeys searched for a way in—any weakness, any latch that would twist or pull out.

"They're really cussing you now," said Bullitt.

Serena sat heaving, her eyes glittering with adrenaline. The monkey's screams began to turn piteous, as though they were begging now.

"Well?" asked Bullitt.

"Well what?"

"Did you *see* anything?"

"Sort of," said Serena. She was putting her hair into a ponytail, rubbing her scalp where the hair had been plucked out.

"You know that scene in *Psycho* . . ." she continued.

"Yes? Which one? The shower scene?"

"No. The one where Norman Bates is talking to his mother, and you just see her in her chair from the back . . ."

"You saw someone sitting in a chair?"

"I think so. By the light. There's a lamp in there. And a big chair with its back to the window, and there seems to be someone, or something, in it."

"Alive?"

"I couldn't tell. I just got a glimpse."

Bullitt stared at her.

"You want to go look yourself?"

The monkey's screams had not abated. Those on the windshield peered intently in at them, looking from Bullitt's eyes to Serena's and back again, like customers who have been bilked by a salesman, demanding satisfaction. Apparently, someone getting out of the car was too much of a provocation, and their frenzy echoed off the surrounding hills.

"Let's go," said Bullitt, starting the car.

The monkeys clinging to the car immediately began to jump off, but did not let up their cries.

As Bullitt and Serena reached the end of the drive, he turned on his lights, only to find that they were almost upon another car. Bullitt hit the breaks, and after a moment, the other car backed up to a wider spot, allowing them to pass. As they drew alongside, the driver rolled down his window and leaned out. Bullitt opened his window.

"Do you know the way to the monkey house?" asked the driver.

From here the sound was fainter, a constant chatter with louder outbursts. It could have been peacocks, or some other exotic noise.

"Yeah," said Bullitt. "Up there on the left."

Later that night they tried to make love, but their bodies felt large and awkward, their hands too clumsy and wide to express anything they might have felt for each other. They put their arms around each other and lay in the silence that fell between them.

A LONG STORY CUT SHORT

Frederick Luis Aldama

I don't apologize. That's what's so nice about dying. You don't have to apologize anymore. Not to anybody. Above all, not to yourself. All's bundled up in one undifferentiated past. Gone. Forever. Nothing to look forward to. Nothing to fret about, past or present. No more struggles to keep up appearances. I don't even care if I soil the sheets or even the whole mattress. Oblivion. Just oblivion. Finally I'm really irrelevant. To myself. To everyone. Just like all those I've known who have died. Including Andrew. The Irish cowboy-dressing, cowboy-swaggering, cowboy-failure I married before the war ended. My choice. My doing. My nightmare. A catch because he could never get a suntan. He had blue eyes. About five-eight tall. Huge next to my five-two. Made sure he couldn't get enough of me. Andrew. A one-way ticket out of Pico Rivera, out of the shirt factory, out of the embarrassing familia always waxing nostalgic about Guatemala. I myself was not *prieta*. Came to L.A. when ten. Grew quickly into the "ay nanita, qué buena estás" on the school premises and walking to the grocer's. Brown eyes, long eyelashes, coquettish smile. Daydreaming I was a fallen woman, but an untouchable one. A virgin. Tight-almost-white flesh. Ida Lupino in that picture with Gary Cooper. Or Louise Brooks in the silent movies. Yes, *Pandora's Box* and that other one I don't remember. *Diary* something-or-other. The flapper look. The femme fatale they called them. I was almost eighteen. He was thirty-four. Strong, fleshy hands always ready to grip. Shovels, cables, monkey-wrenches, wheelbarrows, anything with handles. Meaning his favorite knobs. My tits to squeeze, my nipples to wring and pull. And my flat ass. A stocky, silent old man. Only talked to badmouth Negroes. Or anybody from south of the border. Not much of a brain. Beginning of what became a big gut. And a lousy lover. But what did I care? Who needed a sexy-looking young man, anyway? Andrew's desire was blind. He wanted me bad. I wanted out and up. So I did a decent job. Got him to get me pregnant. Got him to marry me. Got him to put his insatiably grasping hands to work harder. Work for both of us and soon for three. For the little house I dreamt of. With a garden, a backyard. Nice furniture. At least two bedrooms. One for the baby. One for me. Shared with Andrew. But single beds. Like in the movies. Always loved going to the movies. My life would be a movie too. Singing and dancing and smoking and eating in restaurants and traveling and always looking good. No smelling like a wet rag. How I hated it when it got all hot and sticky. Humidity spoiling and curling my hair. Had to have my hair permed all the time. Nobody ever saw me looking like one of those dark-skinned Mexican girls with their hair all enchinado who lived on Pico or worked in the factory. Read a lot too. All kinds of inspiring magazines, like *Life*. It once had these pictures of that couple who owned *Reader's Digest*. The lady, her hat was beautiful. Looked like Scarlett in *Gone With the Wind*. They both looked royal in their mansion with the magnificent marble stair-way. Their magazine became a part of me. I would never give it up. It taught me everything useful and important. How not to be vulgar. How to build a distinguished vocabulary. How to act like a real lady. How great men lived and thought. How will and character can turn a personal tragedy into a he-roic victory. The Most Unforgettable Character stories were always a warm inspiration. The condensed books made you understand the most difficult things, like the evil done by Communism. More and more I became aware that what I wanted was the right thing to want. Year after year I persevered. Andrew took extra assignments to buy a car. It became indispensable. Street-cars, buses, all public transport became rapidly scarce. You no longer could take a tram or a bus from Beaudry to Alsace, from Seventh to First, from Alameda to West Pico. Years later I was driving everywhere, all the time. To put distance between reality and dream, to feel free. A pain-killer and a roving room of my own. Going places while going nowhere. Total stag-nation. Andrew proved to have nothing in him. Never was worth more than the prize of a photograph of John Wayne. Never tried hard enough to raise above his station. An enormous gut but no guts. Always remained a caricature of what I needed. *Caricature*—a good *Reader's Digest* word. My son a lazy bum now hooked to a white trash girl. My house a foul-smelling insignificant farm close to Sacramento with three cows, a horse, some pigs, and some chickens. No silver linings, no matter how hard I looked. No laughter. Only the lasting pleasure of driving. An exhausted body. Lung cancer. Everything wasted away.

Winter is here.

The air is solid.

I can no longer breathe.

I no longer wish to breathe.

THE STRAVINSKY RIOTS

Daniel Chacón

Marianne

When Daddy was a Chicano, he died for 27 seconds. The only version of this story comes from him, his facts, but I see it like one of those corny 1980s movies about Chicano gangs, made way before I was born, films like *American Me, Blood In, Blood Out*. The scene starts like this:

An inner-city street in L.A.

Four silhouettes rise from the steamy grates in the road, Chicano gang members wearing blue bandanas. One of the guys carries a sawed-off rifle in the flap of his flannel shirt. These boys walk out of the alley onto the boulevard toward a lowrider parked in front of the basketball courts, where another gang of boys stands around drinking beer and smoking marijuana.

It's a pretty stereotypical image, isn't it?

I even see tall L.A.-style palm trees swaying in the background.

The four *cholos* in blue cross the avenue to the other *cholos*. Camera cuts again to the sawed-off rifle under the shirt. The boys by the car notice the others and they posture themselves, get into position, ready to fight, two triangles of boys.

One in red says, "¿Qué onda?"

And before you know it, they're fighting. Shop owners close their blinds, kids run in all directions, balls are left to bounce by themselves. The boys fight with roundhouse kicks, punches, elbows, knees. One boy pulls the rifle from the waist of his pants and hits a boy on the head with the butt. The young cholo who is hit, my father at 16 years old, falls to the gutter. (Don't forget, this is a true story.) As he lies there, he feels the barrel of the rifle on his stomach, so he grabs the rifle and struggles to get it away. Daddy says he remembers the barrel was warm in his hands, as if it had recently been shot. He tries to push away the barrel, but a shot rings out. Boys wearing the color blue run away, disappearing into the alley.

My daddy crumples into a fetal position, his blood slowly spreading across the asphalt.

Isn't that corny?

That's not the worst of it.

Daddy told me that his homie Freddy (even the word *homie* sounds so silly) a guy as big as bear, lifts my father from the concrete, and his body curls up like a dead Aztec in the big arms of his friend. Freddy is as fat and round as a sumo wrestler, and even though he squints his eyes to look mean, you can't help but like him the first time you see him. He's got the wide eyes of a little boy. Daddy had his picture on the living room wall next to one of my dead mother.

Freddy places my bleeding father in the backseat of the lowrider, and then he jumps in and speeds through the city toward the hospital, looking into the rearview mirror where he sees my father. Freddy says corny stuff like, "Don't die on me, homie," and "We'll get those vatos!"

I see the 1969 Chevy Impala racing through the dry canals of industrial L.A. The camera pulls back and we see the car speeding through the concrete, sliding up and down the sides of the canal, and the background music is something frantic with electric guitars and a bongo beat.

Cut to Freddy's face, worried, maybe even a tear falling, like a tattoo teardrop under one of his eyes.

(*Freddy is dead now. A few years later, he would die, Daddy told me, from severe diabetes. He was sleeping when he suddenly woke up gasping with a dry mouth, but it was too late; he choked. Anyway, back to the story.*)

The lowrider skids to a stop in front of the hospital. Freddy jumps out of the car and yells, "Help! My homie's been shot."

Stuff like this never happens in real life but always happens in the stories, a hospital crew runs out of the sliding glass doors to care for my father, whose white T-shirt is soaked with blood. They take him in on a stretcher, and when they get him to the emergency room his heart stops beating. He was legally dead for twenty-seven seconds.

He didn't see any great white light nor did he rise above his hospital bed and see himself being worked on by the nurses and doctors, then float out the door. He didn't float like an angel over the city skyline and then the mountains and rivers, he didn't see an old dead family member who said to him, "Mijo, you want another chance at life?" All he remembers in those twenty-seven seconds of death, he told me, is the taste of fried American cheese. The way cheese tastes when it oozes out of the omelet onto the frying pan and you have to peel it off with a fork.

He told us this detail as the waiter was serving our food.

"That's stupid," I told him, looking at my big white plate with fancy food in the middle of it, like a Georgia O'Keefe flower.

Claire had chosen the restaurant, which meant that she was paying. I figured Daddy and I were broke since we hadn't eaten out in a while or taken any weekend trips.

The other reason why I thought we were broke was because Daddy hadn't thrown a party in almost a year, and he loved to give parties.

He did it well, a room full of his friends, all types, from the guy who does our plumbing to the dressed-in-black types, nihilists, you know, artists and workers getting drunk and quoting Nietschze. At one party he flirted back and forth with this woman in a tight black dress, long black hair, and large black eyes, like Morticia Addams from the *Addams Family*. The next morning I saw them eating breakfast together at a wooden table in the sun out back. She was wearing one of his white shirts and they were giggling and kissing between bites of wheat toast and fresh fruit. But it had been a while since there had been a party at our house.

I was pretty sure we were broke.

"I can't believe you were ever a cho-cho," Claire said.

"Cholo," he corrected. "And it's all true," he said. "All of it."

"I can't believe you were ever a Chicano," I said.

"I'm still a Chicano," he said. "¡Con safos y qué!" He tried to make gang signs with his hands, but he was making the movement up as he went along, and it was hard to look like a cholo when you were forty-one years old and wore a sport coat and drank chardonnay.

"We could use that image to market you," said Claire, looking at my father, as if trying to picture him as a cholo, a Chicano gang member.

Claire had pale blue eyes, and even though this was supposed to be a business dinner, she suddenly looked at him as if attracted to him. He picked up a fork and knife and pointed them at the slab of salmon on his plate, and you could see the reflection of his meal in the silver blade. The pink geometry on his overlarge white plate looked too perfect to eat. He looked down at his fish, the chandelier lights above his head. He lifted his eyes to Claire.

"What makes you think I want to be *marketed*?" he asked her, as if the word "marketed" could be replaced with "someone's sex toy." He cut into the salmon, pierced a piece with his fork, and took a bite.

"Mr. Cholo?" she said, watching him chew. "Are you a tough guy?"

"I'm skeptical," I said, nauseated by their flirting. "It sounds like a made-up story." I looked down at my own plate, four perfect white circles of scallops on a big white plate.

"Would I lie to you, Marianne?" He said my name with the Parisian "r," which meant that he wasn't lying. My mother was full-blooded Arab from Morocco, but she spoke only French, which Daddy learned because he loved her so much. Daddy didn't know how to lie in French.

"Non, mon père. Je te crois," I said.

"Anyway," said Claire, "we'll show exclusively California artists who have had international impact. I want you as the feature artist, Victor. I'm talking six, seven pieces. From your early tree images to your hyperrealist stuff. And then we end with your anti-hyperrealist images, *Bleeding Mary, 27 Seconds*, some nudes, which is where I think we should stop." She took a nervous sip of her wine.

She was basically saying that all Daddy had painted since we had moved back to L.A. was crap.

"This is going to be at the LACMA, Victor. They asked me to curate it."

"Why do you want to feature me?" he asked.

"Because I think you're great," she said. "And *not* just because I have your stuff at my gallery. Although we *will* make lots and lots."

Daddy bit into another forkful of fish, enjoying it so much that he closed his eyes as he chewed. Then he lifted his glass of wine and took a sip. He peered over the rim at me. He suddenly tilted his head as if he were trying to listen to something I was about to say.

So I said what I was thinking: "If we're short on cash, it may not be a bad idea."

"We're not short on cash," he said.

"Well, you've been acting like it," I said.

He looked at me as if proud. Then he took a sip, looked at Claire and said, "She's brilliant, isn't she? Can you believe she's only sixteen?"

"She seems so much more mature," Claire said, not really thinking about it.

I didn't like her much. She was a snooty white woman with a thin figure and a tiny nose.

"This could finance your plans, Victor," she said. "Maybe you won't have to sell your house after all."

"Your what?" I asked. "What house? Our house? What's she talking about, Dad?"

He put his wine glass on the white tablecloth, glass sparkling under the lights. He looked at my plate. The white circles of untouched scallops.

"I wanted to be the one to tell her," he said.

Claire clicked her fork down on the plate. She looked at me with those pale blue eyes, then at my father. She had blonde hair, shoulder length, styled from an expensive coiffeur, and she wore diamond earrings. "You mean you haven't told your daughter?"

"Told me what?" I said.

He ran his hands through his hair, a gesture that meant that he was going to tell me something that was hard to say. Father had taught me at an early age that you can predict behavior if you really look at someone. Seeing him sitting there, one hand on his head, fingers sticking out of the thick, black hair—his eyes looking at me —I knew he had something big to tell me.

"OK, OK," he said, looking at his glass. "I'll tell you everything. But first, let me tell you about the Stravinsky Riots."

Victor

My daughter lost her innocence at 16 years old when I told her about the Stravinsky Riots.

I told her that a work of art could be so revolutionary that it could cause violence.

Death even.

I told her that I was in high school when I had first heard about it.

Our honors humanities teacher, Mr. García, pulled a turntable from the classroom closet, one of those old mono systems that looked like a suitcase until you removed one side and revealed a record player. Mr. García told us reverently—as if what we were about to experience was an honor—that the music he was about to play, *The Rite of Spring* by Igor Stravinsky, was so unlike anything ever heard that it had caused a riot in the symphony hall. People threw chairs, punched, smashed heads with big rocks, kicked ribs, just like the Rodney King riots.

Mr. García gently held the album at the edges, not wanting to touch the black surface. He placed it on the turntable and then adjusted the knobs. Mr. García was chubby, shaped like an egg. We students in honors class sat forward at our desks, ready to hear music so powerful that it had caused riots.

The music started, wails and screeches like demonic wind blowing on flowers and blades of grass, and I knew which side I would have taken in the riots.

I had to go beyond trite images of the barrio, lowrider babes and mini trucks and barrio *payasos*, the tragedy and comedy masks, which to Chicanos meant, "Laugh now, cry later." I had to quit doing airbrushes of Madonna, not of *the* Madonna, but Madonna, the blonde singer, who was popular among Chicano boys back then.

Some twenty-five years after Mr. García had told us about the Stravinsky Riots, I wanted my sixteen-year-old daughter to feel what I felt that day, so I told her about the violence his innovation had caused.

We were sitting in a pricey restaurant chosen by Claire, a gallery owner who sold my work. She had picked that particular restaurant because she wanted to invite me to display some pieces for a show at the L.A. County Museum of Art. She must have thought that by spending so much money for dinner, I would understand how big this could be for my career and for both our pocketbooks.

I told Marianne that when the music was over in that East L.A. classroom, Mr. García stood silent for a while, his eyes closed, the cross of the window frame shining white behind him, holding his hands together in front of him like a monk in the afterglow of worship. Then he lifted the record by the edges and slid it back into the jacket.

I looked out the window of the classroom and saw a tree, a jacaranda with two branches growing out of the trunk like thick arms bulging with biceps. The branches reached into the sky. Over the years, Chicano high school students had carved their initials into the tree, *Beto con Alma, El Equis con safos y que.*

Carved hearts.

Crosses.

Like a cholo with prison tattoos on his chest and arms.

I pulled out my notepad, and as Mr. García spoke about the Stravinsky riots, I drew the tree in pencil. I tried to make him look like both a tree and a human cholo at the same time, a sad tree who had lived a hard life, *crying now*, paying for *la vida loca* he had led as a young man. I drew it as if in a trance, the pencil sliding this way and that across the page. Mr. García passed my desk as we were supposed to be writing, and he looked at my drawing. He looked at me, as if shocked.

"What?" I asked.

"I didn't know you could do that," he said.

He ended up hanging my drawing in the classroom. Students started calling the jacaranda "the cholo tree," and Chicano teenagers hung out underneath it before school and at lunchtime, as if the tree was one of the homies. Later I painted it in acrylics.

One day Mr. García asked me where I painted, and I told him in my backyard behind the clothesline and the white sheets that billowed in the breeze. He offered me studio space in his home. He asked me not to tell anyone from the school about it because it might look suspicious to a sick-minded world.

I went there almost every day my senior year, painting in his glass-encased patio while he sat in another room reading books or tending quietly to his plants. I went through my tree phase, drawing and painting trees, all kinds of them. I would walk around the city with a sketch pad looking for any tree that struck me, and I'd sketch it and then paint it later at Mr. García's place.

Then I started adding puddles of water near the feet of the trees. I painted the trees reflected in the water. Sometimes in the reflections I would draw a person who looked like the tree.

Sometimes Mr. García played Stravinsky while I painted, and sometimes I would ask him to raise the volume. I'd paint in rhythm with the springtime violence of Stravinsky's *Rite*.

My paintbrush would slash the canvas like a knife.

I was sixteen years old. The same age as my daughter when I tried to explain to her what the Stravinsky Riots had meant to me—art so powerful that people had killed each other!

We were eating with Claire, the gallery owner, in a restaurant. I had to try to explain to Marianne why I was selling our house, the one she had lived in since she was eight years old, a house, it now occurred to me, that she loved very much. I realized that I should have told her about it before deciding. I tried to frame my explanation in the context of the Stravinsky Riots so she would understand that the decision I had made was revolutionary. It would be life-changing for the both of us, but it was a mistake to tell her about the *Rite of Spring*.

"Yeah, right," she said.

"What do you mean, *yeah, right*?" I asked. "Do you think I'm lying to you?"

"I don't know if you're *lying*," she said, "but you got to be pretty naïve—or think I am—to believe such crap."

"Crap?" I said, offended by the word. "Why would I lie to you?"

"That's what I want to know."

She said she didn't believe that the riot ever happened or that people would react so strongly to a work of art as to want to kill. She said that it probably wasn't a riot at all, just unsatisfied symphonygoers who booed and maybe threw some garbage at the stage as they left. The others, those who liked the music, booed the booers and maybe there were words exchanged, "but a full-blown riot, like the Rodney King riots?" she said, "I don't think so."

And besides, it wasn't Stravinsky she wanted to hear about. "It's the house. What are you thinking of doing to my house?"

"The Stravinsky Riots really happened, Marianne," I said. "The music was *that* radical. *That* innovative."

"Come on, Dad, you don't really believe that, do you? Use your mind for once."

"I don't like the way you're talking to me," I said.

"I'm not concerned about what *you* like," she said. "I'm concerned about the house."

I shook my head, as if to say, "Stupid girl."

I wasn't going to say anything more; I was going to chastise her with my silence, but then I blurted out, "Why can't you just take my word for it?"

She pushed away her untouched plate, crossed her arms, and looked around the restaurant like a bored teenager. I hated it when she did that, because I knew she was smart enough to be doing it on purpose, as if to hide from me behind her age, retreating to a place where she knew I couldn't follow.

I looked at Claire in the light of the candles, into her blue eyes. She shrugged her shoulders.

"The Stravinsky Riots meant a lot to me," I told Marianne.

"Just get over it, OK?" she said.

" OK, forget it," I said. I took a sip of my wine.

After a long, awkward silence, Claire cleared her throat to get our attention. I looked at her and she said, "Victor? Maybe you should tell Mari about the duende."

DODGER DOG

Jennifer Silva Redmond

He is coming back—I'm sure of that. I yawn myself awake and then get up to stretch and circle then lie down again. Up again, around, down . . . No, that's still not comfortable . . .

I get up and pace the floor again, walking the length of the house, checking the front door, though I know it is too early. Stopping by the kitchen, I have a drink, look out the screen door at the backyard—making sure no birds are on the porch, sniff for any missed crumbs in my bowl, then go back to my rug.

The number of times it has gotten dark without him returning seems like too many. I know he has been gone longer than ever before, though everyone knows dogs can't count.

I'm lonely without him, though everyone has been awfully nice to me the last few days. Even the old lady was nice and didn't squeal like she usually does when I greet her at the door. Instead she bent down and patted my head and looked into my eyes. She sounded like she was going to cry and she whispered, "Pobrecito Dodger."

The old lady cried later on, but it wasn't because of me . . . I wasn't even near her. There has been a lot of crying around here lately: Once she cried when she talked on the phone, and once while she was looking at a newspaper, of all things.

My man would usually growl at the newspaper, though. Sometimes he'd talk to it, and even yell at it—"Goddamn *L.A. Times*!" Maybe the goddamn *L.A. Times* made the old lady cry.

But humans do cry sometimes at nothing, so you never know. Once my man cried and all he was doing was listening to music. When I came over to make sure he was all right, he just buried his head in my fur and made it all wet.

I didn't mind, but it was unusual.

I'd be happy for him to cry on me now, if he'd only come back.

The other man who looks like him came—his voice is almost the same, and it fooled me for a second. I ran right to him and almost jumped up before I realized who he was—he even smells a little bit the same, but with cigarette smell added.

Cigarette Man (my man called him "Mano") has been really busy around our house, moving things and packing like he was taking a trip—but he is packing my man's stuff, which I can't figure out. Maybe we are going camping again—all three of us. We did that once, way back when I was still a skinny little pup. I remember swimming after the boat and how they both yelled at me to "go back—go away!"

People say that to me a lot. "Go away!" When they put food on the table, when they clean house, but especially when they open the door and carry things in. They are afraid I'll run outside and run away.

I've never tried to get out the front door before, but that is because I never needed to before. I always liked to wait for my man to come home, knowing he'd sit in the kitchen for awhile, watching the picture box or talking on the phone, but then he'd finally get the leash and take me out.

Our walks are the best part of my day—I miss them the most.

We'd stroll down by the ravine, checking out the sights and sounds and the smells . . . Sometimes the sound of a big crowd yelling would make my man shake his head. "Goddamn Dodgers," he'd say. I always looked at him when he said that because it sounds like my name, "Dodger Dog." I like my name—everyone always laughs when they hear it.

Cigarette Man takes me on walks, but I can tell he doesn't want to. Either he drags his feet and pulls on the leash or he walks too fast and jerks my neck. He growls my name really snarly-low and doesn't even smile. Or he leans on the wall at the park and just smokes, and I'm just supposed to smell the same old bush and clump of grass for ten minutes . . .

Still, it's better than this. Today no one came at all. When it was still dark this morning the old lady filled my water dish and stood for a long time by the door just looking around. She said, "Adios, mijo," (whatever that means) as she left.

My food bowl is empty—though I'm not really hungry anyway. Last night the kibble tasted like the sand in the playground that time I ate the ice-cream flavored stick.

I guess I'll get up and check the door again—it's almost time now. If the old lady comes in the front door, I can look out past them and see the sidewalk. Maybe my man will be outside looking up at the sky, like he sometimes does on our walks. If not, I could still slip outside and look around a little—maybe I could follow his smell down to the park and find him.

But she isn't coming, no one is coming right now. I'll just make another check of the back door and then go back to my rug again.

It's so hard to get comfortable. My rug is all balled up against the wall. He always straightened it out every night, but no one else knows to do that. I can scratch it around a little . . . That's a bit better.

I know he's coming back—but I sure do wish he'd hurry.

DÍA DE LAS MADRES
Rigoberto González

H eriberto sits uncomfortably stiff behind the wheel as if he's riding a roller coaster up the first ascent. I had volunteered to drive but it's he who determines that when it's between him or me. I'm now the passenger to his nervous balking. He balks and balks about how Catarino resents coming back to L.A., that people like Catarino would rather keep it high maintenance in New York City, where they can jump into cabs and get car-serviced everywhere like Miss Daisy, and talk on the cell in the back seat while the driver talks on his cell in the front.

"The only small space he ever jumped out of was the closet. Know what I mean?" Heriberto says.

And I do know what he means. He means this whole rant is about how Catarino left *him* when he couldn't just up and leave for New York City because I was still in junior high and our mother was ill and the only way he could remember not to be like our father was to break open the family album, a thin book with images of a man I don't recognize anymore. When his cell phone rings, Heriberto picks it up and screams, "We're getting there! Chill!"

Heriberto says that New Yorkers should stay in New York because everywhere else they gripe about how it isn't New York. But for everyone around them it *is* New York because there's a loud New Yorker in the room.

But Catarino has to come. Our mother willed it so when she thought she could do one last thing for Heriberto by coaxing Catarino into coming back for him.

Heriberto doesn't let up. "Like a true spoiled New Yorker," he says, "Cata doesn't drive anymore, bitches about traffic and expects me to weave through the highways to pick his ass up at LAX. We have cabs here, too, I'll have him know." But he won't dare say it to Catarino.

Despite his aversion to the West Coast, Catarino has agreed to make the cross-country flight and help drop our mother's ashes into the L.A. River. Our mother always said she wanted it this way, to help clog the toughest vein of the city, just behind Griffith Park, where all the dispossessed converge: the homeless, the aging tennis players, the horse-riding aficionados, Latino golfers, and the bloated blue bodies with their stories locked inside their swollen mouths. "And the homosexuals," Heriberto added. Ma ignored him. But she couldn't ignore how unhappy he became when Catarino went away, waiting for her to get better or to die. She died first, a long, slow race that took seven years to complete.

In those seven years, Heriberto aged fifteen. Maybe twenty. His hairline scuttled back too many inches for his vanity, and he developed those permanent frown lines bracketing his mouth, like Ma had, though hers sunk out of view like the rest of her face because of the sickness.

Finally, we turn into the airport and I'm grateful that at least Heriberto's conversation will change. The tone will stay the same.

We snail-pace up to the terminal and I spot Catarino looking flustered in a black coat while all the other travelers move comfortably in T-shirts and shorts.

"Ahí, ahí," I say, pointing, excited that the search didn't take long.

"Will you look at that? It's eighty-eight degrees but he won't take off his designer coat because then people might think he's from around here or something," Heriberto says as he wedges in between two cars to get to the curb.

"I thought you'd never get here," Catarino says when we pull over. I step out to let him ride shotgun. I take his bag and throw it in the back with me. Once inside he leans in to give Heriberto a hug. He stretches out an arm to draw me into their space.

"Your coat is itchy," Heriberto says.

"And you're bitchy," Catarino says.

We drive out of LAX and Heriberto turns up the volume on the radio as soon as we merge into the flow of the 105 from Sepulveda Boulevard.

"I miss Mexican music," Catarino says. "In New York it's all about salsa and merengue."

Heriberto throws me a knowing glance through the rearview mirror. I try to ignore him.

"So what are you up to nowadays, Helio?" Catarino says.

"College," I say. Then add, "I'm a freshman."

"All growed up," Catarino says. "Studying what?"

"I'm a women's studies major," I say and he raises his eyebrows.

"It's how he hangs around the girls," Heriberto says, making a gesture with his fingers, like he's playing piano. "They're not all lesbians, you know."

"Well they are where I teach," Catarino says. "If I were a dyke I know exactly where I'd go."

"And if you were a fag?" Heriberto says.

"I'd stay in L.A." Catarino says. And they keep talking and laughing like they always have in whatever code they're speaking in. I've stopped trying to crack it long ago, so instead I look out the window and do the only sightseeing that can be done on the highways of L.A.: I check out cars.

I'm not a car buff exactly nor do I know much about what goes on under the hood. What I like about a car is its history, outside and in. Outside I look at the dents and scratches, and those funny bumper stickers people like to flaunt to roaming highway eyes. At the flag decals and those telltale traces of body shop fixtures. I like to watch for antenna decorations and customized tire rims. All of these things give a car its individuality. But when I talk about the inside I don't mean rearview mirror accessories. I mean the people who ride in each distinct vehicle. There's a story moving around within every single car. Like the one I'm in now, an eggplant Jetta with two former lovers bantering because there isn't a bed nearby they can throw themselves onto. And in the backseat is the killjoy little brother with one foot over the urn that holds his mother's ashes.

On the highways our community of stories grows exponentially.

In that forest-green Taurus rides a group of ski bums. They're all excellent skiers except for the chubby college kid in the back who hasn't graduated from the novice slopes. And his buddies poke fun at him but take him along anyway because it's his father's ski rental that supplies the equipment.

That horse trailer carries a born loser with a name he can't live up to like Golden Hoof or Mercury's Wind. He's getting transported to a petting zoo, where he'll be called Pinky or Brandy and he will long for the freedom of the racetrack while some kid cries as soon as he's strapped into the saddle.

"Have you tried out the Velvet Margarita?" Catarino asks. "I hear it's a bit kitschy but the menu's fabulous."

"Overpriced, like every other trendy establishment in the city," Heriberto says. "A taco's a taco in my book. Know what I mean?"

"So are you seeing anyone, Helio?" Catarino says.

"Mesquite," I say.

"What is she, Native American?" Catarino says.

Heriberto laughs. "Mesquite's his car," Heriberto says. "This boy's strange like that, remember?"

When I see Heriberto's eyes framed inside the rearview mirror, it's as if I'm staring at myself. It's the only feature we share besides our dark skins. We have large black eyes that look as if they're perpetually dilated. In high school, both of us came under suspicion for drug use.

"Don't mind him, Helio," Catarino says. "Your brother doesn't understand this love for material possessions."

"And what's yours, your Paul Smith wallet?" Heriberto snaps back.

My first love was Jiminy. He was a cricket-brown Honda Civic with an embarrassing horn that would confuse rather than startle other drivers. He took me out of L.A. for the first time, as far south as Tijuana and as far north as Sacramento. He was the best of Heriberto's hand-me-downs and I would have driven him straight through high school had he not given up on me on that road trip to Las Vegas. Amber broke up with me because we never made it, and because she had to ride to the nearest town next to the smelly tattooed guy in the tow truck. What I lamented most was the loss of the car, and that should have given me a clue that any girlfriend was always going to be my lesser love.

I lost my virginity in Doctor Demented, my beloved ambulance-white station wagon. I was expecting to have the lamest ride in high school when Ma bought this old Chevy from the paralytic neighbor who was letting the car deflate closer to the ground each month. And since I was neither the beggar nor the chooser, I accepted it, then christened it, the letters reading backwards with red spray paint: Doctor Demented. Suddenly it was the coolest car in the school parking lot. At least Daniela thought so. Enough to let me enter her from behind as she leaned over the hood. I tried to do the same with Serena, but she slapped me across the face and yelled out, "Are you demented?" I tried to explain that it wasn't me. That it was my car. The Doctor also liked getting places fast, even though it couldn't take the highways the way Jiminy could. But true to his nature he collapsed at the exit ramp, after having given it one last go during rush hour.

"Isn't that right, Helio?" Heriberto says.

"Right," I say. And they break out into laughter again.

"You're not even listening," Catarino says. "He doesn't change, does he?"

"Nope," Heriberto says. "The boy likes his trips to outer space. Know what I mean?"

Mesquite is my current ride. He belonged to Ma, who gave it that name when I was still driving Jiminy around. Mesquite is a honey-colored Corolla whose only excitement has been watching Ma deteriorate over the years. But Mesquite and I share the most secrets, like when Ma cried that she wasn't going to live long enough to meet her grandchildren. She cried to me because Heriberto sure as hell wasn't going to reproduce. She cried about that as well. It was also the only time she spoke about our father, who was an Elvis nut, apparently. He ran off to an impersonators' convention in Vegas and never came back.

"Probably found a Mrs. Elvis," Ma said, no irony or sarcasm in her voice.

Ma did most of her grieving in that car, on the trips back and forth to the hospital for those blood tests that didn't reveal anything except that she was going to die. She cried that she was going to leave us all alone in the world.

A Corolla passed us by. And then another. They're the most nondescript of cars, but to me they stand out because I'm currently in a relationship with one. I miss him, but I had to leave him parked at home. My brother usually takes control in these situations like carpooling to the airport en route to drop the remains of our mother into a concrete river.

"Are you kidding me?" Catarino says.

"No, we're going to take care of this today!" Heriberto says.

"At least let's get some lunch first and let me shower, for shit's sake!" Catarino says. "I feel absolutely disgusting."

"You're the one who waited to book a goddamn plane ticket until the last minute. It's today or never."

"You know I had to wait for the end of the semester!" Catarino says.

"Go ahead," Heriberto says, "hide behind your fancy job in your fancy town."

"Slow down!" Catarino calls out.

We moved swiftly from the 105 to the 110, but suddenly slowed down to a near halt near the Golden State Freeway exit just before getting on the 5. When we stop altogether, it's a sure sign that there's a bad accident up ahead. In any case, we're trapped in traffic, and the cars going the opposite direction mock us with their steady speed.

"I knew I should've stayed in New York," Catarino says.

"I can drive you straight back to the airport if this it too much drama for you," Heriberto says.

"Cut it out, both of you!" I say. "Fuck! I mean, we're doing this for Ma. Can you stop thinking about yourselves for a minute and think about her?" My flare-up is enough to shut them up. For the moment. We sit there quietly, paralyzed with the rest of the cars around us. Heriberto turns the radio down.

After Catarino came Lamont. He worked for the same bank that Heriberto did. And although he was shaped like a football player Lamont broke down in tears as easily as a girl. I was stunned the first time it happened. But by the fourth or fifth time I became desensitized to it, recognizing it as the same tactic girls used on guys to disarm them with pity. Ma didn't care for Lamont because he was black. I didn't care for him because he was such a wimp.

Kyle was a relief. He was patient, masculine, and polite as hell to Ma, who took a great liking to him. She changed her mind about the black issue, though she qualified it by saying Kyle was a black man from the South and not from Compton. Kyle was the one who taught me to drive since Heriberto has the patience of a dynamite fuse. On those weekend afternoons when Heriberto balanced the books, Kyle showed me the art of parallel parking— the most important maneuver for survival in the residential streets of L.A. And although I love my brother, I couldn't help but let it slip one time to tell Kyle, "You're too good for Heriberto." Kyle laughed it off, but beneath those facial muscles I saw it: he agreed. I have learned to detect such truths within the intimacy of cars. The twitching, the sniffling, the rubbing of the nose with the index knuckle—all of these are signs I can decipher.

When Kyle left, he was replaced by Heriberto's white version, Charlie.

"Stop daydreaming and answer me," Heriberto shouts back at me.

"Quit yelling at him like that," Catarino says.

"Well?" Heriberto says.

"Well, what?" I ask.

"Should we just cancel the ceremony and leave it for tomorrow?"

"It has to be today," I say. "It's Mother's Day."

"You see?" Heriberto says.

"Mother's Day was on Sunday," Catarino says.

"In the U.S.," Heriberto says. "In goddamn Mexico it's always May 10, no matter what fucking day of the week it is."

"Can we cut it out with the expensive words? I'm not sure I can afford to hear them." Catarino looks back at me, sighs and then says, "Fine, fine. Today it is. Hopefully we'll be up and running soon though. I'm tired and I'm hungry."

Heriberto sits back as if this is some hard-won victory for him. Catarino raises the volume on the radio. Next to us, the couple in the jeep is also fighting. None of these people know the trick: roll the window down and let the rage escape. Instead they breathe it back in and back out and back in again, each time making it more toxic.

"Now what?" Heriberto says.

I look out to the side. A man is walking down between the rows of cars. Motorists left and right roll up their windows, lock their doors or check to see if their doors are locked.

The man is a Mexican—I think—in his early fifties, looking as harmless as the ice cream vendor that pushes a white cart that reads PALETAS MICHOACÁN. He's looking discombobulated, stressed, and he turns to peek through each car window as if he's searching for someone. When he gets to our car, he spots me. It is the ice cream vendor who pushes the white cart through our Eagle Rock neighborhood. He taps on the glass. I roll the window down.

"What the fuck are you doing, Helio? This guy could be crazy," Heriberto says.

"I know him," I say.

"He what?" Catarino says.

"¿Algún problema, amigo?" I say.

The man begins to gesture. He's a mute, which makes some twisted sense because the only sound I ever heard coming from his direction was that bell attached to the metal bar. I never purchased anything from him, but Ma did, bringing me back a coconut Popsicle each time. All this time when she was moving her mouth it was a one-way conversation.

"You're not getting out of this car," Heriberto says.

I open the door and follow the ice cream vendor back through the center of the rows of cars. I can hear the police sirens approaching.

"Helio! Get back in here!" Heriberto shouts. I hear him calling my name until I arrive at the accident scene.

The ambulances are sure to follow because it doesn't look good: a cargo truck of ice cream carts has collided with an SUV. The driver of the SUV looks stunned but unharmed. Though injured ice cream vendors sit scattered everywhere, it's the ice cream carts that catch the eye. Some have traveled clear across to the right lane to spill their contents all over the highway. Colorful ice cream bars are tossed about, melting quickly on the hot surface of the highway.

The ice cream vendor takes me to the driver of the cargo truck. I knock on the glass and he doesn't respond.

"Ya viene la policía," I tell the vendor. He shakes his head, insists that I keep at it.

"Sir, sir, are you all right?" I ask. Behind me, other Samaritans have come forward to offer comfort now that the severity of the event has become clear. Mostly they stand over the shell-shocked vendors and speak to them in loud English.

The white man slowly lifts his head and locks his blue eyes on me. I motion to the lock. He lifts it open. And as soon as I open the door, the ice cream vendor rushes forward to attack the driver.

"Whoa, whoa!" I tell him. "Espera."

A cop steps up and pulls the vendor away. The driver slumps back in his seat and sighs. There isn't much guesswork to this story: he's been underpaying the group of undocumented aliens, asking them to work long hours through the streets of L.A. The workers must ride in the back like cattle and are willing to put up with all of the job hazards if the driver promises to stop driving while intoxicated. I can smell the liquor on his breath.

"You need to go back to your car, sir," the cop says. "We've got it all under control."

It's not the phrase that makes me shudder; it's the inflection of the cop's words and the uncanny likeness to another voice I've heard before. I look at him closely, my eyes squinting, and he mistakes my response as a hostile gesture.

"Is there a problem?" the cop says, puffing out his chest like a shield.

The cop doesn't remember me. I look at the tag above the badge and confirm it: Diamonds—the unusual and unforgettable last name of the salt and pepper-haired breaker of bad news.

"Sir," he insists. "You need to return to your vehicle immediately."

"You were the one who found my mother," I tell him. He's unprepared for my statement.

"I'm sorry?" he says.

"My mother, Angelina Ramos. She passed away in her car in our driveway," I say, my voice a little embarrassed suddenly. "She was trying to drive herself to the hospital and you were patrolling the neighborhood. Eagle Rock. You found her because her foot was pressed against the break. You saw the lights."

"I'm sorry, sir," he says. His voice has softened. His hard face has dissolved into a sympathetic one. "I only vaguely remember the incident. It must have been some time ago, right?"

Ma died six months ago. Heriberto was at work when he got the call and he picked me up at the post office, where I was working the seasonal shift, sorting all those letters to Santa Claus addressed to the North Pole. The more I stuffed Christmas-colored letters into bags, the more depressed I became, knowing they were going to get disposed of at the end of the day. The crayon scribbles and homemade stamps were heartbreaking. So when Heriberto arrived, the expression on his face as devastating as the Santa Claus letters, I nearly collapsed. But even sadder than the sacks of blind childish faith, and even sadder than my once good-looking brother, who was getting as frumpy as the mailbag stuffed with that undeliverable hope, was getting told by a man whose last name was Diamonds that the woman who never got to own a single precious jewel in her life was dead. We kept the urn hidden away among her collection of fake china until this afternoon.

I decide to let the guy off the hook.

"Yes," I say finally. "It was a while ago. I apologize, officer, I didn't mean to take up your time."

"No worries, son," the cop says. He pats me on the back gently. "Just get back in your car and let us do our job here."

"Thank you," I say.

As I move down the rows of cars a few drivers roll their windows down and ask me what has happened. I don't speak. Others regard me with the same wariness they had for the ice cream vendor. I'm slow-pacing it back through the stopped traffic, which is surreal enough, but now I'm mulling over the signs: the ice cream vendor, the cop, Ma. Me. We have all crossed paths again. There has to be a message here that I'm not quite reading.

"Read the signs," Ma used to say. And I used to grin, humoring her the way we had learned to do, Heriberto and I, because she was our Ma and she was dying.

"Is that what you do with the sunset?" I asked her once.

"When you get to be as mortal as me, you claim kinship with everything that comes to an end. All I have left in me is the patience to wait for the stars."

"One of these days I'll drive you out of the city," I told her. "So that you can see them big and beautiful. Here they're nothing but pinpricks in the sky."

"But they come," she said.

By the time I get back to the car, traffic patrol has begun to direct the cars away from the accident site.

"What was that all about?" Heriberto says.

"Careful, careful," Catarino says. "Let's try to ease out of here in one piece, OK? God, I hate L.A. traffic."

When we pass the damaged cargo truck, the mute vendor is sitting in the police squad car with a water bottle against his lips. He doesn't see me. The driver of the truck is nowhere in sight and the injured have been taken away rather quickly because this is an inconvenience on the impatient highways of L.A.

"So is the goal sunset or what?" Catarino says.

"You know how it is with doña Angelina," Heriberto says.

He's right, but he doesn't understand why Ma came up with all these little idiosyncrasies, as if she were suffering from OCD. She would never schedule appointments on odd-numbered calendar days, she wouldn't wear red, she answered the phone only after an even-numbered ring, and she didn't read books with images of flowers on the cover. These were all things under her control. She also always prayed during sunset. She never revealed who she prayed to since she wasn't a practicing Catholic. Mesquite's rearview mirror holds Buddhist beads, but there's a small statue of San

Martín de Porres in the glove compartment. The only votive candle in the house is a relic of our father and it bears a picture of Elvis. And though there's an Elvis tape sticking out of Mesquite's player, I never played it. I never bothered to remove it, either, after I inherited the car. Come to think of it, I never heard her play her Elvis music in the house. Our little house in Eagle Rock was always quiet because of the migraines, both hers and Heriberto's.

At sunset, Ma would step out to the backyard and face west, her fingers woven and pressed to her chin. The strange blood disease with the unpronounceable name had turned her skin blotchy, and the dusky light would bathe her with a fiery sheen. But she had been doing this since I was a child. When she became too weak to walk herself outside I'd roll the wheelchair to the window, which is why Heriberto made sure her room looked out the right direction. "For religious reasons," he had explained to the hospital administrators. And Heriberto said they thought we were Muslims making sure we could locate Mecca.

"There are no stars to be seen out here in the summer," Heriberto whispered into my ear as we stood behind Ma one time. "Not with this smog."

"I know," Ma said. "In the fall the Santa Anas will take pity on me and blow the smog away. But I can still sense the stars there, glowing behind the sheet of dirty air."

When I tried to hum "Twinkle, Twinkle Little Star," Ma swatted my knee. Heriberto snickered. And then we all fell silent, wishing out the stars.

We veer off the 5 and onto Los Feliz Boulevard, swerving around to get to Griffith Park. The parking lot is relatively empty but the tennis players are in full swing. The small path that leads to the bike trail lies just behind the courts.

"Why the L.A. River and why at this godforsaken spot?" Catarino says. I'm following close behind with my arm wrapped around the heavy urn. We cross through the shrubs and come out the other side, near the metal footbridge.

"When Ma was a young girl, she used to take care of her old tía in Atwater Village," I say, motioning with my chin.

Tía Lupita wasn't really a blood relation, but she took Ma in since neither of them had any other relatives in California, which is why neither of them wanted a funeral. They believed the saddest thing that could ever happen to a Mexican was an empty wake. After tía Lupita was cremated, Ma dropped her ashes at this part of the river.

When the three of us stand at the footbridge, an awkward silence envelops us.

"What now?" Catarino says, looking down at the small stream of water running beneath us. The bridge vibrates with our weight.

I open the urn and look in. "I suppose we drop the ashes in?" I say.

"We should mark the occasion somehow," Heriberto says. "Otherwise it's going to seem like we're dumping trash. Know what I mean? Catarino, you're our guest. Say something first."

"Me?" Catarino says.

"Go ahead," I say.

"Well, all right." Catarino clears his throat. "I'd like to thank Angelina for allowing me to be part of this ceremony. Indeed, I'm flattered. Though I didn't get to see her as much these last six or seven years, I have to admit she was often in my thoughts. I'm very saddened by her passing, and hope that she's in a better place, at peace, and that she's looking upon us now, and that she's as proud as I am of her two handsome sons."

Flushed, Catarino steps back though there isn't much room on the bridge to move.

"Thank you," Heriberto says, his voice cracking. "Helio?"

I look out at the river dense with debris and a few growths of plants that sprout out of the cracks in the concrete. I hadn't given much thought to a eulogy, and I'm by no means as articulate as Catarino, who socializes a lot more than I do. He once told me it was a necessary survival skill for Latinos in white-dominated spaces like the universities. Ma liked that about him—that his strength came from his skull. She said he was a perfect match for Heriberto because my brother's fire organ was his heart. I'm sure she told Heriberto what rules my nature, but the catch is we're not allowed to tell each other.

I want to keep the speech sweet and simple. I'll let Heriberto deal with the more complicated stuff. He always has, frankly, everything from the finances to my college application. Part of me would love to thank Heriberto at this point, or at least acknowledge him for taking care of me all these years. But this afternoon is not about brotherly love; it's about closing the chapter of our lives called "Our Ma."

I take a deep breath and stare up at the sky. "I'm here to say goodbye, Ma," I say.

I don't get any further because of Heriberto's burst of unrestrained sobbing. Catarino moves in to comfort him and this makes him bawl even louder. At first I'm touched by this display, but five minutes later it's clear Heriberto's not going to stop and that this moment has opened up a pain inside him that only Catarino can assuage. I'm strangely disaffected, perhaps because I can see through the exaggeration of the act—the staged breakdown that was planned from the start, from the moment Catarino stepped into the car.

"Oh, God, I need you. Oh, God, I need you," Heriberto keeps repeating in Catarino's arms. Suddenly, Ma's ceremony seems anti-climactic. So I tip the urn over and watch the ashes plop down on the narrow stream of water that we insist on calling a river. I toss the metal urn in for good measure and it doesn't even make a splash, though the din of the metal makes a quick complaint.

I watch Heriberto sink into Catarino's body, their black attire melding into one mass.

We walk to the car and Catarino and Heriberto take the back seat. Catarino keeps rubbing my brother's back all the way to Eagle Rock and Heriberto mumbles apologies and pleadings into Catarino's shoulder.

The drive home is uneventful. I park Heriberto's Jetta right behind Mesquite and hand Catarino the keys.

"This one's for the front door," I tell him.

"Aren't you coming in?" Catarino says.

He doesn't wait for an answer and proceeds to lead Heriberto to the house. They go in and shut the door behind them. I push in the key to Mesquite's door and am stunned to hear the ice cream vendor's bell. But it's not the mute vendor who tried to strangle his boss just a few hours ago. This is someone else. The lettering on the cart reads PALETAS JALISCO. How quick is the business of moving on.

I sit behind the wheel and close the door. Ma's scent still lingers inside Mesquite. Perhaps it has permeated the seat coverings. In here I will tell Ma that I've changed my major once again because I still don't know what I want to do with my education. Or my life for that matter. That Catarino has returned to take Heriberto back to the East Coast, where he will learn to sip Manhattans and poke fun at Midwesterners. That I can't shake the habit of closing people off, even though I'm as curious about people as I am about cars. That I think I know what she was doing when she was facing the sunset because I do it myself all the time—look for signs of salvation.

Catarino comes out after another twenty minutes. He's stripped down to his undershirt and his ribcage shows through the sides. His arms are long and sunless. I roll the window down.

"I think Heriberto will be OK," he says. "I gave him something from the medicine cabinet. I hope it's Valium."

"It is," I say.

"How about you, are you OK?"

"Fine," I say.

"Are you joining us?"

I think about it for a few seconds. Catarino has slipped back into his old role again. He's the finicky worrywart that Ma's illness didn't allow her to be. I suppose it won't be that bad to have to get looked after for a while longer. Heriberto sure as hell needs it.

"Yes," I say, finally. "But I need to stay in the car a little longer. Know what I mean?"

Catarino bends down and plants a kiss on my head, and then walks back toward the house, assured.

"Cata," I call out. He turns around. "Do you believe in coincidence?"

"Odd question," he says. After a brief pause he continues: "I think I do. But I also believe we make ourselves see what we want to see. To make us feel safer."

Catarino walks inside the house. I roll the window up, adjust the seat, and push the Elvis tape into the player. No music plays. The only sound I hear is the magnetic strip rolling. It's the blank end of the tape. In a moment it will begin playing the other side, but in the meantime I turn the volume up and listen to static, trying to make sense out of it, maybe discover something, maybe a hidden message since I have just figured out what Ma was doing in the car in the final moments of her life. She wasn't trying to go anywhere; she was trying to get to this tape, the only connection left to her husband who never came back—she was going to listen to the end of some sad song as she waited for the last time for the stars to come.

from the novel

THE PEOPLE OF PAPER

Salvador Plascencia

R amón Barreto

Though it was faint, Ramón Barreto could clearly distinguish the melody that entered through his restroom window—a melody he had not heard in more than twenty years. As a young boy, he sat under the weak shade of chaparrals and whistled along with the Oaxacan songbirds. Ramón Barreto's birdcalls were so difficult to discern from the genuine chirps that he was often pelted with rocks intended to scare birds away from the thickets that surrounded the cornfields. But now, as he tried to mimic the tune in his porcelain and linoleum restroom, blood and saliva spilled from his mouth and onto the floor.

Ramón Barreto had slit his tongue and lips while trying to taste the inside of Merced de Papel; he left a puddle of blackening red between her thighs. He ran from the bedroom, through the den, and out to the back deck that overlooked the Hollywood hills. He let his tongue drip on the wood planks until Merced pulled down her dress, walked outside, and helped him wrap his tongue in gauze. The paper cut was so deep that he could not taste the rusty flavor of his own blood.

In time, his lips healed, but the wound on his tongue remained tender and bled so often that he kept a chamber pot in every room where he could spit. Merced de Papel came from a tribe of extinct people and though Ramón Barreto had spent almost a year of his life sleeping happily next to her, he was not surprised when he awoke one day and she was gone. He understood the restlessness of people made of paper.

Often, when a man is deserted, there is a desperate need to fill the emptiness, but for Ramón Barreto there was solace in the loneliness. He felt even a sort of relief: no more tangling with her sharp edges and crumpled legs, waking striped by her dry scratches. Ramón Barreto threw away the dresses and blouses that Merced de Papel had left behind. He scrubbed the newsprint smudges from the refrigerator's handle, from the loveseat's armrests, from the television and radio knobs. The only reminder of Merced de Papel left in the house was a glass jar where Ramón Barreto kept the scraps of construction paper he would sometimes find stuck to his chest or at the foot of the bed.

Ramón Barreto always feared discovering a completely unraveled and torn Merced, and so he was glad that she had gone. But still there were mornings when he woke to a sore tongue and blood on his pillowcases. He would lie there, dabbing his tongue with the sheets, looking at the ceiling and thinking of what he had lost. And on those days, when it was lonely to remember her, he stuffed his mouth with tissue paper and crumpled the Sunday news, and at night he pressed the paper between his knees.

Apolonio

The meat Apolonio bought was carted by Chinese butchers from the stadium to their market stand. While the groundsmen tilled the sand for the next match, the butchers entered the corridor and pulled banderillas and swords from the fallen *toro bravo*. They brought out the hooked knives from their apron pockets and slashed and gutted the bull. The horns and hooves were buried on the plaza passageway, and three wheelbarrows, heavy with warm meat, exited the plaza as the trumpets sounded and the next matador was announced.

The sour steaks were sold to the stone-and-shake prisons lining the border and at the Tijuana central market. Apolonio selected the cuts of beef from the table next to dead fighting cocks. He boiled the tenderloin in brown sugar to counter the acidity of anger and fear, but after a day under the flame the stew still smelled of citrus. It was not until Apolonio added bark from a sweet mesquite that the meat gave up its bitterness. He found a solution to the sourness of ring bulls and soon after learned to marinate uncrested and severely pecked roosters in pear sauce, bringing out the sugar from the wing meat and breasts.

Apolonio was not yet a *curandero*—his broths and fried dishes were intended simply to nourish, not to cure spiritual ailments. Unlike the *curanderos* from the South, Apolonio had come to medicine not through ancestry but by pure accident. His mother had just suffered the third apparition of the Virgin of Trinidad when he stumbled upon his first remedy. The brightness of the holy mother, as she floated above the headboard with her blazing halo, tanned Apolonio's mother's face and warmed the pillows. It was then, looking to calm his mother's neurosis brought by the sacred visitation, that Apolonio discovered the calming effect of tortoise eggs.

One morning—as his mother lay in bed frazzled, praying with her palms pressed and sunscreen on her face—he cracked open a turtle egg, dropping it into the pan and then scrambling it with his finger. Apolonio instantly recognized the soothing properties of the raw yolk. He cracked two more eggs, sifted the whites through his fingers, and walked into his mother's bedroom, carefully sliding the yolks from his palm and onto her belly. As he punctured the soft sacks and massaged the orange yolk into her skin, she sighed and unclasped her hands, relaxing her fingers and falling into a deep sleep for the first time since the Virgin's initial visit.

Apolonio's knowledge was not one of inherited traditions. He was scientific, setting up control groups and administering placebos, all results carefully graphed and cataloged in the index of his recipe book. The remedies were first recorded in pencil and then traced over in ink, once the trial phase was over. Despite Apolonio's insistence on inking only proven antidotes and ignoring the blind faith of the *paisan* healers, his parchment was identical to every other *curandero*'s book—the one exception being an entry that dealt with the music of Oaxacan songbirds.

Santos

In his home state of Jalisco, in front of the mayor, the reigning flower princess, and 14,000 spectators, Santos was unmasked. The challenger, Mil Máscaras, unknotted and unlaced the cloth-and-sequin mask with his teeth as he held Santos's face down on the canvas. He threw the mask out of the ring and two unsuspecting Clandestine Vatican Troops, dressed in their vacationing Swiss guayabera shirts, picked it up from the cobbled floor, placing it in a brown sack bearing the Pope's wax seal. Santos covered his face with his hands and tried to run out of the ring. But

Mil Máscaras knew that he had unveiled a saint, instantly noticing the telltale cowlick where the halo would one day hover. In a choke hold, Mil Máscaras paraded the unmasked Santos from one end of the ring to the other, making sure to stand underneath the balcony of the flower princess. As a fugitive, Santos had found the perfect hideaway in the code of the masked *luchador*, but after nearly four decades of searching, the authorities now knew that Santos was Juan Meza.

After the match, Juan Meza was taken to the dressing room, where a Vatican official touched his Catholic nose and began to administer the qualifying tests of sainthood while the Swiss troops stood by the door. The official, a cardinal on emergency summons, had been educated in Roman seminaries and specially trained in holy and heretic diagnostics.

The cardinal lifted Juan Meza's arm, sniffing the wrestler's sweat, and then shone a flashlight into his eyes. One of the Swiss troops, prompted by the cardinal's command, assisted in the final procedure, slicing the side-welts of Juan Meza's unlaced boots and then peeling the split leather and socks from his feet. It was confirmed: Juan Meza was a saint. His sweat smelled of potpourri, his pupils did not contract, and the soles of his feet were pale and marked by fresh stigmata.

On his saintly honor they released Juan Meza and ordered him to present himself at the Saint Joaquín Cathedral the next day, where the canonization process would begin. He shook the smooth powdered hand of the cardinal, a palm so smooth that it felt like ivory, and promised to arrive promptly and with his hair combed, first thing the next day, and then walked outside to feel the sun on his bare cheeks for the first time in decades.

Juan Meza preferred the life of a Mexican wrestling hero to the quiet, celibate existence of modern saints. He turned down a trip to Saint Peter's Basilica in Rome and a calendar day dedicated in his honor. Instead he fled north to Tijuana, finding refuge in a three-hundred-seat cockfighting ring built on squatted land along the banks of the Tijuana River, where he would fight his final match.

Ramón Barreto

Ramón Barreto remembered the day Merced de Papel wiped the blood from the deck and looked up at him as he stood leaning against the banister.

"I'm sorry, Ramón," she said.

"Not your fault." The blood began to crust on his lips and chin.

"If I had known . . . maybe we shouldn't do that anymore?"

"I'm fine, just a little blood."

"Maybe we should wet it a little. With water I mean. I can do that."

And she did. After Ramón healed, she soaked a face towel and dabbed herself until she was soft and could not cut through the skins of oranges. She put her hand on the back of his head and brought him into her thighs. He opened his lips and put Merced in his mouth. He felt her breaking apart; small wads of wet paper stuck to his teeth, some he swallowed. But instead of facing the fact that Merced was dissolving into his mouth he bit his tongue and drew blood.

"You're still a little sharp," he said and walked over to the sink.

Ramón Barreto wanted to love Merced de Papel from the first day he saw her. He had lived most of his life in Hollywood splicing film. He made sure no one saw Fred Astaire trip on the stairs, cut Judy Garland's temper tantrums, and marked the celluloid where Rita Hayworth botched her lines and cussed in Spanish. One day, as he hand-rolled a reel and stored it in the fireproof safe, he looked out the studio's window and saw Merced de Papel sitting on a bench waiting for a cable car. Ramón Barreto had fled his childhood adobe town and settled in one made of tinsel. As always, with those estranged from their *patrias*, it is a woman who reminds them of the maize fields and songbirds. In Merced de Papel, Ramón Barreto could see the handiwork of the old origami surgeon who made flying swans and leaping monkeys. She bent her knees and then closed her fingers as she lifted her canvas bag, revealing the familiar movements of the paper birds' flapping wings and hinged beaks.

For Ramón Barreto, Merced de Papel was a way to return home without leaving the comforts of central air conditioning and reclining living-room chairs. But soon he discovered that Merced was prone to the same fragility as the eroding adobe walls and the endangered songbirds; and though it was Merced who left Ramón's house, it was he who had pushed her away. Ramón's homeland was disintegrating, a disease spread from the mountain town of El Derramadero, and despite his homesickness he preferred the severe melancholia of Hollywood and its people to the pestilence of decay that Merced de Papel might bring.

Apolonio

Apolonio painted his front door green and lit a red candle that signaled he was open for business. Though he was a self-made *curandero*, his reputation grew, and even stubborn old southern widows knocked on his door looking for a cure for cataracts. A young Rita Hayworth once came to Apolonio's botanica and asked him for plant food and *uña de gato* to rub on her calloused dancing feet. And though Apolonio knew that Rita Hayworth would one day turn her back on the city and people of Tijuana, he treated her kindly and let her follow her path to unhappiness and Hollywood stardom.

The fourth apparition of the Virgin of Trinidad scorched the south wall, the wooden headboard, the grass futon, and the intent face of Apolonio's mother. She died watching the radiating light of the Virgin's halo—a tragedy that only added to Apolonio's reputation and customer base. Against Catholic injunction, Apolonio crumbled his mother into an urn and walked up the *cerro* that overlooked the wood and paper towns and the smoking silver assembly plants. On the hilltop, as the wind spread his mother, he first felt the joint aches of lost parentage, orphan pains that would rankle his body every second Sunday of May and the second to last Sunday of June. With alchemy Apolonio tried to conquer his sorrow, but the concoctions of turtle yolks and minced lemon seeds, the special diet of mesquite beans and palm ash, and candle-burning rituals all failed.

During a hot Tijuana winter the smoke from the television factories lingered and mixed with the odor of meat cuts and *de la hoya* beans. Flocks of migrating Oaxacan songbirds flew over the central market and the *maquilas* but then broke from their formations, dropping like stones onto the Tijuana streets. Some crashed into the chest of a granite Hidalgo raising his shackled hands; the lucky ones collided with the fountains that surrounded the Al Capone casinos. But many broke their beaks against the brick and mortar walls of old slaughter and packing houses.

When Pío-Pío fell, she crashed through the thin layer of burnt shingles and landed safely on the charred bed of Apolonio's dead mother. Pío-Pío could flap her wings but was too weak to fly or sing. In the same room where the intense heat of the halo had spelled death to Apolonio's mother, a faint chirping led Apolonio back into her locked and boarded sleeping chamber. By the third week Pío-Pío was flying around the house and singing concertos with frolicking cadenzas. Alchemy and years of Santería could not alleviate the grief that the visiting Virgin of Trinidad had brought to his home. But now the sorrow that the Holy Mother had brought was pushed out by the melody of a Oaxacan songbird.

Santos

The Vatican official waited for Juan Meza for two weeks before deciding that perhaps the word of a saint was not always to be trusted.

Juan Meza stitched together a new Santos mask, complete with his trademark silver trim that outlined the mouth and eyes. For days he walked around the city of Tijuana with the mask in his pants pocket. No one asked to shake his hand or kiss his knuckles. He bought sugared meat and chewed on it while sitting on the banks of the drained river. People walked by in plastic jumpsuits, passing the cockfighting arena and disappearing into the television *maquilas*.

Juan Meza enjoyed the anonymity of being a Ticuanense, but two days before his final match, he pulled the cloth mask over his face and went to the arena's proprietor, Don Feliz, to discuss the details of his contract. Don Feliz agreed to cut the undercards. There would be no cockfights to upstage, no splattered intestines, shit, or broken blades to slip on. When Santos jumped into the ring, he would smell only the acrid fumes of cleaning ammonia rising from the mat.

Don Feliz offered to split the admission revenue and give the winner fifteen percent of the house bets. And even though Santos refused to acknowledge his own sainthood, he signed over his share to the Virgin of Arcadia, who would be paid in a thousand *veladoras* made from pure bees-wax and braided wicks. Santos agreed to Don Feliz's terms: he would not know the name of his opponent, the thickness of the ropes, or the bounce and pliancy of the mat.

On the day of the match, Santos stretched and oiled his body in the dressing room. He slipped on his wrestling boots and threaded the laces, tightening them to his feet and then shining them with layers of wax, while spectators filed in and took their seats on the bleachers. The Clandestine Vatican Troops were not in the building. They searched for Juan Meza in every farm and church alcove and deployed personnel into the Jaliscon canyons of the Machuca Indians—a tribe notorious for providing sanctuary to AWOL saints. They searched everywhere except for cockfighting arenas and border wrestling circuits.

And while the Pope cursed at the archbishop for losing yet another saint, Chicago gangsters and Hollywood starlets left the horse track, crossed the lounge where the roulette wheel spun, the ball landing on double zeros, and told their chauffeur to drive them to Don Feliz's arena. Don Feliz circled the ring with chairs and made sure to pad the splintering seats and backs with pillows. The gangsters and starlets sat ringside, drinking their own brand of mescal made from tender agave and purple saffron and smoking filtered American cigarettes.

She was wearing a scarf, long gloves, and dark sunglasses, but the distinct wave of her cigarette holder gave her away. From the top bleachers lettuce pickers threw heads of iceberg and chanted, "Rita Vendida!" When she stood up and her bodyguards walked her to the ladies' room, the lettuce pickers whistled and yelled, "Fuck you, Margarita!"

By the time Rita had returned to her seat, Santos had just been introduced, and instead of the pale iceberg lettuce, he was showered with lush romaine leaves and carnations. Santos climbed into the ring. The ropes were unpadded and pulled tight. He undid his cape and hopped on the mat. It was solid. One body slam or a missed flying kick and the match would be over.

Three hours before the match, silk-screened posters were posted on the phone poles, on the bus benches, and in Tijuana's casinos and racetracks. Everybody in Don Feliz's arena knew who Santos was fighting except for Santos himself. Suddenly, from out of the corridor, his head covered with a wet towel, closely followed by his corner man, came the challenger. Instead of flowers and romaine lettuce he was received with animal cookies; loyal fans threw only those shaped like tigers and lions, while the rest of the crowd launched indiscriminate handfuls.

When he pulled off the towel, revealing his orange-and-black mask, the crowd roared the tiger's growl, welcoming the challenging wrestler to the ring.

Santos knew that his old partner was always received with cookies, but it was not until Saturo Sayama stepped over the second rope that he realized that his last match would be Santos versus Tiger Mask.

Ramón Barreto

Minutes before Karen Damen knocked on Ramón Barreto's door, he moved the glass jar that held the scraps of newsprint and colored paper from the bedroom to the kitchen cupboard, next to the pasta and the sacks of bleached flour. Though his tongue was always tender, when Ramón Barreto ate Karen Damen the warm wetness was not followed by the taste of his own blood. There were no ink smudges on his back or on the sofa cushions, and for the first time in years he could make love in the shower with the water running. The moisture from Ramón's mouth did not discolor Karen's chest; water slid across her body and down to her untattered toes. The mundane and simple things that the body could endure were miracles to Ramón Barreto.

Karen slept with her hair wrapped in a towel, and when she awoke in the morning Ramón led her into the shower and watched water bead off her body.

"You've never seen a woman shower?" she asked.

"Not in years," he said.

Apolonio

Pío-Pío descended from one of the flocks that had willingly left the Garden in pursuit of Eve. Pío-Pío's ancestors were faithful to the first couple until they bore Cain. Attending to the duties of a new father, Adam neglected the fields, and when the crops wilted he began to caress the plump meat of the songbirds' wings and bellies. The first bird migration began on the brink of man's discovery of white meat. The flocks were not seen again until the years of Cortez. At that time the mestizos, who had learned from their colonizers, began to cage the Oaxacan songbirds.

And though Apolonio was a perfectly rationed mestizo (fifty percent Machuca and fifty percent Spaniard), he did not cage Pío-Pío. He let her fly through the house and perch on the woven wooden chairs. She ate her fried tortoise eggs and bananas on the kitchen table, and if it hadn't been for the impropriety of lying with feathered vertebrates, she would have slept in his bed. Instead, Pío-Pío rested on top of a redwood table in a nest made from strips of Apolonio's Sunday shirts.

A touring archbishop from Italy had once said, "Where the Virgin touches is forever blessed." And for that reason Apolonio had not informed the local authorities of his mother's cause of death—they would have enshrined her in a glass casket so the whole world could see her burnt face. The house would be surrounded by Vatican officials with pointy noses and Swiss guards, and then they would discover Apolonio's parchment text and Santería potions.

Two months after crashing through Apolonio's roof and regaining her strength, Pío-Pío's fevered flights around the house became quick darts that shot from the tabletop to the kitchen counter and then back, and the excited cadenzas shortened into single chirps. At first, Apolonio worried, fearing that Pío-Pío had contracted an avian flu, but when he saw the three spotted eggs in her nest, he knew Pío-Pío's fatigue was only due to her approaching motherhood.

Santos

Santos and Tiger Mask shook hands at center ring. Rita replaced the cigarette on her holder and the men dressed in their pinstriped suits refilled their silver flasks. Even before the match began, the arena was stuffy and dense with the stench of smoke, sweat, and tub-brewed alcohol.

"Saturo, we can end this quick," Santos told Tiger Mask as they grappled against the ropes that burned and chafed Tiger Mask's back.

Tiger Mask had blown his fortune on Argentine mate and a series of Italian sculptures siphoned from Europe during the war. Now Tiger Mask wanted to return to the foothills of Mt. Tateyama, raise the collapsed roof of his childhood home, and paint the walls where he would hang his championship belts and photographs from every continent he had stepped on. But to afford the voyage he needed to defeat Santos and claim the fight purse.

Neither Santos nor Tiger Mask would throw the match. Despite nearly a decade of touring, during which time they shared a dressing room and won six intercontinental tag-team championships, they were now at opposite corners. The first three rounds were fought conservatively; both were wary of hitting the hard matting and the air in the arena taxed their lungs. The Mexican canto written on the ceiling of the Gran Auditorio de Guadalajara said that in the fourth round heroes were either made or broken. And so it was: midway through the fourth round Tiger Mask lifted Santos over his head and slammed him onto the floor, breaking the back of the most celebrated and beloved Mexican wrestler in history. His spine cracked, sending a wince that frayed the fabric of his mask as he blinked for the final time, his holy eyes never to be seen again. The weight of death instantly dropped his eyelids, while a splintered black cross appeared on every poster and souvenir that bore his face.

The impact tore the canvas and exposed the slabs of concrete upon which the ring was raised. The ropes snapped and the spectators at ringside, except for Rita, rushed forward to see the broken Santos. His body remained still and not even the medics dared to unmask him. When it was clear that Santos was dead, Saturo Sayama knelt on one knee and paid his last respects to his former partner. The lone photographer at the event let the moment pass undocumented. The crowd and even the jeering lettuce pickers were silent. If not for the settling dust and floating cigarette smoke, that section of the world, at 117 degrees longitude and 32 latitude, would have been completely motionless.

Ramón Barreto

Ramón Barreto and Karen Damen ate dolmas and pilaf while bus-boys danced around them and performed Greek somersaults; for dessert they went to the boardwalk and slurped oysters from the half-shell. In their stomachs they felt the aphrodisiacal potency of shellfish, and on their way home made love on the bench seats of the Lincoln while the chauffeur drove around Los Angeles. They passed Japanese gardens with blowfish rising from their waters, towering Salvi banana trees painted in tropical pastels tilting toward San Salvador, and rings of ashes surrounding fur-rowed towns. Ramón Barreto and Karen never looked out of their tinted windows; instead they basked in the glory of wet flesh that withstood the rigors of desire and propulsion.

While love thrived at fifty-five miles per hour, moths invaded Ramón Barreto's pantry and cupboards. They chewed through the flour sacks and ate the pastas. They fluttered throughout the house. The powder from their forewings left beige prints on the walls, on the framed Diego Rivera paintings, on the vases. They punched holes through Ramón's suits and ate everything from the laundry basket, leaving only the zippers from Karen's dresses.

When Ramón Barreto returned to the house, with his shirt unbuttoned and his tie wrapped around his fist, he opened the door to a cloud of flour and insect dust. The jar where he kept the pieces of Merced had burst its lid and was filled with moths and larvae feeding on the scraps. Unbeknownst to him, among the newsprint and construction paper, fertilized moth eggs had also been bottled. Despite his fear of decay and the precautions he had taken against destruction, Ramón Barreto had kept a plague incubating in his kitchen cupboard.

Apolonio

Three days after Pío-Pío's eggs hatched, Apolonio left the house to attend to a woman whose amputated pinky finger had grown back as a brittle mesquite twig. Pío-Pío chewed the fried bananas and eggs and spat the regurgitated food into the beaks of her three hatchlings. After she fed them and picked the ticks from her nest, she began teaching them music scales and harmonies.

Pío-Pío did not feel the heat or see the brightness emanating from Apolonio's mother's old room; Pío-Pío was too busy with motherhood. But the rest of Tijuana—except for those who worked in the *maquilas*—saw the silhouette of the Virgin of Trinidad over the house of Apolonio. The holy mother had returned to visit Apolonio's mother, unaware that she had already passed away. By the time Apolonio returned, the Virgin was gone; the parish priests had surrounded the house, taking notes on Vatican letterhead, and firemen were dousing the fire that blazed on his roof. Apolonio did not want to be under the scrutiny of God, and instead of answering their questions, he went into the house, wrapped Pío-Pío and her hatchlings in their nest, grabbed his parchment text, and ran out. Apolonio did not look back at the smoldering fire until he was over and beyond the chain-link fence and cement barriers that marked the border.

■

When a saint dies, the smell of potpourri extends out to a five-mile radius. But in closed quarters like Don Feliz's arena, what was supposed to be a pleasant tinge of flowery aroma was suffocating and nauseating. In three minutes the arena emptied, leaving Santos alone in the center of the ring. The eyelets from his shiny wrestling boots oozed blood. His arms were spread open and the stigmata on his palms widened. Saints were supposed to die in open fields, not on the mat. Their blood was not supposed to drip from the corners of the ring into the gutters and reservoirs where cock blood was strained and wrapped into sausages.

THE TRUE STORY
Kathleen de Azevedo

In the office of the St. Stephen archdiocese, Gabriella was filing letters, requests for a new church, complaints about lack of funds for a new hall. Her thoughts drifted to Sonny Romero's last healing concert when he cured a man who had both a bleeding ulcer and a fondness for Budweisers with shots of Jose Cuervo. Sonny's music played in the jukebox of Gabriella's heart and he sang to gauchos, *vatos*, tango kings, and East L.A. homeboys. His songs flowed out of the El Corazón Llorando bar near where she worked, and though most didn't know his songs were religious, he preached the word of God from a microphone with music behind him rolling out the sounds of trumpet, accordion, conga drum, *banda* love, samba madness, and rhumba soul. Sonny Romero could convert the most stone-hearted people because his *labios* sounded sticky when he spoke and looked satiny when he sang. He was neither Mexican nor Cuban nor American nor Argentinean, but a passionate mixture—so that everyone could love him but not everyone could know him.

Gabriella picked up the next letter from her stack to be filed. The onionskin paper glowed with longing; it was regarding a priest and his predicament with a young boy. Gabriella trembled and looked away; she could read no more. Did they know about Sonny and his healing powers and how he could heal the soul as well as the body? Did they? Did they? Gabriella heard footsteps of priests approaching the room for their weekly meeting. She stuffed the guilty letter in its place and slapped the drawer shut. The priests entered, rocking along, walking as if their soles were curved like half-moons. They carried cups of coffee and smiled knowingly, hiding their tongues of fire though their faces looked moldy and useless. They'd come to discuss the lust-filled priest and marvel at their own restraint.

■

The Hollywood Freeway at five was jammed. In the hot California sun, headlights appeared heavy-lidded and bored. The drivers all looked as if they'd been crying. A bus, like a silver serpent, barreled between Jaguars exiting east toward Pasadena and Chevys continuing on to South Central. Gabriella drove among the plodding grunting cars, thinking of wasted years. She had graduated from theology school with its lawns and spiked towers to end up as a file clerk at the archdiocese office. She could have been a priest, she had that severe face of one who refuses sin—and she *has* refused it—but the priests tell her that as a woman she is susceptible to lust. But this is not true. She has put off potential lovers by wearing a plain black dress over the squareness of her body so that men felt they were gazing into the big black blank of their own nothingness. Her legs were unattractive and thick, her feet heavy like anvils. But no matter, she was a jukebox and she popped wheat thins in her mouth like quarters and the records inside her went plop-plop-plop playing "Santa Fe Night," "Me crea mujer" and "Dios es mi amigo." Meanwhile, in the smog, the sun was pretending to set and the red horizon played a sweet merengue, God bless and good night.

Gabriella found her roommate crashed out on the couch with her five-year-old son Donovan on the floor beside her. Don't ask how someone so religious could share an apartment with someone like Maxie. Maxie had ruined her hair twice with peroxide and she was so skinny that when she lay down, the waistline of her jeans stood up like the opening of a tunnel. Donovan clung to his mother like a parasitic plant. He was plump and sad and didn't know his father, and to make it worse, he had his hair shagged like Mick Jagger with a small wizened ponytail in the back. But what made the set-up worse still—Maxie worked in the movies.

This late afternoon scene looked particularly desperate; Maxie's rough hair lay flung all over the pillow like a drowning woman's and she had thick slices of cucumbers over her eyes, but her cheeks were smudged as if she'd been crying. Her arm was extended to the side, veins popping as if she'd been walking on her hands all day. Donovan traced words on her arm and spelled out: I love you. Maxie whispered in her husky voice, "Well, I love you too, Donny," and waved her hand, trying to pat his face but he ducked, embarrassed because Gabriella was watching.

Maxie said flatly, "I'm blind."

"You say you're going blind every day when you come home from work. You're tired."

No, I'm blind." And she delicately touched the cucumbers.

Maxie worked as an assistant film editor. Her job was to take the day's shooting and splice all the good shots into one beautiful rough cut—the *dailies* she called it—so the head honcho editor could do his thing. She was working on a made-for-TVer slated for release next Easter called *The True Story*, a religious picture, an "actors in agony show."

Maxie told her how she was looking at the screen when all of a sudden everything got dark. At first, she thought the bulb in the light well had gone out, but she looked up, and everything had diminished into a shadowy khaki color. They took her to a doctor who said the blindness was either permanent or temporary and gave her an appointment for the next day. When she finished her story she screamed, "God help me!" and gave Donovan's hand a squeeze for comfort.

"Let me see your eyes, Maxie."

Maxie slowly slipped away the cukes and started nibbling the edges. Her eyes were puffy and red, the irises blue and twitching. They looked ready to break apart, burning buttons in an overworked face.

Sonny Romero sings songs about women like Maxie: *Oh, mujer, I am blinded by your light, let me hear the one word of love, the one song of sorrow. I am wet with my tears and God knows how I spend my night, praying for you to come in my dreams.*

■

After Gabriella took Maxie to her doctor's appointment to see about her eyes, she went to St. Stephen and tried to pray for a miracle. Maxie would not understand; she refused anything remotely religious. Maxie claimed that Joseph had abandoned Mary somewhere in Tel Aviv and that the Virgin was a single mother, just like her and Don, but the church never owned up to that. Maxie even told her she read somewhere that archaeologists had found Biblical remains of old AFDC checks.

Maxie, all puff-puff with her cigarettes and polished nails, who when Gabriella first met her, had bruises on her face from a broken heart, who referred to crucifixes as wing-dings, who prayed for sitcoms to stay on the air so she wouldn't get the boot; Maxie could now join the ranks of Samson and St. Paul and St. Lucia, holiest of holies who groped their way to Jerusalem. What a perfect roommate! Gabriella could be enraptured by Maxie's sins and ultimate redemption without risking her own fall from grace.

The church smelled like brown resin. Some priests whispered in the corner. Gabriella imagined them getting high, their noses buried in the incense burners, having fantasies of Sonny Romero: Sonny Romero, a grown man and his temple of love songs, Sonny Romero, a young boy and his temple of innocence. Gabriella bowed her head and pressed her nose against the coil of her fist. The white candles seemed to bend as their scented smoke left them like sweet breath.

■

Maxie's blindness was temporary or permanent; they still didn't know, but the blindness made her beautiful. She got a box of cereal for Donovan and sniffed it up and down like a lover and rumbled her fingers inside the package, then she popped a crunchy niblet in her mouth, sucking out the sugar. She opened the refrigerator and her fingers fluttered for the milk. She stroked the silverware, smelled the towels, bit into an orange peel and said how it tingled like spice. Donovan, always enduring, sat in his place at the table like a little pudge, waiting for his mother to stop caressing the food. She put his breakfast in front of him and told him: Even if I can't see, I know exactly what you're doing, you little bugger. Then she groaned to herself and pulled out a cigarette and adjusted her sunglasses, asking out loud (in front of the boy!) if she'd ever get laid in this condition. Gabriella, if I bring home some guy that looks like a dog—you must warn me—I won't be taken advantage of. I'd rather be alone. Then she made a crack about how Greta Garbo was probably blind too. Gabriella laughed, trying to see the humor in it all. Maxie managed to conjure magic with her struts and croons even in the darkest moments of her life.

That afternoon when Gabriella came home from work, Maxie and Donovan were at the front door about to take a walk. Maxie took a breath of electric city air and her body shimmered. Donovan clung to her like a guide-dog, leaning so close that nothing could come between them, not even Gabriella's shadow.

Gabriella followed them, obsessed with Maxie's blindness. As Maxie walked up the hill, a gust of wind parted the back of her hair, exposing her dark growing-out roots and stark white scalp. Her round hips in her Chinos rocked side to side, something she did to drive men wild. A car passed them and Maxie turned her head. Then she put her arm around Donovan waddling in his worn out high-tops. He tugged at her sleeve and she leaned over and gave him a peck on his ear.

They stopped at a chain link fence on top of the hill. At the foot of the hill was a vast field, the studio lot where Maxie was working on *The True Story*. The overgrown anise weed smelled like candy, and the high grass, crisp with summer's tawny dryness, was the perverse promised land of uninspired location shots.

Maxie gripped the fence until her knuckles stuck out like knobs. She let out a few chuffs that could be mistaken for wind tugging at the late afternoon. Then she shoved the top of her head against the fence, and burst into tears that must have poured into her shades like water in small dark cups. Donovan turned his head; this was too much for him to handle. Gabriella hung back in a front yard covered with rocks and pumice and planted with cactus and aloe. The small boy noticed her and they stood looking at each other for a long time. He seemed confused with his mother crying like that, so he scrunched his eyes and wrinkled his forehead and ambled slowly over to Gabriella. They both stood, thick-legged, two square-shaped jukeboxes playing a sad tune, flanked on either side by two giant century plants.

■

Gabriella took Maxie to a Sonny Romero healing concert. Maxie, said she was desperate and would try anything, even dance naked for a voodoo priest. The audience coming through the doors held out prepaid tickets pinched in their fingers or pulled them suavely out of their perfumed coat pockets. Maxie couldn't see that the audience was older and Mexican, and it was just as well because Maxie liked hip places with loud music and singers with sandy hair. The women in Sonny's audience had black polished hair done up in French rolls with long curls spiraling in front of their ears. They wore dark red lipstick and their mouths looked like crimson clams. Their shiny satin dresses captured their butts like jai alai baskets. They wobbled in their thin high heels and linked onto the arms of their men. The men's hair was slicked back and wet, and the overgrown ends formed little curls. The odor of cigars and aftershave clung to their delicately embroidered linen shirts. Maxie, who didn't want to appear blind, refused Gabriella's arm; in fact, in spite of the sunglasses, Maxie gazed around pretending to see because she wanted to make sure all the men understood that she was dangling in the periphery of love and always willing.

The stage was dark and a mysterious cymbal catching some light blinked like an eye. Suddenly, Sonny Romero appeared onstage surrounded by gleaming instruments and men wearing black butterfly bow ties and playing guitars and congas and accordions. Romero, shiny like a pool of silver mercury, danced and swiveled on the soles of his patent leathers; he almost melted into the air, and he threw his hair back, his perfectly waved hair, and sang *mi amor* and he opened his arms to the older women, who flocked to him like pigeons, their minds ablaze with longing.

And Gabriella sat there and saw rays of light coming from his hands and head and saw him being lifted up by overworked cherubs clinging at his feet and she could see why everyone loved him because he seemed to be singing to her, to everyone until the words faded and he was singing in tongues and the roaring crowd was cheering in tongues and the spirit that had hidden itself in churches suddenly roared out like an ungainly animal loose into the crowd, vanquishing all priests in its path, overturning golden tabernacles and spinning crucifixes off into orbit. Gabriella watched groups of people fling themselves against the edge of the stage, tasting the healing music that made them hum deep in their throats. And then the ecstasy in her rose and she shouted PRAY FOR ME! over and over again until her head hit hard against the back of her seat.

Gabriella passed out and woke with Maxie swearing and swatting her face with a mint-scented handkerchief. Their row was empty, with everyone else pouring toward the exits, distant and quiet and discreet. Gabriella experienced the feeling of saints whose passion was so bottled up, they made slashes in their hands, became town fools, threw themselves off precipices.

Maxie threw her head back and laughed and it was hard to tell if her eyes were slit in merriment or in disgust.

■

Sometimes the healing happens after, not during the concert. Sometimes. Gabriella had wanted desperately for Sonny to pull off a miracle. She imagined gentle hands dipping Maxie's two blue orbs into holy water, washing away the haze still cluttering her vision. Perhaps, Gabriella thought, if she threatened, bargained with Sonny: I will sing more praises, no, I will withhold love . . . Sonny continues, he persuades: *My muchacha swimming in a sea of grief, under the rum and colada trees, let me say if you wait long and hard enough, what you pray for will happen, and though a thousand lights may dim tonight, Jesus loves you.* But Sonny, men spew out worthless, empty songs of love. That's why you need to prove yourself. That's what people— ultimately—expect from God.

That evening, Maxie received a call that she was let go from *The True Story*, cut just like that. This made her livid. She did her brassy strut, clamping her fists. Damn those fuckers. They could have waited a few days. Did they think I was gonna be this way forever? Nothing is forever! Some bald asshole executive zilched her without even knowing the facts. Always some asshole with twelve cars. Always has a young girlfriend too. Jesus, I hate men.

Donovan, at the other end of the table playing Zoo-a-Thon, looked up when his mother said that. Gabriella, helplessly entangled in her own frustration, leaned over and said, "She don't mean you." Maxie made an exasperated huff, "Can't you see he's just a boy? You think I mean him. Donovan! Are you listening to all of this?"

Damn. Maxie tore at a pack of cigarettes and groped in the cabinets for some whiskey. She found the bottle, unscrewed the lid, and sniffed. Her polished nails were chipped—polishing nails was something Donovan couldn't do. She pawed over to another cabinet, fumbled out a water glass and filled it with the gold liquid. Then she sat with both hands on the glass, as if protecting it from being snatched away, and she drank in small, tight sips, rolling her lips and sucking. Gradually, her mouth got loose and wet, and her hands drew back from the glass.

Gabriella left Maxie drunk on the couch, put Donovan to bed, then went to her own room. She curled in a tight knot under the covers and squeezed out fervency, shuddering, her prayers clacking in her head until she fell asleep.

The next day as she started to wake, she heard someone thumping around in her dreams. Sensing a miracle with white mothy wings hovering above, Gabriella jumped out of bed and ran into the living room. Maxie was no longer on the couch but on the balcony, looking at the morning without her sunglasses. Gabriella went over to the glass sliding door. Maxie turned. The dawn blushed pink on Maxie's face and damaged hair. The few un-ruined strands reflected the rising sun. Her shirt was half-open and torn, as if she had been fighting with demons. She said in a thick voice that she could see stars—she said she woke up and saw stars out the large sliding door, small lights—maybe it was the crown jewels of Burbank Blvd., of the Ventura, or even the Santa Monica—stars. Gabriella held her breath.

Then Maxie moved the wicker balcony furniture aside with her thighs, holding out her hands until she touched the sliding glass door. She nudged past Gabriella and went into the living room now flooded with the light of dawn. Inside the apartment, Maxie bumped into the table and crashed against the chair, sending a wail of "shit" which roused Donovan's small footsteps coming down the hall. She stumbled out the front door with Gabriella in her nightie chasing her, not sure of Maxie's fate, wanting to hold up two fingers and call, "How many is this, Max?" Maxie's answer: Two! "And this, Max?" Three! Maxie did her jog-walk up the street, weaving side to side a bit, occasionally colliding into hedges as she headed for her *True Story* studio lot. She reached the top of the hill and stopped.

Gabriella joined Maxie at the fence and gasped. The hillside was a crucifixion scene. Fish-white actors with make-up smeared armpits and necks hung onto small pegs on the crosspiece like grape vines in an arbor. Other men carried binders clamped under their muscular movie-time arms and milled around, and a small explosion popped in the distance.

Camera dollies rick-racked through the high weeds. The sky was periwinkle. Maxie leaned her ear in and tried to listen to the chatter of the set. Her eyes were worse, now a pale chalky blue, and her fingers rubbed the air as if to read words that floated around her.

Gabriella turned away and broke down weeping (silently so Maxie wouldn't hear). Oh, Sonny Romero, the word of God coming from your lips that offered a small glimmer of hope to the thousands of women who cling to you in their love-packed dreams, the word of God has turned to the singing of money, the hissing of serpents, and poison that fills the soul.

Gabriella saw Donovan running up the street still wearing his Roy Rogers pajamas. His round face was puckered up like a clean sock. Gabriella knew in a strange way why priests wanted kids like Donovan: helpless like rising bread, puzzled and clingy too, because sad fat boys have a powerful innocence so desperately needed by those spinners of hope.

Maxie raised her head—somehow she sensed her son approaching. She waited, waited for him to tell her what Gabriella would not. In his flat high little-man voice, he would say how the crucifixes looked like wing-ding black birds doing a nosedive. It would sound absurd, like priests trying to profess their love. And Maxie, relieved that she was no longer part of the absurdity, would throw her head back and laugh in her throaty morning-after voice and Donovan would smile, and Maxie would gather his face in her hands and kiss his cheeks, rich with childlikeness, loving him, oblivious to the productions that come and go and the lights that dim and fade.

DRIVEN

Alex Espinoza

1. Agua Mansa

Marcos

I got a tat on my bicep. The black lines are raised above my skin, and you could read it like Braille if you close your eyes and trace the pattern with your fingers.

"A rose?" Cody says. He flicks his cigarette butt on the concrete, and it rolls under the plump left tire of a sweet Chevy S10 parked outside the tattoo shop. "You a hippie? Flower power shit. Why a rose?"

"Rosa Marie," I say.

My daughter. Sofía took off with her in the Honda, so I don't got a ride now. It's been a while and I've forgotten what my baby girl looks like. I got this tat, and once it's healed I'll rub it for memory and hope the petals form something resembling her face. I'm stranded and broke now. Rent's way past due, and I'm about to be evicted. Sofía called the other day, before the phone got disconnected.

"You have to pay child support," she said.

"For what? So you could spend it all on yourself? Find some new Sancho to be my baby's dad? Some fat ex-cholo turned preacher? I know the type."

"Oh, like you're perfect?" She laughed into the phone, and I could hear Rosa Marie in the background, humming the way I'd taught her. "You're one to talk."

"I only sketched that one time," I said.

"That's not the point, Marcos. It's way past over." Then she hung up.

Letters come every day. Stacked next to the dead phone. White envelopes with the county seal. All official.

Like any of it was my fault. Sofía and me hooking up, then the baby coming. My back going out and the disability checks barely enough for diapers. Sofía working fast food to pay the rent. Bringing home bags of cold hamburgers with shriveled brown patties hard as hockey pucks and cups of warm flat soda.

"I need a car. Drive out to L.A. Get Rosa Marie," I tell Cody as we stroll up Rancho toward my pad.

"Shit," he says. "And what'll you do? When you get her? Forget it, man. You and me, we're not meant to be dads."

But I watched her be born. The nurses made me wear green scrubs and put latex gloves on my hands. A mask over my mouth. Her sweaty head resting on my chest as she slept that first night. That small breathing. Clear bubbles peeking out of her half-closed lips. Telling me she was dreaming deep and sweet.

That's how I know different. I'm meant to be a dad. Why else would I remember this?

2. Bloomington

Owen

Owen Thomas wants to die. He's heard that sitting in the car with the engine running and the garage door closed is a pretty good way to go. Just like falling asleep, *he thinks. Only problem is that would take too long.* Maybe I could swallow some pills. *But he's afraid he'll survive and end up brain dead and a vegetable.* That's worse. *Slitting his wrists is too messy and would get all over the place.* A hell of a cleanup job. *He's a practical man, Owen Thomas. No, he doesn't want to die. He wants someone to kill him.*

That's different.

3. Agua Mansa

Marcos

I was a good dad. I sang to her when she was first born. I read her stories even though Sofía said she was too young to know words. But my baby understood. I could see it in the way she blinked. I took her for drives when it was the only thing that would make her drowsy. Just the two of us in the car.

So what went wrong? How is it that a guy like me can go from everything to nothing in such a short time? I had a family. Wheels to rock my baby to sleep on those nights when the air's warm and smelling like wet grass. Slow jams playing on the radio and fools shouting out dedications. The Honda alive, the engine growling big love.

Now I have nada. Zero. Zip. What the fuck happened?

Sofía started going to this church she'd seen advertised on the back of a bus bench. Started carrying a Bible with passages and psalms highlighted in yellow. She even put a fish decal on the Honda and would watch TBN. Pink-haired ladies and fat men in business suits with their arms raised above their heads. Swaying in the aisles like drunks.

"You'll need to watch the baby tonight," Sofía said this one day, changing out of her uniform—the orange pants and blouse smelling like french fries. "We're taking the church van to haul clothes to the homeless shelters in San Bernardino."

"Fine," I said.

She stood in front of the TV. "If it's not too much trouble, give her dinner. Microwave some peas and the chicken nuggets." She folded her arms. "*OK?*"

"You forgetting that I take care of her all day when you're working? I know how to feed her. Go. Stop being paranoid."

Later that night, Sofía came home and found Cody and me sketching in the bathroom. We were so fucked up it took us a few seconds to know she'd come home. Sofía tossed her Bible and purse on the floor and came after me. Her fists thumping on my chest. She scratched my face, and Rosa Marie started crying when she saw how I took Sofía's arm and twisted it behind her back. I laughed and threw her against the toilet and she fell and busted her lip.

"Chill," Cody said, coming up behind me. "Keep it steady, bro." He put both hands on my shoulders. "You don't beat up on chicks." He was right. I calmed down and stepped back.

"What's wrong with you? Here? With the baby?" Sofía shouted, her lip puffed and red.

"Relax."

"Relax? You're doing speed in the bathroom, and she's in the living room by herself, Marcos." She spat blood into the sink. "I can't stand you no more."

"Feeling's mutual," I said.

"I'm gone. I'm leaving you."

"Fine. Go."

"I will. I'll go with my mom and sister in L.A."

"Here, I'll help."

I took her shoes and threw them out into the hallway. The neighbor's kids poking their heads out the door, laughing and shouting shit. I tossed her blouses out the window, and they floated through the air like fucking kites.

"Later days," I told her. "Jesus loves you."

And like that she split and took my baby. And I'm left here.

Stranded.

4. Bloomington

Owen

Owen Thomas is the guy you see in the market with a shopping cart full of junk food and twelve packs of Bud Light. Nothing green. No fruits and vegetables. Everything frozen. TV dinners and prepackaged baked goods. He buys cheap cigarettes that stain his teeth and toothpaste with whitener.

Owen Thomas is a coward. An overweight, balding man who wet his bed as a boy. His mother took him to a doctor who touched Owen's penis when they were in the examination room together. Owen never told anyone until this one time. He told Tiffany, his first girlfriend. They were both eighteen, and Owen thought then that he would marry her. They were making out, and Owen cried when Tiffany touched him and felt that he was soft.

He told her about the doctor. *Tiffany said she understood. She took his head and pressed it between her breasts. She said she understood. Over and over again.* I understand. *Then she didn't return his calls. She moved to Oregon and collects Disney figurines.*

Owen Thomas has skin as tough and dry as an elephant's. He sleeps with his mouth open and has warts on the backs of his hands. His hair is always oily and uncombed. He hardly ever showers.

Owen Thomas has never been anything. Not even a husband. He met Bobbie at the Quick Stop. Bobbie stood in line behind him with a piece of beef jerky and a pack of Certs.

Could I cut, sailor?

She wore perfume and big sunglasses like a starlet. She followed him home and finished the bottle of scotch he once bought but never drank. For days Bobbie didn't leave. Finally Owen asked her to stay.

Bobbie hated Owen and was only after what little money he had. She needed his house for her tricks. She'd tell Owen to fucking leave. You can't even get hard, *she'd shout.* I've got needs. *Owen would go behind the garage and cry, and he would remember the doctor. His soft and beautiful hands cupping Owen's genitals, rolling them between his fingers.*

Bobbie died a few months ago from throat cancer. And Owen took care of her and watched her fade into a shadow. A speck. He's witnessed dying. Slow erosion. Forgetting. Disappearing.

I want to be there.

5. Agua Mansa

Marcos

My tattoo's healing. Skin's pulling together. Itching and it feels like I got a real bad sunburn. In the shower I watch the flakes colored purple roll off my arm and swirl around the drain before falling in and I think, *There I go.* Everything in my life spinning around this gurgling hole. Sucking me down. Then it's adios. More letters come in the mail today, and when the landlord pounds on the door, he says next time he's coming by with the cops.

"You leave me no other alternative," he says. "I'm sorry."

I know he is. I know things got fucked up. I'm trying to straighten up my life here. Right before Sofía left, I went to the junior college and picked up a catalogue of classes. Public speaking. English literature. Political science. American history. I filled out some forms and got financial aid to pay for my books. My registration fees were waived.

I registered today. The lady at the window handed me a printout with a schedule of my classes. She pointed to each one with a pen tied to the counter by a chain. The form's all official. With my student identification number and everything.

I want to be a better person, I think as I walk back home. *I miss my baby. I want to see her.* I tuck the form in my back pocket. I'll use the phone on the corner, call Sofía and tell her I'm a college student now. That I'm not the same. That I've changed. *I'm holding a schedule here,* I'll say. Then I'll read her my classes. Psychology on Monday and Wednesday from eight in the morning until ten. Pre-algebra on Tuesday and Thursday from noon until one-thirty.

All for my baby. All for my girl.

Except when I stroll up to the apartment, there's a padlock on the knob.

I pound on the door with my fists until the neighbor comes out shouting that she's calling the cops if I don't quiet down. I take the school form from my pocket and rip it to shreds.

See? This is what's always happening to me. I kick the door over and over and don't let up until I hear sirens.

6. Bloomington

Owen

We shouldn't feel sorry for Owen Thomas. He could have taken control of his life. Used better judgment. We all know people just like him. Poor excuses. Yes, it's unfortunate what happened to him, the turn his life took. But he could have done things differently. Asserted himself. Taken control. So he was dealt a bad hand. Had a mother who whipped him with electrical cords and made him stand in the closet of her bedroom while she had sex with a man who wasn't Owen's father. He can still remember the sounds. Low, gruff moans. The wooden headboard banging up against the wall. And sometimes he would crack the door open. See her white thigh wrapped around the man's back. Her face pushed up against a pillow. Her mouth opening and closing. Forming words he didn't know.

Owen Thomas is inside his garage now. It's night, warm August. Wild August. *Wind howls through the rafters and everywhere there's the smell of engine oil and dust. The stuff of bad memories. He can hear the roar of traffic from the freeway.*

He wants to go now, so he sits in the car. A green 1971 Challenger with black interior and buttons on the seats. It was Bobbie's, and she never let him drive it. Owen was afraid of the car, of the powerful engine. Of losing control and crashing into a wall.

Owen touches the furry dashboard cover, traces her initials embroidered over the glove compartment. Her cigarette butts are in the ashtray. Her lipstick marks still on them. When he picks one up, Owen starts to cry. Not because he misses her. But because he's alone. Because, even with Bobbie, with her constant shouts and curses, her drinking, the bikers she would fuck in the bedroom with the door open while Owen stood in the kitchen with clenched fists, he wasn't alone. There was someone else. This is what Owen fears the most—the loneliness. The emptiness. The life sucked out of things. He thinks I could rev the engine and just sit here. Let the exhaust coat my tongue and fill my lungs up. I could die now like I need to.

He grips the steering wheel and shouts "Fuck!" *then punches the dashboard until the sting makes him cry even harder. He imagines seeing Bobbie through the windshield, standing there in her housecoat and slippers. Shaking her head. Calling him pathetic and slow-witted.* Didn't your mom have any sense in her to see you were born a retard? They should have taken you to Patton with the rest of the loons. Look at you, *she's saying. And Owen can see her there. Laughing. Her arms crossed.* Could never do nothing for me. No kids. Not that I wanted any. Couldn't fuck me. I don't know why I ever stayed with you for as long as I did. Sure glad I didn't marry your sorry ass.

Owen wants to start the car. To drive it through the garage wall and watch Bobbie break off and disintegrate. But he keeps hearing her voice over and over. Limp dick. Limp dick.

Owen cries harder and shakes. When he turns the car on he tells himself, I'm doing it now. This time. Now. For sure. *But then he pulls his foot off the gas pedal, kills the engine, and steps out.*

Standing in the driveway under the front light, he watches a figure near the sidewalk leaning on his chain link fence. The figure says something to Owen and calls him over.

The problem with people like Owen Thomas is that they lack judgment. We should never feel sorry when something bad happens to them.

7. Agua Mansa

Marcos

"Just tell me where your mom's house is. What part of L.A."

"Like I want you knowing where I'm at," Sofía says. I hear the mom saying something in the background. Talking in Spanish. *Policía*, she's saying. *Policía*.

"Guess what?" I say to Sofía, "Cops don't scare me."

"Leave us alone."

"Just tell me where you're at. Just tell me so that I can see the baby. I'm sorry. Forgive me."

She's silent. I hear her starting to cry. Then the mom takes the phone and says, "Sofía, she don't want to see you no more, Marcos. Leave her in peace."

"Tell me where you're at," I say. "And I'll show you I'm good. I'm straight now. Tell me."

But the line goes dead. When I stick more money in the slot and dial again, all I get is a busy signal.

I spend the night at Cody's, sleeping on the floor of his bedroom. I have no home. No car. No bus fare.

"What are you gonna do?" Cody asks the next day, changing into a pair of jeans and a Raiders jersey.

"Shit if I know."

"What, you gonna go to L.A. and show your wife and baby you're good and straight now? Forget it, man. Let's go. Let's get high." Cody punches the bicep where my tat is. I feel the skin throb. Pulsing angry mad blood through the petals.

"Don't want to," I say.

"Forget about them. You only got a phone number and don't even know where in L.A. they're at. What are you gonna do? Knock on every door?"

"If I have to."

There's shit left here for me in Agua Mansa. I got nothing. Might as well try.

"Like looking for a needle in a haystack," Cody says.

"Maybe it is," I say.

"You're not finding them. Ain't no way. Let's get high. Pick up some chicks. Have fun."

But I watched her be born. I remember that cry she let out. Smooth elbows. New skin. Toes so small and soft you'd think they were made of cotton. All I got left to remind me are these thoughts. This tat.

"It ain't working for me no more," I tell Cody. "I gotta do this."

"How you getting there? You got no money. No ride."

"Walk, I guess."

I leave his house and head west toward Bloomington.

On Valley and Pepper, I stop off at the gas station to use the head. I'm standing in the parking lot thinking what the fuck I'm doing when some old guy in a van crammed with bags full of plastic soda bottles offers me a ride. He has skin like cracked leather and thick black fingernails. When I look at them I remember Sofía spending hours sitting at the edge of our couch, her hands under the lamplight, filing away her nails. Her lap dusted white.

His name's Charlie, and he's on his way to Dos Pasos because his son's getting out today. "Credit card fraud," Charlie tells me. "Dumb ass. Was working at some clothing store in Montclair Plaza. Swiping numbers. Having his friends come in. Charging the shit, then having them move it out. Got me this nice leather jacket. Got his mom one with tassels. Nice and pretty. Real fancy."

Charlie pulls off Valley and hangs a left down a side road. He kills the headlights when we park. All I can see through the windshield are the humps of parked cars lined up along the street.

Charlie says, "You looking to play?" He puts one hand on my leg. "Huh? Come on now. Then I'll drive you where you want."

I give him one hard push, and the back of his head hits the window, cracking the glass. Charlie touches his hair then he smiles.

"Come on, man," he whispers.

"I don't play that way. I'm not a homo."

"Neither am I. This don't make us nothing. Only makes us human. Only makes us wanna feel something else besides lonely."

"I'm on my way to see my baby girl," I tell Charlie. "I'm not lonely."

"OK." He takes a deep breath. "I thought maybe. When I saw you back there in the parking lot you looked, I don't know, like you were hurting. That's all. I thought we could keep each other company."

"You thought wrong."

"Sorry," Charlie says. "I didn't mean to make you feel uncomfortable or scared or nothing."

He reaches his hand out to shake. I jump out the car and take off running. A sign on Valley says

Ontario	12
Los Angeles	48

8. Bloomington

Owen

Owen hasn't bathed, so the man crunches up his nose as he passes through the gate and into the house. He just needs to use the bathroom, he tells Owen.

I'm a student. Going to L.A. To my family.

Owen shows him to the bathroom then sits in his recliner.

He comes out, drying his hands on his pants. You live alone? *On his smooth bicep, black lines forming a flower glisten under the dining room's light.*

Owen nods at the question.

He finds a small space on the couch to sit on by taking the stack of crinkled newspapers and setting them gently on the floor.

You deaf? Mute?

Owen says nothing.

You understand me?

Owen stays quiet.

You cool?

The man gets up and walks around. His shaved head is smooth and waxy. He leans up against the desk, picks up a letter opener, and grips the handle.

What's your story?

Owen wants to leave all this now.

9. Bloomington

Marcos

I stop running when my chest starts hurting. The branches of the trees lining the 10 rock in the breeze from speeding cars on the freeway. It's too far to walk or run. And I think Cody's right. What would I do with her? What kind of father am I? But the thought of some other guy raising my kid, taking all the credit for the shit I did those first few years is what gets me.

Here's what I'm willing to do, and you decide weather I'm crazy or not. Even though I don't know where the mom lives, I can find them. I will. If I have to go down every street in the fucking city I will. L.A.'s not that big, and I'm real patient.

I'm leaning up against the chain-link fence of a house that sits facing Valley, its rear to the 10 freeway. Aluminum foil covers the front windows. The wood's splintered and rotting in spots. There's no flowers. The lawn's a patch of dirt with deep gopher holes. I'm stretching my legs when I turn around and watch a big gray shadow staring at me from the side of the garage. Through the garage's door I see the hood of a car. The gray shadow closes the door and continues standing there.

"Hey," I say. "Could I use your bathroom?"

The shadow's a fat man in a pair of denim overalls. His hair's a mess, and white dandruff flakes dot the back of his black T-shirt. The guy says nothing. He unlatches the gate and lets me in.

Inside the house, the coffee table and sofa and recliner are covered with stacks of old newspapers. A stuffed bear sits on the shelf above the fireplace, an arm raised up so that it looks like it's waving hello. There's no pictures on the walls. Everywhere there's wood paneling. The thick curtains are all stained. There's no TV or radio, and the hallway's dark. More old newspapers are stacked along the wall as he leads me to the head.

"So you don't talk or what?" I say, coming back out and sitting across from him on the sofa.

He stays quiet.

"You slow? You retarded?"

He clears his throat then looks at me. "No," he says. He grips his elbows and rocks back and forth in the recliner.

"Then what?" I stand.

"I'm nothing," he says. "I'm nothing. I'm nothing," he keeps saying. Over and over. "I'm nothing. I'm nothing."

"You on meds?" I scope the scene for a bottle of pills but don't see any. I lean up against a desk, take one of the letter openers piled next to a bunch of mail. I say, "What's your problem, man? What do you need? What do you want?"

"Want," he says, only it sounds more like a question. "Want."

"Yeah. What do you *want*?" I keep fiddling with the letter opener.

"I want to die," he says, starting to cry. "I want to be gone."

A dark patch between the man's legs forms, grows bigger and bigger. Then it runs down his left thigh, down to his knee. Drops of piss small as dimes form on the carpet.

"What's your problem?" I say, pointing at the piss with the letter opener.

"I want—" he says, getting up off the recliner. He comes at me, shaking his fists. Then the guy trips and falls and punches the floor.

I'm afraid to touch him. I jab him a few times with the letter opener's handle. "Get up. Hey, come on. You pissed your pants. You're wet. You need something? A towel?"

In the kitchen the counter's covered with dirty dishes and paper plates with oily stains. There's crusty utensils and glasses with white film around their edges. I look for a rag or sponge, but there's nothing.

I go back out to the living room. "Hey. Dude. I gotta go." His hand is shaking something fierce as he reaches into his pocket. He pulls out a set of keys and points outside. He's gasping and grunting, trying to say something.

"What?" I ask him.

He puts the keys in my hand.

"You want me to drive you to a hospital? You having a heart attack?"

"No," he finally says, getting up off the floor.

"What, then?" I grip the keys.

Only he says nothing. He takes a long look around his place. The chipped furniture and lumpy couches. The shaggy carpet pulled up in parts so you can see the pink padding underneath. Stains on the walls. Cobwebs holding the windows together. Paint bubbling up and cracking.

"Drive me," he says, fixing his hair with a comb he pulls out from his pocket.

I keep looking at the set of keys in my hand. "Drive you?"

"Drive me."

"Yeah," I say. "I guess. Where we going?"

The car's a Challenger. Dark green. The license plate reads 4 *Bobbie*. The thing's in mint condition, and the engine's strong and revs real loud when I give it gas.

I'm not even thinking when I close the door. Through the windshield, I watch the man push the front gate open. "Go," he says, waving me forward, his hands glowing from the headlight glare. We pull out of the driveway. And we take the onramp. West toward L.A.

10. Bloomington

Owen

The roar is the only thing Owen hears. Cutting through the night air. The sound ricocheting in the walls inside his head.

Then it's quiet inside his head. Finally quiet. He squeezes his chest, imagines feeling his warm blood pumping his heart back to life once again.

The wind gets to him. How it stirs his hair. How it whistles inside his ears. How it moves fast through his brain in swift currents. Rubbing away faces. Names. Memories.

Owen reaches for the ashtray. He takes the cigarette butts and tosses them out the window. He rips out the section of the dashboard cover that has her name.

The driver looks at Owen, confused.

But Owen laughs out loud. His mouth opening wide. Gulping gusts of night air that get him drunk. Erase him.

11. Los Angeles

Marcos

I press down on the gas, doing ninety. And I'd forgotten what it felt like to drive. The movement. Darting between semis and cars. Cutting fools off and aggravating them. Tailgating slowpokes. I take to the Challenger real easy. *This is my night*, I think to myself. *I'm driving to get my family back.*

"Where you going?" I ask the old man. He tosses the cigarette butts out the window. He rips out part of the dashboard cover. He holds it in his hands and it looks like the body of a dead rat. He squeezes it, pets it, before tossing it out too.

"Where am I taking you?" I ask him again.

Before long I see the city. Blinking red strobe lights. Tall windows lit up yellow like square lanterns hanging in the sky.

"Where we going, man?" I say again, pulling off the freeway.

"Here," he says after I've driven around a few times. "Stop here." He pats the bald dash.

"What's here?" I ask.

He gets out in front of a building with walls that look like they're made of giant strips of aluminum foil ironed smooth. The old man walks down a sidewalk. He crosses the street and goes over to a bus stop. He sits on the bench and stretches his legs out and gets comfortable. When I see he's closed his eyes, I take off.

I move through the empty streets. I'm driving through a deep canyon of buildings. Looking up, all I see are the smooth edges of skyscrapers sharp as blades cutting up the sky, the stars.

The street names. Alvarado. Olive. First. Flower.

Flower.

Here. Flower. Here's where I'll go.

I stick my head out the window. Catch a scent. A memory. A trace. I rub my tat and think, *I'm not alone. Now. Now. I'm getting it back. And holding on. Her. My baby. What's mine.*

LANA TURNER SLEPT HERE

Sandra Ramos O'Briant

Joe turned off the siren but left the alternating blue and red lights flashing. He got off his motorcycle and walked toward the '76 Camaro he'd just pulled over. Though it had just rained and night was approaching, he still wore reflective sunglasses. He tapped the driver's side window with his flashlight and stepped back. He hated these low-to-the-ground cars that forced him to bend to get a good look at the occupants.

The tinted window slid down and the woman presented her driver's license. He usually had to ask for it, especially on this section of the Pacific Coast Highway where everyone acted innocent, outraged, or dismissive. Joe aimed his flashlight at the picture and then her face. She blinked swollen eyes at him; her cheeks were tear-stained.

"Ma'am . . . ," he glanced at her I.D. again, noted her age, thirty-two, ". . . Ms. Connor, you were going 65 in a 45-mph zone." She sighed raggedly and nodded, turning her face away from the light.

"You're a long way from El Monte. The roads out here are slick and more rain is expected." He lowered the beam so it wasn't shining directly in her eyes. The light brought her mid-section into focus. She was pregnant. About eight months by the look of it. Joe glanced away for a moment. He shouldn't get involved. He'd worked overtime five days in a row, and he should just go home. Home.

He shifted his weight slightly so that his leather boots and belt creaked in the moist night air. His mind made up, he took his sunglasses off and folded them into his front shirt pocket. She needed to see his eyes, and he knew the uniform was intimidating.

"I don't know what's troubling you, ma'am, but you best get off the road."

"I used to come out here every weekend to surf. When I was a kid. With my husband. I know these roads," she said, her voice low and controlled. A tear rounded her jaw and slid beneath her collar. "I'm sorry. I'll . . ." Her voice trailed off into a tight squeak, and she leaned forward as if to rest her head on the steering wheel but her massive stomach got in the way.

Joe looked away again. Then he squared his shoulders and feet. "Ma'am . . . ma'am," he repeated. "I'm going to have to ask you to get out of the car."

"Yes, sir," she said in a little voice, and reached for the handle. He stepped aside to allow the door, which was almost half the length of the car, to swing open. Ms. Connor tilted the steering wheel out of the way and lowered her left foot, swollen and shod in pink flip-flops, to the ground. With effort, she twisted to the side and brought her other foot out. She tried to push herself up, her stomach leading the way. Joe grabbed her elbow and steadied her.

"Thank you, officer," she said, and smoothed her dress down in front and back. The effort involved in getting out of the car had dried her tears. A soft wind came up and blew her dark hair back. She looked up at him. "Now what?"

"Yes, ma'am. I'd like for you to take a walk around the car. Stretch your legs a bit."

She turned away from him, smoothing the back of her dress again, and walked away, her tread steady, each step punctuated with the slap of her flip-flops, loud now, muffled on the other side of the car, growing closer as she came up behind him—he didn't turn—alongside him, brushing so close he smelled her hair. Orange blossoms. Her hair smelled of orange blossoms.

"Orange blossoms," she said. He blinked once, hard. She breathed deeply. "Smell that? After the rain comes the scent of orange blossoms." She smiled up at him. "I'm OK now. I promise."

"There's a coffee shop up ahead, ma'am. I suggest you make a stop there before heading home."

She looked over her shoulder. "The one next to the Turner Inn?"

He watched her ponderous slide into her car, waited until she pulled out onto the highway, and then followed her to the parking lot of the restaurant. He removed his helmet and shut down his motorcycle before taking long strides over to the Camaro just in time to help her out again.

"Thank you, again, Officer. I eventually get upright, you know?" She smiled, and he wanted to, but his face remained neutral. "Well, I'm OK now." She hesitated. He didn't look at her, but concentrated on the brightly lit windows of the coffee shop. "Are you going to give me a ticket?" she asked.

"No," he said, and shifted his weight again so that every metal snap and leather strap on him creaked. Her eyes followed the snap-crackle-pop of his uniform all the way down to his boots and back up to his eyes. He looked away, focused on the coffee shop again.

"Would you like to join me for a cup of coffee?" she said.

"Yes, ma'am, I would," he said without expression. She might get back on the road too soon. Anything could happen if she did.

He walked slowly with her to the door and held it open for her. They took seats in a booth opposite each other and ordered coffee.

"Is coffee OK in your condition?" he asked.

She nodded. "As long as I don't overdo it." The waitress returned and filled their cups. "Do you have children, Officer . . ."

"Salazar. José Salazar," he said. His shoulders relaxed. "Call me Joe."

She reached her hand forward to shake his. "Lydia," she said. "But I guess you already know that." She lifted her coffee and sipped.

"My sisters have children," he said, and stared at her. "They're all divorced and raising the kids on their own." He lifted his cup but just held it. "You're not wearing a wedding ring."

She wiggled her left hand at him. "Fingers too swollen."

He stared at her. Said nothing.

She fidgeted in her seat. Sighed. Then she said, "My husband and I had a fight. He's never home, and when he is it's still like he's not really there . . ." Her voice trailed away and her shoulders sank down inside her skin so that she looked like a little girl being held up by a balloon hidden under her dress.

"He's just trying to make a living," Joe said.

Lydia crossed her arms over her stomach. "What do you know about it?"

"My wife left me. Hailey. She said I was unavailable." He dropped his eyes, but then raised them to Lydia's and stayed there. "I thought I was supposed to work hard—to provide."

"Was she pregnant?"

"No," he said sharply. "But we'd planned on it." Joe sat up taller and pulled a handful of change out of his pocket. He laid it in front of Lydia. "Call him."

"I have a cell phone," she said. She stared at the change. "Did your wife call you?"

He pressed his lips together, and then forced himself to answer. "She left a message on the machine. I wasn't home. Said she'd call back. Tire blew and she ran off the road." Joe swallowed hard; his throat felt raw and tight. He answered the question in Lydia's eyes. "She didn't have a chance."

Lydia dug her cell phone out of her purse and scooted out of the booth. Joe closed his eyes and listened to the slap of her flip-flops recede.

He focused his mind's eye on the laughing image of his wife running to greet him at the door when he returned home after working a double shift or sitting on his lap tickling his sides. He tried to hold her face still, to not allow the slow morph to anger and tears, the slam of the front door and the roar of the engine as she took off. He squeezed his eyebrows together and clenched his teeth trying to rewind, to get back to the smiling face, to stop the internal reel from progressing to the muffled pop of a tire, to the screech of the other three tires trying to gain traction. And then the crash. And the scream. If there was a scream. He concentrated harder, hunching his shoulders forward, as if he could go back to an earlier time by sheer force. This time, he heard the slap slap slap of a tire tread coming loose on asphalt. Not a blown tire, after all, but a tread coming loose. Giving warning. Hailey would know what to do. She'd have time to pull over. Slap slap slap.

He smelled orange blossoms and opened his eyes.

"He's not home." Lydia stood alongside the table and sniffed, her chin trembling. "He either went back to his office as if nothing happened, or he's out running around."

Joe took her hand in his and held it firmly. "Not running around. Never on you, Hailey," he said.

Lydia tugged her hand away and took a step back. One slap of a flip-flop. Joe dropped his eyes to her feet. "I'm staying here tonight," she said, acting as if she hadn't heard him, hadn't felt his hand on hers. "At the Turner Inn. It used to be Lana Turner's beach house."

Joe nodded at her feet. He picked up the check and stood. "Keep calling until you reach him. Hear?"

In the parking lot, Joe sat astride his motorcycle, staring out at the traffic on the Pacific Coast Highway. It began to rain and he raised his face to receive it, eyes closed. He took a deep breath and exhaled, letting his shoulders slump inside his leather jacket. After the rain comes the scent of orange blossoms. He had that to look forward to.

CLOWNPANTS MOLINA
Stephen D. Gutiérrez

Clownpants Molina begs now outside the store in town. A lean figure no longer in clown pants but worn jeans and a workman's shirt blood-spattered and frayed.

"Got some change, man, so I can eat?"

"Sure, Johnny," you start to say, reaching behind you, shaky. You jumped him one time, you remember, three or four dudes from the neighborhood when he first moved in, nothing serious, just a little initiation welcoming him, wrestling him down to the ground and smothering him.

Stood back triumphantly and let him up. Slapped his back for him but still. Fuck. Punks.

"Anytime." And you press a buck into his palm and go off on your own, into your car parked at the curb and down the street, catching him in the rearview mirror moving in front of the store again, begging.

Small store with a sign out front: L&M Handimart. Local store. You're in the neighborhood seeing your mother. Picking up a soda on the way out.

"Clownpants Molina, man," you think, and remember the time he wore clown pants to school. Pink things with wide pockets sewn on to the front, a brass zipper shiny bright and black belt loops.

"Kmart shoppers, under the blue light," you mocked along with all the rest into his ear, cupping your hands into a megaphone and seeing the wide grin spread across his face feeling good after all. He liked this. He didn't mind.

Clownpants Molina was almost a TJ, almost a wetback. Moved in straight from the barrio for a little better life. Caught on real fast. Hanging on the edges of your set but in.

A middle-school dandy. Got rid of the clown pants. Levi's. And flaming Gypsy shirts and sparkling white teeth. Clownpants Molina was good-looking, bright, raising his hand in class to stump the teacher, smartass, breaking into that smile of his.

Inimitable. Special. Clownpants. But he dropped out of school in the ninth grade, cold. Bragged he didn't need this shit anymore. He was cooler then, spoke more English—he was pretty shy still—and wore his hair slicked back, *cholo* style. "Man, fuck school," he said. "I ain't learning nothing." Proved his point by writing some figures in the dirt.

Basic algebra. "What? Rather be making money, dude." Broke the stick in two and walked off down the railroad tracks, leaving you hanging. You and the guys standing around with nothing but your own grins and an empty bottle of wine, Clownpants Molina wiping his mouth as a last gesture, down the tracks.

He was still Clownpants Molina. When you'd see him, "Hey, Molina," and afterwards, "I saw Clownpants down by the tracks with those other dudes he hangs out with, cholos." You shook your head.

Your friends shook their heads. You rued his departure. You missed him. Clownpants Molina the clown always giving you laughs. Kicked out of his house.

Bad years for him, Clownpants Molina drifting from pad to pad in the mean part of town, on the other side of the tracks, staying on the bedroom floors of friends whose parents finally kicked him out, too. Getting a chick pregnant, knocking her up, a handsome *chola* with a beauty mark on her chin, Raquel, who didn't put up with too much shit. She kicked him out. Everybody kicked him out.

Your set watched and told him, "Man, Johnny, get it together." But he didn't listen. He was listing now, lazy, walking around town with a tattoo on his back, Christ in his agony, on the cross, looking up to the sky for help, his father, you realized, absent.

"Molina, why don't you get a job, man?"

"I'm on a mission," he'd say, goldtoothed now for the one knocked out. And wink and not let you know what the hell was going on.

Clownpants Molina was living in the duplexes by the worst factories in town, the soap factory with the two big pipes blackening your sky and the chicken factory that stunk real bad and sent feathers floating into the air that dropped into the front yards of the wetbacks sitting on their porches resting after a hard day's work. "Whew, man, it stinks around here," you said when you bicycled over as a kid, checking out the factories, weaving in the big parking lots toward the action, where it happened, the setup. Diesel trucks lined up at the side of the killing place.

Men standing on tall ladders pulled chickens out of the cramped cages and hung them upside down on the conveyer belt taking them inside in a quick efficient line of death.

Stunk awful. Blood. "Man, let's get out of here."

Clownpants Molina was taken in by a group of wetbacks. "His own people," you said to yourself, quickly, not as if you meant it, but as an old reminder of when he first showed up in town, wearing those clown pants, speaking that clown talk, "Hey, man, how you a-doing?" grinning, and then no more.

And that's where he was now, living. Panhandling on the side and mopping up the blood-stained floor at night. Moving in with different people when he needed to, always the sight of Clownpants Molina at red-burning dusk watering the front lawn of whatever shabby rental he stayed in, cigarette in hand, skinny, wasted, waving to you if you happened to drive by, as if this was his real life, happily home, not begging in front of the fucking store you used to hang out at as *chavalos*. Kids.

Clownpants Molina had gone down fast. First the drinking, you heard, like his old man, a tall sunken withdrawn man always riding him, barking out orders when you picked him up at his house the years he hung out with you cool guys, asking you to meet him on the corner but when he was late, caught slaving at the side of his house, pulling weeds, his old man standing over him, ordering him in Spanish, meanly.

Do it right. What are you, a girl? You caught that much.

And then the needle. How many years later? Clownpants Molina slipping like a clown falling on the floor under the big top, hanging with the bad dudes now, you knew, hardcore *vatos* from East Los who picked him up in a lowered Chevy and scowled if you said anything, "Hey, what's happening?" or "How's it going, man?" sniffing almost with those upturned noses, watching for Clownpants to come stepping down the porch, a Pendleton shirt draped over his arm serving as a hanger, with an abrupt nod for you, the boys, goofy now as you passed in a pack on the way to the store to score a six pack or just sit on the wall for a couple of hours talking shit under the moonlight.

Clownpants Molina didn't say much. But he was cool. Always a friend, just not tight anymore. Involved in his own set away from yours, doing things, you heard, that were crazy and stupid.

Smoking dust. Shooting up. Killing.

"Naw, man, not Clownpants, man."

"Yeah, Clownpants, man, he shanked some dude in Rosemead. He was cruising with the vatos from Los. Got into it down there, he said, at the burger joint where Sangra hangs out. You don't want to fuck with those dudes."

"You don't want to fuck with Clownpants."

"You ever call him that, to his face?"

"No."

Silence. Clownpants. Seventh-grader in pink pants with wide pockets sewn on to the front, a brass zipper shiny bright and black belt loops.

"Clownpants!"

"Hey, Clownpants!"

Vato standing outside the store, hitting you up for money. Still got that grin on his face you thought was gone. Humbled.

"Got some change, man, so I can eat?"

"Sure, Johnny," you say. Reaching for your wallet.

"Anytime." Whip out a dollar and give it to him, folded, neatly in his palm, "Sorry, man, it's all I got."

THE 405 IS LOCKED DOWN

Manuel Ramos

When Alberto Ortiz left a message about speaking on the Cal State campus, Tomás reacted in his usual manner.

Never happen.

A few days later the professor's second call caught the writer in his office. "I'm sorry I didn't return your message," Tomás offered. "You know how it is sometimes."

"Por favor, no se preocupe. We are all too busy these days. That's what life is like in the twenty-first century, no? Especially for us Latinos." The animated professor had the appropriate respectful tone. "I greatly admire your book and the few stories I've found that you've published."

"Thank you," the writer said.

"You and your multifaceted book," Ortiz explained, as though he was addressing a student, "have been a hot topic in my classes several times. The discourse has been quite lively. Clearly, there were two opposing views about your writing. Finally, the MEChA students suggested that I try to get you on campus to speak. It was their idea but I supported it completely and got the department head to approve."

The professor summarized the high points of his proposal—class lecture, evening book reading and signing at the local bookstore where students and faculty congregated, maybe an interview for the university radio station—and when he finished Tomás tried to be polite.

"I appreciate the attention," he said. "But the time away from my writing is too valuable. A trip out-of-state to a college campus has no relevance to putting words down on paper. I've missed one deadline already and spending two or three days in Los Angeles will do nothing for the next chapter in my follow-up book. I'm up against the wire with my editor."

But then Ortiz said, "You're aware that I'm a producer, right? Sure I teach, have for years. Almost ready to retire. Pero, I—uh—we have a production company, Sueños Unlimited. Me and my partner, Mónica Suárez, we've put together a few projects."

"Is the cliché true then?" Tomás asked. "Everyone in L.A. is in the movie business, waiters to university professors?"

"There are days it looks that way. But this is not a hobby for me. Maybe you saw the documentary on PBS last fall, *A Cultural History of East Los Angeles*? We were part of that and now we want to do something more intense, more substantial. We think that project is your book."

He paused and both men thought about an appropriate reaction to the professor's words.

"Tomás," Ortiz carried on when the writer did not speak, "your visit out here would give us the opportunity to talk to you about our ideas, make the pitch for your book. The time is right. There isn't just a Latin boom going on—it's a damn explosion. Music, art, the Internet. J-Lo and Smits still riding high long after they should have burned out. So many Latinos getting attention now. I want to make sure we, the Mexican Americans, get our share. ¿Cómo no? We are taking over. There's no doubt. A movie can be big now. Your book has great audience potential, and that translates to great market numbers."

"It's nice of you to say that about my book. But you actually think there's a movie in it? I'm not sure it's all that visual."

The words came smoothly, as though without effort, but the writer's guts swirled, his tongue felt thick, his heart pumped ambition. A movie, even a small one, could set him up, he thought. Give him the cushion he needed to devote full time to writing. Screw that deadline.

"That's what a good producer can do, Tomás." The professor's earnestness crackled through the phone. "And we, Sueños Unlimited, are good. We get the experts involved to make sure that the film that comes from your book not only does justice to the book but gives a movie audience what it wants. You should come out here so we can talk about that kind of detail. You interested?"

Yeah, he was interested.

They worked out dates, travel arrangements, book orders. The professor sent the writer a standard university contract, a form for the IRS, and a map of the campus with the Chicano Studies building circled in red. Then Tomás waited until the day came for him to begin the adventure that would make his name a household word. And a nice wad of cash.

Outside the terminal the smog and heat greeted Tomás with enthusiasm. He shuddered from LAX chaos and almost immediately a dead weight of doubt settled on his back. He had abandoned the dry, warm, healthier air of Denver and flown into hot Los Angeles for no better reason than the slim chance for some big money. He suspected that too many other people had fled to L.A. for the same reason and that West Coast reality had a lousy way of smashing fantasies and dreams. At least he had a time limit on his hunt for the golden pot at the end of the City of Angels rainbow. Three days and he would be gone.

Ninety minutes later Tomás was on the telephone talking with Professor Ortiz again.

"It's great you could make it for the students," Ortiz said with no hint of sarcasm. The professor and the writer both understood that talking to the professor's post-Chicano literature class served to cover the writer's expenses and a token honorarium. It was not the reason for the trip.

"Glad to do it, Alberto," Tomás said. "I owe you for using my book in your classes. Maybe the students can help me with ideas for the next one."

"Oh yeah. You bet." Ortiz cleared his throat. "Some of them can't wait to talk to you." A slight pause, then he said, "Mónica will meet us for dinner tonight; I'll pick you up in about twenty minutes. We can talk about the class—and the deal, of course. We are both excited about this."

The deal.

The food at the restaurant represented at least four different cultures, and the ambience of the place was cool, hip, so Californian. Tomás ate and drank too much and did not worry about it because he was not paying. He watched his hosts get a bit sloppy on wine and then blue Margaritas. Long after the dessert plates had been cleared, a full carafe of the vile concoction sat next to a pair of empty carafes. Clumps of soggy salt and twisted lemon rinds littered the tablecloth.

Ortiz dominated the conversation with tales of various actors and actresses whose paths he had crossed, with remembrances of past film and theater projects that had almost broken through, with references to friends in the business who owed him favors. He gravitated to an older generation of actors—Tony Plana, Elizabeth Peña, Cheech Marin. At one point he said, "Tony would be great for this project. And he's got the smarts to recognize that this is bound to hit big. I'll see if we can meet with him before you leave town."

Mónica Suárez was about ten years younger than Ortiz and ten steps ahead of him on everything connected to their business. The writer could not gauge the level of their personal involvement, or even if there was any.

The evening stretched on and Tomás started to worry about the professor's inebriation.

When Mónica had a chance she turned the conversation to Tomás's book. "The way it speaks to young Chicanos is so true," she said, leaving the writer thinking about what a false-speaking book might be. "Your writing's not about the new surge of undocumenteds or the old Movement heavies or the slick Hispanic politicians of the nineties. None of that six-hundred-page family saga from Old Mexico to the barrios of urban America. No spiritualism or bruja mythology. Just straight to the hearts and minds of young Latinos, the ones listening to hip-hop and reggaeton. Realism about growing up in this country when your own family is confused about who they are, when you yourself can't figure it out, you can't define your own culture, whether it's that neither the music of José Alfredo Jiménez or Los Lobos relates to you, or that Aztlán sounds quaint and old-fashioned, or that you can't distinguish between Corky Gonzales and José Ángel Gutiérrez and you don't even care that you can't."

"Whoa." The writer held up his hand. "You can take my book however you want. What readers get is not always what I intended."

"There I go again. Sometimes I say too much, too quickly. I have to, to get a word in with him."

The professor fidgeted in his chair. He clinked glasses together, dropped his napkin on the floor and made a production out of retrieving it. His hands did not stop moving. Finally, he blurted, "Tomás, you will have a good, good crowd tomorrow night." His voice was a decibel too loud. "Your signing has attracted a lot of attention. It'll be a late night. Una noche maravillosa."

Mónica groaned. "You don't need any more late nights," she said. "And I can't take any more with you."

"And if you don' make it, so wha'?" the professor growled.

"You can flirt with your students without looking over your shoulder, that's what."

"You're embarrassin' me and yourself. Have some respect for Tomás."

"Keep the dirt to myself, is that it?" Mónica turned to Tomás. "Have I embarrassed us? Or you?"

I'm only concerned about tomorrow," Tomás said. For a second he considered saying something about watching an Albee play. "Is everything OK? Anything I need to do to help?"

"What you mean," she said, "is will this borracho be in any shape tomorrow to pull this off? What do you think, Alberto? You going to be too hungover?"

"Don' worry 'bout me." The professor's head tilted downward and he spoke to a stain on the floor. "I'll be ready. And so will my students."

He stood up awkwardly and excused himself. He muttered something about the *baño*.

Tomás finished his drink and assumed that the evening was over. He needed a good night's sleep.

"Alberto won't be able to drive," Mónica said. "He's never handled his liquor well, especially tequila." She squinted at him over the salty rim of her drink. What he could see of her pupils glistened. The writer attributed both effects to the syrupy drinks. "He drank much more tonight than he's used to. He must have been trying to impress you."

"I didn't think he drank that much."

"Lately," Mónica said, slightly slurring the words, "when we go out we usually end up calling a cab or bumming a ride. Some mornings we can't remember where we left our cars."

"You surprise me," he said. "I have to rely on you. If he can't function tomorrow, where does that leave me? Why bring me out here just for this? "

Mónica looked away. She said, "I'm sorry. But I think he'll be all right. He does recover remarkably well, as long as he gets enough sleep." She sipped her drink. "We're such bad hosts, and you, the guest without a car or friend in this city. Qué mal educados somos."

"I'm a bit tight myself," Tomás said. "But I'll drive if you think that would be better than either of you. You'll have to tell me where to go. I have no idea where I am or how to get back to the hotel. Alberto picked me up and I didn't pay attention to landmarks or street signs."

The squinting had increased and Tomás thought she had closed her eyes altogether. She asked, "What time do you have to be on campus?"

"Alberto said that he would have someone at my place around nine forty-five to make it to his office by ten-thirty for the eleven o'clock class. Then I stay on campus for the rest of the day, meeting with different student groups and some faculty. Hang around until the book signing at the bookstore. I guess eating is somewhere in the plan."

She tried to laugh but it did not quite happen. "He's not a detail guy. At least he thought about getting you to campus in time for the class."

Alberto appeared at the side of the table. He wobbled. His hair was wet and the front of his shirt looked damp. His eyes refused to focus on Mónica or Tomás.

"God, you've gotten drunker," Mónica said. "We should go, Alberto. We have to get Tomás back to his hotel."

Ortiz fell to his knees. The writer looked at Mónica for direction but all he got was her disgust. Tomás grabbed the professor under the arms and tried to help him stand. Ortiz jerked away. "Le' me go!" he blurted.

Tomás released Ortiz and moved away from him. Other customers were staring, some laughed nervously, some glared.

The professor's shirttail hung outside his pants and the laces of his right shoe were untied. Spit dribbled from his lips. "Mónica, I . . . I . . ." He slumped forward. Tomás reached for him but he was too slow. The professor's hand desperately clutched the tablecloth. Glasses, silverware, carafes, and blue liquor tumbled from the table and crashed on the restaurant's colorful tiled floor.

Mónica jumped to her feet. "¡Bruto!" she screamed. "I've had it!"

She turned and bumped a waiter who had rushed to help. He fell against a woman waiting for her plate of food to cool. The plate and the food landed in the woman's lap. Mónica stumbled out of the restaurant.

The writer had to use his credit card to pay the four hundred dollars demanded by the restaurant manager.

Tomás propped the professor against the side wall of the restaurant until the taxi arrived. He squeezed Ortiz in the back seat, then climbed in next to the professor and shouted the name of his hotel to the cabdriver.

"That's gonna be tough tonight," the cabbie drawled. His black skin absorbed the light from the restaurant's entrance and the writer could see the driver's eyes but not any specifics of his face.

"God, now what?"

The driver said, "Your bad luck. The 405's locked down. A high-speed chase on the freeway—dozens of cops and one suicidal white man from up north. But the real problem is that the chase caused several accidents includin' one where a semi jackknifed. Son-of-a-gun blew up. Must've been carryin' some nasty shit. You could see the fireball over in Long Beach. Traffic's stopped for miles. Your hotel's really not that far away, but gettin' there is gonna be a bitch. I'll have to go around, use the 10 or the 110, maybe some of the side streets. It's a ripple effect when this sort of thing happens. Everythin' gets messed up. Sorry, pal, but this could be an expensive ride."

Tomás shook his head. "Never mind. Take this guy over to Cal State, L.A. This is a map of the building where his office is. You can leave him there—a security guard or someone like that will take him in. I don't care what you do with him." The cabbie's face turned even darker when he frowned. "They know him over there," Tomás quickly added. "He's one of their professors. He'll be OK. Here's seventy-five bucks for your trouble. It's all I got."

The cabbie hesitated and did not accept the money. "Gee, pal, that's dicey. It's late to be drivin' around the campus." He stared at the writer. "And what you gonna do?"

The men were bathed in bright white from headlights. Mónica stuck her head out the window of her car and hollered, "Tomás! Come on! Bring that asshole with you."

Tomás stuffed all of his bills in his pocket except for a twenty, which he handed to the cabdriver. He loaded Alberto into Mónica's car and paused before he sat in the front seat but he did not have an option. He listened to her furious condemnation of Alberto on the way back to the hotel. She drove through the residential streets with practiced precision but more speed than Tomás wanted. She avoided the freeways and had Tomás at his hotel in less than a half-hour.

Somewhere during the ride, Alberto woke up. He mumbled incoherently. He tried to apologize but could not finish a sentence. He passed out again.

"I'm not driving him anywhere," Mónica said when she had parked the car in the hotel lot. "Take him with you, let him sleep it off in your room."

"You think that's a good idea?"

"It's the only idea. I'll help you."

They struggled with Alberto through the parking lot and hotel lobby. In the elevator, Tomás said, "That booze hit him hard. He shouldn't drink if this is the result. Getting drunk I might understand, but he's practically comatose."

"It's not just the alcohol," Mónica said. They lifted Alberto and dragged and pushed him to the room. They dumped him on the floor. Mónica sat on a chair and Tomás sat on the bed.

"Why did you say it's not the alcohol?"

"It's everything." She slumped in the chair. "Maybe I don't know what it really is. Being in the film business is so important to him. And his medicines. That started with his bike accident and the broken leg. He denies it but he can't stay away from the damn pills. And I think his so-called energy shake makes it worse. Who knows what's in that? He makes a new batch every morning, as if it was doing him some good."

Tomás rubbed his eyes.

"If he drinks," Mónica continued, "this is what can happen. And sometimes it does happen, although tonight has been the worst."

"Why in the hell does he drink then?" he asked.

"Why does he do stupid things? Why can't he grow up? When will he stop his pendejadas, his flings and personal disasters? I can't answer those questions. Believe me, I've asked them."

She shoved her face in her hands and cried. Hard sobs shook her shoulders and neck.

He escaped into the bathroom and stayed there until he heard her moving around. He flushed the toilet, rinsed his hands, threw water on his face, and walked back in the room.

"I feel like an idiot," she said to him as soon as he appeared. "You must think we're crazy. I don't blame you. We are nuts."

He knew that he should tell her that it was all right; that everyone has a bad night once in a while, that tomorrow they would laugh about it.

"I need to get some sleep," he said.

"Yes, of course," she said, nodding. "You have to be ready for all the students and fans."

Tomás shrugged. "This movie talk. Was that all it was? Just talk?"

"No, no. We need some time. And money, of course. Getting you on board gives us the talking point we need for the people who have to back this type of project. But it takes time. It always does. We'll be another step closer after tomorrow. With the right luck we can do something important. It's all about luck out here."

She picked up her purse. She paused at the doorway.

"I could stay," she said. "He's out cold, dead. I can leave early in the morning. He'll never know."

"You should go."

She didn't even try to argue. She left, no good-bye, nothing.

Alberto's snores filled the room. Tomás slept fitfully and finally at five in the morning he gave up. He called the front desk and asked for a taxi.

"Certainly, sir, where to?"

"The airport."

"Checking out a day early, sir?"

"No. Someone's here, still using the room. He's paying for the room, so I hope you don't mind."

The desk clerk was all business. "Certainly not, sir. The room is reserved and paid for until tomorrow. As long as you don't break any laws you can do whatever you want."

"Good. And I'll need to talk with someone about changing a flight. You got any coffee?"

ACT OF FAITH
Estella González

Once you're married by the Catholic Church you're married for life. "Dicho y hecho, and that's that," Grandma Fina used to say.

So now that Angelina's husband wanted a divorce so he could be with that *desgraciada puta* Claudia Mercado, he had to die. That was the only way. But of course Frank, Marta, *y* everybody and their *madre* were going to put up a big stink about it. So what if Father Jorge wouldn't bless or sanctify it or whatever? Angelina had had enough of his stupid rules. For her, having a funeral for Antonio would clear the way for her. The way to where she didn't know but at least Antonio would be dead and wouldn't be able to stop her.

After she finished chopping the garlic, she checked on the walnuts boiling in the pan. Almost done. Oooh, maybe she should play some Lola Beltrán or maybe Chavela Vargas so the food can be happy? She put on one of the old scratchy albums Antonio had left her.

"Aaaaay que lau-re-les tan ver-des," Lola belted out.

Next she started shredding the flank steak. The hot meat made her fingers feel tingly like they had been asleep a long time. She imagined shredding Antonio's face, heart, and then his *pito*. She popped a piece of steak into her mouth. How would Claudia like that? Too bad Frank wouldn't come but he thought he knew it all just because he was a big-shot college student now. Probably thought she was ignorant like her Grandma Fina, who, up to her dying day, would walk around with coffee grounds stuffed in her socks to cure her sore throats and coughing. What *mijo* doesn't know about women and marriage could fill up this house, she thought. But better he didn't know about his father's girlfriends and God knows how many kids. She quickly crossed herself and started roasting the *poblano* chiles. Next she chopped up the apples, pears, and tomatoes. Frank had vacuumed the living room before he left for classes. He told her he would be going home with his father for the weekend.

"Fine," Angelina said. "Take your father's side."

Frank took his bulging duffle bag and kissed her good-bye. Just then, the phone rang. It was Marta.

"Don't tell me you're not coming," Angelina said.

"I told you I'd come," Marta said. "But I still think you're crazier than a bola de perros juntos. Don't you think it's pura brujería?"

"No," Angelina said. Then she crossed herself.

"Well, doña Goya and all those little viejitas you go to church with every morning think the devil is making you do this. 'Cruz en pecho, diablo en el hecho,' they say."

Viejas metiches, Angelina thought. Doña Goya had been Grandma Fina's oldest friend, always wearing a black veil and black hose and always rubbing her rosary, whispering real hard just before Father Jorge began morning mass. Sometimes Angelina closed her eyes and imagined she was listening to Grandma Fina praying just after she got out of bed.

"I think they're gonna come to your house and pray for you."

"Pray for me?"

"I told you," Marta sounded real tired. "They think your funeral idea is pura brujería. That you're putting a curse on your husband."

"But Hermana Tonia is doing the ceremony. Doña Goya goes to her botica all the time for her sobada."

"I guess she thinks only a priest should be doing this."

"Virgen de la Purísima," Angelina said. "You think they're right, don't you?"

Marta didn't say anything. Angelina knew her friend didn't blame her son or doña Goya. But after the funeral, she'd feel better. She'd be able to look out of her kitchen window and not have to close the curtains every morning so she wouldn't have to see Claudia's house sitting right there in front of her, making fun of her. Once the funeral was over, she wouldn't have to pull out the bottle of Presidente brandy they used to drink on their anniversary, Frank's birthday, or to his promotion at the Checker Auto Parts store. Now the bottle was nearly empty and she wondered if she could get Rudy to buy her another at the corner liquor store. Angelina promised God this would be the last time she took over one of the church's ceremonies.

"I'll be there," Marta said. "How many panes de muertos do you need?"

"Bring ten. Antonio was always a big comelón."

As soon as she got off the phone, she called Rudy and asked him if the coffin was ready.

■

The coffin knocked around the bed of Angelina's pickup truck as she flew around corners and zipped up the steep hills of Boyle Heights, letting the bottom of the truck scrape the street. She liked to think she was banging Antonio around, his bones, though made of paper, cracking with each slam.

"¡Ay qué laureles tan verdes!" Angelina belted with Chavela Vargas. Her veil flapped with the speed of the truck while her rosary swung over the rear-view mirror with each swerve around the corners. Rudy gripped the door handle and with both hands.

"Don't worry, mijo," Angelina said. "I just wanna shake Antonio up a little bit."

When they got to Angelina's house, Rudy threw up into the rose bushes. She laughed and said, "Rudy, you're more of a vieja than I am."

Angelina opened the tailgate of the truck and grabbed the coffin, pulling on it. Rudy wiped his face then grabbed the side of the coffin and helped her carry it to the foot of the steep stairs. He gave a long whistle when he saw them.

"Don't look at me," Angelina said. "Antonio wanted 'the house on the hill' like he was some kind of pinche rico or something."

As they climbed the cement steps, Angelina saw the nicks on the purple paint Rudy had used on the pine box. So what, she thought. Like Antonio deserved a nice, new shiny coffin. He's lucky he's even got one. She should just throw his bones straight into the fire. But she couldn't do that to Frank. She had to keep the funeral somewhat respectful even if her son wasn't coming. If anything, Rudy's artwork deserved some respect, and he was Frank's best friend. Antonio's skeleton, even the skull, was a piece of art like something she'd seen in one of those funny little stores Frank would take her to with all these crazy pictures costing like $500 even though they looked like your own kid could make them in kindergarten.

They hauled the coffin up the stairs, walking real slowly. Angelina tried not to trip over her long red skirt. What if she fell? she thought. The image of Antonio's purple coffin lying on top of her body made her go a little slower. Rudy just kept on lugging the thing. Thank God he could help her. Frank would never do this. When she told him about the funeral, he shook his head and said "Mom, you're creeping me out." Creeping him out, her ass! He was creeped out by a funeral for his father, but he wasn't creeped out when he visited Antonio and his little *puta* girlfriend across the street, was he? No, that was no problem but when his own mother asked him to help burn the coffin with skeleton, clothes and all. Now that was a problem. Angelina got so worked up that she started pushing Rudy harder.

"Take it easy, will ya?"

When they got the coffin to the porch, Angelina told Rudy to take a break.

"Where do you want this thing?"

"In the living room," she said. "We're gonna lay him out and get him ready for the wake tonight."

She noticed him looking at her wall covered with saints, sacred hearts, and of course la Virgen de Guadalupe.

"You sure have a lotta saints here. Didn't you used to have pictures here?"

"Yeah, but that was a while ago."

"Where'd you put them?"

"In a box somewhere."

He saw her bride picture where she's standing by herself in front of these little waterfalls at La Encantada Park. He asked her how old she was when she got married.

"Oooh, mijo, I think I was 17 or 18."

"Wow."

"Que 'wow' que nada. It's not like I'm a hundred years old."

Rudy looked at her and then went up to a picture of Frank.

"Frank looks like you."

"Thank God."

They placed the coffin on the two sawhorses she'd just bought that morning at Home Depot. She had draped them over with a rainbow-colored cotton blanket. Behind the coffin, on the now empty entertainment center, she had placed dozens of multicolored votive candles. As Rudy helped her light them, Angelina wondered why he wasn't "creeped out." Of course she had paid him $100 for the coffin and skeleton, though she still thought that was too expensive. But she knew his mother, Jenny Ortega, former cha-cha girl and the 1983 Tower Queen for Griffith Junior High School. She'd been a bitch but her son was a true gentleman. Very *guapo* too, but of course his father was white. Too bad he had come out *prieto* like his mother.

■

Hermana Tonia started reciting the funeral rites from the Catholic Book of the Dead. The living room was wall-to-wall roses. Angelina had used the last of the money she got from the sale of Grandma Fina's house to buy them. In the candlelight, their shadows bobbed up and down like dozens of mourners. But for tonight, it was only Angelina, Hermana Tonia, and Rudy. Marta stopped by long enough to drop off the *pan de muertos,* but as soon as she saw the coffin and Hermana Tonia, she took off real fast.

"But I thought you were gonna stay."

Marta shook her head, said something about doña Goya, and ran down the stairs so quick she almost flew head first into the rosebushes. Angelina sat next to Rudy, who offered her a shot of the Presidente brandy she had set out on Antonio's altar. Rudy had done a good job. The Virgen de Guadalupe he had drawn on the lid was just like the picture she had hanging on her living room wall.

Dressed in her black rebozo and white tunic and pants, Hermana Tonia looked like one of those Indian women with the red dot on her forehead that she saw at the Catholic school where she worked. Tonia spoke in a low, dry voice about God's mercy for the souls of the dead. Next she sprinkled holy water from the abalone shell. When she began the "Padre Nuestro," Angelina heard them. Doña Goya and the rest of her cronies were praying outside her door.

"¿Ques eso?" Hermana Tonia asked.

"It's only doña Goya," Angelina said.

"Get rid of her. I can't do this if they're making their ruidajo."

Angelina opened the door and told the old ladies to leave. But they kept praying their fifth recitation of the "Act of Faith." Angelina ran around the corner of the house and came back dragging a gushing hose. They finally stopped and looked at her.

"Mija," Doña Goya said. "It's a sin what you're doing."

"It's my business if I wanna hold a funeral."

Doña Goya started crying.

"Your Grandma Fina . . ."

"Don't you dare bring Grandma Fina into this," Angelina said. "I'm not gonna feel bad about this, just like Antonio doesn't feel bad about jack."

"But this curse, hija?"

"Shut up. You don't even know what I'm doing."

"¿Qué pasó? You're acting like you weren't even raised by a decent woman like Josefina."

"I'm acting like I wanna act and I'm not gonna let you, a bunch of old ladies who haven't had sex with anybody for forty years, tell me how to live my life."

The *viejitas* started whispering real fast to each other, shaking their heads.

"Don't shake your head at me like you're some kind of saints. I know about you, and you and you. And I know about your own kids too."

With that, they started walking down the steps, slow at first and then they took little hops like fat black rabbits.

■

After the funeral, Angelina served up the chiles *en nogada* in the kitchen. She kept the window open and sometimes when she passed by it she would look out. Claudia's house was dark. Where could they be? What did she care anyway?

"¿Otro chile?" Angelina asked Hermana Tonia.

"Ay sí. Están pero muy riquísimos," she said taking her sixth chile.

"And you, Rudy?"

"I'll take two more," he said.

"Good! You should take some to your mother."

Angelina scooped out the last of the chiles into a Tupperware bowl.

"Tell your mother I'm sorry I took up so much of your time."

"She doesn't care."

"You sound like Frank. Of course we care."

In the living room, the candles flickered in the dark. Lola Beltrán sang "Paloma negra," scratchy but strong. She poured out another shot of brandy and stood up.

"A toast to Antonio's death!"

After toasting his death, they toasted to the funeral and to Rudy for his work.

"What did you say Antonio was made out of?" Hermana Tonia asked.

"Papier-mâché," Rudy said.

"Then it should burn real easy," she said sipping her glass. Rudy and Angelina looked at each other.

"I don't wanna burn it," Angelina said. "I wanna keep it right here in the living as a recuerdo."

"No," Hermana Tonia said. "You have to burn it if you want the funeral to be complete. You can keep the ashes. Keep them in a bowl or throw them in Claudia's front yard but don't keep the coffin or skeleton enteros."

"¿Por qué no?" Angelina started to think that Hermana Tonia was just like doña Goya.

"Because then you're making fun of God, not just Antonio."

"I'm not making fun of anybody."

Somebody started banging on the door. Rudy opened it and Antonio walked past him up to the coffin.

"So this is it, huh?" Antonio said. "What kind of brujería is this?"

"Get out of here, hijo de la chingada," Angelina said, running over to the coffin. "This isn't your house anymore. Go back to your little whore and marry her."

Antonio reached past her and pushed the coffin over, dumping the skeleton.

"¡Pinche bruja!"

Rudy pushed him.

"¿Y tú buey?" Antonio said. He pushed Rudy over the coffin and waved the skeleton in front of his face.

"Is this supposed to be me?"

"Leave him alone! I'm calling the police," Angelina yelled.

Hermana Tonia came out, her arms heavy with a *molcajete*, ready to smash it over his head. Antonio walked out, laughing.

"¡Brujas!" he said. "I'm still alive and I'm not gonna die."

They watched him walk down the stairs and cross the street back to his house. Through the kitchen window, they saw Claudia waiting in her nightie. As soon as Antonio walked in he shut off the lights.

■

Angelina turned up Cuco Sánchez on the radio so she could hear it over the pickup's engine. The smoke from Rudy's cigarettes made her sing louder. In the setting sun, the San Bernardino Mountains glowed pink and purple.

"Where are we going?" he asked.

"Far," Angelina said.

When they got to Joshua State Park, Angelina drove down the road for a mile or two before parking near a deserted campfire.

"We're here," Angelina said. She jumped out of the truck and straightened out her skirt.

"Now what?"

"Let's get the coffin."

Rudy shook his head, rubbing out his cigarette.

"After all that work I put into it?" he said.

"I paid you for it, didn't I?"

Rudy sat down and lit another cigarette.

"Why do you think I brought you out here?" Angelina said.

He shrugged and pretended to look at the Joshua trees. Why the fuck had she brought him here? The brandy was making her *peda*. He probably thought she was gonna fuck him. And maybe she was. She'd drunk enough Presidente to help her do just about anything. It almost felt like love. Why not make love? But not now. First there was some burning to be done.

"Well, if you won't do it," Angelina said as she walked up to the back of the truck, her feet kicking up dust. She pulled at the coffin so hard it fell to the ground.

"It's your money," Rudy said as he helped her lay the coffin on the dead campfire.

"Too bad Grandma Fina's not here. She liked all this fire and ceremony stuff," she said. "I think this is why she was into the Catholic Church."

Angelina poured brandy over the skeleton while Rudy set the skull on fire. It took about an hour for everything to burn. With the Santa Ana winds blowing, all the ashes blew into the Joshua forest.

"Can we just stay here for a little while?" Angelina said.

Rudy shrugged and his shoulders and climbed into the truck's cab. Angelina climbed into the other side and turned on the radio. María de Lourdes sang, "Tú, sólo tú." Angelina hummed along with it, then started singing with her. Rudy smiled at her and laughed a little.

"You're sooo blasted," he said.

"So what," she said. "I'm a free woman. I can do whatever the hell I want. Túuuuu sólo túuuuuu."

"Are we gonna spend the whole night here?"

"I just don't wanna go back yet. What for?"

Rudy lit a cigarette for her. In the sky, she could see so many stars and wondered if Grandma Fina was looking down at her.

"Grandma Fina's probably getting a place in hell ready for me."

"No she isn't."

Before she knew it, Angelina started crying so hard she started choking on her cigarette smoke.

"She's probably saying 'That sinning whore's no granddaughter of mine. I didn't raise a heretic. Esa mal educada.'"

Angelina wiped her eyes and nose with her skirt. So what if Rudy saw her leg, her old wrinkly thighs with their spider veins. What did he care? He was just a boy starting his life. Just a boy with all the young girls waiting for him. Some day he'd fall in love and get married. Some day he would dump his old ugly wife for a new woman. Just like Antonio.

"Don't ever get married, Rudy."

He almost choked on his cigarette smoke.

"I think we better go," she said, starting the engine.

"Not yet. You're not ready."

"You're not my husband."

"I know. He's dead."

Angelina couldn't make his face out in the shadow of the truck. She turned off the engine and pulled a blanket from behind the seat. Rudy smiled at her like Frank used to when he was little and let her tuck him into bed. Outside, the Santa Ana winds whistled through the cracks in the windows.

■

In the morning they drove back, her head pounding with *ranchera* music on the radio. Angelina felt dry and dusty, like an old empty bottle. On the radio, María de Lourdes sang "Tú, sólo tú" again. Rudy wouldn't sleep even though Angelina told her she was all right. In the sunlight, with his little moustache and beard, he looked like Juan Diego looking at the Virgen de Guadalupe floating near him, his *tilma* filled with roses. His hangover must have been worse than hers.

When she dropped him off at his house she felt cold. She grew colder as she drove back to her house, thinking about climbing up the steps just to end up in an old empty house. She started up the truck again and drove straight back to Rudy's place. His dog Peewee started barking at her as she walked around to the garage where he lived. She just hoped that Jenny didn't come to meet her. *Que vergüenza.* Here she was, a grown woman visiting some twenty-something kid because she was lonely. For a moment she thought of going back home. But the thought of those stairs made her keep walking to the back.

"Rudy, ayúdame," she whispered through the screen door of his window.

His dark shadow moved on the bed. The smell of brandy got stronger as his steps came closer.

"Angelina, what's wrong?"

"Can we talk a little?"

Angelina walked straight into his bedroom and sat on his narrow bed. It smelled like Tide. His mother must have just changed the sheets just that day. Tubes of paint lay on the floor along with some paintbrushes and partly painted canvases. Rudy dragged his chair out hard and sat right next to her.

"Why can't you go home? Aren't you tired?"

"No. Antonio's still alive."

Rudy lit a cigarette.

"According to the Church, Antonio's still my husband."

"According to you, he's dead. We did that little ceremony, remember?"

She had killed Antonio just like he had killed her the moment he started cheating on her. And he had kept on killing.

"Do you wanna sleep here?" Rudy asked.

Angelina choked on her saliva so hard she didn't notice when she lay down or when Rudy took off her shoes. She took off her dress and lay next to him in her bra and panties.

"You won't believe this," she said. "Antonio's the only guy I ever slept with in my whole life."

"I believe it," Rudy said.

GINA AND MAX

Michael Jaime-Becerra

Max has figured out two new ways to annoy me. He found a pair of chopsticks on the sidewalk, and quickly became skilled in using them by picking up every cellophane wrapper, cigarette butt, and bit of paper around the bus stop, placing them in the trash can to his left. When Max tried to pick up an empty beer bottle, it slipped from the sticks like I told him it would, falling and shattering, and I could feel the stares from the people nearby. Now Max is playing the drumbeat to "Bela Lugosi's Dead," a song he's always hated, one he's teased me for liking. Once, when we first started going out, Max stole a set of fake vampire teeth from somewhere and chased me around my parents' house, singing the song through clenched plastic fangs until I let him catch me and kiss me on my mother's couch.

The time schedule posted next to the bench shows that the number 20 bus stops running after midnight. It's almost nine now, and I tell this to Max, and he tells me not to worry as he picks at one of my earrings with his stupid sticks. I get up to read and reread the different schedules. I run my fingers across the map, tracing the red lines marking the 20's route. I try to judge where we'll get off, how far we'll have to go to this Christmas party, and how long it might take us to walk there. When the bus comes, I shield my eyes from its bright headlights. The doors swish open and I'm positive that our last chance to catch the 20 back from Benny's house will be at 11:35.

Max lets me get on before him. I hold the steel rail and look out the broad windshield while he asks the driver if she can break a five. The woman is wearing brown leather gloves with peepholes for her knuckles, and she seems more interested in adjusting her grip on the steering wheel than answering Max's request.

"Sorry, honey, I don't make change," she says.

Max's five is all that he has, so I pay for the bus with the change in my purse, the last of my money until Friday, the day after Christmas, when we both get paid. Max drops the change in the cash box, and the driver yanks the lever that closes the doors.

The bus pulls away from the curb, and we take seats near the back. Max sets his backpack on the ground and tugs at the window, trying to get it closed. It won't budge. He groans and zips up his leather jacket.

"How do you plan on getting us home?" I ask.

"I'm sure someone at the party will give us a ride. You cold?"

Max puts his arm around me before I can answer yes. My coat is long, but it's thin, and my tights are too full of holes to make any difference. I sit with my feet up on the seat, knees together, rubbing the chill from my legs.

Benny is throwing this Christmas party. Seeing as how my mom hung up on me the last two times I called, being with Max at Benny's party sounds better than spending Christmas Eve alone. I start to shiver under Max's arm, and we stay quiet and watch the street go by. Max's tattoo equipment is in his backpack. He's going to get some work done tonight, make some money, which is fine by me, so long as it's not Benny he's working on. Benny's the reason Max is so careful about who he tattoos these days, the reason he hasn't worked his machine in three months.

■

Benny works with Max at the paper tube plant. He's a big guy with six kids by four different women. Each kid's name is tattooed on his chest, and the afternoon he came over, he wanted Max to add the name of his most recent baby, a girl named Suzana. As he unbuttoned his shirt in our kitchen, he said that if he kept up this kind of pace, he'd have to start lifting weights again so his chest could fit more names. I was making a sandwich for my break while they were getting started. Benny folded his shirt carefully and told Max that he had only seen Suzana once, shaking his head as he told him that she had fat lips and a wide nose like her mother. "Ten days old," he said. "Already she's got a nose the size of a Coke bottle."

Suzana was to go under her sisters Abigail and Gabriella, next to her brothers Joseph and Raymond and Moises. The pair of lists on Benny's chest was tattooed in black script, the boys on the right side, the girls on the left. Benny caught me looking at him and he tapped his chest. "They help me remember who belongs to who," he said.

Benny's tattoos reminded me of pictures my dad's cousin has of the plane he flew in during the war, of the little white bombs stenciled by the cockpit that marked the number of cities the crew had destroyed. Later on, Max told me that Benny works at three different jobs—the paper tube factory, the go-cart track, and a paper route—but only sends money to two of the mothers at a time. Sometimes he switches off, and some months Benny's women don't get any of his money. That afternoon Benny asked me if I'd make him a sandwich too, something to keep company with the beer in his stomach. I spread some peanut butter and some jelly on two slices of bread, and Benny ate the sandwich as if it was the last chore on his long list of things to do. He sighed as he watched Max shake a small bottle of black ink. "Let me tell you, Max," he said, "life is so much easier when you keep your dick in your pants."

Suzana was to be spelled with a Z, but Max didn't know this, and after he figured out how to imitate the style, he drew out the name as Susana. He showed it to Benny, and Benny didn't say that anything was wrong. Afterwards, Benny stood in front of our bathroom mirror. He examined the raw rectangle on his chest and came out crazy. He started calling Max names, saying this was bullshit, that he wasn't going to pay. Max was cleaning his tattoo machine, and Benny knocked it from his hand. The motor chattered loudly against the floor as the needle sprayed the last of the ink onto my leg. Benny punched Max twice, once in the stomach and once in the head. That night, the swollen bruise on Max's forehead looked as if someone had glued a prune above his eye. He said the second punch broke one of Benny's fingers. Two days later, Max assured me that things between him and Benny were OK.

■

Max was so excited about my Christmas gift this year that he gave it to me before we left. I shut my eyes so that I wouldn't see it. The things

I bought Max were next to the bed, unwrapped and buried under a pile of my dirty clothes. But he insisted, kissing my eyelids until I opened them, handing me a large envelope made of blue metallic paper. Its tag was cut in the shape of a cartoon bat, TO GINA preprinted on one of its extended wings.

"For you," Max said. "Open it. Come on, open it!"

I peeled tape from the blue paper and found a brown manila envelope underneath. I took my time with this until Max pulled it away. He tore the envelope open and poured the contents onto my lap. There were official-looking papers and forms. A thick pamphlet. Some kind of certificate. I looked among them all and found a bumper sticker that read BATTY ABOUT BATS. There was also a large glossy photo that made me jump. It was a rat with wings. I've always feared these kinds of creepy animals. Last August, a spider in our bedroom had me sleeping on the living room floor, wrapped head to toe in a sheet so that I was practically suffocating. I'd done this for three nights until Max found the spider and brought it to me crushed in the folds of a napkin. When I asked Max what all the papers in my lap were, he seemed slightly disappointed that my face didn't look as happy as his.

"It's a bat," he said. Max took the picture from my lap and held it before me, the excitement shifting from his face to his hands so that the photo shook. "It's your bat, Gina."

Max explained that when he visited the doctor for his aching feet, he saw an advertisement in a magazine. He said he tore the page out and sent them a money order, adopting a bat in my name.

"Somewhere in Texas," he said, "there's a huge hole in the ground where twenty million of these things live. One of them is yours."

I didn't know what to say. I told Max thank you and kissed him and hugged him and made sure to hold him a long time before letting go. I put all the papers and forms back in their envelope, telling Max that I'd read them later, knowing even then that I wouldn't. Max left the room and I finished getting dressed. I brushed my hair, parting it on the left, and made faces at myself as I shaded my eyes the way Siouxsie's were on *Request Video*, purple and black, sexy and threatening. I buckled my boots and was rummaging through my jewelry box when Max came back.

He sat on the bed and spoke to me in a soft and quiet voice. "It's supposed to be a girl. A female. The lady I talked to said they'd make sure and give you a female." Max took out the bat photo, apparently inspecting it for telltale girlie traits. "Anyway, it's a Mexican free-tailed bat." He slipped the picture into the envelope, and put the envelope with the bills on my dresser. "She's supposed to be like you," he said. "She's Mexican and she's Goth."

∎

The bus lurches away from the curb and Max rocks into me. My hands are cold, and I rub them together, but nothing changes, so I tuck them under my thighs. Max's hands never get like this. His entire body is always warm, and I miss this most when one of us gets an odd shift at work. On those nights I sleep alone under thick, woolly blankets, but the cold still manages to creep into my hands and feet.

I rub my hands some more and Max asks if I'm nervous.

"No," I answer. "Are you?"

Max shakes his head and says that Benny's friends will probably just want name tattoos, gang stuff or girlfriends in Old English. "Easy money," he says. "As long as they aren't bleeders, it shouldn't take all night." He shrugs and picks at the rubber molding around the window. "It's no big deal," he says, "just some easy, easy money." Max presses his fingers to his right temple and rubs the skin in small circles. As long as I've known him, he's done this when lying. I take his hand away and hold it in my lap with the two of mine.

Last Sunday I was folding laundry, when I noticed Max's green mug of markers and pens in its spot on our table, their caps fuzzy with crowns of dust. He hasn't drawn much since the day Benny hit him, and, looking at his dusty collection of pens, I wondered if Benny knocked something loose inside Max. The bus crosses Valley Boulevard as I think of a school film I once saw on the nervous system. The filmstrip showed our insides as a bunch of sockets and electrical plugs. There was one for the heart that kept it beating, one for the lungs that kept them breathing, one for the legs that kept them walking. Max pulls the cord to get the bus to stop, and I lose the image of a plug dangling in his head. We get up and step off, and outside the air's been replaced by the odor of wet duck.

■

I've smiled that smile before. This is our third Christmas together, and as much as I love Max, he hasn't gotten any better at giving me gifts. We'd been together five months and three days when our first Christmas came around. Max gave me a pack of multivitamins and a jar of iron pills because I was always tired. His mother said that I was probably anemic, that there was no iron in my blood. Besides the pills, she suggested that Max make me eat more steak. His grandma told him to prepare some *longaniza*, but I've seen other members of Max's family get sick, and that bloody pork sausage seems to be her answer to everything.

When Max and his sister were still talking, he gave me a used camera that she sold him. I was taking a photo class at the time, and the only camera my family had was a Polaroid that refused to spit out its slow-developing squares. We spent ten bucks on gas and took the camera to the beach on the last day of Christmas vacation. I snapped pictures of dogs chasing Frisbees, and old homeless guys passed out on benches, and surfers in black rubber suits running out to ride the water. The car overheated on the way home, and I shot an entire roll on the side of the freeway while we waited for the radiator to cool down. Max posed, the engine billowing steam behind him, and it wasn't until a week later that we found out Evelyn's Kodak didn't work. Every picture I took that day looked as if it had been dipped in milk.

■

Max has Benny's address written on a scrap of paper. He puts his arm around me as we follow the directions, the smell from the duck farm staying with us while we walk. Max covers his nose. As bad as it is now, the stench of wet duck shit is worse in the summer with the sun and heat. We go under the bridge and cross Garvey, ending up on Exline, where every house is next to the freeway, fake snow sprayed in the windows and Christmas lights draped over the wrought iron. The street turns into a cul-de-sac and we come up on a small house with no twinkling lights. A car blocks the driveway and one sits on the sidewalk. Behind them, parked on the lawn, is a light blue pick-up that Max recognizes as Benny's.

The address tacked up on the eave has lost its last two numbers, but the front door is wide open. Max knocks before we step inside and find that Benny's Christmas party isn't much of a party. There are two guys sitting around, drinking beer, one tapping his pack of cigarettes against the table. They look up. In the second where nothing is said I can hear a TV and some oldies playing low. The guy closest to us stands and tucks his cigarette behind his ear. He's tall, thin, and wears only a tank top, like we're in the middle of July. He's definitely not our kind of people. I stand behind Max as he asks for Benny.

"I'm a friend of his from work," he says. Neither of the guys respond. "I'm here for the tattoos."

The smaller guy still sitting nods like this is something profound. "Benny's in the bedroom," he says. "At the end of the hallway."

The hallway is dark, and I follow Max, a giggle coming from an open door on our left. The streetlight comes in through the window, shining dimly on a bed where two blue bodies are pressed together. A second giggle turns into a low moan, but the *cholo* in the kitchen tells us to keep going. There's a second door on the right and a third one up ahead. Max walks up to the one with a stripe of light at the bottom. He knocks lightly.

"Come in." We step inside and find Benny sitting at the edge of a large bed, signing his name to Christmas cards. A bunch of oversized red plastic stockings are piled behind him, and, when we get closer, I see that they're filled with hard candy and cheap plastic toys. Benny puts a card in a red envelope, and licks the entire flap before sealing it shut. He and Max say hello. I wave. Benny sets the card on a dresser, next to some twenty-dollar bills.

"Straight from the bank," he says. "Every year I get my kids new money. It's like they got a copier in the back of the bank just for me." Benny holds one of the bills out to Max, and he inspects it, then passes it back so I can see. The paper's thin and crisp, so crisp that the bill feels phony.

Benny signs one last card and says he'll do the rest later. "I won't see my other kids until tomorrow," he says. Max asks if any of them are here, and Benny says, "Not yet, but Marie is supposed to come by later with Gabriella, Raymond, and Moises." Max nods like he knows these people. Benny gets up and we stand behind him as he flicks off the light switch. We follow him back to the kitchen and the low murmur of talking in the other bedroom stops as we walk by.

■

Two years ago, I had five hundred business cards made for Max's birthday. They were printed in glossy red ink, the Misfits' skull grinning in the left corner, Max's name and his parents' phone number below the word TATTOOS. Max gave some to his friends at a party that Friday. I gave some to mine. On Saturday we took the rest to Melrose and walked up and down the crowded sidewalks, handing cards to people who looked cool. We did this until it got dark, then Max got the idea to head up to Hollywood Boulevard. Both sides of Hollywood were jammed with cruisers, their cars bursting with bodies and bass-heavy music. Between green lights, we mixed with the traffic, cutting through the idling cars and handing out business cards. We gave some to *cholos* who drove their low riders by hanging out their windows, and we gave some to disco chicks in convertibles who waved at cute guys like queens in the Rose Parade.

Max expected calls in the weeks afterward, but there were none, except for one freak. According to Max, this guy first called on Tuesday around one in the morning, but soon after, their phone was ringing five or six times a night. The guy would yell the same thing every time— "GREEN HELL! GREEN HELL! WE'RE GONNA BURN IN HELL! GREEN HELL!"—and one night Max let me answer when he called. The voice was hard to describe, the are calls over as soon as they began, but it did seem muffled, like someone screaming with a hand over their mouth.

None of this was funny to Max's mom. She would hold the receiver at arm's length and stare holes into Max long after this guy hung up. Max swore that the caller wasn't anyone he or I knew, and his mother made him swear on every precious object he owned. Max was still tattooing in secret then, and just in case this guy gave his mom an excuse to go through his stuff, he packed his equipment into a pair of shoe boxes and gave them to me. These stayed in the back of my closet for the month before Max's parents gave in and changed their number. Things had gotten to the point where their telephone would be off the hook for two and three days straight. During one of these times, Max's *tío* in Guaymas died, but his family missed the call and didn't find out until a year later.

One night, alone in my parents' house, I sat with Max's boxes and took out his tattoo machine. Even then he kept the odd-looking contraption in the maroon T-shirt, the material soft and faded. Max had gotten the job at the factory with this machine specifically in mind. It had taken him half the year to save up over three hundred dollars to buy it through the mail. Sitting on my bed, I held the binding post like an iron pencil and examined the simple machinery above it, the polished steel base plates and chrome contact screws. Several times I had witnessed Max take the machine apart the way a soldier in boot camp would dismantle a rifle. I knew that the two silver cylinders were tiny motors, that a thick copper coil inside each of these motors made a needle snap in and out of the skin ten times per second, that some machines worked faster, but that for Max ten was good enough. After a while, I put the machine back and folded the shirt around it several times. I imagined the power one would have when using it, the sudden ability to change a person's body forever, and it seemed inconceivable to me that Max could inspire that kind of trust in anyone.

■

Benny introduces everybody. Frank is the guy with the cigarettes, and next to him is Harvey, who's sucking on his crucifix like cheap gold was a rare and precious vitamin. Max nods and shakes their hands before sitting at the other side of the table to unpack all his things. First he takes out his doctor stuff—bandages and medical tape, latex gloves, cotton swabs and rubbing alcohol—then he lays out an assortment of long steel needles next to a half-empty bottle of black ink. The needles are individually wrapped like Band-Aids, and Max arranges them thinnest to thickest, liners and shaders on the left, the thicker magnums on the right. The maroon bundle with his tattoo machine makes a small thud when Max sets it down. He carefully unwinds the cord to his power supply, smoothing out the kinks, plugging the small generator into the socket behind him.

I take the seat next to Max and look out the sliding glass doors that must open to a patio. The backyard is dark and the doors look like they're made of black glass.

"Did you bring your pictures?" Benny asks.

Max says yeah, handing Benny one sketchbook, though there are many more at home, pages and pages full of Max's designs. Frank gets up and looks at them over Benny's shoulder, but Harvey stays put.

He lets the chain fall from his mouth, and says, "I'm ready. I know what I want."

Harvey takes a folded piece of paper from his shirt pocket and hands it over to Max. "You can do this, right?" I recognize the drawing from Nativity's church bulletin, two hands praying, a rosary draped around the wrists.

"Yeah," Max says. "No problem. I've drawn more of these than the pope." Max laughs at his own joke, but when no one else does, I force a supportive smile. Max asks Harvey where and how he wants it. Harvey puts down his beer and holds his hands about four inches apart. He then rubs the back of his neck and says right here. Max nods. "That'll be fifty bucks."

When Benny says OK, Max smoothes the sheet with the praying hands and starts drawing on a section of transfer paper.

I'm thirsty, and I ask Benny if he has anything to drink, a glass of water maybe. Benny says sure. He gives the notebook to Frank, hands me a glass from the cupboard, and points to the refrigerator. "The tap tastes kinda funny," he says, "but there's some bottled stuff in the fridge."

I go into the kitchen and find the jug of water behind a Styrofoam container and a six-pack of Bud with two cans missing. I'm by the stove, filling my glass, when I notice a bunch of bullets on the tiled countertop. There's eight or nine of them just thrown there, plain as car keys, ordinary as pocket change. No gun. Just bullets.

I stare at them a few seconds, then take a deep breath and ask Max if he wants some water, trying to sound as normal as I possibly can. He looks up from his drawing and says no. Frank goes onto the patio and Harvey takes over the notebook. Benny comes into the kitchen and gets too close to me.

"You need anything else?" he asks.

I tell him no and put the water back in the refrigerator. Before sitting down, I look back at the spot on the counter, and the bullets are gone.

■

My first memory is sitting in a high chair, my *tío* shaking his head at how much I resemble my *abuelita*. I've heard it my entire life. Same eyes, same cheekbones. The same pout when we get mad. Hanging in the hallway of my mom's house is an old brown-and-white photo of my abuelita with her two older brothers. She's just turned seventeen. In two months, she'll be married. In two years, she'll leave for California with my mom kicking inside her. This is who I look like now, and the old woman now living down in La Paz is who I'll be when I get old. I can't imagine my abuelita with something printed on her skin, the letters sagging and misshapen after forty years, the image faded and blotchy. That's why Max has never worked on me.

Not that he hasn't tried. When the Cramps played the Palladium, I drank too much beer in the parking lot, so much that Max left me in the car when the band started. I woke up the next day, startled when I saw my leg. It was covered with a dragon, a wild-eyed Aztec monster that clawed its way from the small knob of my ankle up to my thigh. Its head stretched under my panties and its thin tongue flicked at my pubic hair. I felt my skin carefully, expecting scabs and soreness, but it was a drawing done in black marker, not permanent. I licked my thumb, and as I rubbed my thigh, Max came into the room.

He sat on the bed, chuckling because my spit couldn't take off the ink. My head pounded and my stomach shook from the night before. I thought about the show, about being sick and alone, the smell of barf that's more bubbles and water than barf, about the cool glass of the window against my cheek. My jaw clamped down and my eyes narrowed. Then I thought about what Max had done to me without my knowing, and before he could say anything, I punched him. I aimed for his face and hit him in the neck, but I punched Max all the same. It was the first time I had ever hit anyone. I called Max an asshole and stumbled into the bathroom, locking the door, leaving him holding his throat and coughing wildly. I rinsed my face with cold water and, as I stared at the shiny faucet, the anger came off me in shuddering waves. Max apologized and I yelled.

Go draw on your own fuckin' body!" I screamed. "And when you're done, go fuck yourself!"

I called Max all kinds of things as I undressed. I said he was a worm of a boyfriend for leaving me behind. I got in the shower, grateful for the hot water as I began scrubbing. I worked on the dragon with a soapy washcloth until Max left for his shift. The marker wouldn't come off cleanly. Instead the ink was only willing to fade, especially in the tougher sections, my inner thigh and the patch behind my knee. There it looked like Max had done his work with gray marker instead of black. Alone, I dried off, swabbed nail polish remover on those spots, and spent the rest of the afternoon with my leg splotchy and red.

In truth, it was a good-looking dragon, but I still didn't talk to Max for a week. I slept in our bed and he slept on the couch. We came and went like mismatched roommates. And then one day Max came home from work with his left hand wrapped in a bandage. I was heating some leftover spaghetti at the time. Max sat at the table, and, when I asked, he told me he'd had a small accident, that just before his coffee break, he reached for a quarter he'd dropped, and got the tip of his middle finger sliced by a conveyer belt.

"I'm just lucky it wasn't my right hand," Max said.

He looked tired and sad. He nodded his head when I asked if he was hungry. I gave him my bowl and asked if he wanted some Parmesan, then sat down to listen about the rest of his day.

■

When Max starts working on Harvey, I take my glass of water outside, where Frank's in a lawn chair, cigarette in his mouth, a lighter sparking in his fist. He's sitting between two girls, a thick one who looks familiar and a thin one who doesn't. As I slide the door closed, he whispers something in the thick girl's ear. I make eye contact with her as she giggles, walking past them toward the edge of the yard as she jabs Frank's arm. I take a big drink of water and remind myself that Max knows Benny better than I do, that those bullets definitely don't have anything to do with us. I check the kitchen and everything appears fine. Benny's talking to Max, and Max is dabbing Harvey's shoulder with a paper towel. This will all be over in a few hours, and the best thing I can do in the meantime is stay out here, smell the dirty ducks, and focus my attention elsewhere.

Benny's backyard looks out over the San Gabriel river. There's a half moon out, a moon that casts enough light on the riverbed to let me see the tall stalks of bamboo that rustle in the breeze. The river is dry, and the small pools of still water shine like oil. Beyond this is the 605, tiny red taillights streaming down one side of the freeway, tiny white headlights racing up the other.

Both girls start laughing again, and this time they laugh for real, the thin girl covering her mouth with her hand. Both girls are a few years older than me. They're sharing a cigarette and their bangs are teased, sprayed high and stiff with Aqua Net. The thick girl's named Delia, and she was the only junior in my math class when I was a freshman. Delia reminds me of my cousin Ana, the one who played football in the street and taught my little brother to burp like a bullfrog. Delia looks old, not older, like fifteen years have passed in the four since her graduation. I wonder if she's one of Benny's girlfriends, or if he's seeing them both and they just don't know it. She passes the cigarette back to the thin girl and checks her hair in the glass patio door. Delia nods as she does this, and for a second I think she's nodding at me.

From the freeway comes a sudden screeching of tires. I wait for the thud of an accident, but there's nothing, and the lights continue uninterrupted.

"That'll happen once or twice a night."

I turn around and Benny's standing behind me.

"Some nights I'll be out here, and I'll hear three or four accidents. You can always tell the bad ones by the number of cars that plow into one another." Benny punches the palm of his hand as he says this. "Bam-bam-bam-bam-bam."

"I know about the accidents," I tell him. "My parents live not too far from here."

Benny says really, then asks why I'm spending Christmas Eve here.

"We haven't spoken in awhile."

"Why?"

"Maybe we should change the subject."

Benny smiles. "I'm sorry," he says. "What'd you get Max for Christmas?"

I tell him that I got Max a pair of Winos from the supermarket, but I don't mention that I stole them, the thin-soled canvas shoes jammed inside my purse as I bought groceries last week. I also got Max two pairs of Dickies, one blue pair for work, one black pair for going out. Max has three pairs of pants and the thighs are all worn from the conveyor belt he leans against at the factory. I also spent twenty bucks on a four-ounce bottle of black tattoo ink, Onyx Black, the darkest shade the company makes.

Benny asks if I know what Max is getting me, and I roll my eyes and explain the adopted bat. Benny smiles. He points to the dark riverbed and says, "Max should have told me. I'd have given him a net, and he could've gone down there and brought you the real thing." Benny drinks his beer and shakes his head. "They're in there, but you probably already know that.

When we were kids, we'd throw M-80s into the storm drains. The boom'd echo like we'd chucked a stick of dynamite, and once in a while out would come this mess of bats and smoke."

Frank and the girls go back inside as I ask Benny if he got Marie anything. He says no. "Tomorrow's going to be a bitch," he says, "running around to see all the kids, eating fifty bad tamales before I get to the good ones at my sister's house." As Benny talks, he seems to lose interest in his own sentence. He comes close, puts his arm around my waist and guides me toward a dark corner of the yard. I look back at the window as we move. Max touches the needle to Harvey's neck. Harvey's face squinches up in pain and the girls howl and point.

Benny leans down and his beard scratches against my chin. He kisses me hard on the mouth. Both of Benny's hands clamp my wrists to my waist, and I know I should scream, yell and fight back as our lips touch, but suddenly it isn't in me to do so. I turn my head away and Benny whispers in my ear. "Whatever you saw in there, it doesn't have anything to do with you two. It won't unless you think you saw something. Understand?" I keep quiet and Benny grips me harder. "Remember how easy it was for me to do this, how I could have done more if I wanted to."

■

The night we went to Hollywood, Max and I picked up the business cards that people tossed aside, but most of them were crumpled or ruined with tire prints. Max found three that were in good shape, and on the bus ride home, he talked about making enough money to finally quit the factory. He slid these last three cards into his wallet, where I'm positive they are still, since Max is superstitious about the number three, and he also never gets rid of anything. It was late when we changed buses downtown, and, as we waited for the 176, Max said this starting set of business cards was the first real step to opening his own shop. He said thank you. I sat on his lap as he hugged me, and we stayed like that for a long time among the dark and empty skyscrapers.

■

Max is tearing a strip of medical tape with his teeth and Harvey is holding a patch of gauze over his shoulder when I go back inside the house. I keep my head down in case my lipstick's messy and ask Delia if she knows where the bathroom is, brushing past her friend when she points to the door at the end of the hall. I find the door locked. The person inside says it's busy, sounding startled after I knock. "Use the other one in Benny's bedroom," he says. I think twice, then open the door to Benny's room. I flick the light switch and take my compact and lipstick from my purse. My mouth looks like a smashed grape. It comes off with a Kleenex, and my hand paints a jagged line as I reapply my lipstick. I give up and wipe it away. I sit at the edge of the bed and call for Max.

When he comes, I tell him we have to go. I want to tell him that Benny kissed me, about the bullets on the counter, and the bad things that will happen if we stay here. Max sits next to me and it's as if I'm seeing him for the first time. He's skinny. His chest is flat and the bones in his arms stand out more than his muscles.

"What's the matter?"

I lie. I tell him that I'm sick, that I feel like I'm dying. "We have to leave."

Benny comes into the room and stands at the door. He asks Max what's wrong and looks at me.

"She's sick," Max says. He tells Benny that he'll take me home, that he'll walk me to the bus stop then come back to work on him and Frank. We get up and Benny moves aside to let us leave. I grab onto Max's arm and we go outside.

"What's going on?" Max asks. We get to the curb and walk under the streetlights. I grasp at other excuses. I tell Max to come home, that I can't wait to give him his present, that I want to spend my Christmas with him and not a bunch of thugs. I tell Max that we should leave, but he says he wants to stay.

"Besides," he says, "my pants aren't even wrapped yet." He smiles. "It's OK. I don't care." Max tells me that all this with Benny shouldn't take too long. "I mean, we need the money, and I need to get you something good. Let's face it. My gift's kinda lame."

"That's not important."

"It is to me."

I tell Max that the bat was a lovely idea, and I kiss him to show what I mean. When he holds my neck, his fingers feel slippery from the powder left by the latex gloves. I hope that he's right about him and Benny. Max walks me to the corner, to the bus stop, and we sit and smell the ducks until he puts his five dollars in my hand. "Go home and wrap my presents. Tie them with ribbon, and in three hours I'll be there to help tie the bow."

"What's the use?" I tell him. "The surprise is ruined."

Max pokes at the holes in my stockings and says that the surprise isn't ruined, not if he keeps his eyes closed and pretends.

DE COLORES
Melanie González

"Ki Ki Ri Ki Ki!"

"¡Ay!" Auntie Sofía screams as she burns herself over the pan of refried beans, drawing blood and letting it run into the pot. I stop crying and wonder if that's where all the salsa she makes comes from. She knows that rooster makes me cry in the mornings, or at least they say it's a rooster, *un gallo* like I learned in Ms. Caslon's kindergarten class this year when we sang "De Colores" but my brother Sergio, whose zit face looks like it should be on the cover of *¡Alarma!* magazine says it's a witch's cackle.

"¡Callate, Latricia! You big baby!" Mami yells from the couch as she changes my show with Xuxa to *Regis and Kathy Lee*. Her hair is wrapped in a high pink-and-white striped turban. Auntie Linda's boyfriend, Victorio, grumbles from the bedroom after a night's work at the Dearden's on San Fernando Road, where the Amtrak and tagged-up freight trains flash through, rattling the furniture.

So how does Sergio know about the witch? When he sees my fearful wide eyes he laughs with his big round belly bouncing under his Teenage Mutant Ninja Turtle T-shirt. He's so *panzón* he looks like he could use a bra. If he knows the witch I wonder why she hasn't eaten him yet, like in *Hansel and Gretel*. The witch is an old lady named Guadalupe who wears a kerchief over her balding white head and lives where all the Victorian homes are gated off at Heritage Square. When one of us little kids slips by, she stuffs his mouth with raw pig's feet until he suffocates. Guadalupe leaves dark green feathers in the back parking lot and because she's so small she rides a feather duster instead of a broom.

"Sergio! Stop telling your sister that nonsense!" Mami throws one of her blue jelly Xuxa-style *chanclas*, the kind she wears after a pedicure. On hot, miserable days like this, her feet puff up and get all sweaty, and the toe jam leaves gray oil all over her feet that my Grandma Blanca collects to make candles.

The kitchen fan is blowing the hot air around this tiny apartment like cheap perfume lingering around Kmart. My cousin Nayali, Sergio, and me decide to go swimming. I want to see if this time I can make it to the deep end where it's eight feet deep. Nayali didn't know how to swim before, but a while back she fell in the unfenced pool and somehow, with her miracle light-up L.A. Gears bought up the hill on Figueroa from Mr. Maury's Shoes, she was able to paddle her way up for air. The dead flies, nits, ticks, and mosquitoes all got stuck in her hair. A daddy-long-legs that was still alive made its nest among her black curls, and when she brushed her hair a gray sack of baby spiders fell out of her tangles. Auntie Sofía was already having *cucaracha* problems, so she doused Nayali's hair with Raid and scrubbed it so clean that it was peeling after.

Next door live the Bonillas, who have a daughter my age, Trici. I hate her. She called me ugly when I was coloring and after that I stuck out my middle finger. Trici ran inside and soon came her mother with a big hooked nose that looks like it could be a can opener, trying to convince Mami to give me a good *regañada*, but she says she's too busy, she'll do it later. Trici and her mother bird-nose go back inside. I'm glad they're not at my pool, but standing in front of me is a pale, flabby body in black swim trunks. I don't know who he is, but I push him in as he is almost about to attempt an Esther Williams dive. He turns around as I laugh and threatens to throw me in, so I push him again and run back inside the apartment. Somewhere next door I hear gap-toothed Trici laughing.

Since no one can go swimming now, Auntie Sofía sends us up the hill to Lady's Liquor to get some "Esquirt" soda, as Victorio likes to call it, and Jumex for us kids. As we walk up the hill, the cars on the 110 freeway make speeding, wheezing noises that sound like Sergio's farts. On our way we pass a parking lot with a big red stain located in the back of another apartment building where some *cholo* was shot. I remember passing by the caution tape one night when he was shot; it was a fresh red puddle that looked like Auntie Sofía's nail polish, but now it looks like the orange-red that grows on steel fences. We skip around it to avoid bad luck.

Lady's Liquor has a big white polar bear holding a bottle of Coca-Cola painted on the big white building. I immediately want a nice cool strawberry shortcake ice cream with its pink strawberry filling or a grape Otter Pop, but Nayali wants Doritos and Sergio can't have anything because Mami put him on a diet starting today. Then we see him, the one I pushed into the pool. The little old Asian woman is too slow to take the money, so we run off with our Jumex and two gallons of Esquirt. I hold up the cans of Jumex in my shirt like an apron. When we get back home, the soda will be too shaken and fizzy, and we'll be tired and thirsty. We're almost there and so is that guy. I hop the fence that's covered in guavas and fallen jacaranda flowers behind our parking lot.

"Ki Ki Ri Ki Ki!"

It's the witch! That guy chasing us must have been her evil helper like those flying monkeys in the *Wizard of Oz*. I trip over a water bowl. My eyes look forward to see skinny yellow birdie feet. It's the rooster laughing at me, *un gallo* like we learned this year in kindergarten. My cans of Jumex lay splashed around me, the flavors of mango, guava, and papaya smashed into a pool of fizzy yellow brown.

GHETTO MAN
Danny Romero

The March wind blew trash through the streets. Artie walked the short way home from school, cutting through the alleyway between 75th and 76th Streets. There was no reason to stay after. No detention. And no more basketball practice, since they kicked him off the team.

When he arrived home he found the house key hidden near the faucet in the yard and went in through the back door. He knew the front door was deadbolted and chained by Abuela or his mother, whoever had left the house last in the morning. He stomped up the steps and across the porch. Artie slammed the door good and hard when he was inside.

Sister Dolores had told the class during Religion to plant a bean for Lent and that if they were good and kept their promise to God, the Holy Spirit would come to them, and that little bean they planted would sprout, then grow and be a symbol of their relationship with God.

Artie threw his books across the room, thinking about it. One of them landed in the wastebasket, where he would leave it until someone noticed. The others lay in a heap in the other doorway leading into the dining room, with their pages folded and scattered.

In his mother's room he sat on the edge of the bed and felt his skinned knee through the tear in his pant leg. It was all black and red, glistening, and peeled back and looked like it would form a good scab that he could pick at later. With the cheap shoes his mother bought him he was always slipping and sliding over and across the asphalt at school while he played basketball or football during recess and lunch. He hoped he would get a new uniform, but doubted it, knowing his abuela would just add another patch onto the gray pants.

They had not even bought him a new uniform a month ago when he tore his ass during a game. It was First Friday and he was forced to sit through Mass with his underwear showing through the six-inch long tear on his butt, and the students behind him were laughing and snickering because they could see his drawers and ass even if he had his shirt untucked and hanging out. Then his abuela only sewed it back up so that it looked like he had a scar on his ass with the stitches still in it.

He unzipped his pants and wiggled out of them. His shoes were still on. He struggled with the pants and kicked his legs. Still entangled, he stood and walked around the room, showing his contempt for the uniform by wrestling with it and dragging the pants at his ankles around like some kind of fool, with his chocolate skid-mark-stained jockey shorts itching him when he walked.

In the kitchen he read the note on the refrigerator from his mother. It was stuck up there with a Dodgers magnet. He knew it before he had read the part about asking for credit. Artie didn't like asking for credit from the Food King store, but there it was written at the end of the grocery list, following a gallon of milk. It read: "Ask John if he can put it on the bill."

Artie tossed the paper to the floor and continued around the house in his underwear with his pants dragging behind him. At Food King he knew they were always looking at him strangely when he went in there, as if he was a beggar or thief, and it was all compounded when he asked to put the groceries on the bill. The owner's eyes stayed on him all the while he was in the store. Artie wondered if they thought he was dumb enough to steal while they were watching him. Someday, he plotted, he would rob them blind. There were other stores nearer and cheaper, but with little cash on hand these days he found himself being sent more and more where they could buy on credit, and more and more often Artie went to the Food King.

When Artie hustled bottles they sometimes turned him away or set limits on the number he could sell. More than once the owner had met him at the entrance and told him to "go on back home and clean out all those bottles there, boy, and then I'll take a look at them. Now you know I don't need no ants in my store there, Boy."

He took some jeans out of the laundry basket and put them on. Then he peeked from behind the bedroom curtains at Cynthia, the sixteen-year-old daughter of the Ramírez family next door. She was dressed in her high school pep squad uniform, the white sweater top tight enough around her growing boobs and her brown, tanned legs showing well enough above her knees and up her thighs to get him a little woodie in his jockey shorts. He wished that she could be his and not that jerk's he sometimes saw walk her home from the bus stop.

Artie went over to his corner of the dining room where all his things were and where he set up a cot at night. He had found an old issue of *Cosmopolitan* on the street and hidden it under some newspapers and sports magazines he had piled up there. He went over and lay belly down on the bed and turned the pages of the magazine. The young and beautiful girls, even with clothes on, looked so good to him that he grew hard. He rubbed himself against the soft bedspread and marveled at the breast the French say is the perfect size if it fits into a champagne glass. He thought Cynthia's might be just that size.

Later at the store he picked up a five-pound sack of beans. All the while the proprietor, John, had been following him around the store none too discreetly. Artie bought tortillas also because no one, not even Abuela, made them anymore. Abuela was always over at his sister's, helping with the young children. He was reminded of his bean at school and knew that he was doing none too well, its having not even broken through the soil thus far while the other children's beans flourished.

The boy tried to convince himself that it didn't matter much. No one had mentioned it in his class, or in the entire school for that matter, because everyone knew Artie would have gone loco on their head if it had ever gotten back to him. They all just got very quiet when he was around and the beans were mentioned, or he was standing at the back table where all the plants were with his face in his milk carton, looking, looking ever so hard for a sign of the Holy Spirit.

He had been trying all this time not to say any of those words or think those thoughts, but "tits," "fuck," and "pussy" were forever always crowding his vocabulary and brain. He wanted so much for the Holy Spirit to come into his life that he stopped swiping lemons in the mornings from Pancho's grocery store, though he usually bullied them from some of the other kids, so he ended up eating stolen fruit at recess anyway. But at least his only crime was extortion.

After he had gathered up all the groceries he threw a pack of Twinkies into the cart, hoping to sneak it by. He went over to the checkout counter. Judy, the daughter, stood there. She was in her thirties and still looked like a tomboy. She did not smile much.

"Hi," said Artie.

Judy started taking the items out of the cart and remained silent. Artie walked over to the meat counter on the other side of the room. John stood there watching over the top. His eyes barely showed above the counter.

"I need a pound of hamburger and two dollars of bologna too," said Artie. John opened the sliding glass door and stuck his arm into the display case, scooping some of the meat up with his hand.

"The stuff right there," said Artie, pointing to what looked freshest and not all dried up. John ignored him and scooped what he wanted onto the scale. He then wrapped it in paper and threw the package up onto the counter. He then grabbed a loaf of ham and took it over to the slicer.

"Uh . . . I need bologna," said Artie, "not ham." John turned and looked at him. Artie cleared his throat. "Uh . . . and I wanted to put it on the bill," he said.

John didn't answer him, but put the ham back, and brought out the bologna.

Artie got nervous, wondering why the man didn't answer him. He always acted this way, Artie knew, all silent when asked for credit. Artie couldn't get used to it. He cleared his throat again. "Uh, I need to ask you . . ." The loud whir of the slicer drowned out his words.

A moment later John walked over to where Judy stood at the cash register. Artie stood there also, trying to stay calm. A young girl and her mother walked into the store. Artie grew more embarrassed. The girl was a couple of years older, and Artie had been watching her become more attractive over the years. He knew she would go use the pay phone in the back of the store. He always saw her there talking to her boyfriends, he assumed, while she snapped her gum loudly and twirled her hair, laughing and looking fine to him while she did this.

"Uh . . . John," said Artie. "My mother wants to know if we can put this on the bill."

His words trailed off in embarrassment.

"I know, boy," said the man, looking into the bag of groceries. He took the Twinkies out and scratched the price off the receipt. He handed the bag across the counter.

"Tell your mother I said hello," said John.

Artie left the Food King suddenly feeling tired. He was more sad than angry, a sadness that wrenched at his insides and made him achy all over. He wondered why John, the proprietor, treated him that way. Money was something his family just didn't have. He couldn't help it if he was poor, and he knew it. Artie hoped he was never like the Food King.

The groceries were always heavier walking home from the Food King, no matter how much he actually carried. He thought about walking through the park, but at this time of the day it was filled with the *tecatos*. And they were too much for him, he knew.

Artie saw them at Mass sometimes. A few of them. Mando, Smokey, and Payaso, he knew their names. One or two of them would be there every week, leaning a little on a Saturday afternoon and looking like they had just geezed a good one, ese. Or there on a Sunday morning looking miserably hungover or still buzz bombed out of their skulls on whatever drugs they had scored the night before *y la vida loca*. Artie had no doubt that with the drug and gang lives they led they needed the Holy Spirit and Jesus to look after them.

Stretch *de* 81st Street never once went to Mass, and all through the neighborhood the story was that he and another had robbed the church one night when they were feeling king behind a SuperKool and bold as can be, wheeling the safe through the streets to their garage where they blew it apart with some homemade bombs and rocked the houses all around last June and landed their SuperKool king asses in the penitentiary, where that *vato* Stretch ended up dead.

Artie walked on down the street. Up ahead he saw Rubén and Sammy, two boys from the grade below him at school. He knew Sammy from the basketball team. Sammy was pretty good, thought Artie, but they had fought once during practice. Artie had handled him easily, but the need to push him around subsided and the excitement in it and hate for him went away since he kicked his ass good.

There was a crowd of seven black boys standing around the two of them shouting. Rubén and Sammy were trying their best to ignore the seven, hoping, however futilely, that they would go away of their own volition. Artie saw one of them sucker punch Rubén, who fell. The rest grabbed at Sammy, who was trying to twist out of their grasp. He punched one kid good who had been hanging onto his collar.

Artie looked for a place to hide his groceries. Fight or no fight, he had to get them home. He was near Mrs. Quintana's house. She always came over to visit his *abuela*. He put the groceries on the front porch. In the yard he found a two-by-four and carried that with him down the street to where he had seen Rubén and Sammy and the mob.

The melee was in full swing when Artie came around the corner. It looked like Rubén had never gotten up off the ground. He lay there doubled over in the weeds while four boys traded kicks at his huddled form. Sammy was further to the rear of the lot, cornered with a fence behind him, but swinging a tree branch. Blood ran from his nose into his mouth.

Artie charged toward Rubén first. "What are you doing?" he said. He swung the two-by-four with all his might onto the back of one of the boys standing there, kicking.

"Eh, man, wha's happening?"

Artie went on to the next one.

"Man, wha's goin' on?"

"Hey man, cut it out," said another. Artie swung his board. One of the black boys ran crying, holding the left side of his face where Artie had hit him.

Neighbors started coming out of their houses, hearing the commotion. Artie felt like a crime fighter in his own comic book. Ghetto Man, he thought, swinging the board and beating on the black kids who he knew were always taunting him and making fun of him when he walked home from school with his forehead all black and smeared with a thumbprint on Ash Wednesday.

Artie left the scene when he heard the sirens. "We're gonna get your ass," said one of the black boys as they ran. Artie followed them until he came to Mrs. Quintana's. He wasn't chasing them but kept the bloody board in case he needed it. He dumped it back where he had found it. More important than the sirens were the groceries. They were still on the porch.

While he walked home he thought about the black kids he met sometimes in the street and in the park and how they were always asking him if he was from the "f, x, one, three." And Artie always said no, not liking gangs because they fought in packs like the black kids in the park, chasing the team out sometimes during football season when they were waiting for their coach to come to practice.

Artie knew it wasn't safe for some kids to walk alone. If a kid was in a group of two or three he was better off, but not always.

That night it was his *abuela* who noticed the sliver in Artie's arm and pulled it out. She agreed not to tell his mother. And Artie felt bad about saying "fuck you" to her when he was mad the other day, but he was still not sure if she could understand him because she acted like she did not hear and continued with her words of kindness in Spanish.

Artie said, "Muchas gracias, Abuela," when she bandaged him up.

"De nada, mijo," she said.

When Artie reached school the next day he met Sister Dolores standing there at the fence. "Hello, Artie," she said. "And how are you this beautiful morning?"

"Yeah. OK, I guess," said Artie, nervous and moving past her as quickly as he could. He forced the tittie thoughts out of his mind. He walked, feeling embarrassed about his patched pants and his underwear that he hadn't changed from the day before. Later he saw her walking across the yard, smiling and vibrant. And filled with the Holy Spirit, thought Artie.

When the bell rang he started into the building. He saw Rubén and Sammy standing there at the entrance. "Hey, man, how're ya doing?" said Rubén, shy and reluctantly, but with pride. They exchanged Raza handshakes.

"Hi," said Artie, feeling awkward. Normally he would have told them to get their "candy asses away" before they got hurt. But not this time. Artie guessed it was because they had fought together on the same side, strangers really, but at the same time, as close as *carnales*.

"Hey, you want some potato chips?" said Sammy, extending a bag of them out toward Artie. No one at school had ever offered him anything before, and Artie was taken by surprise.

He stood there for a moment not knowing what to say. "Yeah . . . sure," he finally answered and reached his hand into the bag, grabbing only a few. "I'll have a taste," he said. Artie was surprised at his remarks but not bothered by them. He liked the idea of new friends, which is what he guessed Rubén and Sammy were to him now.

"We'll talk to you later, Artie," said the two of them and walked their black-eyed asses off to their classroom.

"Yeah, all right," said Artie, a little confused. "I'll see you guys later on." He himself hurried off to class, not wanting Mrs. Orcales angry with him. Artie was unsure of how he was feeling. He was a little scared, but at the same time feeling really good about himself. "Those mallates will think twice before they pick on any Chicanos again," he thought, daydreaming in class.

And in his dream he was all khakied down with his hair slicked back and some dark glasses on like Jack's brother Killer on Lou Dillon Avenue. There was a group of black kids led by the Food King himself, and they were trying to rip the clothes off Cynthia, who was looking fine. Artie came along with his two-by-four and saved her, beating on them all over the neighborhood. Then in the dream he was walking with her to the bus stop, and when they boarded, heading to the east side, it was Sister Dolores who sat behind the wheel.

At recess Jerry and the other guys wanted to snap the backs of the girls' bras, but Artie didn't feel like it. He knew that would only cause him to get a woodie in his uniform and then he would have to go to the bathroom to beat his meat and hope no one walked in while he was doing so. But if they did he would threaten them, especially those in the lower grades. But even the seventh- and eighth-graders knew Artie could go loco on anyone's head real easily about anything. Even the silliest thing. And Artie took his masturbation seriously.

Artie left Jerry and the others to themselves. He went and found Rubén and Sammy. The two younger boys sat alone on a bench watching a game of basketball. They both looked badly beaten.

Sammy said, "Yeah, my mother says to me this morning, 'You're going to school all right, boy, or else I'll let your old man know you was fighting in the streets again, next time he's sober. And you know how that will sit and fester in his brain till the next time he's drunk, and then you'll catch it.' So what am I supposed to do? I don't care how many mallates I gotta fight; it's better than getting beaten by that asshole. ¿Sabes que?" Artie and Rubén agreed. "Eh, man, thanks for helping us out there yesterday," said Sammy. "Man, you know they wouldn't mess with anyone from Florencia."

"Yeah, you know," said Rubén, "they're always asking are you from the 'F, X, one, three' before they try and take your money. That's what they did yesterday."

Artie didn't like the conversation and maybe not his two new friends. Things were hard enough with people like *el pendejo*, the Food King, and Mrs. Orcales in a person's life. And on the streets there were *la chota* and the *mallates* to worry about. Who needed the extra trouble, thought Artie, and the constant enemies, whether you're from the "F, X, one, three" or the "H, X, W" *rifamos*. They were all Chicanos, all the same, so why did they end up killing each other? It didn't make any sense to Artie, and he wanted nothing to do with it. Who needed the enemies, he thought, from ten and twenty years past, gangs fighting each other over issues that were long forgotten, though the hate never subsided, the events blurred but the blood all too real. Artie knew it was not like in the movies on a summer afternoon. *Dead End* with Humphrey Bogart as *un pinto*, still strong and not loco and crumbling from booze or strung out on *carga* like those in the park. The streets were filled with shotgun scatters and Uzi sprays. In the movies only a cut on the cheek as the mark of the squealer. And *la chota* was always on your tail with the way they were cracking down on gang bangers and anyone who even looked like one these days. But did he have what it took to go another route? And would the Holy Spirit be there when he needed him? He wondered.

Mrs. Orcales kept Artie in for lunch, along with Jerry and the others for snapping the girls' bras. She could not be convinced that Artie had nothing to do with such "pervertedness."

"I won't believe such nonsense," said the woman.

Artie did not argue about it. He was the first one she went looking for when trouble occurred in the room, the sixth grade, the entire school. She believed delinquents were to be disciplined and constantly reminded Artie and the others that they were getting old enough for juvenile hall and that it would only be a matter of time before they were out on the streets, hanging around with the other little gangsters and headed for jail.

"You can thank your little ringleader for all this," she said, referring to Artie as the rest of the class left the room.

It was a dull three-quarters of an hour for the boys. Three times loud bursts of gas broke the silence. Mrs. Orcales got up after the last boomer and walked through the aisles, stopping and standing near each boy for a moment, sniffing. Felipe, it was concluded, would have to stay after the final bell.

At two o' clock each day all the students in the class stood and lined up for what was supposed to be an orderly walk down to Sister Dolores's classroom for religion. While they went one way, the fifth grade went down the hall on the other side to Mrs. Orcales and her math lesson.

Artie took his place at the end of the line. Mrs. Orcales always had him walk right beside her because, according to her, the *travieso* would start trouble every chance he could get "with his 'hanchmen' to follow course in acts of pervertedness."

Sister Dolores stood outside her classroom and stopped the line of children before they entered. A nun they had never seen before stood there also, carrying a guitar. As they walked down the stairs Sister Dolores explained.

"This is Sister Patricia," said the nun. "She was just ordained a few weeks ago and now she's here to teach. She came this morning on the plane from San Francisco." Sister Patricia was chubby and all red-faced. She wore granny glasses and her hair long, hanging down from her habit.

Nuns and students gathered in front of the statue of the Virgen de Guadalupe that stood in the yard. They stood there for half an hour singing songs to the Virgen and rock and roll. When the nuns sang, a beautiful peace filled the air all around them. The usually busy traffic going up and down Nadeau Avenue seemed to halt and the dogs barking in the alley ceased as the nuns' voices soared. All the children joined in heartily, losing themselves in the music and feeling.

They sang, "Day by day . . . day by day . . . oh, dear Lord, these things I pray . . ."

Sister Patricia strummed the guitar wildly, her big body moving to the music with a grace and energy not expected. The tempo slowed down and a quiet fell over the yard. Sister Patricia plucked at the strings, a hypnotic melody. Sister Dolores began, "Wednesday morning at five o' clock as the day begins . . ."

They sang other songs: "Someone's singing, my Lord, kumbaya . . . Someone's singing, my Lord, kumbaya . . . oh, Lord, kumbaya . . ." And before going inside they did the Johnny Nash hit: "I can see clearly now, the rain is gone . . . I can see all obstacles in my way . . . Gone are the dark clouds that had me blind . . . It's gonna be a . . ."

When they finally went into the classroom the sun was bright all over. Sister Dolores stood there beaming at all the children as they filed past. She had an energy that none of the others seemed to possess.

The children all seated themselves, squirming and murmuring. They turned in their seats, facing the rear of the classroom, then back toward the front. Artie turned also and saw something but could not believe his eyes. There at the back of the room Artie saw how his once barren milk carton had been transformed and was now, this day, grown larger than all the others. Artie's plant dwarfed the other children's, which had all started to grow so long ago. The bean plant overflowed the carton and was a beanstalk. Some branches reached up toward heaven, while others stretched out and blanketed the tabletop.

Artie thought for a moment that he saw a glow coming from his plant and wondered if it was the Holy Spirit, but attributed it to the sun because things like that didn't happen in Los Angeles. But who was he to say if he would be a saint or not, thought Artie.

Sister Dolores went on with the day's lesson, speaking to the class about Pentecost and explaining how they all would be blessed with tongues of fire when they were confirmed the following year. Just as the apostles had been. Artie snuck peeks at his plant standing in the back of the room. He noticed other children doing the same. All day long the day had seemed strange and was more so now, as if he had not woken from the daydream before recess. And now here at the end of the day he knew why. With him sitting there and his plant growing like a beanstalk toward heaven, Sister Dolores went on about the Father, Son, and Holy Spirit.

Sister Dolores said Jesus was love and to love was to have Jesus in a person's life. A real miracle, thought Artie. And where was the difference between what Sister Dolores said to the class this day, and what Don Cornelius said on Saturday afternoons? thought Artie.

Sister Dolores asked, "Does anyone want to explain what I mean by the Holy Trinity?" Chemo raised his hand and said, "The Holy Trinity is like God's gang. You know. And the Father, Son, and Holy Spirit are all like homies. You know what I mean? And the apostles too, they're all homies. Ha, ha, ha . . ."

Sister Dolores said, "You better sit down now, Chemo . . . Anyone else?"

Artie stood and began, "At the end of *Soul Train* . . ." The class started to giggle, but Artie went on anyway. "Don Cornelius at the end of the show always wishes everyone peace, love, and soul. And I think he's talking about the Father, Son, and Holy Spirit. How 'bout that?"

The bell rang and all except for Felipe hurried to the exit. Artie also lingered behind, walking to the back of the room. He picked up his milk carton and touched the branches of the plant. They looked more beautiful than they had from his seat.

Outside the room Rubén and Sammy waited. "Those mallates were looking for you at lunch," said Sammy. Rubén went on, "They're going to be outside." Artie walked past them, heading for the exit, to see what the Holy Spirit had in store for him.

THE LAST TIME
Melinda Palacio

This money's burning a hole in my pocket, baby girl. I had so much of it. You'd be proud of your daddy. I keep the money wadded up in my pocket. I got a fat rubber band around it, you'll see. Soon. I want to put the whole stash in your hands. I know I'm always late for your birthday and sometimes you don't get my Christmas present until the middle of January or well after Valentine's Day. But I remember all the times I've let you down. It pains me and each regret is like a tattoo on my heart.

I'm writing this to you in a little composition book for music. You're so talented at everything you do, I thought you'd want to write a song for me someday. You're always singing to yourself, even when you're not alone. I close my eyes, and no matter where I'm at, I can hear your voice making music for me.

I meant to mail the booklet to you, but now the pages are yellowed and the edges eaten with dust and crap from my car. I can't give this to you. You like nice things, new things, pretty things 'cause you're a sweet girl.

You have a different life without me, but I have to let you know I still think about you, sometimes dream about you. You're with me, even though you don't want to know me. Don't pretend I haven't heard you screaming on the other end of the telephone, telling your mother that you don't want to see me. Your mother says you won't take the telephone to talk to me. I know she's not making it up. She's tried covering up for you too many times. I met your mother when she was a teenager. She could never tell a lie. And that made her more beautiful. However, you, young lady, would lie to please your mother—it's the one thing I taught you how to do. But you weren't lying when you told her you didn't want to see me.

If I bring you something nice that you'd like, I think you'll see me because you'll want to thank me. You have the manners of a little lady and you become more like your mother each day. Soon I won't be able to tell the two of you apart with your honey-colored skin, dark eyes that hide dreams, and hair like a long ribbon of melted chocolate.

■

I worked the carnival last week and I have toys and money. I already wrote that down, but I didn't mention the $150 I had last week. Now I only have $75 left, but I've got even more of the big stuffed animals. Your eyes are going to pop out like a jack-in-the-box when you see the giant white bear I'm keeping in the plastic especially for you. You should see the lousy prizes I started out with a week ago. You would've hated the left-over Kewpie dolls no one else wanted to win. I know you don't play much with dolls, but you'll love the bear because it will remind you of the white pony you like to ride at Griffith Park. And maybe you'll remember how I'd crawl around and give you rides on my back and you'd call me "Daddy Bear" and tug on my beard.

They also had ponies and rides and cotton candy at the carnival. I did try to take you. But your mother laughed in my face when I stopped by the other night after you were asleep. I asked her if I could borrow you for one night, maybe over the weekend, and she laughed. She said she couldn't pay you to go with me. I wish I'd never heard her laugh like that. Her laugh was so ugly that it hurt me.

But I guess I deserve that hiccup-filled laugh. Especially, since I almost got us killed on account of my sleeping problem and that one time I dozed off at the wheel. At least no one got hurt. Except for your goldfish, which I quickly replaced. Remember? I also don't have an excuse for those days I had to leave you at the homes of some ladies you didn't like. I don't need to mention names.

But I still can't imagine why you can't talk to me on the telephone anymore or stand the sight of my face. I'm your father. You won't even smile at me when I happen to be at grandma's house the same time you are. And, by the way, those encounters weren't coincidences. Grandma Henrietta wanted us to be a family. Grandma's always scolding me for screwing up with you. She never acknowledged my second wife. Or my third.

■

I don't remember what happened to the rest of the carnival money. I don't think I gave you the twenty dollars I had after I fixed the van. It never fails. Every time I need to do something important, the engine, she gives up on me. I swear, sweetheart. She broke down on me the day I was going to give you all that money for your birthday. And it's too bad I left the special bear at Jeanine's house because she gave it to her youngest son, Michael. I don't remember what happened to all those other toys I had. But I do remember the day three years ago. It was the last time you called me "Daddy."

DAYLIGHT DREAMS
Victorio Barragán

Tomorrow will be the day. No more putting it off. Fernando has talked himself into risking public ridicule. Tomorrow he will finally speak out loud to the woman on the bus whose tender smile has captivated him.

He has pared down and rehearsed his first words. *Less is more,* he has concluded, concerned he may get tongued-tied and trip over his choppy English. *Perhaps it's for the best or else I may overwhelm her with my feelings.*

∎

Every night for weeks now, Fernando has allowed himself to conjure up a life with her, a long list of imaginings. He would take her to Guatemala. He would show her the highlands where he was born, and share with her the intimate thoughts he had as a child while exploring the caves tucked away in the folds of the valleys.

He would reveal to her the teachings of his people. He would tell her that we are all children of the corn. He would explain to her that the early human inhabitants of the Americas knew of Europe, knew of Asia, and knew of Africa. He would explain to her that the maize foretold it all.

The elders spoke of other peoples, of humanity being scattered kernels. So when the Spaniards arrived there was no stunned awe. And they were greeted like mortals, like brothers, not Gods, for they were the pale kernel my ancestors held in their palms amongst the red, brown, yellow, and purple.

He would introduce her to his relatives and she would have a home, a family, and an ancient lineage. Then he would take her to sit with the grandmothers of his village. In time, they would share with her, teach her womanly things, womanly secrets that would add to her strength, that would help her find her way home through the fog. Yes, she would learn and grow, and in a dream or perhaps a vision, a song would spring from her. She would follow this song to the womb of her own ancestors, and then she would become the embodiment of two bloodlines, a beautiful blend of dark maize, two continents forever drawn to one another.

■

When the clock radio went off, Fernando was not startled. He had been waiting for it. Overcome with nervousness and adoration, he had not slept much.

"Oh, I'm confessin' a feeling . . . Baby, baby, I'm confessin' to you." He smiled and did not tap the snooze button. Instead, he sang along as best he could. When the oldie ended, he thought, *Today is the day. This is a sign that it is so.*

■

Fernando could not sit still. His legs trembled and he shifted in his seat as the bus approached her stop. He kept running his hands down his neatly creased shirt and jeans.

The bus hissed as it came to a jerking halt. Through the partially tinted windows, he saw her idling behind an elderly Asian woman. *No turning back now,* he thought to himself. She was there, about to board the bus, like every weekday morning for the last two months.

Fernando's mouth felt dry. Words saddled up on his tongue and he almost gagged. His nostrils flared momentarily as his body reflexively demanded a greater intake of oxygen.

The elderly lady paid and sat down in the first open seat. She, the woman with the sharp features and braided hair, was in full view now, standing at the top step. She showed the driver her monthly pass and smiled.

Fernando watched her anxiously as she made her way to the back of the bus. All at once, she seemed tender, self-assured, delicate, beautiful, larger than life, and all too human. For him, she held the possibility and potential of a glorious future: she was hope.

She took a seat across from Fernando. *Perfect. It could not be any more perfect.* Fernando took a breath and readied himself to talk.

"Excuse me. Hi. My name is Allen."

Fernando looked to his right. A white man sitting next to him was speaking and looking across at her, at the very same woman to whom Fernando was about to introduce himself. *What is this?*

"Jocelyn," she replied.

"I hope you don't find me disrespectful. I just wanted to say that I think you're very attractive. I've thought so since the first time I saw you."

Fernando's stomach churned with agony. He felt as though a mule had kicked him. *No! It cannot be!*

"Thank you," Jocelyn said in a low voice.

"Would you mind . . . I'd like to invite you for some coffee."

Fernando wanted to rise to his feet, point, and declare: *This man does not love you as I do! Look into his eyes and you will see I tell the truth. For him you're a fetish, an exotic, dark-skinned wonder-thing. See it for yourself. It is there in his eyes the color of a stillborn infant. Somehow this pale man has overtaken my shadow, scurried within me, and stolen my words. I tell you, he is ill intentioned. The truth is in my eyes . . . Look . . . Please, Jocelyn.*

"OK." Jocelyn nodded and smiled.

"I could get off at your stop, walk with you, and we . . . we could find a coffee shop. . . ."

"We could do that."

Fernando did not understand how this could happen. He had prayed. He was certain that the day was to unfold differently, that he was the one who would finally meet her, not this other stranger. *If it was not to be, why did I have to find out like this?*

Jocelyn and Allen sat quietly, staring at each other and grinning. They both looked relaxed. Every so often, each seemed on the verge of breaking out into giggles.

Fernando eyed them both without blinking, without a sense of decorum, without discretion. He was processing, trying to get a handle on what had just transpired. He held his breath. A tear tumbled out of his eye and down his cheek.

A few stops later, Jocelyn and Allen stood up. They made their way to the rear exit. When the doors opened, they walked down the stairs and onto the sidewalk.

The bus pulled away. Fernando watched them until they were out of his sight. Then he hung his head and whispered, "Con o sin razón, la vida puede ser tan cruel."

Fernando felt a sense of betrayal burrowing deep within him. He had been prepared to give of himself to Jocelyn. And now this . . . He was willing to show her his nagging wounds. And now this . . . He was willing to tell her of the degradations he and his roommates faced seven years ago as they made their way through Mexico and into the United States, three seventeen-year-olds ready to sacrifice their youth for their families and for their unborn progeny.

Above all else, Fernando had been certain he had much to offer Jocelyn. He would have worked hard, as he has done his entire life, so he could help her live out her dreams and blossom. And he would have asked nothing in return but love and loyalty, the sort that takes root in deeds, not words.

But now . . . She will not see the world through my almond-shaped migrant eyes. She will not hear the wild aspirations that float out of my cramped apartment window and amuse the drunkards who catnap in McArthur Park. Now, Jocelyn, you will not know me . . . and I will never know you.

■

"Class, let us begin," the professor announced to his twelve students, who sat around the oval classroom table. "The assignment was to put on a performance in a public setting, something that those around you would believe to be real, something that would be eventful in some way. Jocelyn and Allen, why don't you tell us what you did."

Jocelyn spoke up. "We performed on a bus this morning, on the bus I take to school. I got on the bus at my usual stop. Allen was already on it. I sat across from him and he told me, in a voice loud enough for others to hear, that he liked me and wanted to buy me a cup of coffee and . . ."

"What names did you use?"

"Our real names."

"Why?"

"We opted to use our own names so that we would be comfortable, and so our performance would seem more realistic."

"Interesting. Go on."

"I agreed to have coffee, so when we got to my stop we got off the bus together."

"Jocelyn, did you two consider having you ask Allen for coffee?"

"Yes, but I was opposed to the idea."

"Why is that?"

"Because women like *me*, black women with a real shape, fall outside the predominant standard of beauty in our society. This was a way of saying, 'Hey, women who are not white and rail-thin are also beautiful. Men of all types *do* find us attractive.' "

"I see. Interesting perspective. Allen, what did you think of Jocelyn's viewpoint?"

"Like I told her, I never really thought much about the issue before. But once she explained it to me, I felt like we should do it her way."

"Allen, tell me about the audience's reaction."

"Everyone was looking at us. Some looked directly at us. Others tried to act like they weren't interested, but their body language told a different story."

"What do you mean?"

"Well, their eyes shot in our direction and they seemed to lean in like they were trying to listen."

"Anything else?"

"There were a lot of smiles when Jocelyn agreed to join me for coffee. A few people clapped. Someone whistled. That almost made me laugh. We tried really hard to keep our composure the whole time, but, boy, did we want to laugh," Allen reminisced.

"Jocelyn, what did you notice?"

"Pretty much the same thing. But . . . what stood out to me was . . . there was this one guy, a Latino man about our age. He was transfixed on us like he was looking past us. When we were getting off, he had tears in his eyes and his face seemed to drag, or just hang. He looked very sad."

"Do you think your performance had anything to do with it?"

"I think so, but I'm not sure."

"It's quite possible that at that moment your interaction took him to another place, to a memory, one that apparently was not very pleasant. In that way your performance, like any good performance, is like a good song. When done well, it allows the audience member or listener to connect to his or her emotions. In the case of the young man you saw, he might have been taken back to a lost love or a missed chance at romance, a 'what if' moment."

"But it seemed a little different. Like he was experiencing something, living it out, right there on the bus."

"Yes, well . . . that speaks highly of your performance. I'll be interested in hearing if the regulars on your bus route approach you and ask you about your coffee date. Good job, you two. Now, let's move on to the next group."

■

That night Jocelyn could not rest. She was uneasy. She felt as if she had left something undone. She could not pinpoint the feeling, and it persisted.

Jocelyn nodded off, woke up a few hours later, and recalled a dream in which she sat on the ground and before her lay a nearly complete jigsaw puzzle of a spectacular landscape. She could see its lush dark green hills jutting up into a darkening sky with the hint of daylight radiating from behind the massive contours. In the center, there was a man sitting cross-legged on a smooth aqua-green stone. She could not make out his face. That puzzle piece was missing. Annoyed, she began to take the puzzle apart. As she did, the faceless man rose, walked into the hills, and disappeared from the landscape.

■

The next morning Fernando woke up early and began trekking to work. From now on he would walk. *Exercise*, he told his roommates. But the truth is, it would have pained Fernando to see Jocelyn on the bus again, and worse if he saw her with Allen.

Fernando felt somewhat ashamed for expecting so much from a woman he did not know, for making himself so vulnerable to Jocelyn. He felt small and exposed. *But it's not her fault*, he reminded himself.

As for Allen, Fernando had also absolved him of blame. He set aside the anger that had given rise to passing thoughts of violent retribution. He had stopped considering Allen a demon, an evil spirit unleashed on him by a jealous admirer wanting to deprive him of love. *No, he is just a man.*

Walking helped. It calmed Fernando and he was able to concentrate at work. Yet he wished that his walks to and from work were longer so he could get lost in the motions of his body, so he could lose himself completely in his rhythmic breaths as he did during Saturday afternoon soccer games.

One cold morning he decided that come March he would run the city marathon. It was a chance for him to see different areas of Los Angeles and maybe even to match a fellow countryman, or a Kenyan, stride for stride down the final mile. *It costs nothing to dream.*

Though Jocelyn was the impetus for his training regimen, he did not let his marathon aspirations intertwine completely with thoughts of her. He knew that even if he were to win the race, she would not become part of his life. Jocelyn was lost to him, lost in the smog of this alien city.

■

Twenty-nine days later, on the first Monday of daylight savings, Fernando climbed onto a nearly empty bus. The evenings had become too dark and dangerous to walk home from work. He did not want another run-in with gang members who hang out along Sixth Street, young men with wide brown faces just like his own. *They don't fight fair. They pile on and take what you've struggled for.*

Fernando found a seat halfway down the aisle as the bus began to move. He flexed and relaxed his tired muscles. Then he closed his eyes and leaned to his right, resting his head on the window.

Eight stops later, he opened his eyelids slowly. He sensed someone was watching him. Cautiously, he glanced at the reflections in the window.

This cannot be! Fernando made out Jocelyn in the tinted glass. She was sitting to his left, just across the aisle, reading a paperback book.

After a couple of long breaths, he peeked over. He needed to be sure. *Yes, it is Jocelyn and she is alone.*

At the next stop, Jocelyn looked up and then at Fernando. He could feel her gaze. It made him tense up.

Fernando cast his eyes downward. He stared at his flour-covered shirt, jeans, and work boots. He rubbed his broad hands together gently. The smell of fresh dough intensified around him.

Fernando sighed and shut his eyelids. *What a life this life of mine.*

"Are you going to talk to me?" Jocelyn asked.

Fernando's head pulsed. She was talking to him; he was sure of it even though he did not dare look her way. His eyes became watery.

"Well, are you going to talk to me?" Jocelyn asked again, this time in broken Spanish.

Rise. Fernando swallowed what little saliva remained in his mouth. Then, he stood up hastily and, his voice crackling, yelled to the bus driver, "Back door!"

CEMENT GOD

Conrad Romo

We're in the middle of a heat wave. Every window in our house is wide open to coax any kinda merciful breeze that might happen to crawl by. As soon as I open my eyes I brace myself, remembering yesterday's scorcher and the day before that and the day before that. The temperature has been getting over 100 and you just know it's gonna be another hot one.

But this early morning, it's almost cool and amazingly quiet. No sounds of snorin', no sounds from the radio or TV, no horns honkin' or tires screechin' or people yellin', no birds squawkin' or dogs barkin' or cats fightin' or babies cryin' or noise from the train yards or factories at the end of the street. Nothing except for the hum of the refrigerator.

I know it won't last, though, this quiet and the slight cool air of the morning but I just want to hold onto it and make it stretch. It's like some kind of truce, some sort of settlement has been reached in our house and on our block and in our neighborhood. But I know it can't last.

Maybe someone else, one of my brothers or sisters or my mom or dad, is awake too, like me, just lying still in their beds. They might even be pretending to sleep. We do a lot of pretending, my family does. We pretend to know things we don't and to not know things we do. We pretend what matters, doesn't, and that we don't care about the things we honestly do. We pretend things that aren't funny are and that we get the joke when we don't. And we pretend to have a plan and that we know our lines.

So who knows if it's real or pretend sleep that has them all still and quiet but I seize this moment to dress in a hurry and sneak outside. I stand barefoot and stretch at the bottom of our back porch stairs by the banana tree that shades the imprints of feet in the cement. I put a foot in the impression of my big cousin Juno, trying to imagine him when he was my age and our feet were the same size. Alongside his footprints are those of his sister Rachel and the hand and footprints of my older sister Letty and cousins Tino and Yoli and a date scratched in the cement from a time before I was born.

I stretch and look at the cloudless sky and walk down the driveway toward my grandparents' house. The cement is still cool, but in a few hours I'll need *chanclas* or something to keep my feet from frying.

My granddad owns this property. The front and the back houses plus another down the street where my uncle Pete and his family live. My granddad built the *back* house where I live. Friends and family helped with the carpentry, plumbing, and electrical, but the cement work, that was all his. The foundation, the porches and stairs, the long driveway, and the wide yard between the houses were all done by his hand. In fact, he did most of the cement work that could be done on our block. He was best as a finisher, the guy responsible for smoothing and leveling the pour. When he was done there'd be just enough of a grade that water wouldn't ever pool. He was never without work, not even during the depression in the '30s.

But I didn't know any of that then as I walked from the back to the front house. It was long before I was alive, so how could I have known? I didn't know then how he came to have a limp and needed a cane to walk. Years later I learned that he was cleaning the walls and blades inside a big commercial cement mixer when someone accidentally hit a switch, starting the blades spinning in opposite directions. He was cut badly before his cries were heard and the machine shut down.

I didn't know any of this then as I worked my way to the front house, having nothing particular in mind. I didn't know much of anything then and wondered years later if anyone would remember seeing a boy walking with an old man in his piss-stained pants and beat-up hat, one hand on the boy's shoulder and the other on a cane moving slowly, inch by inch along the sidewalk he had poured and made smooth. Would anyone remember them walking to Pierre's Liquor Store to get the old man a couple bottles of muscatel past the walls made of river rock and across Cypress Avenue where people in their cars honked impatiently as the two slowly crossed?

The boy glared back at them—a dare to keep on honking. In years to come they'd never remember the kid and the old *borracho*, the old drunk. Why give them a second thought?

That summer though, that summer morning I found Granddad sitting in a rocker smoking a freshly rolled cigarette from his can of Prince Albert tobacco.

"Hola, Panzón," he said. His nickname for me 'cause I'm kinda fat.

"Hola, Abuelo," I said and sat with my back to him on the green painted cement steps of his front porch and pointed my face toward the sun, looking at the veins through my closed eyelids at a blood-red world as the rays caressed my face. There are some things you are just not supposed to look at directly.

Then again, you just can't rely on your eyes to tell you everything. That morning in the company of my granddad and in no rush to see the summer unfold, there was a contained richness. There was only the up and down of the heavens and the earth. Or in this case, the holy cement beneath my feet.

Some kids may have asked the basic questions of their grandfathers. "Granddad, why's the sky blue and the sun yellow or where do clouds and babies come from and what was I before I was born?" But not me. Not when the mystery was right there beneath my feet.

And so I asked, "Granddad, who made the sidewalks?"

And he answered right back at me without pause, "I did."

And I didn't breathe for a few seconds or it could have been minutes. That's when I knew my granddad was God. I don't remember either one of us saying anything after that. Really, what was there to say? I mean just a moment before he was only my granddad, a mere mortal, an old piss-pants *borracho* and now I'm different and he is so much more.

from the novel

DRIFT

Manuel Luis Martínez

Jerry's brother races Mustangs. Not the horses, but the cars. He actually belongs to a club that races them. I find this out when I get to Jerry's apartment. There's a party going on, and Jerry apologizes for not inviting me. "Dude, I'm glad you're here. I would've told you about this thing, but it's really my bro's doing. These fuckers get together every couple of weeks and race their cars and then party together. Shit's gonna get wild, man. You gonna hang?" He notices my puffy eye and lip and my grass-stained Sizzler shirt. "Hey, what happened to your eye?" he asks. "Did you and Ayala finally mix it up?"

"I need a place to crash. Got home problems, man."

Jerry's cool. He doesn't need to hear the whole story. "You can stay here, but don't plan on getting too much sleep. Not tonight." Jerry gets called into the kitchen and I head off for the bedroom. His room smells like he's cooking old socks and ass soup. It's depressing that I've got to sleep here.

I roll a joint and smoke it next to Jerry's window. I'm all worked up even though I'm so goddam low. I need to calm down, keep my heart from exploding right there. I feel the gun in the waistband of my pants and I think about how close I was to blowing my head off back there. The gun's cold and ready and I get this urge to head right back and put that fucker in my mouth and pull the trigger in front of them all. My moms would feel like shit.

It'd serve her ass right, and I can't think about anything else but how much I wish I could hate her, could just walk back to that house and do it, just blow my fucking brains out right in front of her and just before, shout,

"I'm doing this because of you, you weak, crazy bitch!" But right away I start to repent for it. I ask God to forgive me and I realize that I don't deserve to get what I want, that my moms doesn't deserve such a demented fuck-up son. And I start to panic, wondering what they did to her after I ran out like that. What she must've done when she heard me and my pops fighting. Did he tell her? Did she hear me? And what about Antony? What did he see? What a fucking mess, and I keep saying that to myself in my head, "What a fucking mess, what a fucking mess, what a fucking mess." I want to take it all back, but I know I can't. And I see it in my mind's eye, my insides, all blackened, rotted. My spirit, its outline shaped just like me, but made of ashes, burned and coal-black. I am a piece of shit. "What a fucking mess," I moan from so far deep inside me that I can taste the words sliding out of my mouth, vile and heavy and true.

I hear my voice and it hits me. I'm stoned. I'm tripping. I gotta catch hold of myself. I tighten my fists and slam them against my thighs hard, then harder, then harder still, until my legs are aching and the physical pain tears me away from my thoughts for just a second, long enough for me to take a long peep at myself in Jerry's dresser mirror. I reach back and pull the gun out, put it to my head, and watch my reflection for a second. "Fuck you," I say finally, flipping myself off. I smile big and suave and give myself the thumbs-up sign. I say it: "I am untouchable, goddamn it! I am untouchable. I am untouchable." With that I shove the gun back in my waistband. I walk into the bathroom and stick my head under the faucet, soaking my hair, using Jerry's soap bar to wash off the goddamn grease. I take off the Sizzler shirt, wash my armpits. I look in the mirror, and The Face is there, in the middle of all this craziness. It's there. It isn't gone. It hasn't failed me. I can go out. I have to.

The strange people I saw when I first entered now look a lot stranger, almost like aliens. They are *not* cool and collected. They are freakish, off-the-hook defectives yammering away in a dingy two-bedroom apartment with old, stinky, cigarette-burned carpet and a beer-stained couch. Only the TV is new, a thirty-six-inch model Jerry and his brother probably bought hot. I make my way to the kitchen and to my surprise, it's clean, the only room in the joint that doesn't inspire nausea. I guess it's cuz Jerry's a busboy.

The keg's tapped and I go back out to the living room. I move around listening to conversations, not wanting to join in till I find something that won't wig me out. I don't want to hear other people's horror stories, but I'm damned sure that these freaks aren't going to help. There's about forty people bobbing and weaving in threes and fours, smoking cigs and holding cups that look like they're filled with piss. I walk around listening to them laugh at shit that only a heartless asshole could find amusing. The women look ugly, overly made up, like demonic clowns wearing skanky halter tops and faded Levis. The dudes look mean and suspicious, a roomful of flat-out junkies talking stupid shit about motors and mag tires and horsepower. It hits me that I don't know a goddam person in this city. This apartment has become the center of all loneliness. I am a stranger amongst the strange.

I make my way over to Jerry, who's sitting on his urine-y couch with his girlfriend, Gina, and her cousin Gloria.

Gloria's been drinking all night and she's right away interested in finding out why I'm sporting a shiner. I'm not even close to wanting to explain it. "You get in a fight?" she says. I say no, but she doesn't get the message. "You a boxer? What happened? Does it hurt?" I try and ignore her, but the mystery is killing her and it seems to turn her on. She starts hinting about how ready she is. "I'm feeling *gooood*," she says, trying to wink, but she's so drunk that the wink looks more like a wince, making her almost-pretty face look psychotic, a crazy woman who eats tubes of red, red lipstick. It's scary.

Then from nowhere this goth-looking figure appears. He's wearing a pair of black shorts and an unbuttoned black wool overcoat with no shirt underneath. It's gotta be ninety degrees outside, but the guy isn't even sweating. His skin is white with a rash of ugly pimples and scabs running across his forehead. The dude's so skinny that I can see his spine ridging from below his belly. His face, emaciated, is dominated by black-lined eyes under which he's painted blood-red teardrops. I knew a few goths back home and they were a freaky bunch. But this guy is so hardcore, it hurts to look at him. He seems nervous, one shout away from a meltdown.

It doesn't seem like anyone knows this cat at all. He seems just to have wandered in, but soon he's telling us how blood is the only real bond with chicks that counts. "We cut each other all the time." He's got a bored-like affected tone. It makes him sound sedate and fruity, almost English. "I drink her blood and she drinks mine. You should see it." He pulls the sleeve of his overcoat up and reveals his puny white forearm. Every half inch or so lies a razor-blade-thin red scar. "She'll take our blade and slice me and I do the same to her. It's better than fucking."

I go try to find a beer. I can't listen to that sort of shit right now. It's too much. I focus on drinking. The vampire follows me, though. He wants a beer, too. "I thought you just drank blood," I say.

He smiles at me. "I drink all sorts of things."

From outside I hear a loud motor revving. The Mustang racers are heading out to look at Jerry's brother's car. "We gotta check out my bro's car, dude," Jerry says, poking his head into the kitchen. He's obviously loaded, but people seem genuinely excited to see the car. Jerry explains that his brother has taken the air conditioning out of his mustang to make it even faster. "It's hotter than two rats fucking a wall socket," he tells me as we walk out to the street, "but that bitch moves!"

His brother's car *is* pretty cool. It's a '67 Mustang, bright red, tricked mags, black ragtop, and a kinghell engine that sounds like it's ready to fuck a herd of elephants. I realize right then and there that what I want, what I *need*, is a car. Something that'll move me the hell out of here. "You think your bro or any of his friends can get me a line on a car? Nothing fancy, just something to get me around," I say.

Jerry nods, "Fuck, yeah. You came to the right place for that."

I go back into the apartment wanting to get away from the noise and I find the vampire there alone. He's sitting on the couch, his black wool overcoat splayed out, his knobby, pale chest acting as a resting place for his beer. He has razor scars running across his stomach, too.

"You into that devil shit," I ask him, but in a friendly way. "You one of those goths that go around killing their parents?"

"No, oh no," he says. "Those people are giving us real vampires a bad name. They've listened to too much Slipknot. Now everyone thinks that just by blowing a boy and cutting their wrists, that they're vampires. It doesn't work that way."

"Just how does it work? What do you have to do, watch *The Hunger* and drink blood?"

"Let's not get into it if you think it's a joke." He doesn't say it angry, just like he's getting bored being asked dumb questions.

"I don't think it's a joke," I say. I flash him the smile. "See?" He nods his head understanding that I'm part of the brood.

"So what's there to do around here tonight?"

"What do you have in mind?" he asks.

"Anything, nothing, whatever. I just want to be occupied."

"Well, that gives us a lot of leeway," he says. "How long have you been here?"

"Long enough, but I've been spending most of my time in Mission Viejo."

"Don't spend too much time in Orange County," he says. "Spend time in L.A. It's worlds better."

"To me," I tell him, "this whole fucking mess is L.A. The whole goddam place."

"We need to take you on a tour," he says. "My bar's in Hollywood. Coven 13." He looks me over. "But you're not dressed, Sizzler boy."

"This shirt's got more blood on it than you or your girl could drink in a week," I say.

"Oh, I believe you, but that won't get you into 13. We could go to a rave my girlfriend knows about. It'll get going at about one, out near Laguna, dance till the sun comes up with real children of the night."

"You got a car?" I ask him.

"No."

"You and me must be the only two assholes here without wheels. Do you fly when you need to go somewhere?"

"That's funny," he says making bored. "Why don't you ask that girl that you were talking to if she wants to drive us. She seemed *interested*."

It's only about midnight, but I ask Gloria of the red, red lipstick if she's interested in heading out, maybe drive a little bit. She's cool with it. "You'll have to drive. I'm fucking drunk," she says, giving me a kiss. She's gone, boozy breath sour and not all that attractive, but at least she's willing to roll out. "Let's go, Papi," she says.

She gives me the keys to her (big surprise) Mustang. It's not a show car, but it runs. The vampire directs us to his girlfriend's place. She lives near Newport in a nice house, big palm trees, open, roomy avenues, with a fancy, rich mall featuring all the mind-numbing, asshole department stores. She comes out, a pretty used-to-be-blonde, now jet-black-brunette. She's wearing black, her addict-eyes dark holes. Her name is Blair. "Like in the Witch Project?" I say. She takes it like I'm being an asshole.

"My real name is Blair," she says giving the vampire a big kiss. She calls him Stevie. So much for good vampire names like Cassandra or Victor or Raúl or Lestat. Even Lomos is a better vampire name than that.

The car is almost out of gas and we have to stop on the way. After I pump, I go in to buy some cigarettes. As I walk back to the car, this kid, probably a couple of years younger than me, maybe fourteen or so, comes out of nowhere and he says, Hey, man, hey. Can you help me? I just need directions. That's it. No shit, no joke. Hook me up with some directions." He looks scared, sad, empty, a runaway probably.

"I'm not from here," I say as if it's a mystery to anyone. "I'm just as lost as you." He's lanky, with black hair like me. He's got a scab on his forehead. He says again, "Man, help me out. Help me get home." I look at him trying to figure him. "Help me out, man," but this time he's out and out pleading even though he's trying to smile. "How about a ride? Where you going?"

"Laguna," I say.

"Man, I just want out of here." I feel bad for the guy, but Gloria starts honking the horn. "Let's get the fuck out of here," she yells, laughing.

"I'm lost, too," I say and I throw him a couple of bills, whatever I have in my front pocket. He looks at the money, but doesn't jump at it. I get in the car and drive looking at him in the rearview. He stands watching the car move off and I think I see him bend to the money before I have to turn onto the highway.

■

Gloria is hitting some hash the vampires gave her and I take a couple of hits, turning off where the vamp Stevie directs me. I got no sense of where we're going or how long it takes to get there. These people could be driving me to some demented witch meeting, some coven ritual where they're going to cut me open, take out my burned heart, and whip each other with my intestines in a no-holds-barred satanic fuck frenzy.

That's just what I'm thinking as the traffic drops off to the odd pair of headlights moving in the opposite direction. After a while, though, we seem to be heading toward the beach. Just before we get there, we turn into a warehouse-looking building. There are hundreds of cars in the parking lot and I can see a line of people waiting to get inside the doors, smoke rising above them, music pounding. I try to calm myself down a little. "This is going to be good," Stevie whispers a little too closely in my ear. We get out of the car, but Gloria is already pulling that sick shit, talking about being dizzy and tired and she just wants to lie down for a minute. "Just leave me here," she moans. I got the keys, so fuck her; I say "cool" and we leave her there.

We make our way to the front. It's all kids, hundreds of them waiting in line, talking, smoking, laughing, rubbing each other, a real love fest. "Everyone's rolling," Stevie says right in my ear again. "I'm gonna score a couple of hits for us. This won't be good unless you get some E. Are you going to try it?" I nod although I don't need any more distortion. Already I'm seeing goblins and ghosts under and behind every car. "Twenty bucks, you gotta give me twenty bucks for yours." I hand him a twenty. We get up to the front quickly, but long before that I can hear the bass and computer bleeps pouring through the walls, already making me ever so slightly rock my head back and forth even though I don't want to. The hash was good, good enough to almost drown out my anxiety. The sounds make it seem like I am getting ready to enter a really soothing but haunted pinball machine.

We get in and the place is alive. The place is one big light show with a beat, strong and primitive, flowing, pulling everybody in their own direction. It's Pac-Man gone wild, with limitless silver quarters dropping from heaven, the game gone public—louder and brighter than ever. Motherfuckers are high, hand-jiving, looking like brain-dead hippies just rocking to the beat and that beep, beep, beep, beep, beep. The vampire Stevie sneaks up behind me. He leans toward me and says something but I can't hear a word, then he slips a pill in my hand, blue, small, a cure for what's ailing me. He yells something else in my ear that I don't hear, something about letting go. I pull a stray Dexadrine from my pocket and stick both pills in my mouth and swallow without water. I'm here, I figure, and I might as well go with it.

Just as the beat breaks loose, I look up to see Gloria come running through the crowd like either the greatest thing that ever happened to a human has just happened to her or like she's just woken up to find some horrifying green-eyed demon slurping at her tits. Somehow, seeing her, seeing how confused she looks and how stupidly she runs, gives me the assurance that my mask is still good. I give her the grin, a grinding vampire grin, a friendly warning that I might bite her fucking head off if she gets too crazy. She keeps pulling, though, and we start dancing, rubbing each other, but not like we're horny, just like she's this incredible soft living warm thing that moves with me that's moving with everything else, and I close my eyes and move with her, with myself. I move against the wall, alive with vibration and thunder, as if there's a hundred trapped miners behind it screaming and kicking to get the fuck out before the air ends. Then suddenly it's so loud in there that I can't even hear my own sadness. All of us, deaf to what we don't want to hear, dancing like we're being pursued by some invisible terror, like we can get away from it if we just keep running in place. And I know it's too late, because it will catch me, I know it will, with a bang, and *I don't give a fuck.* Gloria's trying to whisper something in my ear, but all I can sense in this deafening wave is her puky breath. I don't move a facial muscle, I just stare. She won't get to me, no one will. Not anymore. I'm cool, detached, aloof. No one can hurt me now. I'm putting everyone on alert because I'm fucking dangerous.

Hours of bam-dance-distortion and more dance. Thirsty and sweat-drenched, shrunken but still aware, the E fades and I feel my nerves returning to tautness. I can make it out of this crowd now. I need water. I need another Dexy. I say "Let's go" to Gloria. We start to walk out. No water in sight, so I pop the pill dry. I'm ready to get the fuck out of here, out of California. I'm not digging this shit one bit. We hit the door, the vampires Stevie and Blair behind trying to get my attention, but my attention will not be got in here. Not anymore. I *will* walk out of this motherfucker before my skull implodes, and as we make the door, the cool ocean air hits me square in the face like a cold shower the morning after. I feel the up coming on already. I stop to face them. "What?" I say, the first voice I've heard since we came in, my own, sounding small in my numb ears. "We're gonna stay," he says, "but you got some of our stuff in your car."

"Oh," I say, glad that I don't have to lose my shit with these people. There's a crowd outside, no longer waiting, just grouped out there, talking, smoking, laughing. I need to stand there for a couple of minutes, get my senses adjusted, wash out the echoes of the hours' sounds with something close to silence. I pull a cigarette out to buy me some time. I need clarity. Which way to walk? Where did I leave that jacked-up car? If that Gloria moved that motherfucker. . . . Then I hear somebody from behind me say real loud, "Hey, Sizzler, you steal my wallet?"

I turn around and look over at him and he's looking at me, in my direction, a white boy wearing a baseball cap backwards, with three or four other white boys. His nose is pierced and he's wearing a wife-beater, his hair bleached, trying his best to look like that asshole Eminem. Some kid, maybe a couple of years older than me, probably from the valley. I make eye contact and I can tell he and his crew are here to bomb on someone, and they've picked me. I check my mask. It's on straight. Tight. Ready. "Hey Sizzler, I'm talking to *you*," he says.

Gloria and my vampires sense the trouble and try and pull me toward the parking lot, thinking that it can be avoided. But I know better.

"You must be tripping talking like that," I say, but I say it with an out. All he has to do is take it, walk away, just turn around. But I know he won't.

Cuz he's ready. He thinks *he* is cool, detached, dangerous. "You motherfuckers are always stealing." He says this to his friends more than to me. One of them says, "Fuck up that spic, O." O's on it. He starts walking up on me, his boys right behind, and I know it's on. "We oughta call the border patrol on all you wetbacks, especially you, you spic-assed, cockroach-loving motherfucking busboy." But before he can say anything else, I flat out hit him with everything I got as he walks right into the punch. I put all my weight into it and follow through like a homerun hitter swinging pure and swift and *hard*. I know at the instant I make contact that his nose is gone, obliterated, fucked like frozen mashed potatoes. He's got a lump where his shit used to hang and as he falls down he says, "Jesus," and before I can put my steel toes to him, his boys jump in, catching me from all different directions, going wild with their fists, hitting my face and chest and back till I go down and they start kicking. All the vampires watch, clutching their toys, their goddam Big Bird stuffed animals and their Teletubbie backpacks, just a playground brawl set to a pulsating beat. "Motherfucking spic, goddamn Mexican," his boys yell. They want to crush my teeth, to pound my ears flat, to break my last rib. No one jumps in to help me till a bouncer or two comes tearing out of the club, yelling what we already know. "The cops are on their way, you assholes."

They pull back and Stevie helps me up while I look at Eminem, who's still covering up like he's being kicked. His face is lying flat on the concrete and his blood, black in the dark, is pooling and now he's putting his hand in it, trying to roll over, maybe push himself up. His boys pull him to his feet and disappear fast into the parking lot.

"You all right?" Stevie keeps asking me. I don't answer, feeling this sick exhilaration because I've left blood on that concrete, relieved that for a while I can concentrate on the physical pain, that for a minute I can locate its source exactly. I can touch it and see it, not like this other shit weighing my heart down, boiling my stomach, felt everywhere and nowhere. "At least *I'll* know I was in California," I say, walking away toward the car where the girls are already waiting. They're nervous, saying "Hurry up, hurry up," but I don't because I don't give a fuck. I remain cool, detached, aloof. No one can hurt me now. My mask is on straight, tight, ready.

"That was crazy," Gloria says when we pull away. "That was really crazy. Man, that was *insane*."

"Shut up," I say, the adrenaline pouring out in a cold sweat. "Or at least learn another goddam word."

"Fuck that asshole," the vampire says. "Fuck those racist fucks. Why do they have to do that shit?"

Finally everyone shuts up. I drop, just drop, just like that. My energy, the juice, is gone. My heart's beating like hell, though. I need to relax. I feel like my chest is gonna explode, like I'm going to puke out all the acid that's been building up in my stomach all night long. And then I do. Stevie pulls over just in time for me to throw up all over the 5. "Are you all right?" someone is asking me. I wave them off. I just need everyone, everything to be fucking quiet. But of course the cars keep rolling by, a few even honk at me and scream drunken curses.

"Come on in if you're finished," Stevie the vampire says from the driver's seat. "You don't want a cop pulling up with all the drugs we've got. They'll take all of us to jail." He's got a very good point. I wipe my mouth off and swing my legs back into the car. "Do you want some water?" Gloria has a bottle in her shopping-bag-sized purse. Usually those things drive me crazy, the whole bottled water obsession that all these fucking Californians have. Polluted ocean draining into everyone's consciousness. But I take it, grateful to wash out the blood in my mouth. I got to get out of this town, but I know that it isn't just this crazy fucking madhouse. The madhouse is in me, and I can't run fast enough to get away from me. I've tried. I've tried hard. The vampire hands me the pipe. "Take a good, long pull. That's what you need. Chill out."

I suck some smoke in, and feel it rush through my teeth and over my tongue. I try to become that smoke, to get into the rush fast. My window is open and the wind blows over my face, same as the smoke, drying the sweat and blood on my forehead and my eyes that have teared up from the labor of vomiting. I need to calm down, I keep telling myself. I think about where I'm at and who I'm with and what I'm doing and any way I look at it, it just seems completely surreal, completely empty. I feel like jumping from the car right then and there, out into the crazy SoCal night, just get away from the chaos I've invited inside the car, inside my life by coming out here and thinking that I could make my life sane in this insane shit town. This fucking place is as bad as I am, worse, and you can't shake your demons in hell.

■

Gloria's place is way up near Hollywood, but the drive gives me a chance to clear my head a little. The sun is coming up and I can see my face in the rearview mirror. My face isn't so bad. My lips took a couple of shots, but mostly my back and legs got the brunt of it. By the time we get to the apartment, I'm just hoping to get a little rest. The place is nice, soft and girly, with wicker shit everywhere and pictures of flowers. But Gloria's room is different. It's got books and a poster of the Farm Workers' Union eagle. I'm tired, but she wants to fuck. Violence turns her on.

"You like that one?" she says pointing to another poster, this one a nude by some famous painter. "Give you any ideas?" We start to kiss and I've got her half-naked when she reaches under her bed and busts out a Polaroid camera. She wants me to take shots of her giving me head, playing with her own pussy, spreading her legs. She wants the shit down on film, for posterity, for whatever. "I keep the pictures in this box," she says, pulling an old purple school box from under her bed. "You want to look at them?" she says, spreading a handful on the bed next to where I sit. I look down at dozens of pictures of her with other guys and some even with girls. I can't handle this trip. I couldn't get it up right now if she were to break off a lap dance. I say, "I'm going to sleep," and before she can even start to complain, I walk out to her living room and lie down on the couch. "Punk-ass," she says, coming out of her bedroom a few minutes later. She's naked. Behind her she's dragging an old Scooby beach towel. She goes into the bathroom and turns on the shower without closing the door.

I shut my eyes, but I can't fall asleep so I turn on her TV. The morning news is on. Some little girl got hit by a car last night and instead of stopping and checking on her, the fucker rolled over her trapped body so he could make his big getaway. They got her moms on the screen, crying, her eyes looking for someone to tell her that all this is just a horrible dream. I shut the set off and limp out before Gloria can drag herself out of the bathroom.

I stand on the pavement, my Sizzler shirt torn to shit, my face puffed, my legs weak and bruised, and watch the people driving out to the highways to get to work. I only got one place to go and even though I know what's gone down, that I'm not welcome, that sick part of me that hangs on to hope when even God would give up, wants to see the thing through to the very end. So I find a payphone. It's early enough that Naomi answers. "Hello," I say after almost hanging up.

"Robert," she says like she's smelling baby shit. Long pause, then, "you've got a lot of people worried. You need to come here. We need to talk." That's all I need to hear. "I'll be around tonight," I say. Of course, I have no intention of talking to that bitch tonight or any other night. I'm going to wait for her to get out and then try one last time to get through to my moms.

I can't get a cab looking like I do, so I get on a bus. People on their way to work do everything they can not to look at me. I swallow another Dexy to keep from falling asleep and concentrate on not throwing up.

By the time I get to the house, I'm shaking all over the place, like I have Parkinson's or something. My gramps died of that, and I don't remember much because I was so young, but I do remember that his hands were in constant motion, always shaking in time to some deep, unutterable fury, like he was directing some mad symphony in his head. My hands are shaking too. My stomach doesn't feel any too good, either. Between the acid swishing around in there and my jittery hands, I half-turn around and fuck the whole thing off. Just leave. I know this isn't going to get me anywhere. But I push on ahead. I gotta see this thing through all the way so when it all explodes, I'll know I did everything, said everything.

I'm aware that I haven't prepared: no speeches, no laundry list of my best features, or the top ten reasons Moms should forgive me for being such a fuck-up. Nothing. All I got is a nervous stomach, jittery hands, and useless, raggedy vampire teeth.

Instead of knocking at the door, I go around to the back and peer in through the windows. Antony is at school and Naomi is definitely gone. I can see my grandmother napping her old age away, but Moms is nowhere to be seen. I climb up to the second story, to where my room had been. It's not easy. I use the tree, dragging my sore body up a little at a time. The pain is coming in steady and sharp now, my chest, back, and legs begging me to be still, to lie the fuck down.

I go in through the bedroom window that I left unlocked, and real quiet, take off the scraps of my Sizzler shirt. I put on a clean T, rinse my face, cupping big gulps of water because I'm so thirsty I can't stand it. Then I creep downstairs to my moms's bedroom door. It's half-closed. I stick my neck out and take a look. Moms is lying down, her eyelids pressed together, but I can tell she's not asleep because her forehead's knitted.

"Mom," I say, my voice shaking all over the place in almost a whisper. "Mom," I say again. This time she responds but she doesn't open her eyes.

"Mijo," she says. "Roberto. Come here, mijito." Hearing her say "my son" makes me feel so good for a second that I forget the razor blades in my stomach and the blood on my shoes. I walk over to her and before I can even say a word I slide down on my knees right in front of her. I can't even talk. All my energy is gone and all I can manage is to fucking start crying. A perfect beginning. "Stop. Stop." I order myself in my head. I can't, though. I can't maintain my shit. I just kneel there weeping, only no real sound is coming out of my mouth because I'm still hoping I can control it, keep it from her, hide how lost I feel, how lost I am because I don't want her to know that I'm such a goddamn mess, that I need my mommy, a mommy, any mommy. This isn't part of my plan. Goddamn it, I came here to show her that I was past that. That I was gonna take care of her and Antony, and how can a goddamn baby do that? But before I can get it together, she puts her arms on me and draws me to her.

Finally, she says, "I'm sorry, mijo, I'm so sorry." I tell her she's got nothing to be sorry about. Nothing. "You haven't done anything to me," I say, but the words come out small and choked up. "Can't we just be together?" I ask.

"I'm not strong enough," she says, "I can't get away from my sadness. I've tried everything to swim away from it, but it's not something I can swim away from. It's the ocean itself. I thought for a while that I could just float on the top of it, just keep kicking my legs and my arms and that I'd get past it. It's too broad, too deep. I can't find the bottom. It's in me now. I've swallowed so much of it that it's in my blood and I can't wash the smell of all this sadness away." Her eyes are open all the way and she's looking dead at me.

Her pain washes over me and I want to look away because I recognize myself in there. I look closer and I see my father too. I see in that reflection that my father and I are the same thing, are the same *package* for her. We're the Siamese twins of pain and memory. I can see him staring back at me through her anguish and I realize that it will always be like this for her. I'm not going to change that. She says "I'm sorry," again. I hug her tight, tighter than I've ever hugged her or anybody before. I want to tell her that I love her and that it's OK, but I can't move my tongue in my thick fucking throat. Instead I just give her a kiss on the cheek. My lips linger there, and I soak the feel of her skin in for just a few seconds thinking, like a punk, like a sucker, that I better remember that—the feel of my mother's face. In that instant I know that my mask is for shit, because I'm still nothing but a kid, no bigger, no better, no harder than my little Antony.

I stand up and I look at my moms, and I know. I know it's time to leave for real. I limp out of the room like I'm just going to the bathroom or something, but once outside the doorway, I walk up to what was my bedroom, grab my bag, and crawl out the window like a straight-out thief who's found an empty house where he was sure he'd find riches.

JUST SEVEN MINUTES

Wayne Rapp

F‌ADE INTO:

EXT. – FRONT OF MIDDLE CLASS SUBURBAN HOME –
LATE AFTERNOON

Man (GILBERTO MOYA), Chicano, in his mid 30s, well dressed in suit and tie and carrying a briefcase, approaches a house. There is a tricycle in the walkway that he pushes off into the grass as he walks. He enters the house without knocking. Obviously he lives there.

CUT TO:

INT. – ENTRYWAY OF SAME HOME – LATE AFTERNOON

Gilberto enters, puts his briefcase down in the entryway, and moves deeper into the house.

GILBERTO
(loudly)
Hey, is anybody home?

Two young children (HÉCTOR and ÁNGELA), a boy and a girl about five and six years old, come running from one of the rooms and hug their father's legs. He reaches down and picks up the excited children.

HÉCTOR
You can't believe it. You can't believe it.

ÁNGELA
(Talking over her brother)
It's Chiquito. He's so funny. Wait till you see.

An attractive woman (CONNIE MOYA), Gilberto's wife, also in her mid-30s, stands to the side, arms folded, taking in the scene.

CONNIE
Oh, it's quite a sight, all right. Our neighbors are going to learn to love that dog as much as I do.

Still holding the kids, Gilberto moves toward his wife. He smiles and leans toward her, lips puckered.

GILBERTO
With a kiss, I can face anything.

They smile at each other, kiss gently, and all exit toward the back door.

∎

That's the opening of a screenplay that I've written. Nothing very exciting, I know. It's not that kind of film. It's a relationship story, and it's really very moving. A very tender love story. I worked awfully hard and pulled every emotional string I've learned as a writer. The important thing I'm trying to do with this story, though, is to portray a Mexican American family as middle-class professional. Not lower-class fringe people. Normal Americans with normal American problems. I think the time is right. Hollywood seems to be getting away from stereotypes. They're casting different races for parts that were always considered white. Look at *The*

Honeymooners. A black Ralph Kramden? But, think about it, why does he have to be white? See what I mean? That's the whole point of my screenplay. Seeing people in a different light.

My name is Tony Casillas and I live in Tucson. Got my degree in communications from the University of Arizona, and I've been working as a reporter and weekend anchor for one of the local TV stations. Today, though, I'm in Los Angeles. Or as some people call it, "the land of fruits and nuts." Some people. But that's not me. I don't believe in demeaning anybody or any group. That's one of the things I've been able to accomplish in my job at the TV station. It's little stuff that makes the difference. Like people thinking a barrio is a ghetto. I've tried to make the distinction in my news stories that a barrio is just a neighborhood. I know most Mexican American neighborhoods are poor, so I see how people come up with the ghetto comparison, but they don't have to. That's what I'm trying to do with my screenplay. Normal. Middle class. Professional. If Anglos fit this description, why not Chicanos?

This trip to L.A. isn't a social visit. A buddy–a guy I went to college with–lives in Santa Monica. He was in Tucson a couple of months ago, and when he found out I was coming over, he invited me to stay with him. Said he had plenty of room. I told him I'd think about it, but I knew even when I said it that I wouldn't. This is going to be all business for me, and I don't want anything to distract me.

I'm here for what's called in the film industry a pitch festival, or pitch fest. There are several of them every year, and the one I'm going to is considered one of the best. The film industry gets commitments from agencies, production companies, and independent producers who all get together in one place for a day or two and make themselves available to listen to writers pitch their ideas. Of course, they charge you a fee to do it, usually $400 or $500. It's not cheap, but all the literature says it's an effective way to meet producers and get your ideas in front of people who are looking for them. It can really get expensive if you stay at the hotel where the pitch fest is set up. They're usually pretty nice places. When I checked out the price for this one, that free room in Santa Monica sounded pretty inviting, but I needed to be alone. So I went online, lucked out, and found a place in West L.A. on Melrose right across from CBS TV City. This is a great location for me. As soon as I get checked into the motel, I take a quick two-block walk to Farmers Market and have an inexpensive meal. I buy some fruit (fresh figs) for my breakfast and get back to the motel and settle in for the evening.

Now I have time for the important work: rehearsing my pitch. I can pitch to as many producers as I can fit into the day, but I will have only seven minutes to convince someone to buy my idea and screenplay. I sit down in front of my TV set and put on one of those shows that Fox calls news, so I'll pretty much have a talking head on most of the time. This is perfect: an *Anglo* guy staring back at me just as it will probably be tomorrow at the pitch fest. I turn the sound down, check my wristwatch, and start talking to my TV set. Eighteen minutes later I stop. Eighteen minutes! Unless I looked at my watch wrong when I started, that's how long it took me to tell my story. Too much detail. Need to hit just the high points. I take a drink of water and start over. Thirteen minutes this time. Progress. But still taking me twice as long as it should. One more time. Ten minutes. Better, but I don't know what else I can leave out. Finally, I write the pitch out. Keep reading it and changing it until I get it down to seven minutes. There's no way I would read it tomorrow, but if I can go over it enough times, I will pretty much have it memorized, and it should flow.

After a restless night, I get up an hour earlier than I wanted and read it over three times. As I drive to the hotel, I practice the pitch a couple more times. I'm feeling pretty good about my presentation as I reach the hotel and start looking for the registration desk.

Representatives from some of the old-line Hollywood film companies are here: Columbia Pictures, Disney, Fox, Samuel Goldwyn Films, Paramount, RKO Pictures, and Warner Brothers. The new giants of the industry are also here: Dreamworks, Miramax, and New Line Cinema. I don't have appointments with any of them. Maybe I'm making a mistake, but this isn't a big picture, the kind big companies are known for. This is something I think would interest some of the smaller independents, those with the odd-sounding names: Bumbershoot, Catch 23, Handprint, Guy Walks Into a Bar, or Mad Chance, companies that sound like they might be willing to take a risk on a small property and an unknown writer. I have appointments with all of them and also companies that just have people's names in their titles. I'd researched as many as I could for a track record, but I was just taking a chance with most of them, as I hoped they would want to do with me. There really wasn't much of a history of companies making Latino films. At least none that I wanted to pitch.

I stand nervously in a large ballroom looking over a sea of tables with numbers on them. I locate my first appointment and am perched in front of it at least five minutes before I'm scheduled. The man sitting at the table reading the *Los Angeles Times* looks to be about fifty. He is much more casually dressed than I am. He notices me, stands, and smiles. "*Ca-sill-as*?" he asks.

I nod and correct his pronunciation. "*Ca-see-yas.*"

"Whatever," he says. "I'm David Tom from Tom Tom Films." He looks at the bound screenplay in my hand. "You got a script already? Let me see it. That'll save a lot of time."

I hand over my screenplay. He hefts it as if determining its length by weight, then turns to the last page to verify his assessment. "Two hours is too long. Nobody wants to sit in the theater that long anymore." He thumbs through it, stopping at random to glance over a page or two. Then he turns back to the opening and reads a couple of pages. "Slow getting going. What's in the briefcase the guy's carrying?" he asks.

"Just stuff he brought home from the office," I say. "He's a professional."

"I see the character's Latino."

"Mexican," I add.

"OK, Mexican. So is this like *El Mariachi*? If it is, the briefcase could be a little bigger. Like a travel case or something and could have guns and explosives and stuff. Then maybe this gang of bad asses comes to the house, and he has one of the kids crawl away and bring him the case. Did you see that movie *El Mariachi*? Man, by the time they got through the fucking opening credits, I don't know how many people had been killed. Blood and shit all over the place. And they were just getting started. Kept going through the whole film. Made Robert Rodríguez a big fucking name. You got something like *El Mariachi*, but only here in L.A. instead of fucking Mexico, we could talk." He hands me back the screenplay.

"Well, I don't. This is a quiet film. About relationships in a Mexican family, and . . ."

He cuts me off. "I can't use quiet. Nobody wants quiet. Too fucking boring. It's gotta move. Think about what I said. An American *El Mariachi*. I'd fucking write it myself, only I'm not a fucking writer." With that he sits and crosses my name off his list.

I figure there had to be one person in the room who couldn't understand or share my vision, and it looks like I hit him first time out. I have many more people to see, though, so I move quickly away from the rejection and find my next scheduled pitch. This is another small production company, Morgan Town. Nobody is in the pitch seat when I arrive, and I confidently sit down, forcing the elderly man across the table to acknowledge me. "You're early," he says.

"I know. I finished my last pitch early and thought I could wait here as well as there."

"Makes sense. What you got?"

"I've got a young professional Mexican family that lives in Phoenix. It's primarily a relationship story, a love story really. Phoenix isn't that important. I just wanted to place the family in a city location where young professionals tend to congregate and grow."

"Mexican, huh? Thinking maybe a little George A. Romero horror here?"

"No, not really. I don't even think Romero is Mexican. He was born in New York City. Probably Puerto Rican. Maybe Spanish; I don't know. But I'm not thinking horror."

"I think you're missing an opportunity here. Mexican. Puerto Rican. Whatever. The Latinos really dig this vampire horror stuff. All the superstitions. It's part of the culture. You ought to think about it."

"But that's not what my story is about."

"What I'm saying is, maybe that's what it should be about. Look, I need something that's easy to shoot and got good action. And that's not a relationship story. Gotta have actors for a relationship story, so that's expensive, and nobody's looking for a relationship story, anyway."

"How do you explain *Winter Solstice,* then? It's a relationship story. Man and his family. Anthony LaPaglia. It was just released."

"Never heard of it. And I bet in two more weeks hardly anyone else can say they've ever heard of it either. Sorry, kid."

That didn't take long. I've got time to kill now before my next appointment, so I spend it going over the pitch in my head. It seems to pay off, because when I sit down and start talking, the young woman across from me (she doesn't look much older than I am) is really paying attention. Maybe it will take a woman—I'm thinking as I talk—to buy into the relationship aspect of my story and to understand what I'm trying to do with this one.

"You present yourself very well," she says with a smile as I finish. "Nicely done. So nice, in fact, that I feel bad about saying we don't have any room or interest for a project like this."

She must read the disappointment in my face and adds very quickly, "*But* I noticed from your resume that you're from Tucson and you say you live in Barrio Hollywood. Well, we're finishing a pilot for the next TV season, and the story takes place in a barrio. We don't say where it is, but the location is a lot like Tucson. The show is called *Sánchez and Sons*. It's a comedy. People might think *Sanford and Son*, but they'd be wrong. We've got two sons—half brothers, really—and about three ex-wives and assorted girlfriends. It's really funny. Sánchez is a junk dealer, and he gets all this weird stuff from Mexico that he tries to foist off on his neighbors in the barrio, and that makes for some interesting story possibilities. If the pilot sells—we're in edit now— and we get a go-ahead for production, we'll be hiring writers. We probably would be interested in talking to you, and since you actually live in a barrio, that could be a plus. You might go from living in Barrio Hollywood to living in the real Hollywood just like that." I start to explain the word "barrio" to her, but she smiles as she hands me her card and is already greeting the young woman standing behind my chair.

By lunchtime, I have experienced only disappointment. I take a break, too frustrated to eat anything, and continue going over my pitch, trying to find ways to punch it up, to make the person on the other side of the table feel the passion I do for my story.

By mid-afternoon I am losing steam. I get testy with one of the representatives who tries to cut me off when I'm only half finished with my pitch. "I paid my money for the opportunity to pitch my story," I say angrily.

I see his face flush. He looks at me for a moment, then says, "You're right, go ahead." When I finish my pitch—one that I had shortened considerably—he says, "I was just trying to save you and me some time. That's not a story you can sell no matter how good your pitch is." I apologize for losing my temper and walk away.

I am fast running out of time and opportunity, but I throw my shoulders back and meet my next scheduled appointment. Again I am interrupted before I finish. "Look, kid, I can see where you're going, and it's not going to fly." The producer is old enough that I must look like a kid to him, and before I can show my anger at being interrupted, he continues. "You Mexican?" he wants to know. "Or some other Latino extraction?"

"Mexican," I answer.

"If you're a Mexican writer, you've got a hell of a story opportunity right here in L.A. We got a Mexican mayor now. The first one in probably a hundred years."

"A hundred thirty-three years," I inform him. If he'd read my bio, he'd know I was a newsman, and the new mayor was a big story in places other than L.A., especially in areas with a large Chicano population like Tucson.

"You're keeping track. That's good. Then you probably already know what's happening. The Chicanos and blacks have been gang banging all over this city. There's all kinds of shit going on. You know what you call this kind of situation?" He doesn't wait for my answer. "You call it conflict, and conflict—as any writer knows—is the basis of dramatic storytelling. Now, I tell you what, you throw in the Korean gangs and all the Arabs floating into town and you got the potential for a conflict that could burn this place to the ground. That, my young friend, would be quite a story. It's one I'd pay to see. Can't sell me a story without conflict. And it's all right here in front of you." He reaches out and offers me his hand. "Write it and send it to me."

I get up to leave. "Think of Mexicans with guns trying to protect their territory and tearing down the establishment while they do it," he offers as a parting suggestion.

I walk away with sagging shoulders. The disappointment drains through me like water through a sieve. I am totally washed out. I've had it. I don't have the strength for another pitch. Queasy from lack of food and sleep, I head for my car.

As I move through the well-tended lush green of the hotel grounds on my way to the parking garage, I hear two men—part of the landscape crew—speaking Spanish, and the language reminds me of something. Mexicans with guns trying to protect their territory, I think, as I get in my car and open my map. I need to find Olvera Street and the area called El Pueblo de Los Angeles Historical Monument. It's in downtown L.A. Not very far from the hotel.

What draws me to this location is my desire to see a mural painted by the Mexican artist David Siqueiros in 1932. When I produced a TV story about mural artists in Tucson, I cited the influence in this country of the great Mexican artists—Diego Rivera's work in Detroit and New York and Siqueiros's murals in Los Angeles. I am searching for *La América tropical*, the second mural Siqueiros painted and the most controversial. In fact, the work was so politically offensive to the woman who was promoting Olvera Street at that time, that she had the mural covered with whitewash. The work was forgotten until the late '60s when the whitewash began to peel. I remember that eventually the sun began to damage the piece, and it was covered with plywood to protect it. The Getty Museum was scheduled to clean and restore it so that it could once more be accessible to viewers.

I find myself hoping they have completed their effort. I want badly to see this bold work. But when I find the location of the building that was called the Italian Hall and had housed the Plaza Art Center in 1932, I am disappointed. Its second story wall is still covered with wood. The project is not finished, and may not even have been started.

Judging by the wooden cover, the mural is huge, probably twenty feet high. I decide to pace off its width and figure it must be over eighty feet. I return to the center and stand staring at the weathered wood, willing myself to see the mural behind it. The dominant image is a huge double cross on which hangs an Indian peon, his arms tied to the top cross member and his legs splayed and tied to the lower cross member. His head lies at an awkward angle parallel to his left arm. Above his head is the strong image of an American eagle and in the background, a Mayan pyramid overrun with vegetation. Two armed revolutionaries sitting on a wall in the upper right corner of the mural, one aiming his weapon at the American eagle, were the center of the controversy. The mural was considered by many who saw it as an indictment of United States imperialism in its dealings with Mexico.

All this I learned from my involvement in the TV program, but the political statement itself is not what I think of standing in front of the boarded -up mural. It's the fact that, in a free country, Siqueiros's expression was hidden, covered up so that it could not be experienced by the public. This is the same situation proposed for my screenplay. One person wants to cover it with gun-blasting, blood-running death while another wants horror to distract viewers from its message. Then there is the shameful copycat cover-up of the demeaning *Sánchez and Sons* TV pilot. This one comes maybe with a cherry on top, the possibility of a writing job. And, finally, there is the hatred angle of gang warfare to be exploded on the screen, body parts flying in all directions. They want to tie my story of normal, professional, family-loving Chicanos to the cross of commercialism in the most stereotypical and crass way possible. To save my story, I would have to be one of the armed men, sighting my weapon at those who would cover up my intentions.

I leave downtown Los Angeles and drive as quickly as I can back to Melrose Avenue and talk the East Indian man who is at the front desk of my motel into letting me have a late checkout. He charges me a penalty, but it is worth it. I cannot stay here another night. I need a friend, and I have one in Santa Monica. When I call my college buddy, he is more than glad to have me spend the night, so I head west toward the ocean. I know what I have to do now with my story. I need to find some way to produce the film myself, a way to control its content. To keep it clean and honest. Maybe, just maybe, my friend might want to invest in my idea. On the slow drive into the sun, I practice my pitch at a leisurely pace, knowing I will have more than seven minutes to sell the story to someone who cares.

THE COMEUPPANCE OF LUPE RIVERA

Manuel Muñoz

know it's hard to believe, in this day and age, but her name really was Guadalupe. Hard to believe because she was a woman in her late twenties, born right here in the heart of California, with parents who spoke good English. What kind of name is Guadalupe when, these days, it's Terry and Nicole and Kristen? I know some of those girls from the neighborhood who married farmers' sons and dropped their last names. So now they're Terry Westmoreland and Nicole Sargavakian and Kristen Young, but still brown as me and Guadalupe Rivera, my neighbor across the street who doesn't live there anymore. Lupe Rivera. I know some wouldn't care to hear about a woman with a name like that, and I would have to set you up somehow different if this were about Terry Westmoreland. Somewhere along the line I would have to tell you that Terry was Mexican. But with a name like Lupe, you already know. And, for the record, it's Lu-peh, not Loopy, not a butter-fly swirling around in the front yard. I've heard Lupe correct people all the time, very tartly. "It's Lu-*peh*. You speak Spanish," she'd say to the girl at the ballpark concession stand. "Lu-*peh*," she'd say one more time, collecting her change and then, while leaving, she'd mutter under her breath, "Bitch."

With an attitude like that, it's no wonder that not many people in town felt too bad about what happened to Lupe. There was a lot to be jealous of, if you wanted to be. When you're smart like Lupe, you can have a job like union arbiter for the city employees, with your own office and a car to drive around in, even if it is a government one, a beige Dodge Aries. I asked my cousin Cecilia what that job required and Cecilia told me only that Lupe was perfect for it. "You have to have a big mouth, but be a good listener, too," she said. "And a lot of the time you have to tell people what they don't want to hear."

Because of that job, Lupe had a little house on the corner of Gold Street that was all her own because her parents had moved back to Texas. It says a lot about Lupe that she made the side door to the house the front entrance, building a walkway out of brick all the way to the curb, turning on that particular porch light during the dark hours. She liked to say that she lived on Sierra Way and not Gold Street. Not that it matters. Sierra Way is bigger and it has sidewalks and drainage, but it's just as ugly.

You never saw her out on the lawn keeping it green, but there was always her latest man tending to it, always someone different. When Tío Nico let me stay here a few months ago, it wasn't long before I saw Lupe's latest actually putting up a new fence all by himself. This was early in the morning, about seven, when I was getting in my car to go to work at my retail job in Fresno, and there he was getting out of his pickup truck. You start to know things when you live across the street from Lupe. Even though his truck was rusty and the tires rimmed with dirt, I knew who had paid for all that wood sitting in the truckbed. He didn't look like just a contractor—he looked like a Lupe type, stepping out of his truck in a plaid shirt, tight Wrangler jeans, boots. I waved over to him as I drove off, just to show I was friendly to Lupe, and I wondered where Lupe ran into such men in the Valley, like they stepped right out of the advertisements for tejano music, come to life just for her.

That evening, when I drove down Gold Street, I saw the pickup truck still there and heard the hammering even over the radio. Out on the lawn, Lupe's latest had already put up the posts and leveled and nailed in more than half the fence. He tipped his chin to me as I parked, and I pretended to check out his work, flashing him an OK as I made my way inside Tío's house, but he had lost the plaid shirt and was wearing his cowboy hat. Just then, I saw Nicole Sargavakian turn the corner slowly off Sierra Way. So word was getting around about Lupe's latest: handsome and willing to work out in the sun just for her, hairy chest just like Andy Garcia, but better because he was right there on Gold Street for all to see.

I am ten years younger than Lupe and I have to admit that I knew her better when I was a little kid, when I was eight and Lupe was just out of high school and taking classes over at the community college in Reedley. Me and my cousin Cecilia used to tag along over to the Tortilla Flats ballpark by the elementary school, walking with Lupe across the railroad tracks like we were her younger siblings. She would buy both of us sunflower seeds or a cherry soda or a snow cone while she kept the stats for the men's softball game, one pencil behind her ear just in case the other one broke its lead.

Lupe Rivera was always prepared. I don't know where she got the money, but we never had to dig into our own pockets when we were with her. She took us straight to the concession stand without asking what we wanted, and then suddenly we had a treat in our hands, balancing it carefully as we made our way up the wooden planks of the spectator stands. On the field, the guys idled around in their uniforms, some of them tipping their chins and waving to Lupe. I don't know about my cousin Cecilia, but I never knew what I wanted to watch more—the guys who waved over to Lupe or Lupe's fingers on the pencil once the game started, her hand making X's and checkmarks and tabulations that said everything about how fortunate she was, how lucky she was to be so beautiful as well as intelligent. I would watch her make the X's one after another, and sometimes I would forget about the guys who would wave to her, their tight arms gripping the bat, like they were hitting just for her. I would look at the X's and get a little dreamy, thinking about how smart and beautiful she was, how I could be like her someday if I kept studying. Not like my Tío Nico. Not like him, how he had been sitting one day in the kitchen, making little marks on a piece of paper. When I asked him what he was writing, he sat me on his lap and told me he was remembering. He asked me to spell out the names he was attempting for himself, his friends long dead who had been reduced to the one or two letters he knew by heart. When we were done he took my paper like a souvenir and folded it away for himself.

I can admit that I was a sad kid, that I was delicado, as Tía Sara would say when she still lived with Tío Nico. I used to think that meant delicate, but later I realized it meant fragile, dainty, weak, and overly sensitive. How it must have confused Lupe at the ballpark, me staring at the X's she marked on the paper, my wandering to the memory of sitting with Tío Nico, and the tears would start for no reason that Lupe could figure out. I wonder now how she would define delicado, how she would give the word her own nuance. She stopped babying me not long after, one evening when the guys on the field waved as usual and I didn't tip my chin at them like I was supposed to. I waved right back and Lupe looked me straight in the eye and said, "Stop acting like a girl." Her stare narrowed into me like light through a keyhole. After that, she wouldn't let me hold her hand. It made me even sadder as a kid, after she looked at me like that, because she never spoke to me again after she told me who I was.

Despite all of that, I have always wished good things for her. I couldn't dream these things for myself, but I could see Lupe in a bell-shaped dress and getting married at the Baptist church over on K Street, even though she was Catholic. It was the one church in town with grand, wide stairs in front and a towering steeple, the walls built of beautiful dark gray stone and the street shaded with trees that had somehow escaped Dutch elm. That would be the church for someone like Lupe, and we could throw rice without having to stuff it into tiny lace bags first. I suppose it is wrong to assume that only someone beautiful like Lupe could deserve such a scenario and maybe this is where jealousy comes from: the inability to picture ourselves firmly into the lives we can imagine hardest.

That evening, I saw only what the other people saw. I was outside, having decided to wash my car with the hose in the little light before sundown, because Lupe's man was still out in the front yard building her fence. His shirt was draped on the last post like a reward, and he was working fast, as if racing the sunset. I didn't care that Tío Nico kept peeking out the window to disapprove of me. He'd been at his wit's end with me and the way I'd been carrying on. Jilted boyfriends coming by the house and pounding on the door because they found out I'd moved here and wasn't living anymore with Tía Sara in Bakersfield. But in Bakersfield, I'd never seen a man like Lupe's. I'd never seen a man be so willing to give himself over like that, to work under the hot sun to make someone happy. He could have had anyone.

And though I was looking, and Terry Westmoreland kept driving by, and then Kristen Young and all the other metiches in town, we all knew there was something wrong when that car came up the street. We knew it didn't belong here and we knew that it was looking for Lupe's house because the driver paused on Gold Street and turned gingerly over to Sierra Way—he didn't know how Lupe used her front door. We knew the imminent shadow of trouble. We knew that the squeak of unfamiliar brakes meant the men of the neighborhood had to prepare to intervene. And so people stepped out of their houses while that car idled and then killed its engine. I shut off the water hose and Tío Nico came outside and stood on the lawn, the neighborhood slowly gathering into itself as it did through every argument, through the rare house fires, through the fistfights, the car bashings from angry ex-wives, the drunkenness of early evening Saturdays, the beating of someone's mother and the shattering windows, the guns flaunted and then desperately coaxed away. The neighborhood inched out of their houses, hands on hips, eyes shaded against sundown, some of the men already easing into the street with order in mind, the younger boys lurking behind them as if they knew a rite of passage was theirs for the taking. I watched and remembered that feeling, but I had always stayed on the steps.

A man stepped out of that car and shut the door. Lupe's man had stopped working and walked over to the last post to collect his shirt. If a fight was on the way, Lupe's man wasn't about to provoke it. He buttoned the shirt and listened to the other man ask him, "Hey, Guillermo, how come you left my sister?"

That was all he had to say. I immediately imagined Lupe in her bed with the cool sheets lined against her naked breasts, staring at this Guillermo, finding some way to reward him for his day of hard work. I pictured Guillermo's wedding ring sitting by itself in a tiny bowl on Lupe's nightstand, a pale mark around Guillermo's finger like a mark of shame that he would pay no mind. I imagined that scene, of Lupe receiving him with her arms, knew immediately why the women in town hated Lupe Rivera, and what she meant to their own insecurities, the holds on their marriages as tenuóus as spiderwebs. "How come you left my sister?" the man said to Guillermo again, louder, and we all seemed to close in, as if to surround a boxing ring, even me. I was mesmerized by what I had just found out, that Guillermo was a married man, cheating on his wife, and that everyone in this town knew with who. But the men in my neighborhood were watching that man's hands and then the men swarmed suddenly—had they caught the flash of the knife before any of us did? I saw the blood spray and I heard Guillermo choke and collapse, the men shouting orders, everyone in the neighborhood gasping, but I still don't know how the men in my neighborhood sensed it all coming, how they had ever gained that power of knowledge, that readiness to step up to the inevitable.

From inside the house, Lupe rushed screaming to the front yard, but by then it was too late. She wasn't naked, the way I thought she'd be, waiting for this Guillermo inside her house, but had on jeans and a white blouse. The man with the knife knelt in the yard, restrained by the entire neighborhood, and he raised his head to the sky to cry out. Strangely, his cry pierced us more than Lupe's. It was filled with more woe than Lupe's anguished "Ohno, ohno, ohno . . ."

When the town newspaper arrived at our doorstep a few days later, it brought clarity to the rumors that were racing like wildfire around town. The front page plastered with pictures of Gold Street packed with police cars and onlookers. We passed the paper between us, me and Cecilia and Tío Nico, the cheap ink rubbing off on our fingers with each reading. Tío Nico gathered the story as best he could from the pictures, then asked Cecilia to clarify what he might have missed. "That man was getting revenge for his sister," Cecilia answered Tío Nico, raising her voice to him as if he were hard of hearing. "He stabbed him as payback."

Tío Nico seemed to nod in agreement as he studied the newspaper, and then he pointed to the picture of that man kneeling in the front yard, saying sorry to the sky and asking it for forgiveness. He seemed to nod in sympathy, and when he put the paper down, I waited a moment before I picked it up. Lupe's house, dark in the cheap ink of the newspaper. Lupe with her face ravaged by tears. The wailing man in the front yard. A photo, taken elsewhere, of the handsome Guillermo. I couldn't take my eyes off it, remembering his hairy chest, raising the paper a little because Tío Nico was staring at me. He had had enough and got up from his chair, snatching the paper from me. "Give me that," Tío Nico snapped, taking one last look at the front page, his finger pointing to the wailing man. "When grown men cry," he said, "it's usually for themselves."

I thought about that later, when I fished the newspaper out of the garbage can and smoothed its crumpled pages just enough to tear out two pictures: the handsome Guillermo and the one of Lupe ohno-ing in her front yard. If the wailing man cried for himself, then who was Lupe crying for? Who did I cry for when I was a little boy, thinking of Tío Nico? Did Tío Nico cry for himself when he sat staring at his page of X's and O's, trying to remember? Did he cry for himself when Tía Sara left him? I couldn't answer myself, so I stuffed the pictures into my pocket like a terrible secret, but

I knew why I needed them. I wanted a reminder that everyone suffers somehow, that we all make bad mistakes, that bad luck can ruin everything, even for someone beautiful like Lupe. Someone beautiful like her man Guillermo. I wanted something to give me strength to send away those ex-boyfriends who trailed me all the way from where I used to live in Bakersfield with Tía Sara, those boys who made me weak-kneed with their pleading, who confused me with their rage and anger. I wanted Lupe as someone to look up to, even after all of this, that I could set aside the weight of Tía Sara's stare and Tío Nico's disapproval and live my own life, just like she did, no matter that it invited contempt.

"Sergio," Cecilia said to me a few days later, "did you know that guy got stabbed in the neck? Can you believe it? In the neck?" She was helping me wax my car, and we looked across the street. "People are crazy," she said, keeping her eyes for a moment on the half-finished fence. I kept waiting for her to comment on the For Sale sign in front of Lupe's house, the windows suddenly without curtains and the bare walls gleaming through. I couldn't say I was surprised, though no one had run Lupe out of town. I don't know how or when the house was emptied or who did it. I was at work when it happened and so was Cecilia. Tío Nico wouldn't say a word about it.

"Do you know where she moved?" I finally asked Cecilia.

"I have no idea," she answered, but she looked over at me knowingly, and the way she did reminded me of the way Lupe Rivera had looked at me years ago, when I was a little boy, that look of knowing what I was all about.

"I ran into Nicole Garcia," Cecilia said. "She's Nicole Sargavakian now. Remember her?"

"Of course I do."

"She said Lupe moved to Los Angeles."

"How does she know that?" Los Angeles, I knew, was where you could live on a wide boulevard. The men who stepped out of the advertisements for tejano music lived there, waiting to tip their hats to Lupe.

"Word gets around," Cecilia said. "I guess."

I had to look down at the car to keep the knot out of my throat, and then I refused my tears because I didn't want to explain to Cecilia what I was feeling. In looking at the empty house, in knowing that Lupe's whereabouts were already being found out and rumored, I discovered something that made my heart weight down some. I realized suddenly that, during the times my ex-boyfriends drove up to Tío Nico's house with their unfamiliar cars and their loud banging and their threats, the street had been empty. No one had come to see about the car still shuddering outside of Tío Nico's house; no one had come even to check to see if Tío Nico was OK. When I opened the door those times, with the porch light burned out, I saw nothing but the silhouette against the screen coming back to claim me, and the street silent behind.

I let loose the tears, and my cousin Cecilia finally saw. I heard her put down the rag she was using to wax her side of the car and she walked over to me. "Jesus, Sergio," she said. "You're just too sensitive."

"I just feel so bad for her," I lied, but what did it matter? The pictures I had saved to give me some kind of strength would someday fade, and I swore to myself right then that later that night I'd close my eyes and let myself think of Guillermo the way I wanted to. I had no tears for Lupe Rivera, though I still wanted to be like her, to go wherever she was, whatever place she had found that would just let her be. I let loose my tears, Cecilia's arm around me, the way I cried when the ex-boyfriends cried and begged me back. I thought of Lupe in Los Angeles, the way the sun was gentler there, and how you could open a door whenever you wanted. Someone would be standing there and he would be worth the tears, worthy of both praise and longing. Someone in Los Angeles, with its wide boulevards, the long avenues that slithered into the hills with your secrets.

LOS DOS SMILEYS

Álvaro Huerta

My mother often sent me to La Paloma Market while my older brother watched *I Love Lucy* reruns. We lived in East Los Angeles' Ramona Gardens housing project so I had to be selective about the routes I took. Since I feared the barking dogs along the alley, I would take a shortcut through the hill that belonged to the neighborhood gang, the Hill Boys. Those homeboys never bothered me on my daily trip for groceries.

It wasn't until one hot Saturday morning on my way to La Paloma when one of the homeboys called me out for a fight. His name was Martín Chávez, an inductee of the Hill Boys who challenged me about my nickname, Smiley. A *veterano* had given me this nickname because I always made him laugh. Eventually, everyone called me Smiley, including my mother. Although I never belonged to a gang, I could never show signs of weakness or else I would become easy prey for the homeboys. Despite my initial reluctance to fight, Martín and I were to have it out, not for any grudges or personal issues, but for the right to be known as Smiley #1.

Long before our fight, Martín and I would bump into each other at the hill on our way to La Paloma Market. We would acknowledge each other with casual nods of the head. During these encounters we established a friendly relationship despite our obvious differences. While I sported my Los Angeles Rams jersey with my Kmart Lee jeans and Converse sneakers, Martín strutted along with the traditional gang attire—a neatly creased white T-shirt with baggy brown khaki pants and polished black shoes.

But our casual relationship changed that one Saturday during my routine walk to La Paloma. As I took my shortcut, I encountered Martín as he was going through his gang initiation into the Hill Boys. To become a Hill Boy, the inductee had a choice of either walking through two parallel lines of homeboys to suffer hits and kicks until reaching the end, or fight against five of the toughest homeboys while the others counted to ten. Martín chose the latter. As I watched Martín's initiation from a safe distance, I witnessed his futile attempt to fight back against an onslaught of blows.

"One, two, three, four . . . ," the homeboys slowly counted up to ten.

Martín stood as long as he could, but his knees finally buckled at the count of eight. The homeboys finished the last two counts with kicks to Martín's back and legs. It ended with a loud "¡Basta!" One of the homeboys got in a last hard kick to Martín's ribs.

"Congratulations, man, you're one of us," yelled Duke, the gang leader.

Martín slowly rose to his feet and tried to dust himself off. His neatly pressed white T-shirt now sported rips, dirt, and blood. All the homeboys embraced with one big *abrazo*. Almost in unison, they asked Martín to decide on a gang name.

"Smiley," he shouted, grinning through the blood and dirt.

"You know that 'Smiley' is already taken," said Duke as he glanced and pointed in my direction. "Choose another name, man."

"Well, why don't we just have it out for the name?" Martín asked.

"Come in closer, Smiley," yelled Duke as he nodded at me. "You've been challenged to a fight. What's it going to be? Are you going to fight or chicken out?"

As I approached the homeboys, I thought about the promise I made to my mother that I was not to take part in gang activity. Since my nickname was not gang related, I didn't feel that I had to defend it. It was just a nickname, I thought. For Martín, however, it was more than just a nickname. It was his new identity. It represented his new way of life: a proud member and defender of the Hill Boys. And there could only be one Smiley # 1.

As I got closer to Martín, I saw that he was serious. At that point, I felt that I had no way out. I was the only thing that stood in the way of Martín becoming Smiley # 1.

"No, Martín," I pleaded. "I don't want to fight . . ."

Before I could finish, Martín rushed at me, swinging in all directions. "Who are you calling Martín?" he shouted, coming at me at full force. "I'm Smiley # 1."

I closed my eyes and tried to defend myself against a determined foe. After two minutes, Duke broke us apart to see if I wanted to quit. At this point, I knew that my only way out was to give it my all and not back down.

"OK," I said to Martín, "if that's that way you want it, let's have it out."

As I waited for his response, Martín hit me on my chin and I went down like when Muhammad Ali knocked down George Foreman in the "Rumble in the Jungle."

"One . . . two . . . three . . . ," one of the homeboys counted.

"You're out of there," proclaimed another homeboy.

I slowly opened my eyes and tried to bring the homeboys' faces into focus.

"And the winner and new champion, all the way from the big, bad Hill Boys gang,"shouted an exuberant Duke as he raised Martín's arm up in the air, "Smiley # 1."

As their applause dwindled, Martín helped me to my feet and gave me a big bear hug.

"Thanks for helping me up, Smiley," I said to him with a look of defeat. "I have to go now. My mother is waiting for her tortillas and chicken."

When I got home, my mother snatched the grocery bag from me. As she inspected the bag, she said, "What happened to you?"

"¿Qué?" I snapped out of frustration.

She looked up and squinted. "You're a mess, Smiley. And why did it take you so long?"

"Oh . . . uh . . . I was chased by some dogs and fell," I said.

"How many times do I have to tell you to go through the hill?" she scolded me. "Well, I need you to return to the market and return this chicken . . . it smells so . . ."

"Why do I always have to go?" I said as I shot a glance at my older brother, Flaco, who sat on the couch watching TV. "Why don't you send him this time?"

"You know that I can't rely on your brother. He always forgets to get everything I ask him for," she explained.

Flaco kept quiet and concentrated on *I Love Lucy*, but I'm sure he heard everything we said. A little grin crept across his face but I couldn't tell what amused him more, my predicament or Lucy's bawling.

"OK, I'll go back," I said, "but under one condition."

"What?" she asked.

I paused for a moment and coughed. Flaco was still slouched in front of the TV but I saw his eyes shift toward me.

"I don't have all day, Smiley," said my mother.

"Please," I said in a clear voice, "nobody call me Smiley anymore."

My mother shook her head, turned on her heel and walked to the kitchen muttering something. Flaco's eyes turned back to the TV and he let out a little laugh. I walked to the front door.

"Have fun," said Flaco as I stepped out onto the porch.

Lucy let out a long, loud "Wwwwaaaaaaa!" I could only imagine Ricky rolling his eyes and shaking his head.

I let the screen door slam behind me. Nice and loud.

MISS EAST L.A.

Luis J. Rodríguez

My place is too small and cramped to even light up a cigarette. It's a single room on the first floor of a two-story house in a place called the Gully, on Bernal Street just below the Fourth Street bridge. This is the White Fence neighborhood, one of the original barrios of East L.A. There are a lot of longtime residents here—I'm talking four or five generations. I've seen grandmothers with old *pachuco* tattoos up and down their arms, screaming after their grandkids to come home on time.

A lot of the men here work construction. They've built skyscrapers, freeways, roads, and houses all over Los Angeles—with not much to show for it. So, with all the skills they've gathered over time, they stucco their wood-frame homes or drywall an extra room or whatever—most of the time without permits or inspectors.

That's how parts of East L.A. got built in the first place. The Mexicans moved into the most undesirable areas like the ravines and hills and set up their own housing, sometimes without plumbing or sewage. Eventually, the city and county provided basic services. So it's not unusual for small, dilapidated homes to be torn down, added on to, undergo a metamorphosis—like butterflies. If there's anything Mexicans are known for, it's hard work and creativeness.

I've lived here all my life. Not far from downtown is General Hospital—now it's the University of Southern California-Los Angeles County Medical Center. A lot of Chicanos inhaled their very first breath there—and exhaled their last. It's the cheapest and the most overworked hospital in the city. Our hospital. East L.A.'s.

I was born there.

One thing about me is that I've always wanted to be different. I don't want to end up like my *jefito* who worked as a laborer all his life. He worked hard—I give him credit for that—but I want to do something else with my life.

If you can believe this, my goal is to become a writer. I know this sounds crazy. My family thinks so. When I used to be in the *clica* the White Fence Termites, I got into some trouble and even did county camp time as a juvenile. My dad and mom got mad and everything, but they never threw me out of the house. Later, when I told them I wanted to quit work to be a writer, I was out in the street like a flea-sick dog.

"Writing is for bums, for chuntarros," my father yelled, while watching me leave the pad, duffel bag in hand. "You should work like a man—with your hands."

The thing is, I wanted to be a writer even before I knew what writing was about. I wanted to carve out the words that swam in the bloodstream, to press a stunted pencil onto paper so lines break free like birds in flight—to fashion words like hair, lengths and lengths of it, washed with dawn's rusting drizzle.

I yearned for mortar-lined words, speaking in their own boasting tongues, not the diminished, frightened stammering of my childhood—to shape scorching syllables with midnight dust. Words that stood up in bed, danced merengues and *cumbias*, that incinerated the belly like a shimmering habanera. Words with a spoonful of tears, buckshot, boners, traces of garlic, cilantro, aerosol spray, and ocean froth. Words that guffawed, tarnished smooth faces, and wrung song out of silence. Words as languid as a woman's stride, as severe as a convict's gaze, herniated like a bad plan, soaked as in a summer downpour.

I aspired to walk inside these words, to manipulate their internal organs, surrounded by blood, gray matter, and caesuras; to slam words down like the bones of a street domino game—and to crack them in two like lovers' hearts.

Wanting and doing are two different things.

■

Mamá has her own doubts. She doesn't mind that I want to write. She just doesn't know any writers, and she wonders how writers can live without a constant paycheck, which is a good point. But one day, fairly desperate, I didn't go back to my job unloading boxes of fruit and vegetables off trucks at the downtown docks; I decided to get a writer's job, no matter what.

I had taken night writing courses at East Los Angeles College. In high school, my English teachers said I was good at writing. And, like all writers, I read all the time. So I figured I could do this.

There is a free community newspaper sent to our home every week. It's called the *Eastside Star*. Besides pages and pages of ads, the paper actually has articles about local things: people who get married or divorced or die. It even has an advice column by a "Tía Tita."

The newspaper is on the first floor of a renovated warehouse on Brooklyn Avenue (now called César Chávez Avenue—but I haven't quite gotten used to this yet). One day a few weeks ago, I walked into their office. I just pushed in a large wooden door, me with a white shirt and tie, which made my dark skin and thick wavy hair stand out—my family is from Puebla, where *prietos* abound. A plump but pretty Chicana sat behind a desk stacked with papers on the other side of a wood partition.

"I'm looking for a job," I exclaimed, confidence pouring out of me like sweat (actually, it *was* sweat).

The woman stopped what she was doing. She threw me a look, you know, as if I was El Cucui come for her firstborn child.

"What kind of job?" she haltingly asked.

"I want to be a reporter—I can do feature stories or hard news. I can even take pictures."

"Hold on a minute."

She picked up the phone and whispered to someone on the other end of the line. I scanned the place—it had character. There were a few certificates on the wall, dusty, but impressive. Stacks of newspapers in one corner. A handful of desks, all weighed down by boxes, typewriters, phones, and papers. Just like a real newsroom, I thought.

"Mr. Galván will see you," the woman said. "He's the publisher. Through those doors, por favor."

My nerves jumped like drunken crickets. I went through the doors, which suggested a bigger suite than the one I had actually entered. There was hardly room for the massive desk against a bare window. Mr. Galván, a graying full-head-of-hair dude like César Romero, looked up at me with a faint trace of a smile.

"You want to be a reporter . . . have you ever done this kind of work before?" Mr. Galván inquired.

"Yes, I mean, I worked for the high school newspaper, and I wrote some articles for the college paper," I replied.

Then I added, with pride, "I even had a letter to the editor printed in the *Daily News*."

"Well, it just so happens that I'm looking for someone to fill a position," Mr. Galván said, rather casually. Before I had time to take a breath, he continued.

"But we can only offer you a hundred dollars a week, no benefits, and you also have to sweep the floors, take out the trash, answer phones, solicit ads, and paste up boards. What do you say?"

I was making $250 a week, with overtime, on the docks.

"I'll take it."

I said I was crazy, didn't I?

■

Working at the *Eastside Star* barely provides for cigarettes, booze, and rent. The room I'm staying in is only a couple of blocks from my parents' house, even though I hardly visit them, except to get some of Mamá's great *mole*. I feel I have to prove to them and to myself that being a writer is the best thing I can do.

The problem is you can take the boy out of the barrio, but you can't take the barrio out of the boy.

"You gotta leave now," I'm explaining to my *jaina*, a P.Y.T. named Sunni López.

"Why? There's still some time left, ese," Sunni responds, in her usual gruff manner.

"Look, I have a lot of things to do, so if you don't mind."

"But I don't want to leave just yet."

"I don't care what you want—I want you out of here!" I raise my voice.

"That sounds good, but I'm not going till I'm ready," she responds, her hand on a hip and an I-dare-you-to-yell-at-me-again look on her face.

"Oh, did you forget? This is my place."

"Well, let's just see if you're man enough to throw me out."

"What is it with you? You always want me to push you around or something."

"Be a man, then." People around me seem to bring this up a lot, don't they, about being a man?

"I don't have to hit you to be a man."

"Then stop sniveling—you don't want me around, then make me leave . . . I'd like to see you try."

This is Sunni and me going through our standard routine. She is constantly pushing my buttons so that I will smack her and prove, in her eyes, I'm a man. Most of the time, I just ignore her or tell her this is stupid, all this arguing. Once, though, I must admit, I did hit her. Not hard. It was more like a push. I didn't feel good about it afterward, but then Sunni curled up next to me, called me "baby," and stroked my chest. What a life, huh? What a relationship! My mamá taught me never to hit a woman or a child. And here I am kicking it with somebody who wants me to knock her around. Sometimes, though, I feel like really letting her have it—like right now.

But no, I walk out the back door for a smoke. After a few drags of a cigarette, I reenter my room and try again.

"OK, Sunni, let's make a deal," I say. "You leave now and I'll pick you up after work. We can go out. Get pedotes. And come back and make crazy love. What do you say?"

"Benny, you really are a pussy," Sunni says, gathering up a large leather bag.

Sunni is an extraordinarily good looker, which is why I tolerate so much bullshit from her. A homegirl originally from the Aliso Village housing projects, she is part black, part Mexican. She joined the White Fence gang while we were in high school. She's always been tough. That's where the "be a man" stuff comes from.

Sunni's assets are her large hips, thighs, and breasts; she's what they call "big boned." But this also makes her a hard lady to knock down. I actually think she can kick my ass if we ever have a real knockdown, drag-out. She tries to get me there, getting close to my face when we argue. But nothing comes of it. One thing I learned, though, is that Sunni likes it when people stand up to her.

Sunni was the only one who stuck it out with me when the rest of the homies considered me too "out of it" to hang with. She was the only one who *wanted* me to be a writer.

∎

This particular day, I'm eager to get to work. After weeks of carrying out trash, pasting up ads, and taking phone calls, Mr. Galván finally wants me to come up with a feature story idea. His newspaper runs news and other information only when it will sell advertising space. The popular bilingual advice column from Tía Tita is actually written by a man, Genaro, the only Spanish-speaking staff writer on board.

The *Star* has tons of ads for used cars, furniture (with deals almost as bad as borrowing money from crooked shylocks), and supermarkets. Its thriving classified section also carries small announcements for *curanderas*, fortune-tellers, and "under the table" house rehab crews.

But every once in a while, Mr. Galván will run an original researched piece of some interest to the community. This is what I've been waiting for—I didn't want anything or anybody, including Sunni, to make me blow it.

"Drop me off at my crib, then," Sunni says, still angry as we head outside.

We go to the backyard where I've parked my lowrider 1975 Toyota Corolla. It's actually a rusty blue number with overhanging tires, encircling chrome rims so that it looks like I'm cruising all the time—although the Toyota doesn't go too fast as it is. Sunni is pissed off at me all the way to her home, but I don't worry. Tonight she'll be back to her old loving self.

"Hola, Benny, you're on time today, what gives?" asks Amelia, the receptionist who greeted me the first time I'd entered the newspaper's office. Over these past weeks, we've become friends. For one thing, she's good for the *chismorreo*—which, as anyone knows, is what good reporting is really all about.

"Hey, Benny, you missed some fun already," Amelia begins. "Galván found out about Darío."

"What . . . that our dear managing editor has been humping the publisher's wife?" I say.

"Simón, and on top of that, Galván came in and fired Darío this morning—on the spot."

"No me digas."

"Not only that, after he fired him, Galván had the nerve to punch Darío in the mouth. ¡Un chingaso, pero bien dado! Darío fell down, then got up, and Galván hit him again. ¡Zas! Then Darío went down and everybody, including Genaro and me, kept telling him to stay down, stay down, but he got up, and Galván walloped him again. Finally, Darío stayed down while Galván stormed out of here. Genaro had to walk Darío to his car so he could go home and take care of his fat lip. ¿Qué escándalo, no?"

Like I say, Amelia is good for the *chisme*.

As I move toward my desk, Genaro, a middle-aged, heavyset, wire-haired man, and the only experienced journalist among us—he wrote political commentary for a newspaper in Mexico before receiving death threats and exiling himself to Los Angeles—wants to know my opinion on something.

"Benjamin Franklin Pineda . . . ¿cómo lo ves?" he says, knowing full well that I hate to be called by my birth name (my father had a sense of humor, *¿qué no?*).

Genaro displayed on his desk a photo of a man's beaten-up head, without a body, its eyes painted open, and a bad drawing of a bow tie where the neck should be.

"It looks sick, Genaro," I respond. "Where do you come up with these things?"

The decapitated head was discovered behind a trash bin in an alley off Soto Street. The police asked the newspaper for help in identifying the victim. So Genaro figures he can place the photo—with its goofy additions—on the front page next to a cutline that reads: "Does anyone know whose body this belongs to?"

"Genaro, I think you should stick to just doing Tía Tita columns," I say.

"¡Ay, Chihuahua! No tienes la menor idea de como ganar lectores," he replies.

There's never a dull moment at the *Eastside Star*.

■

I'm not sure what I'm going to write about for the feature. I've picked up the morning editions of other newspapers to see if anything strikes me. But it's a slow news day. No mud slides, no corruption cases, no major exposes. Before this day I had tons of ideas; now that I have a chance to actually pull something together, I'm at a loss.

Then Rigoberto, the *Star's* layout guy, who used to work in the production department of a newspaper in Guatemala—another exile— comes down the stairs from the layout room.

"Benny, how you doing, vos?" he says in his heavily accented English.

"Cool, Rigo, just looking for some story ideas—you got any?" I ask.

"Well, I saw something that may interest you," Rigoberto replies, stopping by my desk and riffling through the stack of newspapers. He picks through a few and then takes out the weekend's *Los Angeles Times*. In the Metro section there is an important item, something I had missed, which is not hard to do after I've been partying with Sunni for a couple of days. The article has a photo of an attractive Chicana face and a headline that reads, "Miss East L.A. Found Murdered."

The story begins: *Police say the 18-year-old recently crowned queen of East Los Angeles was found stabbed to death Saturday night at the Central City Hospital where she worked as a nurse's aide.*

According to the account, Emily Contreras, a recent graduate of Wilson High School, was discovered during the night shift with numerous stab wounds, lying on a hospital bed in an empty room. A twenty-one-year-old orderly, Daniel Amaya, was also stabbed a few times but survived. Contreras was selected Miss East L.A. only a couple of months ago after a controversial race.

It seems incredible, but somebody has offed our queen!

"You know, I think you got something here, Rigo," I say.

The Miss East L.A. pageant was actually an entertaining affair this year. At first a rather unattractive, plain-looking teenager won the crown. This brought up more than a few eyebrows—the *comadres* with their *veri veri* had a field day. This vision of unloveliness turned up on TV and everything. Most people just couldn't believe she was the one selected, which is OK, I suppose, if you consider how sexist these contests are to begin with.

But later it's revealed that the winner was the niece of one of the judges, who apparently rigged the voting. Looking at the judge's pock-faced mug in the newspapers, you knew they were related. So *la reina* had to resign and the runner-up, Emily Contreras, was declared the new winner.

Only now she's dead.

Mr. Galván had designated Genaro temporary managing editor of the newspaper before the incident with Darío, so after apologizing for not seeing the thoughtfulness of Genaro's dealing with the bodiless head, I ask him for permission to follow up on the Miss East L.A. murder case.

"Está bien, ya lárgate," Genaro exclaims.

■

The police are not much help to reporters. And since the *Eastside Star* is not considered a "legitimate" newspaper, like the *Times* or the Spanish-language daily, *La opinión*, my chances of getting information from them is . . . well, *olvídate.*

But I have an ace in the hole—a cousin of mine is a detective in the homicide division. It's good to have family in key places.

I decide to jump into my blue "Toyot" and visit him.

"I came to see Detective Dávila," I say to the desk officer.

"He knows you were coming?" he asks.

"Well, not exactly . . ."

"Then I don't know if you can see him. He's really busy," the officer replies. "Why don't you tell me what you want, and I'll see if he can talk to you."

Telling him I work for the *Eastside Star* did not make this any easier.

Finally, after what seems like an hour, a young Chicano in a suit jacket, blue jeans, with badge and gun on his belt, and carefully combed hair, approaches. It's my primo, Detective Raymundo Dávila.

"¿Qué hubo, Benny?" says Mundo, which is the shortened version of his name. He has an outstretched hand and a distrustful rise in an eyebrow. "What in the world brings you here?"

"I guess you haven't heard; I work for the *Eastside Star* now," I say.

"Oh, I heard. I also heard how you broke your mother's heart taking this job."

"Man, not you, too," I respond. "Listen, being a writer is a good profession . . ."

"Save it, ese," Mundo interrupts. "I went through the same thing trying to be a cop, remember?"

Mundo has a point—he was also expected to work in the construction trades like my dad and Mundo's father. Hard-ass work with one's hands was the only kind of business allowed in our families. Being a cop just didn't compute—neither did being a writer.

"Simón, I remember," I ease. "Well, I came for some help. You know about the Emily Contreras murder—Miss East L.A.?"

"Sure, we're working on it right now."

"I'm looking for information on this case, what really happened. You know, whatever is available as far as suspects and motives . . . that kind of thing. I want to do a big story."

"Well, you ought to know, primo, that we normally don't give out 'that kind of thing,' " Mundo says, walking away.

"But I understand you guys will be helping us with the decapitated head case," Mundo turns toward me, and smirks. "So let me find out what I can do for you, all right?"

Genaro, I think, you're an angel with that headless story. Oh, and did I mention it's also good to have family in key places?

Mundo gestures for me to enter his office, a small, cluttered cubicle with wood paneling from top to bottom.

"According to the coroner's office, Contreras was found with seventeen stab wounds in her neck and chest," Mundo explains, getting right to business. "One puncture went directly through her heart. The perpetrators apparently entered the room where Contreras was taking a nap. She worked late. The orderly on duty at the time told her to rest while he kept watch. The perps apparently also attacked the orderly, who was found in the corridor with minor stab wounds to his arms and chest. He says there were at least three attackers, men with masks. They killed Contreras and ran out. There are no other witnesses at this time."

I wait for a few seconds. Mundo looks at me with a tired expression.

"And?" I finally say.

"And what? That's all there is."

"No suspects? No idea of why anyone might want to do this? Nothing?"

"It's under investigation," Mundo says, putting the paperwork away into a file that he casually throws on top of a stack barely balancing on his desk. "That's all we got for now. You should be glad I gave you this much. One thing, primo, you can't mention anything about the number and location of the stab wounds. We need this information to help confirm a possible suspect. You understand what I'm saying?"

I nod.

"Now if you don't mind, I have a lot of work to do," Mundo says, rising to his feet. "Say qué hubo to your mom and dad for me, all right?"

That night, I tell Sunni about the story, and she's intrigued. As always, she has a number of theories on what may have happened.

She paces back and forth.

"I bet you it was a contract hit," she proposes, her imagination getting the better of her. "The queen contest was a fix, right? Maybe there was some money involved. And having her get the crown was blowing it for some people in high places."

"Too farfetched," I counter, while I sit immersed in an old, mildewed bathtub a few feet from where Sunni is pacing. "But it's strange that three men would come into the place and kill her, almost in plain sight. I know it was late, but it *is* a hospital. Where were the nurses, the doctors, or the patients? Something's fishy."

"I got another idea," she says, excited about the prospect. "Maybe, just maybe, she was snuffed out by the uncle of the girl who had to resign. You know, hire a few vatos. Get the queen. He'd be pissed off, right?"

At this point anybody could have killed Miss East L.A., even Sunni. I realize I have to talk to the one witness in the case, the orderly who was also stabbed. Knowing the police, and especially Mundo, I didn't think I would get much help from them on this.

The next day, my Toyot is parked in front of Central City Hospital. Using my skills as an investigative reporter, I forage through the employee file box while the receptionist is talking to the nurse's supervisor, asking if I can discuss the incident with her. So far the hospital has been hush-hush about the killing. I know I won't get any statement from them, but I do find an address for Daniel Amaya, the orderly.

Amaya lives in Maravilla. This is rough territory. Maravilla has a bunch of rival gangs—the biggest is El Hoyo Mara, after the "hole" the residents found refuge in a few generations back. Amaya lives in the barrio known as Marianna Mara. Still, being White Fence, despite my inactivity, I'm *trucha* about where I go and with whom I talk. But I'm a reporter. Somehow I have to get the story.

I wear a long-sleeve shirt to hide the *clica's* tattoo on my arm from coming up in the 'hood. I'm not into "the life" anymore. But like a lot of old homeboys, I still carry the "tats" and scars.

I park in front of a tiny shingled house. There is a wooden archway over the sidewalk outside the front door. A grapevine with small buds of new black grapes curls around the archway. An unpainted wooden fence surrounds the place. Colored flowers and ornate ceramic pots are scattered around the yard, suggesting the hand of a Mexican gardener.

An old woman gently opens the door after I've knocked for several minutes. In Spanish, I ask if Daniel lives there and if he's available for a few questions. It turns out this woman is Daniel's grandmother, small and thin-boned, with deeply creviced brown skin on her face and hands. Daniel lives in an even smaller place out in back. I follow the woman through a walkway surrounded by intense gardenias, roses, and cactuses.

Daniel answers the door quickly as if he's been standing near it. He looks at me intently, suspiciously. His arm is wrapped and in a sling. Despite the alleged ferocity of the attack, there are no bruises or cuts on his face, which is boyish except for acne scars. His grandmother returns to the front house. Standing in the doorway, Daniel is reluctant to talk.

"I've already told the police everything," he says, with a slightly nervous tone in his voice. Otherwise, he's calm. "Why do I have to talk to you?"

"You don't have to talk to me, Daniel," I say. "But I'm doing this story and it would be good if I could get some comments from the one witness. It's up to you. How about it?"

Daniel contemplates this for a while. I'm thinking I have to concoct some scheme to get him to talk when, to my surprise, he opens up.

"I was working the late shift. It was around two a.m. There was only Emily and me on that section of the floor," he says. "The nurses' station is around the corner by the elevators. I could see Emily was tired. She had been real busy since she was named the new queen. I told her to rest for a few minutes in one of the empty rooms.

"There's a back stairway, which is only available to employees. I think the three men broke in there and then walked up. Probably on the stairs, they changed into dark coats and masks. Nobody downstairs saw anybody with those coats on in the waiting area. Anyway, I come out of a patient's room; before I know it a masked man is stabbing me with a knife. He is cutting me on my arm and on my chest. I fall down. I'm hurtin', and I don't know what's happenin'. The man drops his knife and leaves; he meets up with two others, who come out of the room where Emily was sleeping. Then all three of them run down the stairs. It happened so fast. The nurses come running; one of them screams. I didn't realize until later that the two other men had already killed Emily. She was asleep and I didn't hear any noise from inside the room."

I ask Daniel a few questions: Why didn't he yell for help? Did the men say anything? Did any patients hear the noise? What happened to the knife that was dropped?

I don't get much more out of Daniel. I then ask him, "Who do you think would want to kill Emily?"

At this, Daniel looks at me strangely, as if he's trying to read my mind. He then says he has to leave now, that he's had it with these questions, and he would appreciate it if he weren't bothered again.

"Listen, I'm afraid they might come back to get me," he adds as he closes the door.

■

The next day I visit Mundo to find out if there is any more on the investigation. I had just come back from downtown doing research at the library about the Miss East L.A. pageant. I'm really getting into this story. For some reason after I enter the police station, Mundo is standing there, as if he's been waiting for me. He again invites me into his cubicle.

"Yeah, we definitely got something," he says, only in not so helpful a tone as the last time. "But I'm pissed off at you, ese."

"Why?" I ask, although I already know the answer.

"You went to see Daniel Amaya," he looks at me, more as cop than cousin. "What did he say to you?"

"Now, Mundo, you know as a reporter I have the right to talk to him," I respond. "And you also know that I have the right not to tell you what he said. So what's up? What's the latest on this?"

"Well, you're my cousin, ese, but I also have the right not to tell you anything," Mundo says. "The thing is we have a pretty good idea about what happened and why. But I can't tell you just yet. Check with me later. I would appreciate it, though, if you let us deal with this case. We don't want anything to mess up our investigation. Can you do that for me?"

I agree and excuse myself from Mundo's office. I walk fast toward the exit. I can feel Mundo's eyes on my back.

I go home. I should go see Sunni, but I'm not sure I want to. She gets me angry and confused about most things.

After a few chugs on a tequila bottle, I begin to calm down. Well, I wanted to be a writer, didn't I? I just can't seem to piece together what happened to Emily—although I feel I'm at the entrance of a big door where just beyond it lies all the answers. I'm just so new at this that I can't see a way to get through that door.

I lie down on a pile of blankets on the bed. The tequila is loosening me up. I begin to think. By then I had interviewed more people, including the pageant officials, a couple of the princesses, and even the crooked judge (in case he had a guilty look—which he didn't). I also talked to Emily's family—her mother, father, and younger brothers. Although Mundo says they have a break in the case, I still haven't pinned down why someone would want to kill Emily.

I find out that Emily was a good student at Wilson. She was active in student affairs, particularly the Chicano student group and the school newspaper. If she had lived, she might have been a writer, too.

She was extremely beautiful. Photos hang on the walls of the living room and kitchen of her house. Emily had honey-brown skin, elongated indigenous eyes, and a full perfect mouth. Her hair was thick, black, and long.

There is a photo of Emily in a black mariachi outfit, playing violin with other young mariachi musicians. Her mother shows me a newspaper clipping with Emily demonstrating for immigrant rights. She was a budding journalist, musician, and leader—she could have run for office, even become the first Chicana president. Everything I saw and heard emphasized her special nature, and how her death seemed so wrong, so unjust—just plain out of sync with the calling she apparently had in this world.

"She really cared about people, especially those who couldn't defend themselves," her mother states in between sobs.

It appears Emily also lived a decent home life. Her father works as an airplane mechanic; her mother is an involved member of the community, holding school-related meetings at her home. And the brothers are soccer and baseball stars in school. The family resides in a large, Spanish-tiled stucco house in El Sereno, having moved from the Happy Valley neighborhood only a few years back when Dad first got the job at the airlines.

As a child, Emily grew up near Lincoln Park. A tomboy, she played rough with other children, throwing stones into the Lincoln Park lake and running up and down the small grass slopes there. Her mother is the most articulate about her daughter's life. She wants to talk, to reminisce, to let Emily continue to live through her memory, her words. Her father, on the other hand, doesn't say anything. I can tell he's feeling terrible, but it's so personal and deep; I fear he will dissolve if he opens up to the tragedy.

I close my eyes; maybe if I sleep I can get beyond the facts into the real story.

Soon enough, I'm dreaming. I see the unmarred face of Emily Contreras. She is directing me toward a door with those dark eyes of hers. I open it slowly. Then I'm at the *Star* newsroom; Genaro, Amelia, and Rigoberto are there, laughing at me. I start to run. The streets are drenched; everywhere there's moisture, dripping from lampposts, from neon signs, from billboards. Soon I'm in the police station. It's dim and empty. I walk through a wood-paneled hallway. Mundo looks out from his office, staring at me. "We know who did it," he says, then he laughs. Now I'm in a hospital corridor. Sunni stumbles out of a room wearing a hospital gown, bleeding from her chest. "They stabbed me," she screams, then falls. Out of the room, behind her, comes Daniel. In one hand, he's got his grandmother's head.

Talk about cold sweats! I woke up soaked.

■

I've been working on the piece for the *Star* for days now. It's my first feature, and I want it to kick butt. This is East L.A., and nothing is as simple as it first appears. Questions of who, what, and when continue to accumulate around Emily Contreras's death.

Emily didn't seem to have any enemies; she was respectful, endearing. But in a place like East L.A., where almost everyone is from some part of Mexico, lives are entangled, rumors surface: Emily's dad smuggled diamonds on the airplanes. She had had an affair with a prominent businessman who wanted to end the relationship. A close uncle, doing time in San Quentin, may have flubbed a drug deal, resulting in Emily's sacrifice. Then there was the rumor that the police were trying to cover up a police shooting of an unarmed teenager near Emily's home, which she may have witnessed.

I want to provide more about Emily than a short newspaper item and photo. I want to breathe life back into Emily, so she appears to stroll through the living room of whoever reads about her.

So far, I'm the only one writing anything about Emily Contreras. The *Times*'s story is weak; "their" Emily is just a face on a cardboard body.

Sunni continues to be belligerent, but when she reads what I've written so far, she says something she has never said to me before: "You're good."

Doing this story has got me thinking a lot about Emily, about the sweetness of her life and the tragedy of her death. It's got me thinking about all the various ways people can die in this town. Here death stalks us like a sullen figure over upturned sidewalks, like a sleepless guest that fades in and out of dreams—between the solid world and something fluid inside. I had an aunt, for example, who died in a diabetic torture—her eyes failed her and they removed her legs before her kidneys finally gave out. I had a neighbor who owned a taco stand and lost a husband to an armed robber, only to lose a son in another robbery sixteen years later. And there was a whole family—including a six-year-old and an eight-month-old—killed by rivals in a drug deal gone wrong.

Death is on the faces of small children and in the sage advice of old people: It lingers around every card game, converging at every corner, as part of every beer run, next to every family argument, behind every street encounter, and a likely result of every drug overdose or schoolyard dare. Death is like a shadow beneath the body, pulling us down toward its own ground, toward its own mouth, and articulating us in its own measured verses.

Whew . . . I think this story is really starting to get to me.

■

I'm lying in that ancient tub of mine, with cracked tiles surrounding me, letting the warmness of the soapy water seep through my bones, when it strikes me, this idea, preposterous and reasonable at the same time. It comes to me first in a flash. I try to think about something else, then the idea returns, refusing to go away.

What a dummy I am! I know now what Mundo was trying to keep from me.

I pull myself out of the tub, dry off quickly, and put on a pair of jeans, a loose shirt, and a denim jacket. I'm going to see someone who I believe holds the key to Emily's death. Before I do, I make a phone call.

I jump into the Toyot and take off like a mouse with a cat on its tail. I don't care about pedestrians, other cars or *nada*. This notion about who killed Emily is gnawing at me.

I drive a few miles to Maravilla. My mind goes over all the facts, the rumors, and the personalities surrounding the murder, and it all comes back to this—this one house, this one face.

I enter through the wood gate, walk beneath the archway, and swing around to the back. There's a light in the window of the small building there. Out of the shadows, someone emerges; it's Mundo.

"You may as well be in on this, ese," Mundo says, two uniformed police officers at his side. "But remember—you owe me."

Just like before, one knock and the door opens.

When Daniel sees Mundo and the officers, his face drops. He knows what they're here for. He tries to close the door, but Mundo rushes in, holding it open with his foot. I follow behind the other officers.

"Daniel Amaya, you're under arrest for the murder of Emily Contreras," Mundo says. He then proceeds to read him his rights while the officers turn Daniel around to cuff him.

Daniel has this look of incredulity, like if all of us have gone over the edge. But then his demeanor changes. He glances around the room, as if looking for something, a way to get around this. Then he drops his head and begins to cry.

I just stare at Daniel; everything is sharp and clear around him. His voice breaks through his sobs, loud and intrusive.

"Oh, I loved her so much," Daniel says, without looking up. "I tried damn hard to please her, to get her to see how much I cared. But she wouldn't even look at me—as if I didn't exist. I wrote her notes. I left her presents. But she didn't care. Then that contest, that pinche contest! She was getting all this attention. People would call. She would get visitors and compliments. All these guys started talking to her, flirting with her. I was just beginning to get her to notice me, and then this queen thing happened. I knew then that I had lost her."

Daniel looks up, a pained expression on his face.

"I just couldn't stand it," he continues. "I tried to talk to her, but she was cold. Being Miss East L.A., why would she bother with me, right? I told her this couldn't keep going on. I told her. I warned her. But she brushed it off. I just couldn't let her slip away from me, not when I was so close. . . ."

"So how did you do it?" Mundo interjects.

"Man, it was easy," he says, confidently, as if coming to terms with something. "After a while I began to see how I was meant to take Emily away from here. I was doing her a favor, you understand! She wouldn't know real love without me. There are only liars and manipulators out there. Schemers, all of them. So that night I told her to take a rest. I knew she was tired. I even had the room ready for her. At first she wouldn't listen to me, but she finally said OK, that she would rest for a few minutes. I said I would keep a watch out for the nurses. It was a slow night. There were no patients on that side of the floor. I waited until Emily lay down, waited until I knew she was asleep; she fell out fast—that's how tired she was. Then I went into the room. It was dark. But I knew where she was. I put on surgical gloves. Then I took out a knife that had been held by rubber bands on my leg. I walked up to her and without saying anything, I stabbed her—hard, and as many times as I could. I remember feeling the knife enter, how soft her body was, how easily the blade went in and out. I hardly hit bone. I just kept stabbing, placing my hand over her mouth in case she woke up to scream. It happened so fast, I didn't think about it at all. Then I ran out of the room, and I stabbed my chest and arm."

"That's why the wounds weren't deep," I say. "Because you'd done it to yourself."

"I almost had everyone fooled, didn't I?" Daniel continues, suddenly as if he were talking about a prank he may have pulled on a friend. "I threw the knife on the ground because I couldn't get rid of it after stabbing myself. I took off the gloves and hid them in my shoe. I could see blood everywhere. I knew it was Emily's and mine—our blood together. You see, I needed Emily so much. She should have listened to me. She should have loved me."

Daniel stops, closes his eyes, and sobs. The police officers pull him outside by his arms, followed by Mundo. As they prepare to leave, neighbors gather behind fences and parked cars; the only sounds are their whispers, police radio dispatches, and the din of insects. I look up—a slight woman with webbed lines across her face peers through a window in the front house. She sees me, then rapidly closes the curtains, which look like the wings of a ghostly angel turning away.

■

"Amá, you make the best mole," I declare.

Sunni and me are celebrating—my story's on the front page of the *Eastside Star,* with pictures from Emily's home and everything. And where else would we be celebrating but at Mamá's house, eating her *poblana*-style cuisine, guzzling down some brews, and enjoying the good life in the White Fence barrio.

"That's right, ma'am, this is soo good," Sunni adds.

My dad is quiet, but every once in a while he gazes at the newspaper spread across the table. I know there's a *grano* of pride in him somewhere. He won't say it, but I believe my writing life has hit a high mark in this family.

The article appeared the week following Daniel's arrest. It was better than any other news piece on Emily. I was even offered a chance to enroll in a journalism program for emerging writers at the University of California, Berkeley. Nobody in the neighborhood has ever had such an opportunity.

"You did a helluva story, Benny," Sunni chimes in. "Only if you had listened to me sooner, you would have long figured out that crazy orderly'd done it."

"What you clamoring about now?" I respond. "You didn't know he had anything to do with it. You were going on about contract hits and judges out to get people and all that nonsense."

"Now don't start with me, Benny boy, I was giving you the general direction to look—you were just too dumb to figure it out."

"*I'm* dumb . . . the one who has the front page story, who's being recruited to U.C. Berkeley. Yeah, sure, I'm the dumb guy."

"Don't throw that at me—you may think you're so damn smart but I'll have your ass all over this street, ese," Sunni shouts—while Dad gets closer to his food and my mother practically runs into the kitchen to heat up more tortillas.

"Talking tough and doing nothing—that's all you ever do," I say, stuffing a tortilla full of mole and chicken into my mouth.

"Come on then, punk," Sunni stands up. "I'll take you out right now—in front of your family, God, and the whole barrio. I'll show you who don't do nothing."

I get up, wipe my mouth with a napkin, and step outside for a smoke.

from the novel

BARRIO ON THE EDGE

Alejandro Morales

She has always been someone he could run to for security and support. She is a wonderful woman, a great woman who has reared children who are not so bad. She is intelligent; she speaks the language of these parts well and has female friends in stores all over town. She dresses well, and with her increasingly graying hair she walks, speaks, and acts like a queen.

Julián's mother was all this and more for him, but there was still something in their lifestyle or in themselves that prevented them from freely and outwardly expressing real affection. His mother cared deeply for him, and her love was apparent in everything she did for him and the family. Like her husband, she was given to shouting; she used to yell plenty at the two boys. This was good—her husband did it to straighten them out, to make them obey; that is why he did it. She was more of the modern philosophy that the best approach to raising a child is by loving him more. However, she saw that Julián was going astray and she tried over and over again to show him the right path. She tried to help her son up to the moment she died. No one in the whole world can describe a mother's feelings, especially what a mother feels when she loses a son.

Julián knew it all along; he used to live with that grief, the pain of knowing he had really hurt his mother; I gotta protect the memory of my mother. He didn't want doña Matilde to live in the same house with his father.

Julián became more and more suicidal by hanging around queers, whores, and lunatics; the worm in his head gnawed at him and increased the hatred he felt for his father. Julián's mind would wrench with rage upon hearing the gossip and lies the Buenasuerte brothers told him. Your ol' man is layin' Doña Matilde in your mother's bed. They told me that Melón saw him yesterday lappin' her stinky and revoltin' pussy, your mother's portrait watching it all. That little ol' lady ain't so bad, hell, even I get turned on by her. Shut up, assholes, or I'll kill you! The Buenasuertes used to laugh and get a big charge out of making Julián react. Julián was very ill, but the Buenasuertes used him plenty as a source of entertainment.

He decided to settle the debt he owed his mother by fixing the situation between don Edmundo and doña Matilde. He also wanted to take his little brother out of the house in order to help him. That's what I'll do just for you, Mamá, wiping the snot with his knuckles.

And that's how it happened: he went to the house; it was when he started to feel bad, when he was coming down from a delirious high. He preferred not to shoot up because he wanted to avoid feeling good; he wanted to punish himself, wishing for some sort of penance; he would fast; he would not shoot up. He thought he was in the right, doing something good. They all went. The Buenasuerte brothers were very excited. They were happily driving their old clunker. Throw that ol' lady outta the house! She's a whore! Let's do it to her. I wanna fuck her first. Yaaiii . . . Yaaiii, fuckin' high! Far out! . . . Let's poke her and sell her to the ol' men on the corner, just like we did to Bárbara. Yaaaiii! . . .

They laughed and laughed in a broken, rapid-fire machine-gun burst. Nothing could hurt them now; they felt at peace, powerful and lighthearted. They were cruising around with Julián in the car hearing everything and feeling worse; but he could resist; he could hold back from shooting up, knowing he was doing the right thing. He knew it. Admit it, I'm right. Say so, Buenasuerte. Ain't that so, Turco?

One of the Buenasuerte brothers was at the breaking point of his delirium, unable to utter a word; he could only gaze at Julián with his thin lips stretching into a broad smile, his head slowly shaking from side to side, affirming his ecstasy; and he knew, Buenasuerte knew this was the only thing he wanted in the whole world.

The house was the same: a faded white, yellow, and green; an anguished house smelling of lard and old age. Julián stood in front of the torn screen door. The Buenasuertes waited for him in the car. He stepped onto the porch; he didn't hear anyone inside, not a sound. He banged on the door but no one answered. He glanced back toward the car where he could see the Buenasuertes gesturing to him to hurl the chair through the window. Perspiring, he picked up the chair, and in one simultaneous crash the shattering window, the screams inside, and the senseless cackles from the car all fused in the night. Ayy! Back again to hassle me? Go away, you bastard! Help, for God's sake, someone, anyone, help me! Police! Ay, don Edmundo! Grab him, Julián! Yaaiii! . . . Beat the shit outta her! Desperate bug eyes, ripping the curtains, slammed into the bedroom. Those eyes hated doña Matilde. Take that whore outta here! I don't wan'er in this house! Beat it! Haul ass, you goddam pothead, you addict! Get out or I'll call the cops!

The young man glared at doña Matilde; his feet were moving toward her. Glimpsing slivers of light through the mesh of the rear screen door, the old woman's panicked calves held her wobbly ass up as she stumbled back to where the light shone. Her cheek met the staircase, splitting her mouth open; her scream was as sharp as the pain. Aaayy, cabrón, you busted her face! A stifling rage seemed to engulf him, and his eyes popped out even more seeing his father hold the buxom woman. Why didn't you ever help my mother like that? 'Cuz she didn't suck your balls like this fuckin' bitch! Listen, I don't wan' 'er here! I don't want this whore shackin' up with you in my mother's house! You're the one with no respect for my mamá!

He felt a spray all over his face and sensed a thick green glob of phlegm sliding down the side of his nose; from the corner of his right eye, don Edmundo's words battered him. Look here, you asshole, if you ever come back to this house again, I'll kill you. I'll be waiting for you with a gun. Get out of here, you disgraceful, rotten example of a son; beat it, cabrón! You're the one who killed your mother and now you want to kill me, too. Shithead, get out, scram. Murderer, assassin, you killed your mother; you killed your mother! You killed her, you idiot!

Julián's knuckles were bleeding, and his blood mixed with his father's, who continued screaming at him and blaming him. The world also wept; the mechanical sirens brimming with hatred and fear were fast approaching. The Buenasuertes brutally and violently punched the horn of the old clunker, which vomited smoke from its entrails while his own felt parched; he could not scream from hatred and love. Kill me, all of you, kill me! The least you can do for me is to kill me! Fuck the cages! Fuck the world! His eyes expressed this while the Buenasuertes giggled as they stepped into the car.

Román ran toward the house. Come over here, Román! Come with me! One of the Buenasuertes slammed the door. Julián knew he could help his brother; he knew he was doing his best for his little brother's well-being. He was right again when he heard the Buenasuertes burst out laughing hysterically; a head and two hands drove the car, weaving back and forth from one side of the street to the other, relishing the moment.

Cars with screaming, mechanical mouths arrived at the scene howling like *lloronas*. One chased the heads that were barely visible through the Buenasuertes' rear car window. Honking and squealing, the wide-open mechanical mouth tried to catch the car, which was now moving even faster.

El Turco was really jacked up, so out of it that his head could not stay up on his shoulders, bobbing up and down. I wanna get high, and he opened a small package; inserting three fingers, he pulled out a pinch, stuffing it in his nose while inhaling deeply. Román looked out, his back hunched into the seat. They were speeding along that street, racing past the giant eucalyptus trees faster than before.

The foot pressed on the metal below; it couldn't press any harder, and the jalopy, flaunting its clunkiness, reached fifty-five. El Turco could not feel his foot; he could barely see. Hit sixty! Hit sixty! Yaaiii! What a blast! What madness . . . what insanity . . . what bliss!

But Román's screams could not be distinguished from the others' loud grunts and guffaws. Fear, terror crackled. Mamá, mamáaa! But no one stopped the car. Julián fainted; the Buenasuertes were bellowing with laughter. Román jerked at the scrawny, impotent, fucked-up guy next to him. Julián, help me! Someone stop the car! Stop! Mamáaa! Ma . . . ma . . . máaa!

El Turco sank even further physically and mentally into the space he occupied; the head and hands that drove the car no longer did so. The other Buenasuerte made no attempt at stopping the car; he looked around and saw Julián's smudged face banging against the window; he noticed the kid, who was shouting and crying much like the wailing black and white chasing them; he saw El Turco drooling white saliva. No one was steering; the situation seemed so bizarre to him that he simply laughed and laughed. Maa . . . máaa! He simply kept laughing.

Román felt light, floating back and forth and back again . . . everything around him was black pain, abrasive and grating; he cried alone.

Wailing sirens from all sides, people here and there enjoying what they saw, chatting, craning their necks, brushing against each other, hardly surprised at the mass of iron and flesh that formed part of the intense colors of the collage that lay, that hovered and settled on the street. It could not be opened up, it could not be separated; after an hour, more or less, the firemen pulled out El Turco and Román. The hapless Buenasuerte, littered with glass, was glistening on the street. With great care, they lifted Julián, his wounded chest and abdomen torn open from being dragged over the hooks that jutted from the side of the truck. He was face down in a warm puddle. His mouth was ripped in two places from the lower jaw to the Adam's apple. With his arms folded under his chest, he seemed to be trying to prevent all his insides from spilling out.

The brothers were dripping blood in the same ambulance, where Román saw Julián's blood saturate the floor and the sheets; the assistant could not stop the flow of blood; Román was unable to cry.

BENDER

Daniel A. Olivas

This will not do, says Raúl. No, this will not do at all.

Raúl stands up, pushing back his chair with the insides of his knees. He stands before the table for a moment with his hands on his hips.

No, this cannot be left as it is, Raúl says.

He turns on his heel and marches barefoot toward the bedroom. Raúl shakes his head from side to side. This will not do at all.

He finds María sitting on their bed cutting her toenails with a large pair of clippers that she purchased last year at the Santa Monica Pier. On one side of the clippers, the part you put your thumb on, is an elongated version of the Mexican flag with the eagle looking as though it has been stretched out like Silly Putty. A flailing serpent hangs from the eagle's beak and looks like an evil penis or a goose's neck. María lets her nail clippings fly up and land throughout the rumpled sheets of the unmade bed. She wears no clothes and sits with her left leg out, her right leg bent, and her foot pulled up close to her face. Perspiration drips from her face and rains on her round, firm toes. The Los Angeles summer sun shines hard and heartlessly through the large window and lights up the bed like a Broadway stage. María smells ripe and delicious to Raúl, but he has some other business to take care of right now. Otherwise, he would pull off his boxers and slide across the sheets and put himself into María.

Have you seen it? Raúl asks María.

Yes.

Well?

Well what, mi cielo?

She clips the nail on her big toe and a hard crescent moon flies up and almost hits Raúl on his knitted brow.

Raúl scratches his small hairy belly and then his head and then his belly again because scratching his belly feels more appropriate at that moment.

What should we do about it? he continues. It presents a problem, doesn't it?

Donde una puerta se cierra, otra se abre, says María without looking up.

How does this present an opportunity? asks Raúl in all sincerity but getting a little irritated.

El que mucho habla, poco logra, she answers, spreading out her right leg and pulling her left foot up toward her face. Her wavy black hair tickles the tips of her toes and she laughs a little before starting to clip the next set of toenails.

You're right, says Raúl. Enough talk. Time to act. He turns and walks back to the kitchen table.

By the time he gets there, it has moved from one corner of the table to the other. Raúl pulls his chair under him and sits down with a little grunt. Perspiration drips from both armpits and down his sides.

OK, says Raúl. Look at me.

It turns and looks at Raúl.

OK, begins Raúl. Let's deal with this now or else I can't get on with my day and I have a lot of plans, you know.

It looks at Raúl with large sorrowful eyes and Raúl fears that it will start crying at any moment if he doesn't watch his tone.

Do you understand me? asks Raúl in a softer voice.

It nods slowly.

María yells from the bedroom, Ask it if it's hungry, mi cielo.

No! yells Raúl without moving his eyes from it. That will defeat the purpose. But as Raúl says this, it lets a tear drop slowly first from one eye and then the other.

OK, OK, says Raúl. Are you hungry?

It nods and smiles, displaying many sharp little teeth.

OK. Raúl stands up and walks over to the refrigerator and opens it. This is what we have, says Raúl. We have applesauce, bread, flour tortillas, grape jam (not jelly), fat-free half & half (how is that possible?), Egg Beaters, and Diet Coke.

It makes a snide comment.

I know, I know, answers Raúl. I have a cholesterol problem.

It asks a question.

My LDL is way too high and HDL too low, says Raúl.

It asks another question.

Of course I work out, answers Raúl.

It says something.

Well, I'm glad your numbers are good. OK, says Raúl in exasperation. If you don't make a choice, I'll choose for you.

It makes a choice.

Good, says Raúl and he grabs the applesauce, shuts the refrigerator door with a flick of his wrist, and grabs a spoon and bowl from the cupboard. He sets it all on the table, scoops a large spoonful of the applesauce, and plops it into the bowl. There, he says. Eat up.

It lets out a little laugh before sticking its tongue into the applesauce.

María walks into the room still naked, but her toenails are nicely clipped. Her chocolate skin shines with perspiration.

Well, she says. What's up?

Raúl looks at María. Her wide brown hips and the large inverted triangle of black hair between her muscular thighs make Raúl hard and he quickly sits down before María and it are able to notice.

María, Raúl says. Get a robe on or something. The windows are open.

María yawns and stretches her arms up over her head. This makes her breasts bounce just a little. Raúl grows harder.

María, please, says Raúl. For me.

El tiempo perdido no se recupera jamás, she says with a lascivious smile and walks slowly to the bedroom.

I know, says Raúl. But this is not the time. I need to deal with it.

It is still lapping up the applesauce while making a sound that is a cross between a purr and a dentist's drill.

María comes back into the kitchen wearing a tiny Mel Tormé T-shirt, but her bottom is still naked. She plops down on one of the chairs and leans close to it while it slurps the applesauce. The perspiration on her buttocks makes it difficult to shift on the vinyl seat cushion without her skin sticking and making an unpleasant sound.

It's very nice, María says.

That's not the point, says Raúl. It will grow, like the other one, and then we're going to have trouble. Don't you remember?

El que no arriesga, no pasa el charco, she mumbles, avoiding Raúl's eyes.

You're full of dichos this morning, Raúl says. It's not a matter of taking risks or gaining anything. We already know what's going to happen if we don't deal with it now.

Raúl turns to it. Finished? he asks it.

It nods, wiping applesauce from its large pink lips.

Ask its name, says María.

You're here. You ask it.

What's your name? asks María.

It answers and smiles at María's breasts.

I like that name, says María. Bender. Bender.

It's a stupid name, says Raúl.

It laps up the last of the applesauce, ignoring Raúl's insult.

Oh, look! It finished, says María.

Good, says Raúl. Time to go.

It opens its eyes as wide as it can.

Time to go, repeats Raúl. María feels a pang of sadness.

It looks at Raúl. It looks at María. It lets out a sigh. Slowly and with great effort, it leaps from the table and lands on the hardwood floor with a thump. Raúl and María do not move. It shuffles to the front door and manages to open it. It lurks in the doorway for a moment looking forlorn.

Well? asks Raúl. What are you waiting for?

It sighs before turning and slamming the door behind itself. The sound reverberates throughout the room.

Raúl and María sit silently staring at the closed door.

There, says Raúl. It's done.

Yes, says María. It's done.

María stands up and walks back to the bedroom. The floorboards creak under her bare feet. It's done, she says again.

Raúl sits at the kitchen table with his hands folded as if in prayer. A gardener starts up his leaf blower and the motorized roar invades the apartment through the open windows like a reckless burglar. After a few minutes, Raúl stands and picks up the empty bowl and places it gently into the sink. He then closes the applesauce jar and puts it back into the refrigerator.

It's done, he says again to no one in particular. Raúl turns and walks to the bedroom where María already lies in bed waiting for him. The floorboards creak under his bare feet.

SWEET TIME

Lisa Alvarez

Bayshore Harbor is like other hospitals in that the administration thoughtfully provides enough clocks so we can see just how fast or how slow time is passing, how much is gone, how much may be left. Our mother though, as usual, is defiant. Audrey is taking, as she liked to complain of others, her own sweet time. The landlord took his sweet time fixing the heater. The mechanic took his sweet time with the alternator. The boss took his sweet time cutting her paycheck, she explained to the landlord. The post office took its sweet time delivering her alimony payment, she complained to the mechanic. Sweet time. The bartender took his sweet time pouring her drink. Her latest man took his sweet time calling back. Sweet time put Audrey out, made her wait. And now we wait for her. Her sweet time. And we, my sister Cassie and I, are, with every clock's help, marking it. We wait on the fourth-floor terrace, the only place beyond the reach of the mounted clocks.

"This is," I say, "the only goddamn thing she's ever done slowly." Cassie stiffens and I realize that I've hurt her though I didn't mean to.

"What time is it?" I ask, as if I haven't complained about our mother's unseemly loitering. Which, of course, Audrey isn't doing at all. Not yet anyway. I'm simply anticipating the inevitable.

Cassie swivels her left wrist to check her watch. It is of a modest, sensible design. The tiny face is as big as her thumbnail. She bought it for herself.

When I need to know what time it is and a public clock is not available, I glance at people's wrists and try to decipher the hour and minute. The old-fashioned faces are easier than the digital ones. I don't like to ask, but sometimes people catch me looking and I have to. My sister's watch, however, is too small for me to read.

I don't wear a watch, though I remember as a child wanting my own, just as I wanted my birthstone, a sapphire, glinting on a ring. And a charm bracelet jangling on my scrawny wrist. Other girls told time by locating Mickey Mouse's white gloved hands, proudly revealed their birth months by flashing red, blue, and green gemstones and recounted trips to Disneyland and Sea World, San Francisco, and nearby Mexico as they fingered miniature Tinkerbells and dolphins, trolley cars and sombreros. Soon enough I learned not to want Snow White watches and souvenir jewelry. I looked, I admired, but I did not desire. I learned to ask for nothing and to expect less. I learned the difference between want and need. I needed very little. That hasn't changed.

But it's not like my life, then or now, fills with appointments or deadlines or occasions. Any honest charm bracelet from my childhood would either be a slack, bare chain or else ornamented with tiny martini glasses, televisions, slot machines, pistols, police cars, and dented automobiles. Who would have tooled such tiny mementos? Who else would have purchased them?

Out on the hospital terrace, our backs to the round cement tables and their umbrellas as festive as those stuck in tropical drinks, my sister Cassie smokes a cigarette she knows she shouldn't. Usually she's the first to scold herself, but today she cuts herself some slack. She's already stubbed out two in the squat pillar of sand provided for that purpose. She stands while I pace the cement slab terrace, which protrudes, a wide, compliant tongue. She's looking at the view, as you're supposed to do. That's the point of elevated terraces, especially in places like this, but me—*me*—I watch how my feet measure the cement squares. My black flats and brown feet against the gray. I watch our dim reflections in the glass doors. My sister's slim back, my own slouching profile.

"Was I born here?" she asks. It's a funny question for most people, but not for us. Except for a rare moment like this one when she sounds like a kid sister, like a teenager, like a sibling who turns to an elder for an answer, Cassie generally appears as if she's leapfrogged over her twenties past her youth and landed somewhere deep inside her thirties, anxious for middle age. Her sudden maturity is abetted by her choice of outfit, a two-piece pastel skirt suit with a silky blouse that ties in a bow at the neck. Nylons. Short-heeled pumps in the same inoffensive blue as her suit. She's pinned a gold brooch of indefinite shape to her lapel. Her make-up is comprehensive but subdued, none of the dazzle young women her age are apt to adopt.

I shake my head. "Audrey worked here, that's all," I tell her. "You were born at Harbor View." I move toward where she allows herself to lean against the railing and gesture widely toward the docks, the downtown tangle of warehouses and commerce, the spidery snarl of power lines and cables strung above and between it. There are two hospitals in San Pedro. This is the better one. You can stand, as we do, on the elevated terrace of one and see the windows of the other. Bayshore Harbor, where we are, has the view but Harbor View County has the name. San Pedro is all slope, a wide, sweeping descent from the hill that is Palos Verdes to the oily rim of the L.A. harbor.

There is quite a view after all from the sixth-floor terrace of the intensive care unit at Bayshore Harbor General, a harbor view. I try to locate some detail of our past to point out to Cassie, to distract her. I consider the lighthouse; old Fort MacArthur; the brick face of the junior high that I attended and she did not, its playground devoid of students and filled instead with hungry gulls doing the job of the janitors, feeding on the food left behind; the old Grand Theater on Sixth; the pink units of the Rancho housing projects where we lived once, twice, three times; the distant flags on the slow-moving tankers. But I choose San Pedro's most obvious feature: the Vincent Thomas Bridge.

"I've always liked that bridge," I say, pointing to the green span. It's true. I did. I do. It's no Golden Gate, but there's something about a suspension bridge, its soaring defiance, even if it really takes you nowhere, like the Vincent Thomas does: picking you up at the heel of San Pedro and depositing you on the bleak industrial flats of Terminal Island.

This doesn't work. My sister is not some tourist and my delivery, well, lacked conviction though the bridge is nice enough, especially at night when it's lit like a necklace. It makes you look up and away from where you are.

"Is this where my father died?" Cassie asks, though she looks obligingly enough at the bridge.

"I never thought about it," I tell her.

It's the truth. Until she asked, it hadn't occurred to me that Glen Cassidy may have been taken here that night. I suppose he was.

"Could be, either here or Harbor View," I say. "Audrey would know." I could tell her that Glen probably arrived DOA, having expired at the intersection of Gaffey and Sixth, just up the street from the old theater, equidistant from both hospitals and a block from where Phil Stanley found our mother, but I don't. I suppose it's better to die in a hospital on a gurney surrounded by health care professionals rather than on the asphalt surrounded by strangers. "He was probably here though," I decide to add. I figure it's better to die at the better hospital with the better view than in the noisy pungent halls of the county ward. But I'm too late.

"It's not important. I was just wondering. You know." She smiles a bit and keeps her eyes on the bridge. It's always been green, the minerally green that grows in the crevices of some old pennies.

"He'd take me over it, the bridge, your father would," I say, still trying to salvage the moment. "Just for fun. In his red truck." Cassie has heard about the red truck before. It's one of the few details about her father that I can offer her. I have to be careful. Some are acceptable. The truck. His sideburns. His love of Neil Diamond. Some are not. His drinking. His gun. How he left us just like all the others.

When my sister finally takes her eyes off the bridge and looks at me, I see what the hospital wants from our mother. Cassie has them too. She didn't get her father's.

Audrey's eyes. Her green eyes. They'll end up in somebody else's head. Two hours earlier I had printed "green" in the box marked "eye color."

The admitting doctor, a man named Davenport, had already discreetly brought up organ donation. That told me all I needed to know. Begin saying goodbye now, he advised. And consider signing the organ donation form, he added.

There's not much else to say now. Cassie and I watch the tankers, the gray-tipped wings of white gulls. Cassie smokes. I pace. The shadows of the two umbrellas move like huge sunglasses across the pavement.

We're waiting, waiting to hear how long.

Not how long she'll live. We know, more or less, about that. It is, the staff agrees, a matter of time. If Audrey's heart and the rest of her organs were in better condition, chances of a limited recovery would be improved.

Still, that morning the doctor did push organ donation. He added the form to my stack.

"You're kidding," I had replied. "Something works?"

He winced.

That was earlier, before Cassie arrived, back when I could barely finish the sentences I began in the emergency room. But those questions, those two came out before I could stop them. Other questions, simpler ones, more difficult ones, were not so easy to ask.

"How long," I had asked Davenport, "how long did she . . ." My right hand made a spreading motion, as if I were smoothing a wrinkle in the air. At that point, after my shocked outburst about the startling viability of my mother's vital organs, the doctor wanted to finish with me and move on to someone else. I could tell. But I had to know.

And Davenport knew what I wanted to know; he knew the end of my question even if I couldn't get there myself. "We won't know for awhile," he said, "and besides, that's not important. What's important is that she's here and you're here and we're going to find out what we can do to make your mother as comfortable as possible and we're going to do just that."

That was hours ago. Hospital hours. Long ones measured in breaths and heartbeats and clocks and my sister's cigarettes, slim, smoked to the filter and kissed by her frosty pink lipstick.

Both Cassie and I are waiting for the answer to my stuttered question, the one that Davenport recognized and brushed away.

We're waiting to hear how long our mother lay there unconscious in her one-room apartment, how long before Phil, the landlord, became disturbed by her absence. We're waiting to find out how bad it was, how bad we were.

■

I had done my big sister best to break it to Cassie, as they say, easy. She is, after all, still my baby sister. She calls Audrey "Mom." Not me. I'm not that generous.

"Where are you?" she asked after I'd give her the rundown, such as it was. There wasn't much to report.

"At the hospital," I told her, though I was sure I had already mentioned this fact. Except for me, the shiny bank of pay phones was unoccupied. But all around, echoing from the nurses' stations and patients' rooms, telephones rang, answered and unanswered, blending in with the industrial chorus of machines and workers, the noise a single building and the people in it can make when everyone and everything is being used. It was loud and quiet at the same time. A noisy hush. The clock on the wall told me the time whether I wanted to know or not.

"I cut my hair," she blurted, her voice hard in my ear. "You're not going to like it," she continued. "Mom'll like it but you won't."

"Cassie," I said. Perhaps it was easier for her to talk about her hair. Maybe this was what the experts call shock.

"I know you're going to hate it," she declared.

"Cassie, I want you to come to the hospital now, OK?"

"My haircut. Mom hasn't seen it yet," she said. "I was going to drop by this week."

"Just come," I told her. "I'll be waiting for you on the sixth floor." I hung up and returned to the lounge. I watched while others disappeared, following nurses down the hallways. It was a version of "Ten Little Indians" that never quite played out. Before the lounge could empty, another always arrived and took a seat with the shocked decorum that seemed to mark us all. I sat where I could see the elevator doors open and close and discharge passengers. I waited for my sister with her newly-coifed hair to become one of them. I practiced what I might say. I pretended to be an Indian, a polite survivor of the waiting lounge, and remembered the first time when I was an Indian, a Thanksgiving play in first grade. The teacher plaited my hair into two long braids and, like all the other squaws, I was speechless. We were all suspiciously Mexican and each toted two ears of corn, one in each hand, held up as if surrendering. Our hair, I heard the teacher exclaim, was just perfect.

Cassie had indeed cut the long blonde hair that I once braided, though no one would ever cast my little sister as an Indian. "I like it," I told her as I rose to greet her, even though I didn't. I was surprised at how much older the short feathery cap made her.

"Really?" A small smile transformed her otherwise worried face. Cassie can't resist a compliment even though she never goes looking for one. When she smiles, I see our mother in her cheeks, those eyes, that easy blonde beauty.

"You look my age," I go on.

Her smile disappeared. "Everyone is wearing their hair short," she said. "Not just me."

I nodded. We stood in the lounge. Sofas. Tables. A prominent clock. A television suspended above our heads in the far corner. On screen, people sat in chairs and spoke energetically, waving their arms, pointing, accusing each other. The family resemblance to each other was sadly obvious. Thankfully, someone had turned the sound down.

Cassie had landed a clerical position in the Harbor Division of the L.A. Police Department. She has a desk and her own telephone extension. When I called her this morning, she answered the phone and said, "Cassidy Vincent, Community Policing Unit, can I help you?"

My little sister now resembles a particular contingent of the flower shop's clientele. Low-level professional women, skin faded to the color of those file folders they shuffle all day, the ladies who my high school sociology textbook referred to as "pink collar." They stop by the shop on the way home to buy themselves flowers, choosing the sale blooms and jealously monitoring me to make sure their bargain bouquets rate ribbons and bows, plenty of greenery to fill out a vase. I imagine how these strong, lonely women carefully remove each bow, how their cool irons press out the ribbons so that they can used again. Perhaps, like Cassie, their paychecks go only so far. The rest of the way is up to them.

"They let you off work OK?" I asked.

She nodded.

"What are you waiting for?" Cassie asked me. She put her purse down on the nearby end table but remained standing. The toes of her sensible shoes were bluntly squared, grown-up shoes that matched the right angles and sober colors of the lounge.

"They told me to wait."

"Who?"

"The nurse." I pointed. I was willing to wait. At this point, I was willing to do whatever they told me. I offered up the clipboard and the forms with which I had made little progress.

Cassie crossed the corridor and approached the nurse at the station. She identified herself and began asking questions. At one point, Cassie moved her head in my direction. Her eyes and the nurse's simultaneously swiveled toward me. Cassie whispered something and the nurse nodded. It was becoming clear to her now. It was all making sense.

Nearly an hour earlier, the same nurse, a woman perhaps of my mother's age, had suggested that I take a seat until my sister arrived. Her demeanor implied that I was being uncooperative. But I wasn't. I just found it difficult or impossible to answer her questions, most of which required either unknown decisions or unknown information. While I did fine with the simple stuff—eye color, hair, height, address—other information eluded me. Past medical history? Allergies? Living will? Organ donation? Resuscitation? Do not resuscitate? It didn't help that the nurse first spoke to me entirely in rapid Spanish that rolled like marbles dropped on a slick floor.

"No, no," I told her. "No hablo español, sólo inglés."

The nurse had paused and considered me carefully, her broad face as powdery and pale as a biscuit. She was trying to figure out how she'd made the mistake. I'd seen this look before. My skin, my color, my name, yes, but there was something else too, bones, expression, attitude. The traces of The Girl behind the counter, ready to take orders and do what's wanted, the first-grade Indian with her hands full of corn. For the nurse, it all added up to the Spanish language. Spanish. That was the nicest name I was called when I was growing up, as if the language one spoke was what one was. But I, of course, didn't speak Spanish. Somehow that didn't change anything for me back then, me the beaner, the wetback, the Mexican, the spic, the Spanish girl. No matter who said them, none of them sounded very nice.

The nurse began again in American English, this white woman who was, no doubt, trying her best to be nice, who had, no doubt, taken evening classes to become bilingual and earn more money only to have me undermine her efforts.

Cassie relayed more information to her. The nurse nodded, then their gazes slid to the clipboard on the counter. I had been dealt with, our unlikely sisterhood explained. Cassie had, no doubt, made up for my shortcomings, provided reassurance where I had only offered doubt and anxiety.

Somehow, in the past couple years, Cassie had acquired a self-assurance I had yet to achieve. She understood this and moved to fill the gap between my abilities and the expectations of the rest of the world, which were, at this moment, personified in the competent figure of the bilingual nurse.

I heard her ask about the private room that Audrey had been assigned to, if Medicare covered it.

The nurse said something. Cassie nodded.

She turned and walked toward me with the clipboard. "We've got some decisions to make," she announced, tossing her head back, as if her hair were still long like mine and needed to be pushed out of her way.

■

Some kind of seizure, inducing organ failure. And—Cassie read this part aloud carefully—sounding out the syllables like a child learning compound words, *acute hemorrhagic pancreatitis.*

We've returned to the lounge. There's just us two. Two Little Indians. As Cassie reads passages aloud from the paperwork, a laborious process, I decide to turn off the television. Though someone has already hushed the sound, even so, I still stare at the screen, and so does Cassie, when she isn't busy deciphering medical jargon. It's a soap opera set at a hospital, medical melodrama—cover meetings in the linen supply closet, feverish junkie orderlies. A family gathers to weep at the bedside of an ailing teenage girl, her head swaddled in bandages. A nurse moistens her lips with her tongue over and over while riding in an elevator with a handsome, shy doctor who wears a prominent wedding band and glances at his watch when the elevator slows. I fear for the young doctor's virtue even though I think I should empathize with the nurse who is forced, no doubt, to use her feminine wiles in order to succeed in a man's world. Mostly, I despise the television itself, how the world within it goes on without a burp, a smug reproach to everything outside it. It hangs above us, suspended out of reach. My eyes follow the cord down the wall to the outlet.

Since I can't reach the dial, and don't want to approach the nurse, I crawl under a table to unplug it. Cassie watches me.

"Do you have to do that?" she asks, her voice low.

"Yes," I reply from under the table. One tug does the job. The moment of release is accompanied by sparks.

"I don't believe you," Cassie says. "I really cannot believe you sometimes."

"Sorry," I say, resuming my seat, the screen now satisfyingly blank.

"You didn't have to watch it," she says.

"I couldn't help it," I say.

She returns to the papers. "What about esophageal varices?" asks Cassie. "Have you ever heard of it?"

"No," I say. "Never."

"Fine," she says, shuffling the papers together and capping her pen. "I'll just wait for the doctor." She looks around the lounge. It's a living room with too many couches and chairs. I understand another reason why people bring flowers and plants to a hospital. The place needs it.

Cassie reaches for a magazine. "I wish you hadn't done that with the television," she says. "Now look what I have to read. It's old." She holds up a glossy housekeeping magazine advertising a Halloween theme. "I've already read it. Last year."

"Nobody's making you," I tell her.

"I'm not like you," she says, flipping open the magazine. "I can't just sit here."

But she does. Even though she flips the pages and peruses the articles, feigns interest in the sweatery fashions and the ten-minute dinner menus, my sister just sits there, as I do. Our thoughts are down the hall, or so we imagine, in the room with our mother who waits or doesn't, who, for the first time in our lives, simply is.

■

When the doctor shows up, a short time after I have disabled the television, Cassie is ready. The magazine is tossed on the tabletop and the clipboard is across her lap. She introduces herself, again slipping into the role of responsible daughter, the spokesperson for the family, all two of us.

"You've met my sister," she adds, gesturing my way. I nod and the doctor glances at me. His double take is less pronounced than was the nurse's. His steady blue eyes just take us both in.

"What is acute hemorrhagic pancreatitis?" Cassie asks. Dr. Davenport seems impressed. I guess her pronunciation is good.

He smiles now. He pulls a chair closer to where we sit.

Cassie returns his smile.

He leans toward us, clasping his hands.

"It's what happens," he explains, "when the liver ceases functioning.

When it," he looks at me, as though I might have difficulty following him and require this simpler translation, "stops doing its job." I consider the fact that Dr. Davenport might have seen me crawl under the table. It's what Cassie fears. Shame. Embarrassment. She's had enough already. Me, I don't care. I know what people think doesn't matter—that is, I know there's little you can do to stop them from thinking what they want.

I nod and he goes on.

"The pancreas takes over at that point. But it can only do it for so long and then . . ." He opens his hands, palms out. "This development is not uncommon in, uh, such advanced cases."

"Advanced cases?" My question leaps. I have to ask, even though I recognize a euphemism when it's used on me. I have to ask, even if I know the answer. I want someone to say it, even if Audrey can't hear. This is the part of me that unplugs televisions in public spaces. This is the part of me that crawls under tables to do it. This is the part of me that doesn't care what people think. This is the part of me that was an unsuccessful waitress so many times. The part of me that resists The Girl. My big mouth. I got it from my mother, though I don't use it that much. Only when it can hurt, it seems.

"Yes. Advanced. Alcoholism."

Professional that he is, he's uncomfortable. His whole face stiffens noticeably. His gray eyebrows, which presided amiably enough over his blue eyes, drop. Perhaps he's embarrassed for us, these two nice young women. Or perhaps he feels just for Cassie and not for me. After all, I asked the impolite question. I was the one under the table disabling the television. And Cassie, I've noted, generally appears more deserving of sympathy. Unlike me, Cassie is incapable of suspicion.

Twenty years ago this man might have accompanied my mother home one night, the gold band on his stubby ring finger or not. He might have been one of those men who carried me in his arms to my room, closed the door and returned to where she waited. By then she would have restored her mouth with fresh lipstick and begun mixing drinks. For a man like this, a professional, the kind with a clean, paid-for car and clean fingernails, only the best. She'd search out the Glenlivet or Royal Canadian, bottles she pushed to the back for special occasions. She'd let him do what he wanted, all the while hoping it was enough. I scan his name tag again—Davenport—his aging good looks, a rugged but spare face tanned from golf or tennis, sailing, or open sea fishing, a lean physique, buffed fingernails with white moons rising in unison from the cuticles. I am looking for a memory as I do when searching out our former homes.

Does Davenport suspect anything? Of course, Audrey bears that ridiculous surname now. Jubilee. And landlord Phil referred to her as a widow. Only her first name remained constant through the years. But the connection between the vibrant, willing woman she was and the desiccated figure she became is hard for even me to see, let alone someone who, like the good doctor, might have caressed her once, twice, never imagining how she could change, how time would take back what it had given. But which lover does? I think of those young men I knew fifteen years ago, the backseat boys with their smooth shoulders newly broadened, the slim hips and firm jaw lines. The guys who crept the streets in their big cars and waited for slow-walking girls like me to look twice and smile, to look up and look willing. We were.

Who are those boys now in the daylight of adulthood? Perhaps I drove past them today or sold them flowers last week. Maybe the young man who has spent the morning with his aging father, the one with the prematurely graying hair and the lanky build, maybe he once offered me beer, a drive to the beach, an ear, a shoulder, a good time. Maybe he gave me all those.

I wouldn't know any of them if I met them today. I doubt they'd know me, either. You remember different things. You imagine different things when they're moving under or over you. You don't imagine how they'll end up or, if you do, you don't fathom a fate like our mother's.

"How long have you been at Bay?" I ask Davenport. I'm chasing my intuition, counting years, measuring how something begins to shift in him whenever he looks at Cassie. My sister is the same kind of big blond our mother was, but fresher, less flashy, her lips a soft pink. With her legs crossed, her modest skirt reveals more than intended.

But Davenport takes it wrong. "Cases like your mother's don't generally require a second opinion, but . . ."

"That's not what I meant," I say. "I'm just curious, that's all. How long have you worked here?"

Now they both look at me, Cassie with a weariness I recognize all too well, Davenport with a look that suggests that I am not rising in his estimation. Some questions should not be asked by a thirty-year-old woman.

After a certain age, apparently, one should not be idly curious. It implies a certain lack of maturity, an absence of decorum. No wristwatch. A person who doesn't know what time it is and has to ask. The Girl never asks questions.

"I've been at Bay for twenty-five years," he says. He glances down at his jacket. My eyes follow his. The fine weave of his lapel is pierced by a tiny gold pin, the kind given to denote service. A green jewel winks from the center.

"That must be wonderful," Cassie says. She means it. She goes on to explain how she's hoping for the same kind of career commitment from the police department. "Of course, I'm not a doctor," she continues, "or even an officer, but . . . who knows? I'm just starting out." She is, of course, making up for me. It works.

If Cassie is impressed by him, so is he by her. They exchange small smiles. Me, I count the years, shuffling through the friends and boyfriends, the husbands, the so-called fiancés and the one-night stands, as if their faces survived in some deck of ancient playing cards. Jacks, kings, aces, jokers. Spades, diamonds, clubs, and hearts. Davenport could be a card in the deck. Selected but played, with his own consent, early. He's the type. His smile switches on, switches off. He takes everything in. He knows his place, his power. He flirts with a dying woman's daughter as a matter of routine. He knows what he wants and what he wants to give in order to get it. Not so different from Audrey herself. I begin to think that the bashful doctor in the soap opera, the one in the elevator wearing the ring, was just feigning timid fidelity, all along knowing how attractive women find a man who's already taken.

I excuse myself before I smirk or otherwise further misbehave. "Be right back," I promise, though my intention is to wait out Davenport. I wander down the hall to the terrace, now occupied by two smokers, the father and son I'd seen earlier, the man who could have been my parking-lot lover. The man I silently identified as the father and husband looks up and nods. We're old friends now. At his side is his son, a young man who inherited his broad shoulders, lanky stature, and smoking habits. They're waiting for news about his wife, his mother. I didn't ask, but I didn't have to. Through the hours, such details become part of the public record. They know about my mother. I know about theirs.

I let them have the view and slide instead onto the cement bench, taking the shade of one of the umbrellas. The two wear nearly identical clothing, the uniform of the working class Latino, plaid shirts the color of old leaves tucked into chinos washed almost white, barely rumpled by today's labor considering they began their hospital vigil before noon. White cotton T-shirts peek out from their necklines. Their clothes are clean and ironed, though softened by age and work, pressed and washed, perhaps by the woman who had suffered the heart attack. Wife and mother.

I haven't seen her, of course, but I can imagine what else she may have given her son. It's a game I play. To get one parent, look in the mirror and subtract the other. It's not perfect math, but it works well enough. The son can thank his mother for his healthy hairline at the same time he may blame her for the premature gray that undermines its vitality. And those cheekbones rising like arrows almost to his eyes. But aside from that, he is mostly his father. They bend now at the hips and lean on the railing, smoke trailing behind them, two lean grim men with not much to say to one another. I see now that the wife, the mother, is the one who talks, the one who makes them talk to each other. Without her, they don't know how to begin. Perhaps they worry that this is what life without her will hold for them—silence, cigarettes.

My own mother was stingy with me, her firstborn, withholding the hereditary grace, the large bosom, the blond hair and fair skin. My father's rod-shaped chromosomes filled in the blanks abdicated by Audrey—aided, of course, by the natural dominance of Latin darkness over the singular passive attribute in my mother's make-up—her recessive and pale Northern European roots. So, although I never knew my father, I experience the world through him, colored by his potent Latin ancestry. My broad forehead. My black hair. My brown eyes. My skin the color of tree bark. My exceptionally high cholesterol count. His name, four musical syllables, imported from Mexico, a place I've never been. *San. Ti. A. Go.*

I have seen only one photograph of my father. In it, he stands beside Audrey and they both smile dutifully for the camera. They don't appear to touch each other, or if they do, it's behind Audrey's back, where her hands disappear from sight, perhaps to meet my father's left hand. But cameras can't see through matter to reveal what's hidden or, if lenses could, I would know whether my parents held hands or not and I could perhaps see myself, curling alive inside, hidden from all but my mother. How I wished as a child when I studied that photo, that they did hold hands. How I wanted them to be affectionate, to be unable to keep their hands off each other and for me to be a product of their love. But my father never wanted children of his own. Or so Audrey always said. He wanted a wife. That's all. And, like so many men, he didn't even know he wanted that until he met Audrey.

In the photo, Audrey looks young, her mouth made red, her short blond hair curled. Her sleeveless shirtdress is white, sprinkled with polka dots the size and color of pennies. Her narrow waist is banded by a belt and four loops of pearls perfectly fill the modest V neckline. Red toenails blink through her flat white sandals. Her legs are bare. It's summer and she squints ever so slightly, her full mouth pinched by the effort to hold the simple pose under the glare.

My father, standing beside her, is solid and dark. Tall. Older. Combed back from his broad forehead, his black hair is a gleaming wave. His brown skin shines like mine in the sun, a thin patina of oil catching the light on the brow, the cheeks, the nose. The white button-down shirt is tight across a powerful chest and tucked neatly into his dark trousers. The toes of his shoes point out, down the cement path.

The three cement steps behind them lead to a white single-story bungalow I can't remember, though occasionally, in my neighborhood cruises, I have tried to locate it. A red straight-backed chair waits on the slab porch. Venetian blinds hang in the windows. Trimmed shrubs grow from hard-packed dirt and the lawn is scant but mowed and edged. A slice of driveway reveals the rear fender of an old Plymouth sedan. The car has been carefully backed into the driveway, so exit will be easy.

It was 1960, somewhere in Los Angeles. That much I know. My mother has recently become Mrs. Richard Santiago. She tells my father it was her second marriage. I know it is, at the very least, her fourth. But who's counting? Audrey is, as she probably reminds herself, settling for something less than she deserves. But she is thirty, though she tells my father and anyone else who asks twenty-six. My mother is good with numbers. Very good. But even she knows the inevitable product of nine months. The pregnancy is stubborn. And besides, these days, many, many people, Audrey no doubt consoles herself, are marrying Mexicans—or are even Mexicans themselves. Ricardo Montalban. Rita Hayworth. Anthony Quinn. Vikki Carr.

The photo was there for years, like so many things, in a drawer or a closeted shoebox. Once it resided in the medicine cabinet filed away, unlikely enough, in a Band-Aid tin, and then, one day, it wasn't. I knew better than to ask where it had gone. Besides, I'd studied it so often that I can, even now, years later, conjure it up for myself as I watch a man and his son who know each other so well that they don't need photographs to remind them of the features they share and the ones they do not. Of course, people like them have plenty anyway, framed, hung in places of honor in their homes, fattening thin-with-cash wallets with the smiles of school photos and studio shots.

In the photo of my parents, the Southern California sun shines and the ephemeral newlywed Santiagos smile into the Brownie camera. Years later, their daughter wonders who they were smiling for. I wonder who my parents imagined would cherish this photograph with its wavy white border, its oddly tinted colors. Who did they imagine would look at it? Who would recognize Richard and Audrey? Who would know why they stood together and where exactly they were? Who would care? Me?

LAX CONFIDENTIAL
Rudy Ch. Garcia

The headline on February 20 read "Hunter S.T., 67, Author, Commits Suicide," which didn't surprise me as much as the first thing I thought of. Would *he* reappear now?

Not Hunter S., of course. I meant one of his old "friends." One that had mysteriously disappeared back in '74 off the coast of Baja, the "Samoan" in one of his books. The *vato* who had·maybe even invented gonzo lit.

Not that I knew what gonzo meant, or cared; I had never read any of it. Not even back when I first took a shot at tracking down the *vato* worth fifty grand to some unknown party. All I knew was that fifty thou was a lot of bread, as we said back then. I didn't know what the *vato* had done to deserve the bounty, but I knew I deserved to collect it. That's what I do between real low-paying jobs. Hunt down people.

In the late seventies, I'd put out feelers around San Diego and L.A., including over on the Tijuana side. My gut feeling told me I should sprinkle a few twenties here and there to pushers, snitches, and some LAPD as an investment. Turned out to be a bad one. All I got in return at the time were collect calls asking for more of my twenties and vague assurances of sightings. They all turned into caca.

So why had the suicide headline resparked my gut feeling? I didn't know for sure, but I had to do something or it would act up as much as my ulcer, not leaving me alone unless I applied something soothing to it.

I did what any half-assed, part-time sort-of-detective-without-a-license would do. I took out an ad in the *L.A.Times* under the Personals, Women Seeking Men. "Vata Buscando Old Samoan" was all I could think of. I didn't flesh it out much, so it only cost me a single twenty for a change, and at least my gut stopped bothering me.

I only had to disappoint one male who really was ethnic Samoan. Actually, he wasn't disappointed I wasn't female; I guess he went at least two ways. He was just pissed I didn't live in the L.A. area.

I'd already considered my options, made plans. I'd checked that the blood money was still out there—now up to 75K. I'd fly standby and keep my expenses down. But I decided if I got any kind of real nibble, I'd have to head west.

A week later, *he* called, sounding not at all like someone from the South Pacific. He left a voice message: "I know you're probably working for them, pero a mí, ya no me importa. The pinche cowboy's dead. That's what matters, as you undoubtedly know. Meet me at the _____ Motel by LAX Saturday night at ten. Don't keep me waiting."

The voice on the machine was gruff like an old alkie, raspy like a confirmed smoker, and the accent sounded college-educated mixed with *puro mexicano*. I was about to find out what twenty dollars had bought me.

■

I caught the plane Friday to make sure I didn't get bumped at the last minute. Problem was, now I was stuck with an extra day of expenses in one of the most free-spending societies on the planet.

People go to L.A. for the Hollywood shit, the beaches, Dizzyland, etc. All the times I'd been there, I'd never seen the insides of any tourist trap. It was usually fly in, pick up a package or a bail jumper, and fly out. Suited me fine. I hated L.A., Southern California, the beach-blonde-bimbo culture and the cool-sounding West Coast jargon and arrogance the natives emitted. Reminds me of Texans—another one of God's gifts—just a different accent.

When I reached the terminal, I checked the marquee showing hotels and motels nearby. I planned to stay my first night where he'd told me to meet him. The photo on the wall only showed the motel drive-up, but looked clean enough. I didn't even have to stay my first night there if they were all booked, since I'd already made my reservation for Saturday. Now I just had to find a cheap way to kill the rest of Friday, lugging around my lone backpack.

I knew better than to rent a car; I'd gotten carsick one time, trying to learn and maneuver the highway system. But I also knew cabbing around too much would kill me. Venice Beach was only a few miles away, so I figured I could hang around there until nighttime. A cab dropped me off right at Ocean Front Walk. The smog quality to the air made mockery of the California sunshine in all those old Beach Boys songs.

The palm trees, sand, Pacific Ocean, and bikinis almost made you believe you'd found some fabulous place, somewhere that only let the coolest people walk down its cement boardwalk. They sell a better caliber of junk on that strip than other places I've been. And some nice artwork and craft stuff. But I couldn't help feeling that, except for families of tourists, the beach groupies and the weightlifter klatch, nobody knew anybody.

Not much else to tell. I ate and drank a few things. Bought some handmade trinkets my nephews would enjoy. If I'd had a fatter wallet, I would've picked up more, like others around me who seemed to believe purchasing a piece from Venice, California, would somehow make their lives purer, better. I finally took a nap out on the grass under a palm and wondered whether my own life would be better after that weekend. Seventy-five grand better.

I waited until seven to head to the motel, hoping the worst of the traffic would be over with. It almost was.

After paying for one night, I followed the clerk's directions into a huge, tunnel-like hallway. Halfway through I realized the place was transform-ing—from the prim accommodations captured in the airport photo into a scene that wouldn't have made it into Quentin's cut of *Reservoir Dogs*—for lack of taste. If I'd only gotten just a little more pissed off at that point, I would have turned around and demanded my money back. Luckily, I decided not to pay attention to my gut.

The place looked bad. The smell was worse. And the noise. (I never did find out how the motel had earned a marquee spot at LAX. Cultural inertia, I suppose.)

If someone had swept a few hundred feet of Denver's East Colfax, or scraped up some of the old side streets off Times Square, or airlifted a block of Juárez on a Saturday night when the college boys shell out money for Mondo Cane—none of that would've felt out of place in what I entered in the central so-called pool area of this degraded stopover.

The pool itself would've passed for La Brea Tar Pits, it was so black, with a few feet of what had mostly been water maybe, at one time. The floating beer and whiskey bottles and cans were sinking much as the saber-tooths once had. But this pit smelled like prehistorics that hadn't completed the rotting stage. Or maybe the odor came from the people.

The residents of this oasis proved that not everyone made it in Lalaland. I didn't have to see any IDs to know these people had come from everywhere, from all over the world. But they had flunked the all-American-success-story exam or had never been allowed to take it, maybe because of their accents, because of their skin, or maybe just because Californey needed to pummel people into this condition to hold up the other, beautiful-people culture. A jet very low overhead leaving LAX made me flinch.

I can't tell you all of what went on there. I didn't have to see exchanges of money and little bags to know I could probably have gotten anything illegal there. Nor did I have to hear the price for twenty minutes with what looked like the hardest ridden, oldest, and unluckiest collection of prostitutes you'd never want to meet, to know that some of the rooms probably even specialized in WMDs or illicit harvesting of vital organs. It wouldn't have surprised me.

I would have left then, except I thought it might be more dangerous to turn around to find someone behind me than to continue to my room. Upstairs, I could see a very angry man slap a large woman across the face. She returned his affection with a brown-bagged bottle that smashed and wet his bloodied cheek. Then they made up and went into their room.

A couple of clients who passed me gave me that "I wish I hadn't already eaten" look, like I was a holiday ham. I pushed out my chest, tightened my stomach, and assumed my tough-detective grimace. I avoided locking on anyone's eyes. It didn't do much good; my legs wobbled, threatening to drop me in the middle of hyena country.

The key stuck bad in the door, and by the time I shut it, I had to tighten my fists to stop from shaking. I didn't switch on the light; just grabbed a chair I could see by the light coming through the blinds and jammed it under the doorknob. Waist-high, a three-inch-diameter hole went right through the hollow door. I could hear beds banging walls and stereos and televisions blasting from other rooms. Most of the profanity coming through was too muffled to make out.

I sat on the bed, wondering what the hell I'd done to myself, whether I'd make it through the night, and realizing that seventy-five grand wasn't really that much money. I'd have been a lot better off getting a ticket for napping all night on Venice Beach.

Before I could decide whether to forget it all and try to make a dash for the relative safety of the lobby, a chair shifted behind me. I realized the cigarette-smoke smell was fresh, unlike the other reeking from the room. And the husky breathing to my rear was no air conditioner, as I'd first hoped. I reached for the switchblade I'd bought on the Walk and remembered I'd stupidly stuck it in the backpack. I let out a "Shit!" and groped at the bag.

"Forget it. You won't need it. I'm not carrying." It was the voice from my message machine. "Want a shot of Presidente? I got us some ice and clean glasses."

I didn't want to say anything until I got my shivering and shaking under control; I couldn't afford to show any weakness. So I nodded, knowing he could see me from what little came through the window.

"What are you? Fed, private, contract?"

I took a quick sniff of the glass he handed me. The booze wouldn't let me guess anything, even if it had been filled with arsenic. I took a sip. "Private. I've been retained to locate you, by some of your friends."

"Friends—my ass. The only putos looking for me wear stinkin' badges or don't ever show up on anybody's computer database. Drink it. I told you on the phone I don't care anymore. And I was never interested in murder, not really."

He was here, in front of me. I had a photo in my pack I'd memorized, descriptions I'd copied from articles and books. But all I could make out amounted to a burly blur of shadow. The so-called Samoan countless people had searched for or conjectured about and even revered was not five feet from me.

In my earlier searches I'd met umpteen university types, once-upon-a-time-militant Chicanos, government Hispanics, and the regular people who had been his friends or acquaintances. Any one of them would have given their left nut or last twenty to be in my spot unless they'd heard about the motel.

I knew offhand that somebody else might have asked him if he could prove who'd invented gonzo journalism. Or what it had really felt like in the middle of those crazy years of the Chicano movement. Or a variety of other questions about literature, his loves, or how his beliefs had changed down through the years. But "Where you been hiding?" was what came out of my mouth.

"Ay por ay."

"I've been searching for a long time."

"You and a shitload of other pendejos. For a few years there, I couldn't afford to take a piss without having to shave my head and wear one of those sissy robes."

"You were a Hare Krishna?"

"It was a joke, ese, a joke."

A woman's voice filtered through the ceiling as if she had a bullhorn set at max volume. "*Stupid* dickhead, I told you—the red one!" She switched off then.

I squinted, tried to make out his face. "You knew I came early. How'd you get in here?"

He pointed his arm to the door. "I could have come through that hole there. Or I'm still solid enough to have lifted the door off its hinges." The cubes in his glass clinked. "Nah, ese, I still have lots of contacts in low places."

"Low places? This dump's more sordid than a toxic waste site." I was playing at Mr. Suave, hoping to get him on my side so that I could at least eventually reach the safety of LAX.

"This? This is nothing. You should see some of the culos I passed through. Oh, don't bother trying to be cute. I won't like you no matter how intelligent or comical you are. We're not here for you to impress me."

"Why *are* we here?"

"You called—I rang. ¿Que no?" He sounded as if I'd ordered a pizza and handed him too small of a tip.

"But why let yourself be found after all these years? And why to me? Why not contact your family or someone?"

"Paisano, you're just lucky, maybe the only one who made the connection to the suicide, thinking it might bring me out. It did."

I felt like this once-in-a-lifetime-kill had nothing to do with any of my past work. Almost like Prince Serendipity had found me, not the reverse.

"As for mi familia and such, I'm content not to be found. It's what I've done for decades. I stopped being a person a long time ago. I am legend, almost myth, perhaps one day even a literary icon. Myths and icons cannot go gentle back into the daylight. The burden of fame, notoriety, and history—yes, even history—sometimes cannot be borne by mortal shoulders. An Aztec god would not have found the load so onerous, perhaps. As a man, I couldn't have carried all this with me for long."

After a few long minutes of both of us drinking, listening to the building's goings-on, I broke the silence. "Lots of people liked your books."

"Liked them? They loved them, vato! And I hear even more love them now. You sound like you've never read any of them."

"Never read much of anything, yours or otherwise."

"You're here to take in this mass of a legend, a literary myth, and you haven't even read my stuff?" He moved forward in the armchair to where I could see shadowed accents of his face.

"I never thought I'd find you."

"Baboso, that's no excuse! Didn't the Chicano movement bequeath you anything? You should have found some pride in your people, your culture. And at least *read* about it. Found out the true story, what really happened during those years. Ah—such a wondrous time!"

I felt like his eyes had taken on a sparkle.

Above us, the female bullhorn turned on again, but I was too wrapped up in the dark shape I faced to worry about whatever had upset her. "I heard stories about how it wasn't all good times. Some of the leaders weren't what they claimed. A lot of women got the bad end of the macho treatment. Drugs, beatings, political gangs. And lots of money disappearing. Some say you were . . . less than a saint."

"Less than a . . . ah, qué chingaos." He stood and went into a bellowing laughter for so long, I couldn't stop myself from joining in, even though I didn't know all of what had hit him.

"The leaders, the women, the beatings and money—if they only knew what I've learned on my travels though Aztlán these past years. But they will one day. It's the responsibility of those who know the truth to write it. There's much left that needs explaining, exposing. As for myself, we can leave it to the critics and such to analyze the little things about us for posterity. I am too cansado to contribute."

When he got up, I moved back, even while laughing, as if the air pressure itself had changed in the room. After he sat again, I felt like something had been strained out of my body, right through my skin and clothes. I tried to shake it off. "So what happens next?"

"First, we finish this bottle, compa'. Then *you* will tell me what happens next. It's your jale, not mine, ese. I am only along for the ride."

We talked for hours, sipping the Mexican brandy at a rate that never got me very high. Overhead, Mistress Bullhorn regularly handled new clients in her same hostess-like manner. LAX regularly contributed muted thunder to remind us where it was. Once someone tried pushing in the door. Sounds of a scuffle followed.

"Don't worry, nothing will make it through the door alive," he assured me. No one bothered us again.

I have to say *we* talked, because it didn't turn into one of those Q&As other people might have pulled on him. I didn't know enough to ask anything specific about his life or writings, so we just talked the way old men who meet in a bar would. About special episodes in our lives, close encounters, lost loves, failed ventures. Mine didn't compare to his, though he laughed or asked questions as if they did. The few personal things or pieces of history that I heard, he asked me to keep to myself.

I knew it was almost morning when the noises started dying down. I rose, tempted for a second to open the blinds.

He cleared his throat hard, freezing me in place. His last words came slowly: "Gracias por todo."

At that moment we both knew I'd leave the motel without him, without phoning my money contact, without understanding what the hell was wrong with me, how I was walking away from a grand prize. I still can't say why it turned out that way.

As the cab took me into LAX, I didn't worry about how my financial future was worse than when I'd arrived. I didn't worry whether anyone would ever try to force me to tell certain bits of what I'd learned because I'll simply *never* reveal those things.

I did wonder though, whether this stuff of legends, ego and all, the *vato* I'd just killed a bottle with, whether he'd ever find whatever he still sought, the reason he kept on living, wandering Aztlán.

And my gut needs to know that reason.

■

Postscript: Oscar Zeta Acosta, author of *Autobiography of a Brown Buffalo*, disappeared somewhere in Mexico in spring 1974, by causes unknown, though often speculated. He is presumed dead; the speculation continues.

ADRIANA

Reyna Grande

I know my sister is out there hidden in the darkness. Her eyes watching me dance. Did she notice that I just missed a step? Can she tell that my arms are tired now, and this Jalisco skirt is so damn heavy, I can hardly twirl it anymore? I try to forget that her eyes are watching me. I tell myself that next time I won't invite her to another performance. But I know I will. I always do. *I'm* the one up here on stage. Not her.

Ben is somewhere out there watching me, too. He doesn't make me feel weird. He likes the way I dance. Besides, he's a gringo, and he wouldn't know any better. But Elena can tell every time I miss a step. Fuck her.

The lights blind me for a second. I look down at my skirt, watch the red, pink, blue, and green ribbons swirl around and around. José's crooked teeth gleam under the lights as he smiles. We circle around each other. I keep an eye out on the seven other couples and make sure I keep up. I force my lips to match their smiles. I make my feet keep the rhythm of "La negra." I let the strumming of the mariachis guide me. Why is it that my feet drag behind? Why is it that they slow down for a moment, unsure of themselves? My fucking feet, I can never get them to do what they need to do.

I give José my hand and let him twirl me around into his arms now that the dance is over. I hide behind his big sombrero, trying to catch my breath. The clapping thunders out of the darkness like the sudden flapping of bats that have just gotten spooked. It scares me for a moment. "You did good," José says in a voice that makes it sound like he's saying that at least I didn't step on his damn feet this time like I did in Nuevo León. He's so close to me I can count every single drop of sweat on his forehead. As we take a bow, my eyes search for Elena in the darkness. I wonder if she liked the performance. I tell myself that I did good. I was great. I let José guide me out of the stage as I swallow the sour taste in my mouth.

When I come home I see Ben's car parked in front of the apartment building. The lights are out in his apartment. I hiccup as I go up the stairs to my place. I hold on to José's hand because I feel that I might fall. I shouldn't have drunk so much tonight. But the after-party was good. They always are. These dancers are crazy. Too bad most of the male dancers are gay. And they're so fuckin' cute, too. It's a waste. That's why I asked José to bring me home. *His* dick is available. Even if it's so fucking small. I swear even my middle finger is bigger.

"Thanks for the ride," I say.

"Es un placer," he whispers close to my ear. A pleasure. I smell the alcohol on his breath and I feel a rush of desire like faint electric shocks tickling my pussy. Alcohol makes me horny.

As I fish in my purse for my keys I notice a bundle right outside my door. I bend down to grab it, even though the movement makes me squirmy and I feel that I'm going to barf. I hold it in, though.

White roses. I breathe in the pungent scent and feel sick again.

"Secret admirer?" José asks.

"Nah." I open my door. I throw the roses onto the coffee table and turn on the light. "My neighbor," I say.

José laughs and walks over to the coffee table to pick up the card that came with the roses.

He reads it. "You were wonderful tonight. Ben."

I grab his hand and pull him with me onto the couch.

"Did you really like how I danced tonight?" I ask him.

"Ah, yeah," he says. He looks at the card from Ben and reads it again. "You were wonderful tonight." Then he bursts out laughing. A little bit of his spit sprays my cheek. I look at my guitar leaning against the wall next to the night table, so lonely in the shadows. I look at my Frida Kahlo prints hanging on the walls. None of them speak to me now. They are silent. Even the two Fridas are quiet. They don't like José being here.

I feel his hand rubbing the inside of my arm. He slides closer to me, his breath on my cheek. I look at the two Fridas, afraid to turn his way. His tongue slithers over my earlobe like a snail, leaving a trail of saliva.

"C'mon, Adriana, why do you always pretend you don't want it? You know you wanna fuck, too."

I hear a voice inside my head. It's the other me, the other Adriana telling me I should have listened to her and asked Yesenia for a ride instead of this *baboso* that now wants to screw me. But my hand reaches out to touch him, to feel his warmth. José's lips suddenly latch onto mine and he drools all over me like an over-friendly dog. But I hold on to him because I'm afraid, I'm afraid of the loneliness of my apartment and the memories that come creeping out at night. Memories of a mother who died. Memories of a father who doesn't give a damn. I tell myself that at least for tonight José is here to chase all those memories away.

The next day I go to Highland Park, and because next week is my birthday, I have the guts to knock on the door this time. My grandmother opens the door and right away I feel like a stupid fourteen-year-old girl, scared shitless. She does this to me.

"What do you want?" she asks in Spanish.

"I want to see my father." I try to stand up straighter.

"He doesn't want to see you. Now go."

She tries to close the door, but I'm a young woman and she is an old *vieja*. I push the door open and yell my father's name.

He comes to the living room, holding a beer in his hand.

"What are you doing here?" he asks.

My mouth feels like if it's stuffed with a rebozo. I can't talk. I look at my grandmother. She's holding the door, one arm on her waist. Talk, Adriana. Talk.

"I—um. It's my birthday next week, and I was wondering if we could have dinner together at La Perla."

Too late, I realize that La Perla was my mother's favorite place to go. I bite my damn tongue. Stupid, stupid, stupid.

He takes a drink of his beer and walks over to me. I can smell the alcohol on his breath. I look at him and I see the anger in his eyes. "Don't look for me anymore, do you understand? I don't want to see you. You and that sister of yours are not my problem. Get out of here, Adriana," he says.

I look down at the floor. I turn my neck a certain way to show him the scar—remind him of what he did to me. But instead, he pushes me out the door.

I stand there and look at the wooden door in front of me for a few seconds. When the thunder hits the sky, I bounce off the porch and run out to the street.

Sin madre, sin padre, sin perro que me ladre. Without a mother, without a father, without a fucking dog to bark at me. This Mexican saying was created just for me, I swear it. I rush down Avenue 50, rubbing my watery eyes so I can see where the fuck I'm going. By the time I get to the bus stop on Figueroa, the rain has already started. I stand there and shiver in the rain, in the darkness, in my solitude.

Goddammit, why can't he love me? I'm his daughter. How long do I have to beg? What do I have to do for him to finally want me?

The headlights blind me for a second. The beams shine on the raindrops. I watch them fall in front of me.

"Wanna ride?"

I look at the man waving at me from the car. I don't know how many of them there are. It's too dark to see. I wrap my wet sweater tighter around me.

"¿Sí o no?"

I look up the street. There is no sign of a bus. At this hour of the night, who knows if and when it'll come.

"¿Cómo te llamas?" the man in the driver seat asks me as soon as I take a seat in the back with one of his buddies.

"Jennifer," I lie.

"Where do you want us to drop you off?" he asks in Spanish. The red light turns green. He pushes the gas pedal and the car lunges forward.

"Drop me off on the corner of Fourth Street and Mott, please," I say in Spanish. These guys don't speak any English. There are empty Budweiser cans on the floor and the car stinks of weed. The man sitting next to me looks to be in his late twenties. He's clean shaven but his hair is shaggy and badly needs a haircut.

"I'm José," he says. I roll my eyes. The world is full of too many Josés.

"I'm Uvaldo," the driver says then he points to the man next to him in the passenger seat, "and this here is Artemio."

I turn to look at the street in front of me. The rain is coming down harder now and the wipers swish up and down trying to clear up the windshield but failing. I put my cold hands in front of the back heater vent to warm them. My clothes are soaking wet, even my damn underwear.

Uvaldo takes a joint from his pocket and hands it to me to light it for him. I wonder why he didn't give it to Artemio or José. When I hand it back he refuses and tells me to take a few hits. Part of me doesn't want to. I promised I wasn't going to do that shit anymore. But there's a pain in my chest I need to numb, and there are thoughts in my head I want to forget. I lean back in the seat and do as I am told.

Artemio turns on the stereo and Chalino Sánchez fills the silence with "Nieves de enero."

"You like Chalino Sánchez?" he asks.

"Yeah." I think back on my high school years and remember how most of the ESL kids I hung out with were crazy about Chalino Sánchez, though the guy had been killed years before. I remember Héctor. That motherfucker took my virginity in the storage room under the bleachers and then never looked at me again. The asshole loved Chalino Sánchez.

I feel warm all over. The heaviness I felt in my chest eases up and now I can breathe. I feel as weightless as the smoke coming out of my mouth.

"So where are you guys coming from?" I ask. They are all wearing tight-fitting jeans, cowboy boots, and long-sleeve shirts. I can see their Tejana hats next to José.

"From a friend's house."

"Do you like to dance?" Artemio asks.

"Yeah," I say. "I'm a professional dancer." It's true. I mean Eduardo only pays us for our Christmas performance at La Golondrina restaurant, but that still puts me in the category of being a paid dancer—that is, a professional dancer, right?

"Chale," Uvaldo says. "So do you strip dance?"

I laugh. "No, tonto, I dance folklórico."

"That's too bad," José says. "I would've liked to have seen you strip for me."

The guys laugh. The car exits the freeway and makes left turn. We're almost home. I hand the last of the joint to José, who quickly puts it in his mouth.

"So, you got a boyfriend, Jennifer?" José asks.

I try to sit up to look at him, but I don't have the strength to do it.

"Why do you want to know?"

"I'm a curious guy."

"And what else are you curious about?"

"I'm curious to know how it would feel like to have your legs wrapped around me," he says.

The guys burst out laughing. "Chale, José, you don't waste any time with the ladies, do you?" Artemio says.

We're now at the intersection of Fourth and Soto. The clock in the car reads 9:33.

I tell Uvaldo to pull over as soon as he passes Roosevelt High School.

I look outside. My apartment is right across the street. All the lights are out in Ben's apartment, like I knew they would be. He's out of town until tomorrow. I sigh, feeling disappointed. Artemio opens the door and gets out of the car to let me out. The rain has now turned into a drizzle.

"I need to piss," he says.

I get out of the car and thank them for the ride.

"Hey, how about letting us use your bathroom?" José asks. "I really need to piss, too. My bladder is going to burst."

Even though my brain is numb with all that crap I just smoked, I am aware of what they are really asking for. I look back at Ben's dark, empty apartment. There's no one there to talk to.

"OK," I sigh. They cross the street with me and they follow behind me, drooling like dogs after a bitch in heat. My apartment is freezing and it smells of rotten food. I have forgotten to take out the trash for a few days now. I light the candles and an incense stick while they take off their leather jackets and hats. Then they take turns using my bathroom. Fuck, I hope it's not too dirty.

"Do you have something to drink?" Artemio asks while he walks around my living room looking at my Frida Kahlo paintings.

"Who's the ugly bitch?" José asks as he points at the frames.

"Frida Kahlo," I say.

"Oh," they say, but I know they don't have a clue.

"You know, I think she looks like Salma Hayek," Uvaldo says. "I remember seeing a picture of Salma dressed like this Frida woman." Uvaldo is messing around with my guitar. He puts it down carelessly on the end table and my guitar topples down to the floor. *Cabrón.*

"You really have the hots for her," José says as he parts my Frida bamboo curtain and goes into my kitchen. "Mira la Jennifer, she has some good stuff," he says when he comes back. He holds my bottles of tequila and vodka I keep on top of the refrigerator. José hands everyone a shot glass and they all toast to me. Artemio turns on the radio and starts dancing to Shakira. The guys start hooting and throwing coins at him. My apartment feels like a closet.

"What's wrong?" Uvaldo asks. "You look sad."

I feel tears welling in my eyes. Damn alcohol. It's getting to me.

"It's nothing," I tell him.

"Nah, you have a broken heart," Uvaldo says. "I recognize the symptoms."

"Yeah, you should," Artemio says, "all your girlfriends dump your sorry ass in a day or two."

"We'll make you happy, corazón," José says as he runs his hand over my arm. It's rough. It reminds me of my father's hands.

"Why don't we get going, guys?" Uvaldo says. He looks at me with tenderness, and I can almost see Ben in him.

"Nah. We can't leave her alone," José says. "Dance for us, Jennifer," he says as he pulls me up to my feet.

I shake my head. I don't want to dance. José hands me his shot glass and I down its contents in a big gulp. I feel my throat burning.

"Come on, Jennifer, dance for us," Artemio urges me on.

Uvaldo stands by the door, as if he doesn't know what the fuck to do. Then the hombre in him takes over. He goes to clear the coffee table and puts the candles on the floor. Artemio pumps up the volume and I let Shakira's voice take me out of myself. I see the way they look at me, see the hunger in their eyes.

They don't know how much I want to be seen, how much I need my presence to be noticed.

The sane Adriana tells me I shouldn't do this. I don't need to stoop this low. "Have some pride," she tells me. But the other Adriana, the other Adriana has this overwhelming need to feel wanted. Loved.

Don't do it. Don't do it.

I get up on the coffee table and begin to dance. My clothes come off one piece at a time. I see Uvaldo lick his lips. José puts his hand over his hardening dick. Artemio's nostrils are flaring, his chest heaving. I see their eyes, their unblinking eyes filled with lust, with want. I let them hypnotize me. The power of those eyes focused on me fills me with warmth, and I forget the pain and the loneliness and the emptiness.

I smile. You see, Adriana? Someone does want you.

■

Adondequiera que voy, me acuerdo de ti. Adondequiera que estoy, te estoy mirando. El viento me trae tu voz, no hay música que no oiga yo, que no me deje llorando.

I lie on my couch listening to this song over and over again. I like the repeat button on my stereo because that means I can lie here until the cows come home and "Corazoncito tirano" will keep playing and playing even after they do.

I nurse my empty tequila shot glass in my hand, wishing it too had a repeat button so that it could fill up again and again without me having to get my flat ass off the couch to fill it.

I close my eyes for a moment, feeling the room spinning around me. Or maybe I'm spinning around it like a *folklórico* skirt that twirls around and around on the stage.

Estoy sola. A-L-O-N-E.

Ben left me all alone again and flew to Washington DC to spend Thanksgiving with one of his sisters. And Emilio, where the fuck is Emilio? I don't know. He comes and goes like diarrhea—when you least expect it.

Elena invited me to her house, but I didn't feel like going. It's weird enough spending time with Elena without having strangers around.

Laura invited me to her place, too, bless her little dancer's heart. She didn't want me to be all alone on this special day of Thanksgiving. But I say, man, what's there to celebrate anyway? Besides, I don't fit in at Laura's house. I was there last year, and I can still remember all those cousins, aunts and uncles, nieces and nephews, and the cute white-haired *abuelitas* you just want to cuddle with. And I remember her mom, you know, the way she smiled at me and put her hand on my shoulder and pulled me away from the little corner where I was already building a nest. I still remember the softness of her hand.

I told Laura I already had plans. And I do, I guess. I plan to stay here on my couch, surrounded by my dripping candles and Frida's art.

¡Viva La Frida bigotona!

¡Que viva!

Nah, don't believe that shit. Elena thinks I like Frida's mustache and that's why I have her paintings all over my house, but that's not the truth. She thinks that just because I'm not e-du-ca-ted like her I can't think deep thoughts, or feel *hasta adentro* in the deepest part of my heart. But I can.

Te lo juro.

I remember that day at Olverita's Village I stood in the middle of the store, stunned. I had never seen that big painting before—*The Two Fridas*. I stood there looking at the reproduction hanging on the wall, thinking, how did she know? How did this woman know this is how I feel?

The two Adrianas. I struggle to understand them. They share the same heart, yet they don't think the same thoughts. One Adriana wishes she was free, free of those memories that hurt her, free to live her life in a better way and to love and be loved in the purest way possible. And the other Adriana . . . Aha! That's the one that's fucked up in the head.

Completamente loca.

The thing that struck me about the painting was their hands. The two Fridas holding hands, as if they're trying to reassure each other. And that's what the two Adrianas do. Because one can't live without the other. Both are so vulnerable, you know. Especially the Adriana that wants her mommy and daddy. She's like a baby that wants to be sung to and told that she is loved. But who will sing to little Adriana to sleep when she's afraid of the dark? Who will sit by her side and reassure her that there are no monsters in the closet eating her dance shoes and waiting to eat her, too? Who will tell little Adriana that she is their *estrellita*, their little sky, and their moon?

No-bo-dy.

That's why I sit here and wrap my arms around my legs. My right hand holds my left and won't let go, won't let go because if it does, little Adriana would be lost. And the cows would come home, and "Corazoncito tirano" would keep on playing, and the candles would keep shining their little lights, but Adriana would be like this empty shot glass. This empty shot glass with no one to fill it with that holy tequila that burns your throat and turns you inside out.

from the novel

CHICANO

Richard Vásquez

Pete Sandoval parked his battered old pickup truck carefully next to the curb on San Pedro Street in downtown Los Angeles and got out. He stood on the sidewalk a moment, looking up a little apprehensively at the large brick building with a sign reading CONSTRUCTION TRADES UNION— American Federation of Labor. He seemed to brace himself as he pushed the door open and entered.

He walked uncertainly down the hall, reading the signs on the doors until he came to: "International Brotherhood of Cement Masons—AF of L." He stood looking at it a while, his hand stroking his clean-shaven chin in what he hoped appeared a casual manner. He pushed the door open and walked to a waist-high counter in front of several desks. A half dozen men and two women were working. One man looked up and came toward Pete.

"Can I help you?" the man asked. Pete did not allow himself to become rattled.

"Is this where you join the union?" he asked in his broken English.

"You want to be a cement finisher?" the man asked. Pete nodded. "Yes, this is it," the man continued. "You had any experience?"

Pete knew the answer could be incriminating. It was expected that any good union man would never dream of scabbing, yet it was impossible to become a union member without experience. "Only when I had to," he answered, actually believing this to be an original and believable excuse. "I been doing some labor for some companies, and sometimes when they pour cement somebody gets sick or something and then I pick up a trowel and get a little experience."

The man eyed him severely, yet Pete sensed friendliness.

"Been doing quite a lot of cement finishing, eh?"

"No," Pete explained, "I don't believe anybody should do certain work unless they belong to that union."

"Well then what makes you think you're qualified to be a finisher? We don't want men in here who will go out and mess up a sidewalk job and get the contractor down on us. We have enough trouble with them."

"Well," Pete swallowed, but he knew he was good at making logical excuses, "I didn't do very much—like I say, only when it was to save the concrete from drying too rough—but what little I did, I learned very fast."

The man eyed Pete with a trace of amusement. Pete continued.

"I thought that before I do very much more, I should come in and get a union card, so I won't be breaking the rules anymore. So here I am."

The man forced himself to remain serious. Pete's naïve sincerity, his simple logic built on simple lies, plus his appearance, would cause anyone at least to smile.

He eyed Pete's five feet, three inches, his bald head, the beautiful set of large teeth in a big mouth set in a prematurely wrinkled face, and knew the Los Angeles local cement finishers' union had another brother.

He sighed, guessing accurately what was coming next.

"OK. You got a job to go to? As a finisher?"

Pete pondered a moment. "No. How can I? Nobody will hire a cement finisher who doesn't belong to the union." He got a little indignant. "That's why I came here. To join. So I can go . . ."

"OK, OK," the man said hurriedly. He extended his hand to Pete. "My name's Harrington. I'm one of the business agents. What's your name?"

"Pete," Pete answered. "Pete Sandoval."

"You know it costs a hundred bucks to join the union, don't you?" Harrington again guessed what was coming.

Pete reached his hand into his pocket and felt the five twenty-dollar bills nestled there. His face showed a little dismay. "A hundred dollars? I don't think I can pay that much 'til I'm working. Another cement finisher said you would let me bring you twenty dollars each time I get paid until I pay it."

Harrington gave a disgusted grunt and started writing on a form.

"OK, Sandoval," he said as he wrote, "we'll let you in. You bring me in twenty bucks every time you get paid, understand? And you got to have three of your amigos who are members come in and sign that you're qualified to do the work. Can you do that?"

Pete grinned broadly. "Sure," he said. The "sh" being an alien sound combination to his native tongue, the word came out "Choor."

Harrington helped him fill out the necessary forms and gave him a book of union rules and a badge which read "I.B.C.M., A.F. of L., Local 627, L.A."

By the time Pete had walked back to the tired old pickup truck his usual swagger had returned. In fact it was a little more pronounced. He coaxed the engine to life, smiling with satisfaction that, after many generations, a Sandoval in the family was finally a highly skilled, highly paid worker. He was so pleased with the events of the past half hour, so pleased he had saved himself a hundred dollars—at least for the time being—that he failed to see a car coming as he pulled out from the curb. The car slammed on its brakes, wheels locking as the driver blasted the horn and barely avoided a collision. Pete got a glimpse of the freckled-faced man glaring at him as he swerved out and passed the old pickup. Pete glared back at him accusingly.

"Look where you're going, you Goddam dumb Oakie son-of-a-bitch," Pete muttered as he coaxed a little speed from the reluctant motor. And his last word came out "beach."

Pete headed down San Pedro Street to Fourth Street and turned toward East Los Angeles. He smiled again over his good fortune.

To him, he had just made one hundred dollars. And he wanted to share it with Minnie. True, it was she who had saved and skimped for months to save up that money they knew the Union would demand as an initiation fee. But it was still just like finding a hundred dollars not to have to pay it. The fact that he would have to pay twenty dollars each payday until it was paid off was canceled out by the fact that he would be earning at least that much more than he would have as a common unskilled construction laborer. And when it was eventually paid, it would be like getting a twenty-dollar-a-week raise. This also pleased him. Yes, he wanted to share his good fortune with Minnie.

He frowned now as he thought of something. He wanted to give her $50 and tell her Harrington had insisted on half payment. But he had only five twenty-dollar bills, and you couldn't divide that in half. He thought about giving her two twenties and saying Harrington had taken $60. But $60 was too much to hold out on a good wife like Minnie. After all, she had saved it. Giving her only $40 would hurt his conscience. She was too good a woman for that kind of treatment. But on the other hand, $60 was too much to give her unexpectedly—and that would leave him only $40. Well, only one thing to do. Stop and change one bill. Then he could split with her. And he might as well stop at a bar and have a drink while he was changing it. That way he could hit two birds with one rock.

The next day Pete approached the gringo boss and showed his union card and work permit, which entitled him to do work as a qualified concrete mason. He reminded the boss he'd been promised the job.

"I can handle it," Pete said, with what he hoped appeared to be typical Yankee confidence. But inside he was in doubt.

"Good," the boss said. "It's settled, then. Come with me and I'll show you what our pour schedule is."

For the first time in his life, Pete felt important. As the dozens of other workmen sawed and hammered and chiseled and welded and operated the huge machines, Pete accompanied the boss around the job.

"Tomorrow," the boss explained as they stood near one bank of the approach, "we pour this little bit of the deck. Only a small pour compared to what's coming up. How many men do you think can handle it?"

Pete's mind raced, but he appeared calm. "Give me two laborers to shovel, and one more cement finisher," he said casually.

"You get your own finisher. Either call the Union Hall or bring a skilled man. But I want a top-notch job here. I'm having enough trouble with the state inspectors. Just make sure it's done right. Now come over here and I'll show you what we got lined up for Friday, Monday, and Wednesday . . ."

That evening after work Pete again drove straight to Angie's Bar and Grill. It never occurred to him to call Minnie to say he'd be late.

He ate dinner and then had a few drinks. Before long the men with hard hats began arriving. They traipsed in in steel helmets, dirty khakis, huge heavy shoes, sweaty, grimy-faced, but somehow laughing and not tired.

They ate and drank, shouted and quarreled, half in English, half in Spanish. Another day was over for them, and a night was beginning. None thought of the wife and children waiting at home. None brooded over the day's drudgery. All took pride in telling how hard they had worked, yet how much strength and energy they had left. Many would drink until the small hours of the morning, then stagger home to say "shut up" to the wife and sleep until dawn, at which time they would get up and do it all over again.

Angie's waitress circulated among them, taking orders, swearing loudly and slapping at gnarled, black hands that tried to feel the ample buttocks. The juke box roared the latest hit tune from Mexico, and everyone in the place outroared it.

Truculently, Pete wandered among the groups at the tables, casually— or so he thought—bringing out his new union card. He pinned his I.B.C.M. AFL badge to his baseball cap which he always wore to cover his baldness when he wasn't wearing his steel helmet.

Presently Pete saw the man he wanted to talk to enter. It was Antonio.

Old Antonio was the resident and reigning old-timer at concrete work. Many years before, he'd been one of the first to join the concrete finishers' union. He was an old man now, and he spoke practically no English, but many were the gringo bosses who breathed a sigh of relief and relaxed when they saw the union hall had sent out Old Tony. He knew everything there was to know about his trade, and when he told a boss a certain job was worth more than the usual wage scale, there was no argument.

Old Tony, Pete knew, made a great deal of money and was revered among his peers, although all generally agreed he worried too much.

Pete sat Antonio down and showed him his new union card and badge.

"Qué bueno!" the old man said. "You have graduated."

Then Pete told him what was on his mind. He was very worried about the pour the next morning. He knew it was completely unlike troweling sidewalks, floors or finishing curbs; in fact, Pete knew, no trowels were used on a deck pour. He described what was to be done in detail and asked Antonio to tell him how to do it. Antonio shook his head.

"No," he said, "it cannot be told. I will go to your job in the morning and help you. The bosses are Americanos?"

"Sí."

"Bueno. They will not understand as I show you what is to be done. Believe me, I know how to handle this so they will know they have made a wise choice in promoting you. Do not worry about my job. We are doing nothing important and I will call and say I am sick."

Pete gave Old Tony instructions as to how to get to his job and soon the old man, after a serious good-bye to many friends, left to go home.

"Hasta mañana," he said to Pete as he left, waving a gnarled hand.

Pete suddenly didn't feel like drinking and being carefree anymore. A vague uneasiness gnawed at him, and he kept thinking of the pour coming in the morning. He grew quiet and suddenly decided to go home.

At home he was unusually noncommunicative with Minnie. He was a little irritable and when in bed he lay thinking to himself a long time, worrying. What if his truck didn't start in the morning? He sat up, wanting to go out to make sure it was reliable. What if he overslept? Maybe he'd better not sleep. He got up and tested the electric alarm clock. He adjusted it to go off at four-thirty instead of five-thirty. Twice during the night he decided he couldn't hear the clock motor humming, and he got up to check it.

He was awake at four o'clock, getting dressed. Minnie got up and made his breakfast, but before he was half through eating he found himself looking at the clock. Maybe Old Tony would oversleep. Maybe he wouldn't be able to find the job.

He said good-bye and told Minnie he might work late and went out to his pickup truck.

Dawn was breaking as he parked beside the project and climbed up the approach to the waiting bridge-to-be. He looked around. The 600-foot-wide strip of fresh dirt splitting the city looked raw and primitive to him. The freeway bed stretched out to the horizon, gently winding among the factories and buildings, disappearing somewhere near the mass of structures that was the Los Angeles civic center. From the bridge's height he was about even with the tops of most of the packing plants, storage silos, assembly plants, steel mills and industrial complexes which stretched out before him, behind him and on either side as far as the eye could see. In the brightening morning light he could see the huge earth-moving machine abandoned at quitting time the previous day lined up on the dirt right-of-way. A few men were appearing here and there, starting the little auxiliary engines which, when warmed up, would turn over the main engine in each machine. He heard one start, blatting like an outboard motor. In the relative quiet the engine's raucous sound sputtered and coughed, then steadied to a high-pitched whine, then the pitch suddenly dipped as the clutch was thrown to engage the main engine, and in a few moments the boom . . .

boom . . . boom, boom of the diesel engine's thunder drowned out the outboard sound. The operator moved the earth-mover along to scoop up dirt where the freeway would dip below street level and deposit it on the approach where the freeway would rise to the height of the overhead bridge. As he watched, another earth-mover began moving, and then another and another. A bulldozer began spreading the earth evenly, a huge water truck saturated it and a compacting machine followed, packing the freshly deposited dirt to granite hardness.

A grader put the finishing touches on a temporary approach from the nearby street, and any minute the great transit-mix trucks, with black spirals painted on a gray drum to give the illusion of motion, like a barber pole on its side, would be turning in, anxious to disgorge their semi-liquid cargo and then, empty of the awful weight, go bouncing ridiculously over the rough dirt, to bring back another load as quickly as the driver could maneuver through the traffic-congested streets.

The men concerned with the deck pour began arriving. The boss, looking worried and then relief obvious in his face at seeing Pete waiting atop the bridge, waved from the little house trailer that served as an office near the end of the bridge. The state inspectors, breast pockets bursting with notebooks and pencils of various colors, their belts laden with plumb-bobs, hand-levels, slide-rules and measuring tapes, began a systematic check of reinforcing steel and metal plates to be left in the concrete. Pete pretended to understand as they set up telescope transits and checked the positions of everything to be covered by the concrete, including the forms and false work.

The boss came running to Pete from the trailer.

"Concrete company on the phone," he said seriously. "They're ready to send the first loads. Be here in twenty minutes if they leave now. Shall I tell them OK?"

"I'm ready," Pete said, and his heart leaped as he saw Old Tony climbing up on the deck, ready for work. The boss ran back to the office. He returned soon, and stood with the state men, who had finished checking positions. Pete knew the boss was uneasy, and he made a show of casual talk with Old Tony. This pour was to be part of the decking over which traffic would move at high speed. Pete understood it had to be level, even. The state allowed only a sixteenth of an inch irregularity in ten feet. It took experts in the field to finish concrete according to highway specifications. Finishing machines, which would be used to pave the freeway over the dirt bed, could not be used here because of their weight. This part of a bridge had to be done by hand and had to be perfectly smooth, Old Tony explained, because if there were any bumps, causing traffic to bounce when the bridge was eventually opened, it could conceivably endanger the structure. An uneven concrete deck would have to be torn out, at prohibitive cost to the contractor.

The giant trucks full of freshly mixed concrete began arriving. The company supplying the concrete allowed each truck only so many minutes standing time after arrival on the job. After that the contractor was charged standing time for both the truck and the driver.

The first truck made a wide arc on the dirt approach and then started backing up, the engine thundering as the huge drum revolved slowly, churning the twelve tons of concrete inside. The driver expertly stopped inches from the one-and-a-half yard bucket attached by a steel cable to a tall crane. The state inspectors made a final quick check of the wooden forms. The project boss ordered a check of all equipment; compressors, vibrators, and machines. Nothing must go wrong. Once started, under no circumstances could the pour be stopped for any length of time.

Pete was standing next to Old Tony, watching the activity. He suddenly realized everything had come to a stop and all eyes were on him, expectantly. The boss cupped his hands to his mouth and shouted mightily above the rattle and roar of equipment and machines: "Whenever you say, Pete!" Old Tony, without looking at him, said: "Tell him to begin."

Only vaguely was Pete aware this was the high point in his life. Heart pounding, he cupped his hands and shouted, "Let 'er rip!" in what he thought was good gringo English, but the last word came out "reep."

The boss signaled the truck driver, who threw levers this way and that and wet concrete began pouring from the rear of the truck. Within seconds, there were two tons of concrete in the bucket, and the crane operator threw the throttle forward and the shiny steel reel started winding up the slack in the steel cables, lifting the bucket up and over the heads of the workers, then gently down to within a few feet of the wooden forms at the far end of the pour where Pete and Old Tony stood. A worker tripped the handle on the bucket and the first two tons of concrete emptied out onto the forms, its thick, jamlike consistency causing it to form a knee-deep puddle. The common laborers wearing high rubber boots waded into it, bent almost double, grunting loudly as they plunged their short-handled shovels into it and began spreading the concrete around to the approximate depth required. Old Tony stood beside Pete and the two watched.

"We do nothing until they pour the entire width of the deck and move up out of our way," he advised Pete in Spanish quietly.

The pour was underway.

Back and forth across the width of the deck the bucket unloaded its heavy contents, and the laborers evened out the puddles, until the concrete was placed fairly evenly more than a dozen feet from the beginning of the pour. Then Old Tony quietly told Pete how to move out the low scaffolding over the wet concrete which would allow them to work with their finishing tools without walking on the fresh surface. The workers involved in placing the concrete all moved up another dozen or so feet to repeat the whole process while Old Tony and Pete smoothed the deck to paved finish.

As the pour progressed the length of the deck, Antonio kept up a steady stream of quiet instructions to Pete. Pete relayed this to the workmen, the man operating the crane with the huge bucket, the laborers placing the concrete. Ostensibly, Pete was running the pour as a good cement foreman should. The other workers, Spanish-speaking almost to a man, quickly saw what was happening, and all on the job except the gringo boss and the state inspector, joined in the silent conspiracy to put Pete across as the hero of the day.

By noon the pour had reached the halfway point. Stopping for lunch was inconceivable. The boss and the state inspectors stood watching the work proceed, the worried lines lessening in their faces as they saw the smooth, even pavement Pete and Old Tony left behind each time they moved the low work scaffolding ahead to keep up with the pouring. Then near-disaster struck.

While they were waiting for the pour to progress enough for another "bite," Pete saw Old Tony squatting beside the section just finished. Almost imperceptibly, Antonio moved his head, beckoning Pete. Pete approached him and knelt, looking out on the newly finished still wet deck.

"See the spot near the center where moisture is standing?" Tony asked without pointing. Pete strained to see. The wet concrete glistened all over, but in one area a puddle of water perhaps a quarter of an inch stood. Only an extremely practiced eye could have noticed. Pete nodded.

Old Tony explained quietly, "When we finished it, it was perfectly even. But the forms beneath have given under the weight and vibration. That little puddle indicates a depression."

They both squatted silently, Pete waiting for him to continue.

Antonio said, "The inspectors will not check it with a straightedge until it becomes hard. Then it is too late to do anything about it. They will blame you."

Pete panicked a little. "Can we fix it?"

"Do just as I say," Tony said, still speaking softly, not looking at Pete. "I will return to the pour. Stay here a while, then call the gringos here and show them the little puddle. Tell them what I told you. They will check and find you're right, and they will get very excited. Then you call for me. I can fix it."

Pete was a good actor. He remained kneeling, squinting at the finished deck. Soon he caught the eye of the state inspector and the boss, and beckoned them. They hurried toward him, worry on their faces.

"Something wrong, Pete?" the boss asked apprehensively.

Pete pointed to the wet spot. "See that water standing there? I think the forms gave way underneath a little bit. We better check it now."

Quickly, the boss produced a straightedge ten feet long, and they placed it across the deck, spanning the little puddle of water. Where the moisture stood, the deck was nearly an inch lower than the surrounding areas. The inspectors looked accusingly at the boss. Their reputations were at stake and they would hold him responsible for a poor job.

The boss was near panic himself. It was one thing to be able to spot a bad place, quite another to be mechanic enough to know what to do about it.

"Should we stop the pour, Pete? Can you fix it?"

"Yes," Pete said wisely, "it's still fresh enough to be fixed. Lucky we caught it in time, though. I'll call Old Tony back here and tell him what to do."

Pete summoned Old Tony. The boss and the inspectors stood watching as the two jabbered at length in Spanish, and then Antonio shouted for two shovelers to bring shovels full of fresh concrete. He took one shovelful and with the expertness of a basketball player threw the concrete out onto the wet spot. He then quickly nailed a long handle to a flat board and, standing at the edge of the deck, he gripped the handle and expertly guided the flat board over the area where he'd thrown the concrete until suddenly as if by magic the wet spot was gone. The inspectors checked the deck again and found it perfectly level. They broke into big grins. The boss beamed at Pete. But Pete didn't have time for compliments.

"Come on, Tony," he said impatiently, "they're ready for us to move up again." By quitting time the last great transit-mix truck had roared away. The deck was poured out, smooth, perfectly even. The boss was delighted. Not a single delay had cost truck-and-driver standing time. The highly paid equipment operators did not go on overtime. Pete's handling of the pour had been a model of efficiency, and saving of time and money.

The boss' praise for Pete was brief but sincere. The next day another pour was scheduled. And again Old Tony saw Pete through. And again on the next pour.

Time flew. After a month, Old Tony left Pete on his own, to hire his own skilled men and make his own decisions. The state engineers assigned to the job, whose reputations were at stake in seeing that the contractor did quality work, were delighted with Pete's work. The contractor was delighted that the state's men were delighted.

Pete wallowed in the glory of his newfound skills, his newfound importance, and his newfound wealth. His reputation for his special skill spread, and he found his earnings increased in proportion to the demand for his work. And when Minnie told him the doctor said she was going to have twins, Pete nodded casually. After all, what would you expect from such a man?

Contributors

KATHLEEN ALCALÁ is the author of a short-story collection and three novels set in the Southwest and nineteenth-century Mexico. She teaches creative writing at workshops and programs in Washington State and elsewhere, including Seattle University, the University of New Mexico, and Richard Hugo House. Alcalá is also a co-founder of and contributing editor to *The Raven Chronicles*. A play based on her novel, *Spirits of the Ordinary,* was produced by the Miracle Theatre of Portland, Oregon. She serves on the board of Richard Hugo House and the advisory boards of Con Tinta, Field's End, and the Centrum Writers Conference. Her books include *Mrs. Vargas and the Dead Naturalist* (Calyx Books); *Spirits of the Ordinary* (Chronicle; Harvest Books); *The Flower in the Skull* (Chronicle; Harvest Books); and *Treasures in Heaven* (Chronicle; Northwestern University Press). Alcalá's first collection of nonfiction essays, *The Desert Remembers My Name,* was published in 2007 by the University of Arizona Press. Web page: www.kathleenalcala.com.

FREDERICK LUIS ALDAMA obtained his Ph.D. from Stanford University and is a professor at Ohio State University, where he teaches Chicano/a, Latino/a, and postcolonial literature and film. He is the author of several books, including *Dancing With Ghosts: A Critical Biography of Arturo Islas, Postethnic Narrative Criticism, Spilling the Beans in Chicanolandia: Conversations with Artists and Writers,* and *Brown on Brown: Chicano/a Representations of Gender, Sexuality, and Ethnicity.* He is editor of *Arturo Islas: The Uncollected Works* and

Critical Mappings of Arturo Islas's Fictions. Aldama's articles and interviews have appeared in such journals as *Aztlán, College Literature, Poets & Writers, World Literature Today, Cross Cultural Poetics, Lit: Literature Interpretation Theory, Lucero, Comparative Literature, Callaloo, Nepantla, Journal of Interdisciplinary Literary Analysis, American Literature, Latin American Research Review, Modern Fiction Studies,* and *Modern Drama.*

LISA ALVAREZ'S work has appeared in the *Los Angeles Times, OC Weekly,* and in the anthology *Geography of Rage: Remembering the LA Riots of 1992,* edited by Jervey Tervalon. "Sweet Time" is a chapter from her novel-in-progress. She grew up in and around Los Angeles but now lives in Orange County, where she earned an M.F.A. in fiction from the University of California at Irvine and now works as a professor of English at Irvine Valley College.

VICTORIO BARRAGÁN is completing a collection of short stories and two novels. He is a founding member of Collective R.A.B.I.A., a Los Angeles-based collective of urban artists.

DANIEL CHACÓN is an assistant professor of English with the M.F.A. bilingual program at the University of Texas, El Paso. He is the author of *Chicano Chicanery* and *And the Shadows Took Him.* His stories have appeared in such journals as ZYZZYVA, *The New England Review, Quarterly West,* and the *Bilingual Review.*

KATHLEEN DE AZEVEDO'S stories and articles, many on Brazilian and Latino life, have appeared in various publications, including the *Los Angeles Times, Boston Review, Gulf Coast, Tampa Review, Michigan Quarterly Review, Green Mountains Review, Hayden's Ferry Review, Greensboro Review, Américas, TriQuarterly,* and *Gettysburg Review.* Her novel *Samba Dreamers* (The University of Arizona Press/Camino del Sol), about Brazilians in Hollywood, was released in March 2006. Information on *Samba Dreamers,* as well as other links on Brazil can be found at www.kathleenazevedo.com. She was born in Rio de Janeiro and currently lives in San Francisco.

ALEX ESPINOZA was born in Tijuana, Mexico, and raised just east of Los Angeles in the city of La Puente. He has worked as a used appliance salesman, a cashier, and a retail manager. He holds a B.A. in creative writing from the University of California at Riverside and an M.F.A. in writing from the University of California at Irvine. His first novel, *Still Water Saints*, was published by Random House in 2007. He lives and teaches in Southern California and is currently at work on his next novel.

RUDY CH. GARCIA originally started writing as a *Denver Post* editorial columnist in the 1970s, and after a few decades of sabbatical, returned to write speculative fiction. He is a semi-active member of Northern Colorado Writer's Workshop, works in Denver as a bilingual first-grade teacher (with a writing B.A. from the University of Colorado), and is a founding member of *La Bloga*, a literary blog dedicated to Chicano/a literature.

ESTELLA GONZÁLEZ was born and raised in East Los Angeles, which serves as the inspiration for most of her writing. Her poetry and short stories have appeared in the literary magazines *Sandscript, Eleven Eleven,* and *Puerto del Sol.* She has been recognized with the Pam Mayhall poetry award by the Tucson PEN Women and the Martindale Literary Award by Pima Community College. In addition, *Sandscript* has recognized her short stories with first- and second-place awards. She graduated with a B.A. in English from Northwestern University and is an M.F.A. candidate at Cornell University.

MELANIE GONZÁLEZ is a Chicana who has been published on poeticdiversity.org and in the anthologies *Pieces of Me* and *Nothing Held Back*, both published by WriteGirl Publishers.

RIGOBERTO GONZÁLEZ is the author of two poetry books, *So Often the Pitcher Goes to Water until It Breaks*, a National Poetry Series selection, and *Other Fugitives and Other Strangers*; two bilingual children's books: *Soledad Sigh-Sighs* and *Antonio's Card;* the novel *Crossing Vines,* winner of *ForeWord Magazine's* Fiction Book of the Year Award; a memoir, *Butterfly Boy;* and a biography about the Chicano writer Tomás Rivera forthcoming in 2007. The recipient of Guggenheim and NEA fellowships, and of various international artist residencies, he writes a monthly Latino book column, now entering its sixth year, for the *El Paso Times* of Texas. He is contributing editor for *Poets & Writers Magazine*, a member of the National Book Critics Circle, and an associate professor of English at Queens College, CUNY and M.F. Steinhardt Visiting Writer at Rutgers University. He is on the Advisory Circle of Con Tinta, a collective of Chicano/Latino activist-writers. Web page: www.rigobertogonzalez.com.

REYNA GRANDE was born in Guerrero, Mexico, in 1975. She entered the United States as an undocumented immigrant at nine years of age. In 1999, Grande obtained her B.A. in creative writing from the University of California at Santa Cruz and was a 2003 PEN USA Emerging Voices Fellow. She is the author of the novel *Across a Hundred Mountains* (Atria Books, 2006). Grande currently lives in Los Angeles. Web page: www.reynagrande.com.

STEPHEN D. GUTIÉRREZ grew up on the outskirts of Los Angeles in the City of Commerce. He attended public and Catholic schools, and holds degrees from California State University, Chico, and Cornell University. His short stories and essays have appeared in many publications including *Puerto del Sol, Santa Monica Review, Fiction International, The Quarterly, pacific REVIEW, Fiction, San Francisco Chronicle Sunday, Fourth Genre, River Teeth, ZYZZYVA,* and in the anthologies *Latino Heretics* and *Fantasmas: Supernatural Stories by Mexican American Writers.* In 1997 he received the Charles H. and N. Mildred Nilon Excellence in Minority Fiction Award for his short story collection *Elements.* His one-act plays include *A Chicano Experience, Tamales on Christmas Eve,* and *The Performance,* produced in local theaters. Since 1992 he has taught in the creative writing program at California State University, East Bay, and is currently serving as director.

ÁLVARO HUERTA was born to Mexican parents from Michoacán, Mexico, and raised in East Los Angeles' turbulent Ramona Gardens Housing project. Growing up in the projects, Huerta never dreamed of going to college to become a community activist and writer. Like many of his peers, Huerta was not encouraged to attend a university either by his public school teachers or Spanish-speaking parents, who had no formal education. When the pressure to join a gang and take drugs became intense, he desperately sought a way out of his neighborhood through higher education. Being the first in his family (both immediate and extended) and one of the few from Ramona Gardens to attend a university, Huerta felt a great responsibility to succeed academically for his family and community. Upon entering the University of California at Los Angeles as a freshman in 1985, however, Huerta became shocked by the lack of Latinos on campus and aware of the social inequalities impacting his community. Not satisfied with pursuing a professional career upon graduation, Huerta dedicated himself to a life of social activism, scholarship, and writing, shedding light on the social and economic inequities impacting Latinos. Through his writings in particular, both nonfiction and fiction, Huerta portrays Chicanos in their daily struggles for democracy, dignity, and respect in this country. Currently, Huerta is a graduate student in UCLA's Department of Urban Planning program and will pursue his Ph.D. at UC Berkeley in this same field of study. Huerta resides in Los Angeles with his wife, Antonia Montes, and their son, Joaquín Montes Huerta.

MICHAEL JAIME-BECERRA is a native of El Monte, California. A graduate of the University of California at Riverside's creative writing department, his early work, under the name of Michael Jayme, was first collected in 1996 as *Look Back and Laugh* for the Chicano Chapbook Series, edited by Gary Soto. The following year he began publishing under the surname "Jaime-Becerra" and shortly thereafter, a limited-edition collection of prose poems, entitled *The Estrellistas off Peck Road*, was released locally by Temporary Vandalism. He studied in the University of California, Irvine's Master of Fine Arts in Fiction Program, completing work toward his degree in 2001. His debut collection of interrelated short stories, entitled *Every Night Is Ladies' Night*, was published in 2004 by Rayo, the Latino imprint of HarperCollins. He is an assistant professor in the M.F.A. writing program at the University of California at Riverside.

MANUAL LUIS MARTÍNEZ is an associate professor at Ohio State University in Chicano/a literature, postwar American literature, and creative writing. He is the author of *Countering the Counterculture: Rereading Postwar American Dissent from Jack Keroauc to Tomás Rivera* (University of Wisconsin Press), and the novels *Drift* (Picador) and *Crossing* (Bilingual Press). He earned his Ph.D. from Stanford University.

ALEJANDRO MORALES was born in Montebello, California. He received his Ph.D. from Rutgers University. He is a professor in the Department of

Spanish and Portuguese and the Chicano/Latino Studies Program at the University of California at Irvine. His writing focuses on chronicling the Chicano/Latino experience past, present, and future. His works include *Barrio on the Edge/Caras viejas y vino nuevo*, *La verdad sin voz*, *Reto en el paraíso*, *The Brick People*, *The Rag Doll Plagues*, *Waiting to Happen*, and *Pequeña nación*. *The Place of the White Heron*, *Volume Two of the Heterotopia Trilogy* is being considered for publication. His latest novel, *The Captain of All These Men of Death*, is scheduled to be published by Bilingual Press in 2008. Currently, he is working on several projects, including a novel with the working title *The Los Angeles River, Bridges, and a Love Story*.

MANUAL MUÑOZ is the author of *Zigzagger*, a short-story collection, published by Northwestern University Press in 2003. He is the recipient of a Constance Saltonstall Foundation Individual Artist's Grant in Fiction and a National Endowment for the Arts literature fellowship for 2006. His work has appeared in many journals, including *Rush Hour, Swink, Epoch,* and *Boston Review*, and has been aired on National Public Radio's *Selected Shorts*. Algonquin Books of Chapel Hill published his second collection of stories, *The Faith Healer of Olive Avenue*, in 2007. A native of Dinuba, California, Muñoz graduated from Harvard University and received his M.F.A. in creative writing at Cornell University. He now lives in New York City, where he is at work on a novel.

DANIEL A. OLIVAS is the author of *Devil Talk: Stories* (Bilingual Press, 2004), *Assumption and Other Stories* (Bilingual Press, 2003), *The Courtship of María Rivera Peña: A Novella* (Silver Lake Publishing, 2000), and a children's book, *Benjamin and the Word/Benjamín y la palabra* (Arte Público Press, 2005). His writing has appeared in several anthologies and many publications including the *Los Angeles Times, El Paso Times, MacGuffin, Exquisite Corpse, Tu Ciudad, Multicultural Review,* and the *Jewish Journal*. Olivas is a member of Con Tinta and shares blogging duties on *La Bloga*. He received his B.A. in English literature from Stanford University and his law degree from the University of California at Los Angeles. Olivas practices law with the California Department of Justice, specializing in land use and environmental enforcement. He makes his home with his wife and son in the San Fernando Valley. Web page: www.danielolivas.com.

MELINDA PALACIO grew up in Huntington Park, California. She holds two degrees in comparative literature, a B.A. from the University of California at Berkeley, and a master's from the University of California at Santa Cruz. Palacio began writing professionally in 2000 after a short stint as a news assistant for the *Arizona Republic*. Her articles have appeared in *Phoenix Magazine, Get Out*, and the *East Valley Tribune* and *Scottsdale Tribune,* where she was a frequent contributor. In 2001, she moved to Santa Barbara and became a staff reporter for the *Goleta Valley Voice*. In 2003 she won first prize in poetry at the Santa Barbara Writers Conference and in 2005 she won an honorable mention for her entry in the conference's 1000-word fiction contest. Her latest venture is an online magazine, *Ink Byte: Everything for Writers* http://inkbyte.com, where she is a co-editor, reporter, and columnist. Palacio is currently working on a collection of short stories, *Bathroom Girls: Coming of Age in South Central L.A.*, and a novel, *Ocotillo Dreams*.

SALVADOR PLASCENCIA is author of the novel *The People of Paper* (McSweeney's Books). His writing has appeared in *Tin House, McSweeney's,* and *Salt Hill*. Plascencia received his B.A. from Whittier College and his M.F.A from Syracuse University.

MANUEL RAMOS, an attorney who also has taught Chicano literature cours-es at Metropolitan State College of Denver, is the author of several crime fiction novels. These novels have garnered critical and popular recognition such as the Colorado Book Award and the Chicano/Latino Literary Award (University of California at Irvine), as well as an Edgar nomination from the Mystery Writers of America. Born in Florence, Colorado, his grandfathers included a coal miner and a veteran of Pancho Villa's army. His father, a construction worker, and his mother raised Ramos to appreciate education; accordingly, Ramos eventually graduated from Colorado State University with honors in 1970, and received his law degree from the University of Colorado in 1973. After a few years in private practice, Ramos accepted a staff attorney position with the Denver legal aid program, and the bulk of his legal career has consisted of providing legal assistance to the indigent. Today he is the Director of Advocacy for Colorado Legal Services, the statewide legal aid program.

SANDRA RAMOS O'BRIANT'S work has appeared in *Whistling Shade, AIM Magazine, Ink Pot, NFG, Café Irreal, Flashquake,* and *Best Lesbian Love Stories of 2004,* and appears in *What Wildness is This: Women Write the Southwest* (University of Texas Press). Excerpts from her first novel, *The Secret of Old Blood: The Sandoval Sisters,* have appeared in *La Herencia, FriGG,* and *The Copperfield Review,* a journal devoted to historical fiction. Her book reviews have been published online at *La Bloga* and *Moorishgirl.* Web page: www.sramosobriant.com.

WAYNE RAPP lived in the Los Angeles area for ten years and worked as a writer-director in the motion picture department of a major corporation. He was born and raised in Bisbee, Arizona, and traces his Mexican roots to the Figueroa and Valenzuela families of Sonora. His fiction has appeared in various publications including the *Americas Review, Grit, Chiricú, THEMA, Vincent Brothers Review,* and *High Plains Literary Review.* His short story, "In the Time of Marvel and Confusion," was nominated for a Pushcart Prize, and he has twice been honored with Individual Artist Fellowships from the Ohio Arts Council. His collection of border stories, *Burnt Sienna,* was a finalist for the 2005 Miguel Mármol Prize for Fiction. A book, *Celebrating, Honoring, Valuing Rich Traditions: The History of the Ohio Appalachian Arts Program,* was recently published by Lucky Press.

JOHN RECHY, born in El Paso, Texas, is of Mexican Scottish descent and has written novels reflecting his background as a gay Mexican American. He is the author of many books including *City of Night, The Fourth Angel, Bodies and Souls, Marilyn's Daughter, The Miraculous Day of Amalia Gómez, The Coming of the Night,* and *The Life and Adventures of Lyle Clemens.* Rechy is also the author of the off-Broadway play "Tigers Wild." His work has been translated into fourteen languages and into Braille. Rechy's reviews and essays have been published in newspapers and journals nationally. He is a recipient of PEN Center West's Lifetime Achievement Award. Rechy is a faculty member at the Master of Professional Writing Program at the University of Southern California.

LUIS J. RODRÍGUEZ has emerged as one of the leading Chicano writers in the country with ten nationally published books in memoir, fiction, nonfiction, children's literature, and poetry. Rodríguez's poetry has won a Poetry

Center Book Award, a PEN Josephine Miles Literary Award, and *ForeWord* magazine's Silver Book Award, among others. His two children's books have won a Patterson Young Adult Book Award, two "Skipping Stones" Honor Awards, and a Parent's Choice Book Award, among others. A novel, *Music of the Mill*, was published in 2005 by Rayo/HarperCollins; and a poetry collection, *My Nature is Hunger: New and Selected Poems*, 1989-2004, came out in 2005 from Curbstone Press/Rattle Edition.

DANNY ROMERO is a Chicano writer who was born and raised in Los Angeles. He is the author of the novel *Calle 10* and two chapbooks of poetry, the latest of which is *Land of a Thousand Barrios*. Romero's poems and short stories have been published in journals throughout the country, including *Colorado Review, Drumvoices Revue*, and *Ploughshares*. His work can also be found in such anthologies of California and Chicano writers as *West of the West: Imagining California, Pieces of the Heart: New Chicano Fiction, Los vasos comunicantes: antología de poesía chicana* (Spain) and *Under the Fifth Sun: Latino Literature from California*.

CONRAD ROMO is a native Angeleno. He is the producer of a monthly reading event, Tongue & Groove (www.tongueandgroovela.com). He is also a contributor to *Wednesday Magazine* and Pale Horse Press. He has studied with Lynda Barry and Jack Grapes. He grew up on the other side of the tracks short, stocky and swarthy. He'd like to be thought of as a ladies' man, a man's man, and a dog's best friend. He earns his daily bread as an entrepreneur/raconteur, and is compiling a collection of short stories and several CDs.

JORGE SARALEGUI was born in Havana, Cuba, graduated from Antioch College in Ohio, and now lives in Venice, California. His stories have appeared in several journals including *ZYZZYVA* and *Santa Monica Review*. He is currently writing a novel.

JENNIFER SILVA REDMOND was born in Los Angeles and grew up in Venice, California. She attended United States International University (both the London and San Diego campuses), majoring in dramatic literature, before moving to New York City; she worked extensively as an actor/playwright in New York City and on tour with the Asolo State Theatre of Florida.

After marrying artist Russel Redmond in 1989, and spending two years on a sailboat in Mexico, she began writing about "finding her roots" in Baja California (her grandmother, Edmee Silva, is Mexican). She sold stories to *Cruising World, Sail, Latitude 38, Dog Fancy, Science of Mind,* and the poetry journal *Cicada,* among others. Back in Baja in 1996, Silva Redmond became involved in local writers' groups and cofounded the *Sea of Cortez Review,* a literary publication that premiered in 1998; two more annual issues were published in 1999 and 2000/2001, to critical acclaim. In 2000 she joined Sunbelt Publications, an award-winning small press, as acquisitions editor, and in 2004 she was named editor-in-chief. Silva Redmond is a popular speaker for conferences, writing groups, and other cultural organizations. Editing is still her passion, but she also finds time to work on stories and essays. She is currently at work on a novel based on her theatrical background, and recently finished her first screenplay.

MARIO SUÁREZ (1923-1998) is a key figure in the founding of Chicano literature and was among the first writers to focus not only on Chicano characters but also on the multicultural space in which they live, whether a Tucson barbershop or a Manhattan boxing ring. Many of his stories have received wide acclaim through publication in periodicals and anthologies. In most of his stories, Suárez sought to portray people he knew from Tucson's El Hoyo barrio, a place usually thought of as urban wasteland when it is thought of at all. Suárez set out to fictionalize this place of ignored men and women because he believed their human stories were worth telling, and he hoped that through his depictions American literature would recognize their existence. By seeking to record the so-called underside of America, Suárez was inspired to pay close attention to people's mannerisms, language, and aspirations. And by focusing on these barrio characters—the deviant and the virtuous, the mischievous and the mysterious—he also crafted a unique, mild-mannered realism overflowing with humor and pathos. Along with Fray Angélico Chávez, Suárez stands as arguably the mid-twentieth century's most important short story writer of Mexican descent, and his writing can be appreciated not only as fiction but also for the human element it offers in the study of Chicano culture.

LUIS ALBERTO URREA, 2005 Pulitzer Prize finalist for nonfiction and member of the Latino Literature Hall of Fame, is a prolific and acclaimed writer who uses his dual-culture life experiences to explore greater themes of love, loss, and triumph. Born in Tijuana, Mexico, to a Mexican father and an American mother, Urrea has written extensively in all the major genres and is currently published by Little, Brown and Company. *The Devil's Highway*, his 2004 non-fiction account of a group of Mexican immigrants lost in the Arizona desert, won the 2004 Lannan Literary Award and was a finalist for the Pulitzer Prize and the Pacific Rim Kiriyama Prize. Urrea's first book, *Across the Wire*, was named a *New York Times* Notable Book and won the Christopher Award. Urrea also won a 1999 American Book Award for his memoir, *Nobody's Son: Notes from an American Life*. His short story collection, *Six Kinds of Sky*, was named the 2002 small press Book of the Year in fiction by the editors of *Fore-Word* magazine. Urrea's most recent book, *The Hummingbird's Daughter*, won the Pacific Rim Kiriyama Prize for fiction in 2006. Urrea lives with his family in Naperville, Illinois, where he is a professor of creative writing at the University of Illinois at Chicago.

RICHARD VÁSQUEZ (1928-1990) worked for several newspapers, including the *Santa Monica Independent*, the *San Gabriel Valley Tribune*, and the *Los Angeles Times*. His novel, *Chicano*, reissued in 2005 by Rayo/HarperCollins, was a groundbreaking bestseller when it was first published by Doubleday in 1970 at the height of the Mexican American civil rights movement. In addition to *Chicano*, Vásquez published two other novels, *The Giant Killer* and *Another Land*.

HELENA MARÍA VIRAMONTES is the author of *The Moths and Other Stories* (Arte Público Press, 1985); *Under the Feet of Jesus*, a novel (Dutton, 1995; Plume-Penguin, 1996); and the coeditor, with María Herrera Sobek, of two collections: *Chicana (W)rites: On Word and Film* (Arte Público Press, 1985/1995) and *Chicana Creativity and Criticism* (University of New Mexico Press, 1996). Her latest novel, *Their Dogs Came With Them*, was published by Atria/Washington Square Press in 2007. She is the recipient of numerous awards and honors, including the John Dos Passos Award for Literature and the 2006 Luis Leal Award. Her short stories and essays have been widely anthologized and her writings have been adopted for classroom use and university study. A community organizer and former coordinator of the Los Angeles Latino Writers Association, she is a frequent reader and lecturer in the United States and internationally. Born and raised in East L.A., Viramontes now lives in Ithaca, New York, where she is a professor in the Department of English at Cornell University.

Permissions
and Source Acknowledgments

Kathleen de Azevedo. "The True Story." First published in *Writers Forum*, 1996. Reprinted by permission of the author.

Estella González. "Act of Faith." *Eleven Eleven*, 2004. Reprinted by permission of the author.

Michael Jaime-Becerra. "Gina and Max." From *Every Night is Ladies' Night: Stories.* © 2004 by Michael Jaime-Becerra. Reprinted by permission of HarperCollins Publishers.

Manuel Luis Martínez. Excerpt from the novel *Drift.* © 2003 by Manuel Luis Rodriguez. Reprinted by permission of St. Martin's Press, LLC, and Matt Williams of the Gernert Company on behalf of the author.

Alejandro Morales. Excerpt from the novel *Barrio on the Edge.* © 1993 by Bilingual Press/ Editorial Bilingüe, 1998. Reprinted by permission of Bilingual Press/Editorial Bilingüe.

Manuel Muñoz. "The Comeuppance of Lupe Rivera." © 2006 by Manuel Muñoz. First published in *Swink*, Issue 2, spring 2005. From *The Faith Healer of Olive Avenue*, Algonquin Books, 2007. Reprinted by permission of Stuart Bernstein Representation for Artists, New York. All rights reserved.

Daniel A. Olivas. "Bender." First published in *Pacific Review*, spring 2000. From *Devil Talk: Stories.* © 2004 by Bilingual Press/Editorial Bilingüe. Reprinted by permission of Bilingual Press/Editorial Bilingüe.

Salvador Plascencia. Excerpt from the novel *The People of Paper.* © 2005 by Salvador Plascencia. Reprinted by permission of the author.

John Rechy. Excerpt from the novel *The Miraculous Day of Amalia Gómez.* © 1991 by John Rechy. Reprinted by permission of Georges Borchardt, Inc. on behalf of the author.

Luis J. Rodríguez. "Miss East L.A." From *The Republic of East L.A.* © 2002 by Luis J. Rodríguez. Published by Rayo, an imprint of HarperCollins Publishers. Reprinted by permission of Susan Bergholz Literary Services, New York. All rights reserved.

Danny Romero. "Ghetto Man." First published in *Ishmael Reed's Konch* (1991). Reprinted by permission of the author.

Mario Suárez. "Kid Zopilote." First published in *Arizona Quarterly*, summer 1947. From *Chicano Sketches: Short Stories by Mario Suárez*, edited by Francisco A. Lomelí, Cecilia Cota-Robles Suárez, and Juan José Casillas-Núñez. © 2004 by the Arizona Board of Regents, 2004. Reprinted by permission of the University of Arizona Press.

Richard Vásquez. Excerpt from the novel *Chicano*. © 1970 by Richard Vásquez. Published by Rayo, an imprint of HarperCollins Publishers in 2005 and originally in hardcover by Doubleday in 1970 and Avon Books in 1971. Reprinted by permission of Stuart Bernstein Representation for Artists, New York. All rights reserved.

Helena María Viramontes. "Tears on My Pillow." © 1994 by Helena María Viramontes. First appeared in *Currents from the Dancing River: Contemporary Latino Fiction, Nonfiction, and Poetry*, edited by Ray González and published by Harvest books, an imprint of Harcourt. Reprinted by permission of Stuart Bernstein Representation for Artists, New York. All rights reserved.